The Unfinished World

.ll.

Heraclitus says, you know, that all things flow and nothing abides, and he likens the things that exist to the current of a river, saying that one cannot step into the same river twice.

—*Plato*

Dolls are not inanimate. Rilke's exasperation with the unresponsive doll is an admission that he expects life from what seems lifeless. In the complete world, not this imagined world divided into convenient categories by thought, there can be no absolute divisions, either between life and death, thing and spirit, or anything else. There is only transformation.

—*Idris Parry*

One boat
two—
    pointed toward
        my shore

—*Lorine Niedecker*

More than anything, she likes to swim. When she swims, there is nothing to think about but making the turn at the end of the lane as smoothly as possible. To and fro, to and fro while memory gathers its forces into a tale she can live with. In the water, all wounds heal; in the water she heads for her beginning, over and over, until she gets out of the pool, showers, and dresses. And re-enters the world.

The Unfinished World

a novel

MARILYN BOWERING

Linda Leith Publishing, 2025.

Prepared for the press by Edward He, Shakiya Williams, Anna Dunlop
Cover design by Debbie Geltner
Cover image by Marilyn Bowering
Book design: DiTech

Library and Archives Canada Cataloguing in Publication
Title: The unfinished world / Marilyn Bowering.
Names: Bowering, Marilyn, author
Identifiers: Canadiana (print) 20250245191 | Canadiana (ebook) 20250245205 | ISBN 9781773901800 (softcover) | ISBN 9781773901817 (EPUB) | ISBN 9781773901824 (PDF)
Subjects: LCGFT: Novels.
Classification: LCC PS8553.O9 U54 2025 | DDC C813/.54—dc23

Printed and bound in Canada

Legal deposit - Library and Archives Canada and Bibliothèque et Archives nationales du Québec, 2025

The publisher gratefully acknowledges the support of the Government of Canada through the Canada Council for the Arts, the Canada Book Fund, and of the Government of Quebec through the Société de développement des entreprises culturelles (SODEC).

Linda Leith Publishing
Montreal
www.lindaleith.com

For ASBE and MSE

Table of Contents

PART I

THEANO: The Philosopher's Tale

There are eighty-five generations between Theano and you, Nora wrote. When you write the story, don't forget to put that in.

When Pearl was young, strangers came to the house, dropped off by van, by bus, or on foot. There were times, too, that her grandmother Nora brought them home after rescuing them in *SeaPin* as they swam from dinghies listing dangerously in the channel. Those were cold nights. Nora at the tiller, Pearl scanning the waves with a flashlight. With no thought for the risks she took, Pearl would dive in and tow survivors to *Seapin*'s stern where Nora helped adults and children scale the boarding ladder. The children—faces soapy with fatigue, slack with shock—were always smaller than robust Pearl with her shoulders sturdy from swim practices.

Later, in Nora's house, with whole families settled on couches, in chairs, and on the floor in Nora's living room, the children slumbered with pillows clutched for companionship. The adults rarely slept. Their late-night conversations scribbled the walls.

This period, which lasted from when Pearl was about fourteen until she finished high school, was a time of exhaustion. Upstairs in her room, after completing her schoolwork while Nora busied herself with asylum applications to file in court the next morning, Pearl tried to sleep. Instead, the murmured exchanges and cries from nightmares in the rooms below kept her awake. She worried about the people she failed to rescue. What would happen to them? Why couldn't Pearl save everyone? The questions went on for hours.

"You're doing all you can," Nora told her each day. "You have an ability to find people even when it seems hopeless."

Pearl would nod in agreement, but it was not like that at all. In the water, she felt at home and was never lonely or cold or afraid. She did not *find* people; they came to her. How could she explain this to lawyer Nora?

Yet, Pearl felt lucky. Lucky to have Nora, lucky to be able to help. Every day, so many people looking for sanctuary began this journey, passed overland from one smuggler to another, or from 2,500 miles away in a container on a ship, eventually to be transferred to speed boats and then into small craft along the coast. There they would meet Nora and her granddaughter, waiting for them in the darkness. After coffee in the morning they would leave the house, relayed to someone else to guide them on the next stage of their journey.

Pearl had grown up with her grandmother, in her grandmother's house. She does not complain about those years. She acknowledges that everything she is, is because of this. Her father, Harry, had lived nearby as long as he could after her parents' divorce, until he accepted a job with Broadcast News in Vancouver. Retired now, Harry and his third wife, Loretta, run a motel there. Pearl has never been to see them, but she stays in touch. Her mother, who lives in New York, visits when it is convenient to a book tour, but otherwise Pearl has spent little time with her since Sara left when Pearl was three years old. Overall, though, because of Nora, Pearl has had more of a family than most people she knows, including friends whose parents *had* stayed together.

It is not usual for Pearl to let her thoughts run on this way. She prefers focusing on goals and *moving the pieces forward* to revisiting the past, especially where it concerns her parents, but an out-of-the-blue summons from her grandmother to meet for coffee has stirred things up. These days, Nora provides a few lucky immigrants with legal support and a safe and stable place to live, through her foundation, Refuge House, in British Columbia. The house is a hunting lodge left to Nora by her second husband.

"It makes a difference, Pearl," Nora had told her granddaughter, "but it isn't enough."

"You can't save them all," Pearl had replied. "Aren't you the one who told me that?"

Pearl and Nora have not seen each other for months.

Inside the van in which Pearl lives unseen by passersby, but near enough to the beach to hear the waves, she pushes aside the curtains. Morning sunlight filters through the trees and bush where she is parked. She stitched the curtains herself, threaded them on elastic runners and hung them using eye screws when she and Gerry-David first lived there together. A tiny fridge and a propane stove made enough of a kitchen for them to cook their meals. They fitted a shelf below the side bubble window so that the one who got home first could light a welcoming candle for the other.

Pearl shuffles on her knees to tidy the duvet and pillows, gathers what she wants to take with her, and places it in her rucksack.

Gerry-David, whose van this is, has left her. He and his new girlfriend live in the condo Pearl and Gerry-David bought together and registered in his name so he could use it as a tax-deductible business address. It had never felt like home to Pearl; she always preferred the sequestered world of the van in which for a time they had been happy. It isn't that Pearl is sorry about the break-up, either—far from it. She is glad that Gerry-David has someone to love him—she had found that difficult. The trouble is that he hasn't paid for her half of the condo, and without it she does not have the money to find another place to live, which is why she has hidden the van and is staying in it over Gerry-David's objections.

Pearl closes and locks the van's sliding door, hefts her pack onto her shoulders, and checks the time. The walk to the coffee shop should take half an hour. She wriggles through the brush surrounding the van, taking care not to break branches or leave any other evidence of her passage. The regular walking trail begins behind the park washrooms. The rough track she drove in on is accessed on the far side of a fenced enclosure for park vehicles. She is friends with several of the workers—fellow conservationists who showed her the spot and will not give her away. They watch the SaveOurSouls cooking videos Pearl makes and posts online. Her niche is environmental consciousness matched to simple seafood dishes, and the vlogs are attracting attention. She is negotiating with advertisers; she has magazine commissions and an expression of interest from an online streaming platform that could mean a profitable SaveOurSouls series in the future.

In the long run, Pearl is going to be all right. But at the moment, things are not easy—especially given that she has to face her grandmother this morning.

"How does it help anybody but yourself?" Nora had asked when Pearl described her work to her. "What is it you do for others?"

"I connect people to the environment, to sea life in particular, Gran. I encourage them to think about their overall relationship to life."

"To life? Good! But it's how you make your money, isn't it? I hope you won't confuse business with philanthropy, Pearl," Nora had said. "You have abilities you should use. Don't leave it too long. Real gifts don't wait around forever."

"I know what I'm doing," Pearl had said.

But did she? Pearl had borrowed money from Nora for projects and investments she'd entered into with Gerry-David and is awaiting an accounting that he keeps putting off. In the meantime, if she is to work her way out of her difficulties, Pearl needs to focus on next steps.

After she reaches the shore road, Pearl encounters a woman on her knees on the verge pulling out invasive pampas grass that's overwhelming the native sage. They smile at each other because the regeneration of native species will help heal the environment. Pearl scuffles through piles of dry eucalyptus leaves and burnt-brown pine needles that the wind has blown onto the path, adjusts her backpack and confronts the barrier of bluffs she must climb to the business district.

One summer morning shortly after Pearl had completed college and an IT teaching certificate, she'd fled Nora's attempts to get her to apply to law school by heading to the beach with a book. Pearl's academic program was a mix of environmental and communications studies, biology, and history. The IT certificate was her insurance: all writers needed an alternative plan. Harry had gone to broadcast school; Sara had an editor who took an interest in her and whom she later married.

Pearl had not been reading long when Gerry-David spotted her through binoculars from a beach house he was borrowing. He had skidded down the cliff path, squatted on his heels an unthreatening distance away, jerked a thumb over his shoulder at the wood-frame and glass cottage from which he'd emerged and said, "I've got cold beer in the refrigerator, and you look thirsty." He raised his eyebrows.

"You can't be serious," she said. It was 9:30 in the morning.

"Sure, why not?"

Pearl returned to her book.

"Well, okay then," he said after she had turned a few more pages. "Let's talk."

He pattered on until she closed the book, dribbled sand through her fingers and listened. He had a temporary job with a driveway paving company while he established his business, he said. Every day, he scoured the ads for real estate; ran a few miles or worked out at the gym. Work was mostly cold calls to get signed paving contracts. As soon as he got home, he'd pursue the best of the property deals, negotiate, place a deposit on anything promising, and "look for girls as pretty as you on my days off." He smiled.

She rolled her eyes.

"Why not make money *and* be happy?" he said. "No, really, tell me! What I do takes discipline, but I enjoy my life. Do you?"

Pearl looked at him. He had blond curly hair, a tan, and firm abs. Sunny good nature shone from him. The in-breaths he sipped through his teeth between verbal paragraphs were endearing. He was harmless. Every sentence ended with a grin. She grinned, too.

Gerry-David needed no further encouragement to keep on talking, but he didn't mention beer again, and he stayed put and didn't invade her blanket. At noon, too hot in the sun, Pearl gathered her belongings, ready to depart. He did not get up to follow, only called after her, "You forgot to give me your cell number."

"No, I didn't."

"I'll phone you anyway!"

"Sure!" she said. She did not expect to hear from him.

On their first date two weeks later, he served cocktails and snacks inside his van, then walked her along the coast to the "best rocks from which to view the sunset."

"So much we still don't know, Pearl," he'd said. He placed his arm around her in a friendly fashion. "Why is the sky blue, where do stars come from? What makes all these colours?" He gestured at the hues shimmering the horizon.

Pearl watched the light drain. She isn't sure why she answered the way she did, but likely she thought it amusing that he really did not know. She did not mean to be cruel.

"The sky is blue because the Earth's atmosphere scatters light, and blue is scattered more than other colours," she said. "Sunlight takes a longer path through the atmosphere at sunset than it does in the middle of the day. When the path is long enough all the blue and violet light disperses, but the other colours, like yellow, orange, and red, persist." Pearl had learned this on a visit to the observatory with Nora.

Gerry-David removed his arm from her shoulder, and they sat in silence. Later, he smoked a cigarette in the dark and said, "My van is paid for, I buy my clothes with my own money, I've put an offer on a condo big enough for two and I've got a good business going, but if I fail, there's no safety net. I never went to college, and unlike you I've got no family to help me out *or* get in my way."

"My family isn't in my way," Pearl had said, flushing.

"No?" He'd stood and brushed invisible dirt from his chinos. "Then why are you trying so hard to ditch them?"

It was a good question.

Nora waits near a window, two large cappuccinos on the table in front of her. A sunbeam highlights the barista's flower creation in the creamy frothing.

"Oh!" Nora says, taking in her granddaughter's appearance. "You've changed your hair! I like it!"

Pearl brushes her hand through the cut she gave herself to eliminate years of bleaching and sits down. Her jeans and T-shirt need washing. She resists the impulse to hunch her shoulders and cross her arms to cover stains. Her grandmother is dressed in expensive, sturdy, woven taupe garments that drape her gaunt figure. Her bobbed, steel-grey hair gleams. A tapestry holdall of Nora's occupies most of the table's glass top.

"I hope the coffee isn't cold," Nora says. "I went ahead and ordered. Here, I've got something for you." Nora leans forward and pushes a legal-sized envelope across the table, her necklace of amber beads knocking softly on the table's edge.

"Open it!" Nora says.

Pearl has missed her grandmother's enthusiasm. She pauses with her thumb hooked in the corner of the flap. "How are things up north?" she asks.

"Go ahead, Pearl!" Nora says. "It's for you. Open it."

It takes a moment for Pearl to absorb that what is inside the envelope is not a cheque or anything else she might have hoped for, but an airline ticket. An itinerary lists a series of destinations that mean little to her, except that her parents live in two of the cities.

"Will you come?" Nora says. Pearl sets the envelope down and takes a sip of coffee. Nora's smile fades. "You're disappointed."

"No, not at all." Pearl takes another swallow. "It's just … I'm not sure I understand."

"Say you'll come. It won't be a long trip, and it will be fun. We'll visit Harry and Sara and some other people I want you to meet. Your friend can get along without you."

While Pearl is considering what to say, how to tell Nora what she must do to make a living and that she now lives on her own, Nora asks, "What did you mean, 'How are things up north?'"

"I meant Refuge House."

It's Nora's turn to fiddle with her coffee. She stirs it, drinks, puts the cup down, and covers Pearl's hand with her own. "Refuge House has been closed for some time, Pearl. It ran into problems; nothing I could solve on my own, unfortunately. I would have told you earlier, but I didn't want you to worry."

"I'm sorry, Gran," Pearl says. She slips her hand away and takes a breath. "About this trip. I don't know what to say. It's a great idea, but ... "

"What can be more important than time together?"

"I left him," Pearl says. "Well, he left me, but it's the same thing. I didn't want to tell you." She gazes at her phone which shows three more texts from Gerry-David. They'll be about the van.

"You're not together? You thought that would bother me? Even more reason to come on this journey, Pearl."

"You don't understand. I have real opportunities, and I can't afford to ignore them."

"What aren't you telling me, Pearl?" Nora asks, taking in the state of her granddaughter's clothing, her general air of neglect. "What are you living on? I bet he's got the condo, hasn't he."

"It isn't like that, Gran," Pearl says, although it was. "I'm looking for a place, that's all; but I *am* busy."

"You could come home in the meantime, while you're house-hunting," Nora says. "I've got plenty of room. Why didn't you tell me earlier? Honestly!"

Home. Nora's home is where Pearl was raised. It was built with wood salvaged from shipwrecks on Pink Pelican Island and inhabits an acre of garden. The island was the birthplace of Nora's grandmother—Pearl's great-great-grandmother. There is a story about this; there is a story about everything in Nora's world. But home? To her childhood?

"Come with me on the trip and then move in," Nora says. "Just for a while, until you find your feet."

"I really can't," Pearl says. "It's bad timing." She explains about the streaming platform's response to her vlog. "It isn't solid yet, but my agent said if I show them how good it could be as a series—well, you never know. They've asked me to write a pilot; well not a pilot, exactly, but a demo."

"A series? About SaveOurSouls cooking?"

"With seafood. Yes."

Nora looks away, her eye caught by a movement near the door.

"Then I'd be able to repay the loan," Pearl says.

"Would you excuse me, darling? I have to talk to someone." Nora pushes her chair from the table, and leaves. The man waiting at the doorway looks like an accountant, a lawyer, a doctor, or maybe the director of a non-profit. He's more presentable than most of the people who seek an audience with Pearl's grandmother. Nora must have told him where she would be.

Person to person is Nora's style, but it is annoying that she's let a stranger interrupt them. Pearl's phone rings and she answers without thinking, "SaveOurSouls?"

"Tell me how to find it and I won't call the police," Gerry-David says.

"I'll give you the van if you give me the money you owe me," she says. She has said it before.

"You can't drive it anywhere; I cancelled the insurance."

Pearl ends the call and watches Nora finish what seems to be an intimate conversation. She is proud of Nora's successes, yet much of her grandmother's world is a mystery to her.

Nora returns to the table, pushing her half-empty cup away. "Are you sure you won't come with me, Pearl? Final offer?"

Pearl shakes her head. "You know I would love to."

Nora pulls the holdall off the table onto her lap. She closes her eyes for an instant.

"Who was that man you were talking to?" Pearl says. "People take advantage. He has made you tired."

Her grandmother briefly touches Pearl's cheek, and smiles. "He didn't make me tired. It's not him, darling, it's really not anyone." She shifts and searches their reflections in the window.

"You know," Nora continues, "I still think of you as the little girl who played at the dining room table with dolls propped up on chairs. You would read to them from a book of blank pages."

"Yes," Pearl says, "I remember. You stapled the pages for me."

Nora releases the holdall catch and opens it. "I've brought some of the dolls with me. I want you to have your favourites," she says.

Each of the half-dozen dolls Nora lays in a heap on the table is four or five inches tall. These are not conventional dolls, and they're all in varying states of disrepair.

An odour of must spreads from the mound of painted wood, bone, straw, and cloth. A woman at a nearby table sniffs and turns her head away.

The dolls bring mixed feelings. When she was small, Pearl imagined they were alive, her true companions; so much so that she can picture them resolving into life-sized figures in the smoky blue haze at Nora's shoulder. She blinks the haze away. Their tales—Nora's tales—had made her feel part of a different world, a world that tracked through centuries. It has been a long time since she's thought of them.

"I would love to have them at some point, Gran," she says carefully.

"What point might that be?" Nora says.

Pearl is about to respond but Nora adds, "No, I'm sorry, I shouldn't have said that. I don't want us to quarrel, and I have a favour to ask. Do you remember the stories that went with the dolls? You promised you wouldn't forget them; but can you recall enough to write them down for me? If there's anything you've forgotten, you can ask; but the stories don't stop growing, Pearl, they'd be your own work, too." Nora touches the dolls with long fingers knotted with arthritis. "It would mean a lot."

"What's going on, Gran? Are you alright?"

"Why should anything be wrong?" Nora asks.

"You're sure you're not worried about anything? You travel so much—should you really be going on another trip?"

Nora glances at the door, but the man she had spoken with is gone. "You didn't answer my question," she says, shifting her attention back to Pearl.

"Yes," Pearl says. "Yes. I will write the stories as soon as I have the time, but I don't have time right now and I can't take the dolls with me. I have no place to keep them. I'm living in Gerry-David's van."

"Pearl!"

"Look, Gran," Pearl says, "how about this? If you are going to be away, I could house-sit. It would help me out. I could use your kitchen to film a SaveOurSouls episode, the demo I told you about that might turn into a series, and I wouldn't be in your way."

"Of course," Nora says. "If it would be helpful to you, but I'd rather you came with me."

Pearl likes the idea of having Nora's house to herself. She slides the dolls across the table and watches Nora put them into the holdall.

"When are you leaving?" Pearl asks.

"Soon. Right away. I have no reason to wait."

"And when are you coming back?"

"I have four to six weeks, Pearl; three at the very least." Nora holds her granddaughter's gaze. For a second Pearl wonders if she has missed a piece of the conversation. Then her phone rings. It is Gerry-David again, so she shuts it off.

They hug goodbye at Nora's car. Pearl is surprised how bony her grandmother's shoulders have become. "Give me a call when you know your schedule," she says. "I'll drive you to the airport, so you won't have to leave the car there."

Nora gives her a final squeeze and climbs into her green RAV with expandable seating and tinted windows.

Perfect for picking up refugees; but if Nora waves as she drives off, Pearl doesn't see.

At the beach, Pearl changes into her swimsuit and dives into the swells beyond the breakers. She floats—held, lifted, and rocked in the water, her eyes closed against the light. Lazy strokes idle her in place until something brushes her arms and legs, and she finds she has drifted into a kelp forest. Gulls and terns wheel overhead, and a school of tiny fish sweeps through the seaweed and transits her body on the hunt for food.

It is not until Pearl has finished dressing and is groping for a scarf in the pocket of her hoodie that she finds the napkin-bound doll Nora had stashed there when they parted—that final squeeze. Pearl does not want the doll; not this one, not any of them. There will be a time for such things later. Right now, she needs to focus on her career. She thought she'd made that clear, but now she'll have to resolve the issue before Nora leaves, or it'll go on and on. Once Nora wants something, she does not relent. It makes her an effective attorney, but it isn't great to live with.

It takes Pearl an hour and a half to walk to Nora's. She does not mind the exercise, but she had hoped to work on her script before it grew too dark in the van to see. However, the house gate is in shadow, and the bougainvillea that foams over the garden walls is muted and silvery. Inside the yard, Nora's sunflowers, mustards, cresses, morning glory, buckthorn, peas, wallflowers, and grasses—even the scrub oaks—are leached of colour; all of them transplanted from Pink Pelican Island to join the berry bushes and fruit trees that were established by Nora's own grandmother.

Pearl's shoulder brushes the glossy leaves of an avocado tree as she steps onto the unlit porch and shifts her shoulder bag so she can open the front door. She tries the handle, but the heavy wooden door is locked. Luckily, she has her key.

The house is quiet. The curtains closed. Pearl turns on the lights. "Nora," she calls, "Where are you? Nora?" A note for Pearl is weighted by an empty vase on the dining room table. Nora, without saying goodbye to her granddaughter, has gone.

Pearl takes a quick look around to check that everything is as it should be. This house means a lot to her, its rooms full of artefacts from Nora's travels: paintings, rugs, books. Pearl leafs through a book from the coffee table—*Spanish Colonial Portraiture*—her eye caught by the women in elaborate costumes.

Upstairs, at Nora's closed bedroom door, Pearl listens for a second or two and enters. The bed is made; the curtains undrawn. From the window there is a view of the darkening harbour to where it leaks into the channel. Amber light pools beneath the dockside streetlights; blue light outlines the docks themselves; strings of white lights trace yacht masts; green and red navigation lights mark the paths of ships conveying food, fuel, and lumber along the coast. California produce voyaging northwards into the cold; oil from rigs all over the world moving in tankers to the Navy yards; east-coast steel brought through Panama for construction that will transform scrub-land into cities; car carriers heading in from Tokyo, and garbage scows leaving for China. People openly, or in disguise, or stowed away, travelling in all of them, engaged in visions of a better, more profitable world.

On an impulse, Pearl opens Nora's cupboard. Her suitcase and a small amount of clothing is absent. At the rear, half-obscured by the hems of party clothes, relics of Nora's charity fund-raising days, is the rosewood sea-chest in which Nora stores the dolls. Pearl lifts the lid, and the room fills with their scent of must, sandalwood, and tobacco, but the chest is empty. Maybe Nora is thinking of moving and got rid of them. Without Pearl in it, the house is too big for her. Downsizing: it is what older people do, but not what Pearl had pictured for her grandmother. Or for herself. She had thought the house would be hers one day. If she were planning to sell it, Nora should have said. She should not be giving away the dolls.

In her own dark room down the corridor, Pearl undresses, dons the worn wool dressing gown that hangs on a hook on the door, and gets into bed under a quilt Nora had made for her from clothing left behind by immigrants. Scraps of embroidered cotton, handwoven wool, and spider-web silk Nora had reinforced with linen; fragments of school uniforms: bits and pieces to which Nora, and at a certain period, Pearl, could have associated a person, if not a name.

A stir of loneliness makes Pearl get out of bed and retrieve the doll Nora had tucked into her pocket. Its name is Theano. Dark curling hair, blue eyes and full red lips painted on one end of an oblong of olivewood form its minimal portrait, and yet Theano is warm to hold. A square of undyed linen, tied at the neck, drapes the body-handle. The cloth is embroidered with spirals of gold thread. Theano, Nora had said, was a teacher, a mathematician and philosopher who lived in the middle of the fifth century BCE. Pearl is glad to have the doll after Nora's quick departure. If she were younger, she would sleep with it under her pillow. She stretches to put it on the shelf above the bed on which Nora has always kept dolls that were special to Pearl—the ones that she had tried to give to Pearl that day—but the shelf is empty. Pearl sneezes from the dust she has stirred, and then with a heartache she is loath to acknowledge, slips the little Theano doll under her pillow.

Those dolls! Inevitably, on Pearl's birthday, Nora would unearth another and give it to her granddaughter along with the story that went with it. The dolls were old, most of them handed down through generations. Every so often, a replacement would appear. Sara, Pearl's distant mother, had tried to add a model of herself to the collection, to "take my place in our history," but Nora had quickly mislaid it.

Pearl had begun to mislay dolls, too. Other girls had dolls that could wet themselves or talk, or dolls that came with exotic wardrobes. They could be taken to school and their high-heeled shoe straps unbuckled, saris unwound, hats rejected or changed, and hairstyles rearranged. Her dolls—Nora's dolls—were garbed as if they had tumbled out of bed or returned from long journeys. They showed up with scars and disfigurements, or with unlikely companions such as tiny birds and skinny horses. Some of them carried little packsacks, and miniature scrolls imprinted with Bible verses or poems. They were not dolls that had been featured on television or in movies or even in books, like the dollies of Pearl's friends. Some of them appeared to be in distress, hunched into oddment coverings as if they were wounded and cold.

Nora had managed to rescue most of the dolls that Pearl threw in flower beds or sneaked into the trash. She tucked them away in the chest in her cupboard until Pearl changed her mind and asked for them. Some of the dolls, though, Nora could not find, and Pearl had forgotten where she'd left them.

It's quiet in the house with Nora away, and Pearl soon structures a routine. Although her nights are full of dreams, she sleeps soundly and rises refreshed, full of ideas. She runs through the neighbourhood, or practises yoga for half an hour on the deck; showers and makes breakfast with an avocado from one of Nora's trees, spreading the fruit thickly on toast. She turns off her phone to avoid Gerry-David's calls and texts, and places it in a running shoe in the closet so she will remember to take it with her when she goes out. The van nests, hidden at the beach.

Pearl seats herself at Nora's dining room table and catches up on her blog. "Living a simpler life due to changed personal circumstances," she writes, "has helped me appreciate the basics. I have several new recipes to share, but this one is my favourite."

It really is a favourite. In its way, it embodies her entire philosophy: explore, improvise, do no harm, learn something new. Pearl notes to her followers that unless they need to purchase algae, this dish—Diatom

Soup—costs nothing to make. "Process and intention are free," she writes. "Diatom Soup helps underline the lesson."

> *You will need a bowl or a watertight basket, several egg-sized rocks, and a greenwood stick for stirring coals or moving stones. If no algae bloom is available for the broth, you can order jars of pure algae from my website. Build your fire on the beach or on a cliff and watch the sunset. Remember that hardwoods, which burn slow and hot, are preferable, although some of you may like the cooler and faster softwoods. Heat the rocks in the fire and drop them into your bowl or basket of algae mixed with water. The heat in the rocks will make the Diatom Soup boil. Sip the soup with a wooden spoon or scoop and enjoy your reconnection to the natural world.*

Pearl's two-minute vlog, the one the streaming platform liked, featured Pearl and several companions collecting mussels, and Pearl serving mussel stew for dinner. The expanded version—the demo—will be more detailed so that people can follow along, but it will still feature Pearl and her friends gathering ingredients for seafood dishes in the wild, and cooking and eating them together. Over time, if a series evolves, her friends will become recurring characters whose careers and relationships intertwine with the rising challenge of sourcing high-quality foraged food.

The fishing boat *Solar Ray* leaves harbour at dawn with Pearl's friend Jack at the wheel, his girlfriend Debbie navigating, and Pearl filming. Ahead, as they enter the open channel, is the heave of a fast-running sea; behind, the land dwindles to mist and smoke. On the way to Pink Pelican Island, Jack cuts the engine, and they haul in the homemade shrimp traps he set out the day before.

"It may be easier to buy fresh shrimp in the fish market," Pearl says to the camera she is handling, "but catching them yourself is more rewarding." She lifts one of the pink glistening shellfish from a bucket. Its eyes are glossy and moist, its feelers wave, sensing the air.

"Here, catch!" Pearl cries and tosses the shrimp at Jack. He ducks and it misses him, but as Debbie stoops for it, a wave splashes over the bow and soaks her. By the time she emerges from the cabin with a blanket draped over her swimsuit, they are at the sea cave opening they've been aiming for. "This is where we'll find the rest of the ingredients for dinner," Pearl says.

Jack waits for a break in the waves and steers the fishing boat into the gloom. Inside the cave, Debbie plays a spotlight over stone that shimmers red and yellow and green. "The colours come from minerals and algae," Pearl tells her video audience. The cavern narrows. "Shut the engine off, Jack," she murmurs. As *Solar Ray* drifts, the spotlight illuminates rock outcroppings of anemones, urchins, and sponges. Sea cucumbers, disturbed by their presence, flatten, contract their bodies and inch into the shadows.

"How do they do that?" Deborah asks.

"They have suction-cup feet," Pearl says. Echoing seawash thickens their voices. She leans from the boat and pries a retreating sea cucumber from its shelf to show Debbie. It shortens into a smaller sausage shape and deposits dark linear material into her palm. "That's its guts," Pearl explains. "They self-eviscerate when they're frightened, but their insides do regrow." She passes the invertebrate to her friend.

"How can you tell the males from the females?" Deborah asks, casting an eye over the other sea cucumber colonies. "They all look the same to me."

"You'd have to dissect the gonads if you wanted to know for sure, but in a clean environment, sea cucumbers expel innumerable eggs and sperm—gametes—into the sea where a chemical attraction brings the eggs and sperm together."

Outside the cave, Pearl films the rolling, ruffling sea, wave on wave piled and columnar from the deep. Within the sea's lifting, tumbling microscopic detritus, aquatic life searches and finds or fails to find what it needs.

In town, wet fog blows through the streets, weaving scarves through the garden of Nora's house, and softening the clack of eucalyptus leaves. Inside the house, Pearl tidies Nora's clutter from the dining room, and runs upstairs to change into a black dress and a pair of heels from Nora's closet.

The dining room table is set with Nora's linen, good china, and crystal glasses. On a long metal stand behind the table, an aquarium gurgles and fizzes oxygen. Intended for species that might appear in future episodes, Pearl has left it empty for the demo. Laughter trills in from outside: Pearl's glance through the French doors confirms that her friends are drinking the cocktails they'd filmed themselves making earlier. Together, the three of them had peeled, boiled, and iced the shrimp. Next, Pearl had shown them how to clean sea cucumbers by slicing off their ends, inserting the knife into the resulting tubes and splitting them down the centre. Once the remnants of guts were wiped away, they'd begun the long process of paring away the long grey strips they'd be eating. With the strips in boiling water (it took about an hour for them to cook) and starting wild rice cooking on "lo," they'd sat at the kitchen table drinking wine and mashing cream, sour cream, salt, and lime juice with avocado; and blending coconut cream with finely minced chilis.

Pearl looks at her watch: the strips should be about done.

In the kitchen, she films herself testing the boiling sea cucumber for tenderness and sieving the strips to put onto plates. She makes sun patterns with them and distributes generous dollops of coconut-chili cream and trails of avocado sauce over each serving. After stirring the rice with a fork to fluff it up, she knocks on the glass to bring Jack and Deb indoors.

At the table, candlelight softens the faces of her friends. Deb's blonde hair acquires an aureole; Jack's beard and deep eye-sockets lend him gravity. He yawns and takes Deb's hand. She is draped in a poncho belonging to Nora. It has slipped a little: her bare shoulders display the sheen of old varnish. She closes her eyes and hums. Between the three of them they've eaten all the shrimp and most of the rice and made inroads on the sea cucumber which, admittedly, takes some getting used to.

"I'll make coffee and bring in dessert," Pearl says.

"We've been cooking inside today," she adds, getting up, "but you could do all we've done today, outdoors. Next time, I'll show you how to prepare sauces in sea-shells and bake them over a campfire."

If there is a next time. Pearl is too tired to know if any-thing they have filmed will be worthwhile. She screws the camera onto a tripod in the kitchen.

"I've had a ginger-maple syrup glaze—as simple as it sounds: maple syrup and grated ginger—cooking at low temperature with diced leftover sea cucumber. Let's see how it turned out." She scoops golden candied chunks from the pot and drops them into tiny antique bowls; re-boils the kettle, makes coffee in the French press and places it all, along with three mugs, on a tray. Taking the camera with her, she returns to the dining room.

"It's the unpredictability that will make people like the show, Pearl," Jack told her. Deb added, "You've got to let it flow." It had not flowed. She should not have worn Nora's dress.

Debbie and Jack's places at the dining table are empty. Pearl's eyes roam the room: after all this effort how could they have left without telling her? The tray trembles in her hands, but she settles it on the table without incident. As she does, she hears a whiffling noise near her feet. She lifts the curtaining edge of the tablecloth, and there are her friends, asleep on the Persian carpet in each oth-er's arms. Debbie snores and bubbles. Jack's breath lifts a strand of her hair. Pearl fetches a blanket from a chest in the living room and covers them; and then she sits and films herself eating ginger-and-maple-syrup-glazed diced sea cucumber and drinking coffee alone.

It takes a week for Pearl to edit the footage. The seascape and cave shots are fine, even spectacular; and by splicing in a mix of Jack and Debbie's comments, Pearl comes across as no more than quirkily awkward. The food looks good, and the journey from sourcing to dining is slow-paced but not boring. The ending, instead of showcasing Pearl's loneliness, as she'd feared, is low-key and sweet.

Pearl pauses, about to email the file to her agent. What would she do if a SaveOurSouls cooking series caught on? She envisions people combing coastal sea caves and stripping them of their bounty. But no. That would never happen. Pearl hits *send*.

That evening, after checking her email for messages from her agent or Nora, or a transfer of funds from Gerry-David, Pearl fetches the Theano doll from the shelf in her bedroom and places it in front of her on the table. Being in the house and recollecting how Nora *is* and what the stories mean to her, Pearl has decided to accommodate Nora's request sooner than she planned. Pearl dreams about the dolls. The stories that accompany them swirl through the air. The only time they are not on Pearl's mind is when she swims—an activity that has always cleared her thinking. In any case, Pearl will write the Theano story, hoping it makes things better between her and her grandmother.

Pearl opens her laptop. She straightens the little doll's linen dress and traces its embroidered spirals with a finger. In the golden spiral, each quarter turn widens by the factor φ (phi)—the golden ratio, the proportion for beauty characteristic to all arts and sciences—which Theano is said to have discovered. The fabric feels thicker than Pearl remembers. She turns it inside out. On its underside is a wide strip of masking tape marked with the Greek letter φ and a sentence in Nora's writing: *There are eighty-five generations between Theano and you. When you write the story, don't forget to put that in.*

With a sigh, and a surrendering to the tools of memory and writing that Nora has taught her, Pearl begins.

~

The Philosopher's Tale

Fifth-Century Greek Colony, Croton

Eighty-five generations ago, on a day etched into history by the actions of earth and water, Theano, a teacher of mathematics and philosophy at the Academy founded by her husband Pythagoras near Croton, sat with her students on cushioned stone benches indoors. The poet the class had come to hear had only recently arrived. He had made a long journey over snow-capped mountains and then a dangerous crossing by sea after his patron was killed in Athens during a political uprising. Why he had fled to the school for refuge, he had not said. Theano's husband had not even greeted the younger man and had moved his classes elsewhere, claiming the poet had nothing to say of interest to them or to him. Theano on the other hand, who had known the poet before her marriage, hoped that the story he chose to tell this morning would reveal his thinking.

She listened; but the students braced their heads on their arms and yawned, scarcely pretending to pay attention as the poet recounted the well-known tale of the goddess Demeter's search for her daughter Persephone who was abducted by Hades, the god of the dead, who wanted her for his wife. Those nearest the window watched waves wash onto the shingle at the foot of the Academy hill. Even the poet's dog sighed in the doorway, lay down, put its paws over its ears, and slept. Theano shifted to ease her back. So far, the poet had told them nothing new. He had not helped his standing with the students by introducing himself as one who believed in telling and retelling the old stories. "Why taint great myths with the trivia of daily life?" he said. "Everything mankind needs to know is retained within them."

Theano herself believed that tales of ordinary people were as valuable as those of gods and heroes and could guide her students through their lives.

With few fresh details to add, the poet relied on dramatic recital. The longing of the goddess for her kidnapped child was heartbreaking. He clutched his heart. The violence of the god of death was reprehensible—the poet raised his fist—but because Hades was a god he could not be held accountable. What, then, were they to learn? The story set the creative force of the goddess of fertility's maternal love against the underworld god's annihilating will. It was life against death, but since creation and destruction both were vital to existence, the lesson lay in the struggle between them. The poet lifted his hands in front of him as if each held a weight, raising one hand and then the other.

Theano adjusted a cushion. What about a third point of view? Shouldn't Persephone have a say in what happened to her?

The poet came to the final act of the narrative. God and goddess agreed to share the girl, allowing her six months with her mother in spring and summer, and six months in the cold and dark with her captor. The poet's voice shook with emotion. His lip quivered. He looked directly at Theano. Theano gazed back. What was he trying to convey? When they were lovers, they were young, neither giving way to the other. Had he regrets? Did he mean that he and Pythagoras should share her? Was that why he had made such a long and arduous journey? He had never lacked audacity, but to cast himself as her rescuer, as spring itself, and her husband as Hades! Where was the consideration for her vocation, for her?

The room they sat in was open to the air; the doorway where the dog lay led to a colonnaded porch. In the lengthening silence, the animal pushed to its feet and growled.

Theano's thoughts continued. Perhaps the poet believed, wrongly, that she pined for him. Her marriage wasn't perfect, but she had learned that love required tolerance and sacrifice. Yet, misguided and threadbare as he was, she had to admire the muscles of his arms and shoulders, and the swell of his calves above his shoddy footwear. It would be a while before it was safe for him to return to the city and find a new patron. For the sake of old friendship, nothing more, she would persuade Pythagoras to ask him to stay.

The students stirred, sensing too late for politeness that their lecturer had finished his talk and would require a response. The dog's growl changed to a whine. It ran to the poet, latched its teeth onto his wrist and tugged him towards the doorway.

A loud bass rumbling rushed through the Earth. Theano thought of the ghosts that leapt from holes and frightened horses at chariot races, the horses so terrified that the charioteers crashed into one another. The building shook, the floor swayed and buckled. She grabbed the nearest students and pulled them down with her, crouching and covering her head with her arms. Several ceiling beams shattered and fell, one of them onto the tile on which the poet had been standing moments before.

As soon as the shaking ceased, Theano crawled from the debris, and called, "Quickly! Everyone outside!" She said the name of each student as, coughing and sobbing, they stumbled past her into the sunshine. "Keep moving! Hurry! Hurry!" she cried. More stones came loose and tumbled into the classroom. They were lucky. In this small class all had come out safely.

The sun was high in the sky; no shadows softened the damaged buildings. A few cypress trees were uprooted, but the gardens around the classrooms were little changed. A student sobbed. No birds flew between branches of the upright trees, and the dog stared silently at the sea. As they clung together and watched, the frill of waves that rinsed the shoreline below, thinned.

Holding the poet's hand, Theano turned to offer reassurance, but the pressure on her ears increased, and she struggled to breathe as air rushed out of her lungs taking with it any words she might have spoken. The dog lifted its head and howled.

The expanse of beach grew, broadening and extending south-eastwards at a gallop. Shipwrecks long erased from memory lay exposed to view. A trickle of figures scurried down the rocks from the caves at the northern curve of the bay and ran onto the sand. These were teachers and students who used the caves as private classrooms. For a reason Theano could not understand, they paused to stare seaward as the horizon began to rise.

"Run!" she screamed. "Run!" If they heard her and ran, she did not know, for the poet was hauling her behind him, and the roar of the rapidly advancing wave masked all sound except for the shrieks of those beside her. For a moment, thinking that with her ability to swim in treacherous waters, she could help the drowning, she let go of the poet, but then she grabbed onto a nearby girl who took hold of the boy next to her. Forming a chain, Theano, the students, and the poet hove, staggered and pushed each other uphill as quickly as they could. When they turned around at the crest of the promontory, they saw that the wave had scoured the harbour and the fishing town, mounted to the Academy precinct, and smashed its buildings and walls. Already it had begun to recede, leaving a grimy remnant draining down the hill from the ruins to the sea.

At once, they built a fire and posted lookouts for survivors. A chain of beacons sprang high along the coastline giving Theano hope that many had escaped; but the stragglers who found her group brought little good news. Instead, they gave the names of those they knew were killed in the earthquake or taken by the sea for Theano to tally. Each account piled horror on horror and bore witness to the rapidity with which their friends had shed their bodies. No one could begin a search for the missing before the waters dropped completely, but the granting of immortality through remembrance of the dead was a task that had to start immediately.

"The past cannot be changed," Theano counselled, talking with her students as they began their labour.

"Destiny may be destiny, but it is susceptible to will." The students nodded: Theano had screamed *Run*! while those on the beach had gawked and done nothing. "It is all too easy in the scattering and grief that follow a tragedy, for forgetfulness to erase the record of the lost from existence," she told them.

The poet stood listening, biting his lip, standing aside. Theano and the students remembered locations in the Academy and its gardens for each of their vanished colleagues. The order of encounter was by class, youngest to oldest, and then by employment, along a route Pythagoras and Theano had taken at the beginning of each year. Those who knew each person best, assigned them objects and articles of dress to prompt recall of their family name, birthplace, attributes, and field of study or work.

"Each person has a gift," Theano had told them on their arrival at the school. "Your task while you are at the academy is to find it." Opportunities presented themselves from the storehouse of infinity but retreated into it if they were not seized. The enemy of creation was invisibility; failure to attain potential was a misuse of life, but many of the departed had scarcely begun their search.

The memory task complete and the fire burned down to coals and radiating a steady heat, the students went to gather what they could for food before darkness fell. Theano said to the poet, "The recollection of individual stories is a gift to us and to the families of the dead. Even the most frightened can feel there is a lifeline out of the evils of this day. Too often the old narratives have been emptied of emotion and do little to help."

The poet said, "The traditional tales are deep, unchangeable containers of proven worth. You put your trust in personal accounts which rarely plumb the depths. Nothing I have heard today, no matter how poignant, convinces me otherwise."

"But, this morning," she said, in an attempt to be conciliatory, "you talked of ancient matters with passion. What you spoke of touched you closely. Feeling is coincident with meaning, don't you think?. Will you tell me, friend, what lay behind those emotions?"

"You dwell on details and neglect the larger view," he said. "Human life is brief and full of suffering; it has nothing lasting to teach. Unshakeable truth resides in tales of beings greater than us; they are the only accounts worth preserving. Your efforts are medicinal and nothing more. Your work with theorems, however, demonstrates the permanence brought into being by the gods. We are not as far apart as you might think."

"I do not think of permanence but of discovery," she said. "What is certain now may become a record of our mistakes."

A girl returned from foraging and sat beside Theano with the herbs and greens she had gathered in her lap. "I have heard you say that the soul may be reborn in animals and plants as well as in humans," she said, her eyes downcast.

"Of course. It is why equality between life forms is more valuable than dominance, one over the other."

"Plants and animals!" the poet muttered. "What about the infinite!"

"Will those who died *today* reappear?" the girl asked.

"That is what I believe," Theano answered.

"How will we recognize them?"

Theano let a few seconds pass, then said, "We are given clues to the reappearance of those we love by the attraction which draws them to us, and by a feeling of familiarity; but we cannot know for certain."

The girl lifted her eyes to her teacher. "But how will I go on without the companionship of those I love? Who is going to help me through the days and nights to come?"

The poet and the teacher each took one of the girl's hands. "Your gods are deaf to human need," Theano murmured to the poet, but no helpful story sprang to mind, and she had no more comfort to give.

The child of a servant in Pythagoras's household slipped away from the fire and down the hill to the wreckage of the Academy quarters in which until that day, she'd lived with her mother, two brothers and a sister. Her father had died in the winter. The little girl, Aya, had not gone with her family that morning when they'd left carrying food and water for the teachers and students in the caves. Instead, she'd stayed home to practise her letters. When the earthquake struck, she'd grabbed her mother's shawl, dashed outside, and joined Theano and her students as they ran uphill. Her family was already dead—killed in a rockslide before they'd even reached the caves.

From a high cupboard in an intact wall in one of the ruined rooms, Aya retrieved her mother's sewing basket and the little dolls that were her mother's inheritance. Aya's grandparents had escaped their homeland ahead of an advancing Persian army, hoping to build a future in the Greek islands for themselves and their daughter. But as they'd neared the island of Samos (Pythagoras's birthplace), their boat had overturned. Aya's mother was the sole survivor. Pythagoras had found her on a beach with a package containing the dolls, wrapped in oil-cloth, bound to her body. She'd been part of Pythagoras's household ever since.

Aya swaddled the dolls in her mother's shawl and remembered the stories her mother had told her. She reclaimed her sister's earrings from behind the stone where her sister had cached them, and put them on. The ceiling over her brothers' room had collapsed, but she dug out a few damp wooden toys and buttons they'd played with and added them to the basket along with a candle she'd found.

As dusk neared, Aya returned to the fire, placed the dolls on the ground, lit the candle, and began making outfits for them with the scraps from her mother's sewing. They were simple clothes. She used her mother's dressmaker's knives to make a hole in the material to go over the head, and stitches to join the sides under the arms. As she stitched, she said the name and told the story of a member of her family, and attached an object or two, or embroidered symbols onto the costume. For her sister she made a wooden bird, because her sister had loved birds and could call them to her. On the brothers' clothing she embroidered fish, because they liked to swim and dive, and took pleasure in the underwater world. For her mother she devised a tiny shell comb because her mother had beautiful hair. All this she did to store in her mind those she had lost. She even made a doll of herself with a stick family tied to it, and an acanthus embroidered on its garb as a sign that all living things return. Out of gratitude for Theano's teachings, she made a doll of her as well and decorated its dress with gold thread. She made another doll of the poet because she liked him. When she finished, she gave the basket of sewing scraps to the student who had spoken of missing her friends. Then she nestled all the dolls close in her arms and lay down and spread her mother's shawl over them and herself, but not before tying seed pods as floats to each of them, just in case.

After everyone else had eaten and gone to sleep, Theano and the poet huddled together for comfort, and kept vigil, and told each other what was in their hearts: of the unrelenting speed of time, of the rarity of a second chance.

At dawn, Theano's husband breasted the hill in the company of his students, and Theano stood to greet him.

"I was forewarned," he said. "When the birds flocked and fled inland, we followed them."

"Did you give everyone you met the warning?" she asked him. "Did you light the beacons?"

"All of us lost valuable time although we had none to spare, Theano."

She nodded and embraced him. The poet moved over to make room for him to sit down.

"Look," Theano said, pointing to where the waves rolled gently in as if nothing had happened. A line on the land marked the furthest advance of the wave. Survivors trawled through the debris, filling baskets, pots, and bags made from rags—anything they could find—with stranded fish. "At least no one will go hungry," she said. "Some good can come from this misery."

"Good?" the poet said. "Not for the drowned."

"What shall we be when our souls transmigrate after death?" Theano's husband said, looking not at the beached sea life, but at the bodies along the shore. "Shall we be fish or birds like these we see on land and in the sky, or will we be new versions of ourselves? What about the poet? What will he be? What is his future?" Pythagoras held the poet's eyes.

The poet patted the dog, which had come from its nosings in the night to lie next to him. The little girl with the dolls woke and came to sit with the dog. The dolls slumbered on under the shawl.

Theano said, "Time is our future. Our poet is going to teach with us for now. Things will settle and then we will see."

"I will take responsibility for the servant's child," the poet said unexpectedly. Aya and the dog looked at him. Theano's eyebrows rose. "I have no family and no other ties," he said. "I must do what I can."

"Her name is Aya. To raise a child is a life's commitment," Theano said.

"She can care for you in old age," Theano's husband said. "That is not a bad idea."

"Old age?" said his wife.

"To raise a child is to hope," the poet said. "What is your hope, Theano?"

"How is your writing on virtue coming along?" Pythagoras interrupted.

"Surely, virtue is to choose," Theano answered. The poet's dog shifted and rested against her legs.

~

Pearl hesitates. At this point in the story Nora would ask Pearl to decide whom she thought Theano would want to be with—the poet or the husband; or for Pearl to imagine a different possibility because stories *could* change their endings.

Once or twice, Pearl said "the husband" because Pythagoras, although elderly and jealous of the poet, was reliable and seemed kind. At other times, she chose the poet because he was more romantic. He and Theano might argue but they liked each other. Pearl's favourite idea, though, was for Theano to pick the dog because Pearl, herself, longed for one.

But, "She might choose the little girl," Pearl told Nora. It was after she spent the day making images of her absent parents from paper towel and toilet paper rolls, tape, and a marking pen.

"Umm," Nora said. "I wonder."

Adult Pearl has another idea. She forges on.

~

Theano got to her feet and gazed at the sitting men. Her husband's lips tightened; the poet canvassed the horizon. The dog stretched as if it might rise and accompany her, but instead it inched closer to the child. Each was as determined as the others.

Theano sighed. "Virtue also lies in action," she said, and turned on her heel to go down the hill and try to repair the damage.

~

Pearl yawns, shuts down the computer, turns out the lights, and heads upstairs. She stashes the Theano doll beneath her pillow, gets into bed and pulls the quilt up under her chin.

What happened to those in the story? Did the earthquake and tsunami change the trajectory of Theano's life? Was she happy? Did the dolls and their stories help Aya, the servant's child, or the girl with the questions, or any of the others to get safely through the nights?

Pearl listens as the house settles. In the darkness, with the honk of fog horns heralding a sea haze in the straits, she is conscious that she is waiting for what Nora called the nightly closing of flowers, petal after petal folding into an evening hush. Close on that thought is the recollection that Nora stores an emergency disaster pack in the cottage off the veranda, another in the garden shed, and a third onboard *SeaPin*. Pearl is glad this is so, but it will not divert a catastrophe if one is on the way.

In the night, in the small hours when if something important needs doing, it gets done, Pearl awakens thirsty. As she passes by Nora's bedroom on her way down to the kitchen, she hears snoring. Quietly, she opens the door to find Nora in bed, snuffling. After a couple of snorts, Nora rumbles full bore. Her unopened suitcase leans against the closet.

Pearl glances down the hallway and sees that Nora has taped a note to Pearl's bedroom door. She closes Nora's door softly and continues on her way. She is happy to have her grandmother home. It means she can talk to her sooner than she'd expected about staying on *SeaPin* instead of in Gerry-David's van, until she can rent a place of her own. Pearl is pleased to have finished the

Theano story; to be able to give it to Nora as a sign that she loves her grandmother despite their differences. It has been more pleasant spending time in Nora's world than she anticipated, and now she wants Nora to tell her what she has done with the other dolls.

From the top of the stairs, Pearl scents sandalwood, earth, and fish. She treads carefully and descends to find what look like Nora's dolls, but life-sized, flocking round the dining room table—as if the dolls she had seated there years before as a little girl had kept on growing. She runs a hand through her hair, tightens the belt of the dressing gown and moves past the gathered figures to the kitchen where she runs cold water into a glass and drinks quickly without looking round. Odd things happen in Nora's house. She used to be accustomed to it. They are illusions, not real, caught in the web of a suspended childhood imagination. They will subside as soon as she confronts them. She closes her eyes and opens them again, aware of an unpleasant sensation. A fishing net slung over a dining chair has sprawled across the floor and caught on one of her toes. She has dragged half of it with her, its clammy strings lapping her ankles. Behind her, floorboards creak and a breeze gusts through an open window. Pearl inhales perfumes of the sea and the garden. The leaves of the avocado tree clack. She drinks another glass of water, turns, and looks through the kitchen into the dining room. The figures are still there.

One of them enters the kitchen and unfastens the cupboard doors. As Pearl is about to speak and put an end to whatever is going on, the phone in her dressing gown pocket chirrups. Pearl turns it off, and trailing the phantom, replaces everything the visitor removes—a jar of honey, a bottle of whisky, and a jug of milk from the fridge. Then, reconsidering, she takes it all out again and makes two hot toddies: one for herself and one for Nora. She puts the drinks on a tray, and ignoring the intruders, retraces her steps.

Upstairs again, Pearl opens her grandmother's door. Moonlight sheds through the window and reveals Nora awake. She is sitting up in bed, her grey hair tucked behind her ears. She's holding a pillow to her face.

"Nora? It's me. Are you all right?" Pearl puts the mugs on the bedside table. One slops and burns her fingers.

"I hate tea," the muffled voice says.

"It's not tea. What are you doing with that pillow?"

Nora lifts her head: flakes of blood clog her nostrils. A dark stain dampens the pillowcase. "Do you know, Pearl," her grandmother says, sniffing and dabbing at her nose with a corner of a sheet, "it's the funniest thing, but I thought I was talking to my mother; I wonder what happened to her?"

"You've got a nosebleed. I'll get some ice and towels." Pearl wants to ask, *Why are you home early, like this?* and *Help me, please!* but she can't.

"She was a dressmaker."

"Who?"

"My mother: she worked at the Emporium, but really she was known for her good taste. She was a beautiful dresser. I learned how to sew from her."

"I'll be right back. Do you want me to bring anything else?"

"No. Wait—my workbag from the guest room."

"Pearl?" Nora says. Pearl turns from the door. "I'm glad you're here."

Nora's nose gushes fresh blood, and Pearl dashes downstairs.

The dining room is empty, but the chairs are askew. The French doors are open. Out of the corner of her eye, Pearl confirms that the life-sized *dolls* have moved outside. She has no time to decide what this means. If she has a foot in two worlds, so be it: Nora needs her.

Pearl takes an icepack from the freezer, and towels, clean sheets, and pillowcases from the linen closet. In the bathroom she runs cold water into the sink, soaks two small towels, and fills a bowl with water to take upstairs. With the linen under an arm, the bowl and wet towels in her hands and the ice pack balanced on them, she pushes Nora's door open with her shoulder. As she does, she feels someone passing ahead of her into the room. Quickly, Pearl places a wet towel on the nape of Nora's neck and gives her the other towel, folded over the icepack, to hold to her nose. She drapes the bath towels over the bedclothes. Then she consults the list by Nora's bedside, and calls Nora's doctor. She leaves a message with the answering service even though Nora discards the towel pack, sniffs experimentally, and says, "It's all right. I'm fine. Did you bring the workbag?"

"I really think you should rest."

"Don't fret, Pearl. Please, just do what I ask."

When Pearl returns, Nora is dozing. Pearl does what she can with the bloodstained linen, lays the workbag by Nora, then fetches a quilt and a pillow from her own bedroom and settles herself in an armchair. She is asleep in a minute, exhausted by the happenings, but is awakened by the bang of the front door.

"Who is it?" Pearl calls. She is on her feet, but Nora says, from the bed, "Just leave it, Pearl." Pearl makes another move to go and investigate, but Nora says, "Wait." She struggles upright, opens the workbag, and sifts through an overflow of fabric scraps, ribbons, sequins, thread and feathers. "I have it somewhere."

"Gran?"

"Half a sec. Now, where did I put it?"

Pearl sits on the bed. Her fingers clench the sleeve of Nora's nightgown. "What do they want? Why do I see them, Gran?"

"We weren't born just to pass the time, Pearl. Ah, I've got it! It belongs to Rosa, of course." Nora closes the fingers of Pearl's free hand on a swirl of tiny blue and green feathers she has mined from the scraps. It is a miniature cape; a new version of the ratty one Pearl remembers tied round the shoulders of one of the missing dolls. "The feathers were coming loose; I've been trying to fix it, but I've had to do it over. How do you find cormorant feathers nowadays?" Nora says. "You will finish it for me, Pearl, won't you?"

Pearl covers Nora's hand with her own, then lifts and kisses it. "I can't do the things you can, I never could." Time is carrying them quickly.

"Your question about why they come …" Nora closes her eyes and leans against the pillows. There are spots of blood on her nightdress.

"Don't!" Pearl says.

Nora opens her eyes, smiles and says, "Oh, look, Pearl! My mother has made me a birthday cake!"

Pearl springs to her feet to prevent what must be coming, but she cannot stop it. Blood floods from Nora's nostrils and mouth. In seconds it has soaked through the towels Pearl is holding. Then, Nora's absence from her body is so emphatic that it must be a mistake. People do not vanish like that, one second to the next. Pearl glances round the room, sees the closed suitcase and looks out the open window at the path to the street, as if her grandmother might have decided to take it. The blur of the harbour comes from her tears, not from the knot of indistinct figures at the end of the garden beneath the transplanted oaks. Pearl sits with her grandmother's body and sponges it. She changes the blood-soaked nightgown and linen and throws them onto the floor, and then she lies down and lays her head on Nora's shoulder. "I wrote a story for you," she says. "Why couldn't you wait?"

When Pearl reaches the doctor, he says, "I am sorry, Pearl. It's what we expected, but I would have liked to see her again."

He pauses then, and says, "I gave her the lab results and she asked me how much time she had left." He sighs. "It was just a guess, but it was less than I'd hoped."

"I didn't know," Pearl says.

"You were in the café where I brought the test results. I'd promised to let her know right away. Didn't she say anything?"

Pearl does not respond. He goes on, "The undertakers will come soon for the body; I have papers for you to sign."

"Shouldn't I be the one to … ?"

"I'll make the arrangements. Nora and I agreed I would when the time came."

Her father, Harry, answers her call at the reception desk of his motel, Casa Rocinante, in Vancouver. "Ah," he says. And then, "Nora asked that you scatter her ashes on Pink Pelican Island and other places important to her. Can you do that for her?"

"How could you know what she wanted, Harry! She's only just gone!"

"I'm her executor. She's been trying to visit everybody she needed to say goodbye to." He pauses. "Unfortunately, your mother was away. Sara disappears at bad news, always has. Anyway, I'll call her agent."

"But if Nora knew she was dying why didn't she tell *me*?" Remorse twists Pearl's entrails. Nora had asked for her company on this last journey—such a small thing—and Pearl had turned her down.

"She didn't want you to be upset. It was important to her that you make your own decisions. Anyway, everything has been arranged. You're to have the house and *SeaPin*. The Foundation gets the other assets. There isn't much else. We have to decide between the four of us what happens to her effects."

"The four of us?"

"You and me—as I said, I'm also the executor—and Sara and Joachim. Loretta's mother, Judy, gets a stipend as long as she lets family stay in the cabin."

"Who is Joachim? What cabin?"

"The cabin on Nootka island. Judy said she would take responsibility for it. It's complicated. Look, first things first, Pearl." Then he tells her of Nora's illness, so recently diagnosed. "The doctor said she could go quickly. The body gets overwhelmed. From what you say, I don't think she suffered."

"Everyone knew but me," Pearl says. "I wish ..." but what she wishes has opened an unutterable chasm.

When Pearl eventually goes downstairs, the dining room is shipshape, bereft of spectres, spilled food and drink or noticeable odours: everything she feared and half-hoped she might find has evaporated with daylight. She checks the other rooms. They too are in order. The night might not have happened, except that Nora's lifeless body is upstairs; and whatever that will mean to the rest of Pearl's life lies ahead.

As soon as the undertaker leaves—Nora's body on a stretcher under a sheet, the tight turn in the upstairs hallway, a slip and a stumble on the stairs, the final closing of the solid oak front door behind the stretcher-bearers—Pearl goes into Nora's room.

She opens the night table drawer, a jumble of pens and safety pins, then the shelf below and its stack of maps, brochures, and books. She shakes out the pages of each tome—*History of California Missions*, *Troubadour Poetry*, *Medieval Crusades*, *The Horse from the Deriivka to Master Kikkuli*, and others—and dislodges some bookmarks and a grocery list. To the chest of drawers then, through underwear and keepsakes (Pearl's baby things), knitted bonnets, and booties and sweaters, a crocheted jacket, a christening shawl, and white kid slippers that must have belonged to Sara, or maybe to Nora herself. Then through T-shirts, sweat pants, gloves, and nightgowns; and in the closet, tall boots, hiking boots, ballet shoes, sandals, big swingy skirts, evening gowns, cocktail dresses, a woman's tuxedo, white shirts and silk blouses, and hats with netting: Pearl riffles, rummages, and combs.

Back in her own bedroom, she searches drawers, the cupboard, and among toys and tennis racquets beneath the bed. In the sewing room she rakes through boxes of patterns and materials, bags of clothing set aside for refugees, and through Nora's desk stuffed with letters from teachers, missions, the United Nations, scrawled notes in alien penmanship—all the texture of Nora, but never a shred of a message for Pearl.

Downstairs next, she trolls through columns of CDs and rows of vinyl records, shakes out sheets and pillowcases in the linen cupboard, and empties ice cube trays in the freezer. It is a madness against which Pearl is helpless.

Then to Nora's room again, to confirm … what? Nora's presence or absence? Her aura is palpable. Pearl catches sight of herself in the hall mirror, pulling at her hair *like a maenad*—a Nora phrase, words from a story—wild, in fragments, overcome. Death the thief. Death that offers nothing but stones in place of living comfort.

It is barely dawn when Pearl awakens on the fourth day after Nora's death in the only place she is able to sleep: on the floor beneath her grandmother's dining room table, on the Persian carpet for which Pearl's grandfather had traded whisky from Pink Pelican Island. Her great-grandmother's portrait hangs on the wall. Each night Pearl has the same dream of digging in beach shingle with a toy shovel while Nora walks away until she is out of sight.

Nora's friends have brought casseroles which Pearl puts in the freezer or warms to serve visitors who need to sit and talk. Some of them bring bottles of homemade wine, uncork them and fill glasses; others have made themselves useful by cutting the grass, pruning canes, keeping the kitchen swept, even washing windows. Pearl has accepted their condolences, tried to smile and think of Nora anecdotes to share, and find Nora photographs to show, but all she can focus on is her failure to understand what Nora had needed from her in the café. They had been such simple demands: that Pearl accompany her grandmother on a journey, and that she record the dolls' stories. What else in Pearl's life could have been more urgent?

Pearl showers and dons the black dress and heels she had taken earlier from Nora's closet. She makes coffee and sits down to wait. Nora's doctor has offered to collect the ashes from the crematorium and bring them over. He has been kind. He helped Pearl pick out a wicker coffin for the cremation and made it possible for Pearl to sit with Nora's body at the mortuary those first few days for as long as she wanted.

Pearl has not asked anyone to mark today's occasion with her, although any of Nora's friends, or her own, would have volunteered. Even Gerry-David had texted a brief, "Need me?" It was Pearl's task to receive her grandmother appropriately, with respect and without fuss—as

Nora would have wanted—and get on with the task of carrying out her grandmother's final wishes.

An indistinct noise draws her to open the front door. It might have been nothing but the wind blowing offshore, but at the top of the steps, she finds the container of ashes the doctor has left, along with a note: *I didn't want to disturb you in case you were sleeping.*

The box of Nora's ashes in her hands, Pearl is about to go inside when she senses a weight behind her. Someone touches her shoulder. She pivots, expecting to see the doctor. But it is not the doctor. It is Gerry-David.

"What about the keys, Pearl," he says. "I guess the timing's awkward, but were you going to give me the keys? I found the van, no help from you." While he waits for her to comply, he leans over her shoulder to look into the house. "I guess all of this is yours, hey? Things are looking up." Pearl sets the ashes on the doorstep.

The van keys are inside the door on a table in an envelope she had planned to mail. She tears it open, balls the keys in her fist, and looks down the driveway at a waiting car, engine running.

"New car?"

He shifts his feet. "No, no, not mine."

Pearl thinks for a moment, wonders if any of it is worth it. She does not trouble to define what *it* might mean. It is not the fault of the woman in the car though. "I'll just go and check," she says. The passenger window is open, so all Pearl must do when she is close enough is call out, "Your car or his?"

"His," she says. "It's brand new!"

"You'd better have these, then" she says, and tosses her the keys to the van.

PART II

ROSA: The Castaway's Tale

Six generations ago, Nora wrote, my grandmother's grandmother, Rosa, washed ashore on Pink Pelican Island. When you write the stories, don't forget to put that in.

A miracle. A little bay Pearl has known since childhood but never seen like this. She crouches on the deck of *SeaPin*, balanced against the rail, dawn light on her skin and on the wheat-coloured grass of the point to the east; but it is the water that holds her attention. From the foot of the granite cliffs to the rocky little beach and to *SeaPin*'s keel—a shallow cut in a glassy sea of silver and grey—float millions of tiny crustaceans. They are an inch or two below the surface, so that looking at them is like peering inside the orb of a clouded eye. Pink and coral, they quaver as if in a medium of jelly: thousands and thousands of them, thumbnail sized and less. Pearl finds the word for them: *krill*. They are their own primal soup.

As to what could have driven them inshore, she has no idea. It could be whales, or a raft of sea lions, or strong winds and tides, yet she cannot recollect any of these things from her journey through the sea lanes on *SeaPin*. She can recall little since she arrived in the bay. Judging from the evidence rolling on the deck, she had finished the bottle of tequila she'd found in Nora's onboard cabinet. Fortunately, both she and *SeaPin* appear to be unharmed.

Pearl tightens her stomach against a wave of nausea and tries not to move. Beneath a heavy sweater scrounged from Nora's locker, Pearl wears Nora's good black dress. On the deck beside her, Nora's workbag gapes open, revealing the Theano doll in one corner and a tumble of scraps and furbelows flattened by a squat cardboard container. One flap of the box is open: inside the box is a plastic bag stuffed with coarse grey powder.

Pearl does not make coffee or busy herself with the puzzle of why things are as they are; she does not set to tidying lines or clearing the deck. She doesn't even close the workbag: she is as immobile as her jittery muscles will allow, absorbing the message of the clouds of creatures in the water. Whatever lies in wait for her beyond the limits of drink-induced amnesia can wait a few minutes longer. All she thinks of now, is the beauty of the krill: no matter how brief their lives, regardless of the predators patrolling beyond the sheltered waters of the bay, there will be this yellow dawn, and what it is these primordial creatures do together that they cannot do on their own.

With the sun fully risen, *SeaPin* shipshape, and the krill following the welling of cool coastal water out of the bay, Pearl fires up the zodiac and takes it around the point, and along the base of the sea cliffs to the sea cave. She waits for the tide to drop so she can nudge the zodiac round a turn at the rear of the cavern. The cave roof is so low she must lie flat; the craft scrapes forward until it emerges into a large domed space with a cobble beach. It is cold, but a natural rock chimney admits enough light to illuminate cave wall paintings—red, black, and white spokes, wheels, cogs, mazes, winged-creatures, and bug-eyed beings so mysterious they must belong to an alternate evolution or be a catalogue in an ancient repository of dreams.

Pearl gathers dry beach dross and lights a fire for warmth. At the zodiac, she opens a waterproof flap, withdraws the cardboard container she had taken from Nora's workbag and tries to summon thoughts and words for a service. The first time she'd come to the cave it was with Nora and Harry. "Do you know how old the cave is?" Harry had asked his daughter. She was only eight years old. She shook her head.

Nora said, "Don't tease her, Harry."

"It was three thousand years old when I first saw it four years ago, so it must be three thousand and four years old now." Did he smile and tickle her under the chin? Had Pearl believed him? She didn't recall. How old was anything. Did it matter? Most of what Pearl knew was measured by her life in the eternal present. Why should a cave be any different? No reason, except that it was.

As Pearl scatters a thermos cup of Nora's ashes and asks the cave to fold her grandmother into its scale of time, some of the ash flies and dusts the cave walls. The rest settles in streaks on the beach stones. She closes the box, replaces it in the zodiac, draws the craft onto the shingle as far as it will go and loops a mooring line around a rock outcrop. The tide will have to finish rising and ebb again before she can leave. She makes herself comfortable inside the inflatable and listens to the hiss of steam as the water drenches the fire. No one knows where she is. Above her, she can hear birds twittering through the narrow chimney which opens into an inland gully near a fern-fringed pool of clear water. She is cold, hung over, and thirsty. If she cannot leave the cave, she will die. It is better not to think of it.

Pearl's hand slips into a pocket and finds the comforting shape of Theano. Theano: beset by disaster and competing men, yet with the best part of her life and work ahead of her.

On board *SeaPin*, with a bottle of water to drink, and before she investigates the stores in the galley, Pearl goes to her berth in the bow. She lifts the pillow to place the

Theano doll safely under it. The doll is her talisman. She has written its story for Nora. It is evidence of a thread—a lifeline—between her and her grandmother; of the possibility of making peace with her failings.

But beneath the pillow is another of Nora's dolls, Rosa, the doll Nora spoke to Pearl about on her last night, when she took the doll's tiny cloak-in-progress from the workbag, and said it was up to Pearl to finish it. Nora must have placed the doll in *SeaPin* for her to find!

The ice in Pearl's heart thaws. Pearl, who after hearing from Harry how Nora had spent her last weeks visiting everyone important to her, had looked obsessively through the house in case Nora had left something—anything!—to show that she had been thinking of Pearl as well. She lets out a cry; a gull in the rigging squawks and flees, and Pearl sobs with no one to hear her, except for a seal that has popped its head above the waves.

Later, Pearl brings the Rosa doll into the galley and props it on the shelf above the propane stove. The dark hair glued to the doll's head is coarse animal hair; the head and body are whalebone; the doll wears sealskin leggings along with the original balding cloak. A grass basket tied to one arm contains a tiny scroll on which Nora has written: *Six generations ago, my grandmother's grandmother, Rosa, washed ashore on Pink Pelican Island. When you write the story, don't forget to put that in.*

Pearl boils tank water, adds porridge oats, and stirs. Evaporated milk from a tin and a few crumbled cubes of sugar make the meal palatable. While she eats, and brews coffee with bottled water, segments of Rosa's tale assemble around the core Pearl recalls from her childhood.

More than ever, she wants to do as Nora asked and write the stories down. It will not be easy.

Nora had told the young Pearl, who liked to sit with the dolls in chairs around a table, a book of blank pages in front of her from which she pretended to read, that Pearl could learn to tell the tales on her own. Their source was a pool into which anyone could look but only storytellers would see figures looking *from* the pool *back* at them. Nora said that Pearl was a storyteller, too.

"Sometimes," Nora had added encouragingly, "it's like fishing. You must drop in a line and wait."

Pearl searches in a drawer for paper, then remembers that she has brought her laptop with her. She fetches it, and places it on the table beside Nora's workbag. She turns the computer on, and rummages through the bag until she locates the Rosa doll's new cloak. She holds it for a moment, breathing in the memory of Nora's touch. Then, she switches the doll's old cloak for the new, in-progress garment and straightens it on "Rosa's" shoulders.

Pearl waits, gazing into the pool, and writes.

~

The Castaway's Tale

San Blas, Mexico, c.1803

They say you shape the future with the purpose for which you came into the world, but how do you know what that is?

Six generations after Rosa's lifetime, the question still stands. A life without a compass is hardly a life at all: it simply passes the hours. Pelicans lift from the rocks to fly into the wind and scout for fish. The mosquitoes drawn to Rosa's sweating skin as she sits and waits, are after her blood. Rosa's mother, Beatris, shoes sunk into the mud at the water's edge, shades her eyes against the sun and tries to see if today will be the day that Rosa's father comes. If Rosa believes her mother, he will arrive without warning, muscles thickened by months of travel, carrying with him a vision of a coastline haunted by sea lions and whales, along which the San Blas ships journey to supply the presidios and naval yards, and the Franciscan missions of Alta California. His arrival, the result of a resolve to reunite with Beatris and Rosa at all costs, would demonstrate that it is no good weeping and lamenting over small things, such as the cleaving away of Rosa's childhood; you must simply endure.

"Your grandparents have spoiled you," her mother said, turning to Rosa. "I was against it all along. It gave you impossible ideas and it has had to stop. I have tried to teach you, but did you want to learn?"

"*You* did impossible things. Why shouldn't I? You stowed away as a boy, you told me!"

"What do you know that is useful? Most of it comes from books! What would you do without me?"

Rosa wanted to say, but did not, "You are always here, how would I know?" and "I have learned more than you could imagine," and "What about fighting with knives?"

She glanced at a cluster of children replanting swatches of grass torn from the beach by passing donkeys. Not long ago, these children were her friends. She shared the dolls that her mother gave her, with them, and no one—except her grandmother, who did not count—said she should not. Everything she did amused grandfather, and nothing was forbidden. But ever since the maid had found blood stains on Rosa's underclothes, nothing was permitted. Grandmother took the dolls, gave away the comfortable outfits Rosa loved, and made her wear tight bodices and corsets. Grandmother would have taken the knives as well, but grandfather intervened. "More than ever," he said to his wife, "Rosa will need to protect herself. What I can do is at an end." Rosa was not meant to overhear, but she knew where to secrete herself to listen.

Today, instead of doing what she liked, Rosa eyed the donkeys that carried corn, tobacco, bananas and coconut to the scows and barges that rowed to the ships in the outer harbour. The inner harbour, joined to the outer by a narrow passage, admitted only small ships and those destined for repairs in the shipyards. Not far from Rosa and her mother, a schooner lay under construction. The port's small factories produced resin, varnish, and paint. Contracts with nearby indigenous villages like Tequepespan, brought in pitch and tar for waterproofing from the forest. Cedar and other woods—pine, gum, cacao, lemon, orange, tamarind, and the mesquite used for firewood—were stockpiled in the vicinity of the dockyard; enough to provide for the colony's needs for years.

Without thinking about it—why would she?—Rosa had assumed she would always help grandfather, the Commandant at San Blas, with his tasks, and that someday all she knew about the running of the port and timber yards would be called upon. He had treated her as if her opinion mattered. He had asked for her comments on construction plans: she inspected ships from holds to masts with him and made lists of needed repairs. Without notice and for no good reason, because of this first bleeding, which was not her fault, all had changed.

"He is to blame!" Rosa's mother said again. "Letting you think! And as for her!" *Her* referred to Rosa's grandmother who had helped make Rosa unfit for reality. For every morning that the tutor her grandfather hired instructed Rosa in mathematics, astronomy, and navigation, Spanish history, and literature, straight-spined grandmother had scheduled an afternoon of needlework, lessons in etiquette, or visits to dressmakers and the priest of Nuestra Señora del Rosario la Marinera.

"They were out of their minds! What did they think would happen to you?"

"They took us in when we had no one!" Rosa said to her mother. "Why are you so ungrateful?"

"Did you notice you had no Spanish friends? Did you hear what they called you? '*Bastarda*'? '*Naboria*'?"

"You knew this day would come," her mother, Beatris, had said to Rosa's grandparents. "How often have I warned you? You have ensured Rosa's unhappiness by pleasing yourselves. She will never be content."

You were not content, Rosa had thought from her listening post in the library. *Why should I be*?

"But so soon? I believed her only a child," grandmother said.

"You and he are the children," Beatris said. "We will have to leave, the two of us, and make our own future if she is to have any life at all."

"You, a woman without protection—what will you do? Train horses, with Rosa a servant to be taken advantage of by whoever comes along?" grandfather asked.

"I will do what I have to," Beatris had said.

This morning at breakfast, after grandfather said Rosa was not to come on the jaguar hunt in the mangrove swamps as he'd promised she could, she had placed her hands on the table to show the calluses and cuts on them. *They* would attest to who she was and what she could do, unwelcome womanly bleeding or not. But instead of nodding approval, he had grimaced, stood, and left without speaking. Her grandmother had said, pouring out coffee, "That will teach you to neglect your gloves."

Why had he left her behind? She shot well and was expert in the use of the *navaja*, the long Sevillian knife her mother had taught her to use. She could only have been an asset, more so than the newly arrived naval officer who had gone in her stead.

Through her dress, Rosa fingered the knife she kept strapped to her thigh. Grandfather used to watch her and Beatris practise in the trees below the lip of the *cerro* on which they lived. He said he was proud of her skill. The knives Rosa and her mother used were not toys: the blades were steel and drew blood at a touch.

"We were their pets," Beatris said to Rosa, breaking her vigil once more. "You more than I. You have matured; they cannot disguise the fact there is no place for you here."

"Whose fault is that?" Rosa said. "I did not choose my parents! I did not choose to be a woman! Why has grandfather turned against me? I am the same as always!"

Her voice rose to a cry. "Being a woman didn't mean you couldn't do what you wanted!"

"And why," Beatris said, "would you think you knew what that was?"

Rosa hated her mother. Everyone knew that the husband Beatris waited for would never come for them. Nevertheless, Rosa liked to picture herself in another family with people who would love her, people who knew her worth.

Nearby, labourers loaded a flat-bottomed skiff with salt. Rosa knew how much the skiff could safely carry. Automatically, she counted the sacks until the men shoved off and headed out to the anchored ships. Far off, a lighter left the side of a packet boat; sunlight glittered off the gold braid of the officers' uniforms.

Beatris said, her eye on the traffic, "You are right: it is my fault. I have left it late, but you will see. We will make a new life."

"I don't want another life! Grandfather needs me!" Rosa's wail ascended with the birds that flapped above the children who turned to stare at her.

Because the river flooded in the rainy season, mud and debris swept into the harbour and created shifting sandbars. No matter how often the harbour was dredged, sandbars remained a problem. Rosa noted the lighter's progress with concern. Whoever was piloting the craft was letting the tide carry them too far south, where it could run aground and overturn. Rosa waited anxiously in case she needed to go to the rescue of those on board, but the lighter swerved and went safely on to the landing.

Her mother lowered the hand that shaded her eyes and seated herself on a rock near Rosa. Her leather boots were salt stained. Rosa bent, scooped a fistful of sand, and let it run through her fingers.

"What have I told you of our history?" Beatris asked.

"More than enough," Rosa said.

"Tell me."

"Not now. There isn't time." Rosa thought of grandmother's thin upright figure, her lips pursed in disapproval if they took too long coming home. She tried tightening her mouth to make it as small as grandmother's. She narrowed her nostrils to make her nose more aquiline like grandfather's. This was her family, hers.

"Please." Hesitantly, Beatris touched Rosa's arm. Beatris rarely begged, and so Rosa relented.

"You left Spain to come to New Spain. I was born during the passage. My father went on without us and the ship voyaged northwards from its port of call in California. The ship was lost; he was lost. That is why we are in San Blas on our own. My father will never reappear, and you know it. Grandmother says you are wasting your life."

"That is *not* our story, and you *know* it. You said yourself I was a stowaway! I dressed as a boy!"

"It is what grandmother says to anyone who asks."

"I thought you were interested in truth."

"Truth! What does truth matter! Do you tell the truth? I wish I were dead," but Rosa did not wish that at all. She did wish she looked more like her mother. Beatris's skin, despite her age—she was just past thirty—was a smooth, pale olive. Rosa's skin was brown. Grandmother had told Rosa that she tanned easily and should wear a hat. Grandmother's complexion was like bleached linen. Rosa pulled at her sleeves until they met the gloves at her wrists. Then, changing her mind, she stripped off the gloves and tucked them into her bodice. She examined the sunset.

Her mother sighed. "You were not born during a voyage. I followed my brother onto an expedition ship at Cadiz. I was only a girl, not yet fourteen." Then Beatris, without apology and for the hundredth time, told Rosa the story of her journey, replete with death and birth and drama, but Rosa heard only what matched her life as she wished it to be.

With the dropping of the wind, mosquitoes rose in drifts from the debris of the shoreline. Rosa swatted them away. Her mother's voice joined with the droning of the insects. "Yes," Beatris concluded, "you have a father, a father of the heart. A true one who cared for us and made sure we were looked after. He is the one I have waited for. That is the truth." She sighed and added, "But it was all so long ago."

On the three-hundred-feet-high *cerro de basilio* where Rosa and her family lived, the houses and official buildings were built of stone. Sea breezes cooled the air and kept mosquitoes away, but on the plain fronting the harbour, poor people lived in palm-thatched huts. The humidity all year and the heat in summer bred fevers—dysentery, typhoid, and malaria. People talked of moving the port, but that would never happen.

"Grandfather was not born in Spain, but in Lima," Beatris said, looking over at her daughter. "In part, that is why he has been sympathetic to you. He has had to rise with nothing but the strength and intelligence he finds within himself. He has loved and taught you as long as he could, but you are a woman now and he can do nothing to help with that or the facts of your parentage. He—all of us—must face this. A woman depends on the judgments of others, but you and I must rely on ourselves, and on those we alone choose to be with and who in turn, choose us.

"However hard it may be to accept, you must trust the story of your origins if you are to make your way in the world. Do not waste yourself on a delusion." From the small bag that hung from her wrist, Beatris brought out a doll. "I have made two sets of clothing for her. In this set she appears to be a boy." Her mother smiled and held out the figure.

"Is it supposed to be you?" Rosa asked. It was, even to a mark under its chin to mimic her mother's scar.

"I will also make dolls of my travelling companions and a model of the horse that arrived with us, because you love horses, Rosa, and the horse brought all of us together."

"I do not like horses," Rosa said, examining the outline of a horse stitched onto the doll's plain shirt, and fingering the small *navaja* strapped to its waist. The doll carried a little satchel. Rosa undid it, peered inside, and found a miniature wooden sailing ship and a stick doll with a leather hat. She knew the horse her mother meant: it was so old no one could ride it.

"She takes those with her for luck on her travels," Beatris said, referring to the contents of the little pack.

~

Pearl pauses. Rosa's mother is right. A girl of unknown family could run into difficulty; any racial divide or religious difference from the settled majority would make it worse. Denying that reality would only leave Rosa helpless. Pearl retakes the story's thread.

"I feel like a fool," Rosa said, turning the doll this way and that. "Everyone must be laughing at me."

"You are as foolish as your nature allows but consider, too, that you have been free of the constraints of most girls your age. Unlike them, you can make your life your own."

"Free," her mother had said. Was it free not to be wanted?

"How many of them can fight with knives, or fit out a ship, or speak to *los Indios* in their language? Or swim! Remember when we used to swim together at night?"

"That was long ago," Rosa said, in an echo of her mother. She gave the doll back, brushed sand from her skirt, and shook out her shoes.

"Not so long ago," her mother said. Beatris grimaced and layered her palms on her stomach. Her complexion was green. She was not pretty now.

Rosa hung back when her mother said they had to leave, and then had to hasten after her along the path to the hill. Grandmother hated them being late especially when an official dinner was to be followed by dancing.

Rosa's knife rubbed against her thigh. As she drew close to her mother, she imagined lifting her skirt and withdrawing the *navaja* from its sheath. Since grandfather had turned against her, an angry twin had grown inside Rosa: one who blamed Beatris for what had gone wrong. But on reaching her mother, she threw her arms around her mother's soft waist instead.

"I am sorry, so sorry," Rosa wept against her mother's breast. Rosa's moods swung like a pendulum. Beatris stroked her hair.

"No, I am sorry. We have been happy, have we not? So, let us go home and behave."

The grandparents' house, like the *contaduria* next to it, was built of great blocks of stone heaved and levered into place by Mexican labourers. Its ceilings were made of timber, the beams carved from trunks floated down river, then towed uphill on rollers to the building site.

The rooms were fitted with heavy Spanish furniture from grandmother's family. Only the grandparents' bed was made in New Spain, its frame and posts shaped to resemble a ship; its drapes bound or unfurled like sails. The kitchen, with cauldrons, huge clay pots, and ovens as big as caves, had been Rosa's favourite place to play. She had only to enter it to be petted and given treats. Not any longer though: the kitchen was barred to her.

Rosa's new dress lay ready on her bed: it was made of gold satin cut low across the shoulders and trimmed with lace at the sleeves and hem. Rosa put it on, then Beatris helped with her hair, piling it high and pricking it through with yellow silk flowers. Rosa gazed in the mirror. Her mother had better eyes than her (they were green) but *she* had prettier hair—black tresses brushed daily by the maids, washed in rainwater and rinsed with herbs. Beatris, busy with grandfather's horses or wandering and waiting, allowed her hair to puff and frizz.

Rosa leaned forward. For a moment, a younger Rosa, one who did not care how she looked, stared back. *This* Rosa had loved to swim at night in water phosphorescent with plankton, pillowed by the deep ocean before it tossed her and her mother to shore. Once, they had crossed the sand against a surge of turtle hatchlings heading for the creamy waves. The night was warm, the star-etched sky opened and filled with the stories her mother told her.

"You were born to love the sea," her mother had said. "You can swim forever, even underwater, and you don't mind the cold." The shallows glittered with hatchlings and tiny silver fish. But it was her mother who could swim like that, wasn't it? Always, she talked about herself, whatever else she pretended to say. Rosa touched the mirror, and the girl and the memory died away.

Beatris stood behind her, adjusting her own indigo and lace gown, then pinning her own hair. She smiled at Rosa in the mirror. Rosa turned to her and said, "Do not say I look like anyone, especially not like you."

The Commandant and his wife kept an open table in the French style for officers, bureaucrats, and travellers whose rank made an invitation appropriate. Often on evenings like this, especially when there was to be dancing, grandfather gathered his resources with a brandy and a browse through newly arrived books in the library. Rosa admired the way he handled them, his fine thin nose lowered over the pages, his hands encased in white gloves, his dress impeccable with matching coat, waistcoat, and breeches, with lace on his shirt neck and cuffs. Rosa hoped to catch him there, in good humour because of the day's successful jaguar hunt (the predator's body lay on the terrace, protected from dogs by a cage). Perhaps if he approved of how she looked, he would show her more consideration, more patience, and restore her to his confidence.

The library was fitted at one end with a semicircle of shelves that rose to the ceiling. A door cut through the middle of the curve into a recess in which Rosa often read and studied (and eavesdropped), invisible to all and at liberty with her thoughts. Grandfather's paper-strewn desk was in the larger room, set at an angle below a window. Rosa noted as she entered that the fire was lit, chairs spaced nearby, brandy and glasses arranged on a low table: he would arrive soon. Nevertheless, she slipped a book of French engravings out of its place on a shelf and took it with her into the nook. Maps that traced unpublished routes of Spanish expeditions, and texts that contradicted the priest's version of Creation were kept here. In this room, Rosa was privy to grandfather's most secret opinions: how could she and he be in conflict?

She set the book of engravings aside and opened *Arca Noë*, one of the books which could have had him excommunicated. Kircher, the author, had written in contradiction to the Biblical account of Creation, that after the Flood new species emerged because surviving animals moved to different environments. In a colder climate, deer became reindeer; in other circumstances, species bred with others to form hybrids such as the combination of turtle and porcupine that produced the armadillo. The possibility of spontaneous generation was not to be dismissed, either. Illustrations of what these creatures might look like interspersed the text.

Rosa closed *Arca Noë* and opened the French volume. To look at it was a risk, but she would hear grandfather coming in and could quickly cover it and replace it on the shelf later.

In one print, a young woman flew high on a swing, her legs spread wide beneath billowing skirts; hiding above her in the brush edging a gully, a young man spied on her. The feelings that came as Rosa viewed the engraving spread from her belly. Rosa closed her eyes. Sensations like this had begun even before the first bleeding, but she knew they were connected: *these feelings* were what told her she was becoming a woman.

The outer door opened. A chair scraped in the library's main room. Rosa covered the engravings with a map, straightened her shoulders, and prepared to greet her grandfather.

A stranger stooped over grandfather's desk reading grandfather's papers. His sharply cutaway coat and plain shirt collar and cuffs exhibited the latest fashion. Dark curls straddled the nape of his neck. He glanced at her without surprise.

"You must be Rosa. Your family has spoken of you; I hoped we would meet," he said. "Miguel de Roca, at your service." He clicked his heels.

Rosa strode forward. "You have no business at the Commandant's desk! Get away from it!"

"Forgive me!" He bowed and revealed an even parting in his shining head of hair. When he unbent, he said, "I was hunting with the Commandant this morning. He asked me to wait for him here before dinner. I am sorry if I startled you."

Before she was able to reply, grandfather entered the room. "Why are you here?" he said to her. "I did not ask for you!"

To Miguel he said, "I would never have suggested meeting here if I'd thought the child would intrude." The stranger nodded politely. Rosa's cheeks flamed.

"I have only followed our long-established custom," she said to her grandfather, grateful that her voice did not tremble. "Forgive me if I have misunderstood. I will go."

"Wait, no," the stranger, Miguel, said. "Please, not on my account." He smiled at her and turned towards grandfather.

"It is my fault, Señor Commandant," he said formally. "Your granddaughter thought I was prying." He indicated the desk. "She could not know I was asked to read these materials. Sir, please, allow her to join us."

"As you wish," grandfather said, but to Rosa he added, "From here on, you will ask permission before you use the library, and you will leave the door open if you are inside."

The role of the soul is to question itself. It is best done in the quietness before sleep. Sor Juana, a nun, another writer of whom the priest would not approve, wrote that at night the imagination contemplates the whole of creation. Reason cannot comprehend these matters; they are too large, and reason exhausts itself in useless effort. What is the nature of a flower? Or of a stone? Reason has no answer and abandons the soul to its enquiries. In the morning, the soul and body reunite, without recollection.

As she walked beside Miguel de Roca with the rest of the dining party, Rosa said, "My grandmother says you have been to the port before and did not care for it."

"Yes. Some months ago, I arrived in poor weather, thought the town unattractive and the environment oppressive, and hurried away. My opinions were superficial." They halted on the terrace outside the banquet hall; the other guests were several paces ahead. Below them the *cerro* fell away to the breathing sea.

"My work brought me back a short time later," he said. "Your mother and grandparents welcomed me as an old friend. Their kindness made me willing to change my mind. Now, I feel at home. On the hunt today, I saw so many birds! And look at the palm groves, Rosa," he said gesturing to the trees that fringed the beach below, "see how they move in rhythm with the wind and waves. It is like a dance." Miguel smiled. "You are lucky to live here; it is like a dream."

"When *you* dream," Rosa said carefully, her eyes on the Piedra Blanca, a thumb-shaped islet in the wrinkled ocean distance, "of what do you dream?"

"I am a surveyor by profession. In my work I must be a realist; but I come from the mountains of Aragon. When I dream, I am an eagle."

To be able to see the world from on high and to be master of it! Rosa's heart swelled with warmth.

At dinner, grandmother took the head of the table, with Adelina, the Comisario's wife, on one side of her, and Rosa on the other, an honour doubtless meant to soothe the Rosa's wounded feelings. Grandfather's place was at the foot, with Miguel de Roca next to Beatris on his right and the Comisario and the priest to his left. A servant showed the other guests to their places. After the soup, the servants brought in dishes of meat. At a nod from grandmother, the first slice of jaguar went to Miguel. "A fine shot!" grandfather said to him. "A pleasure to hunt with you!"

Rosa looked away from the bloody meat at a salver containing the carapace of a turtle. Mixed in with the turtle meat were several dozen baby turtles; their tiny brown legs splayed from infant shells. A mound of turtle eggs with a pink piping of shrimp made a bull's eye in the centre of the tray. Rosa's stomach heaved and she covered her mouth. Grandmother whispered, "What is it? Your time again, so soon?" Rosa lowered her head to hide the red flooding her cheeks.

"I am not hungry," she said quietly. She sipped from her wine glass.

"Eat." Grandmother motioned to a servant to fill Rosa's plate.

The Comisario's wife leaned close to grandmother. "Beatris spoils the effect by how she holds herself. And that scar at her throat, how did she acquire it?"

Grandmother smiled at her. "More wine Adelina?"

Beatris's swimming and her practice with the *navaja* had developed corded muscles in her shoulders, arms, and wrists. The shoulders of the other female guests were narrow, their upper arms and wrists, thin. Rosa watched her mother toy with a water glass, displaying a thumb thickened from handling the reins of horses. How had these other women done *anything*? Was it as her mother had told her, that the skills they had set them apart, made them free?

Rosa would rather be like her mother, even to the scar. It drew interest; although not even Rosa knew what had happened to make it. It wasn't anything her mother talked about. From under her lowered lashes, Rosa examined the fragile ladies and wondered what men saw in them.

The Comisario's wife persevered. "She is pretty, in her way: such good skin. Not at all like her daughter's. What has she said about the father?" Rosa did not need to turn her head to listen; each word was destined for her ears. "The Commandant is used to darker skin from his upbringing, naturally, but still, it is kind of him." Moisture stood on grandmother's brow, but she did not blot it. Her Spanish ancestors, large-nosed and haughty, passed judgement from their portraits on the walls. At table, as in the life-sized painting on the wall behind him, Rosa's grandfather wore the chivalric Order of Santiago. The portrait was a Royal commission made to commemorate his time at the Naval Academy at Cadiz.

"He has the ear of the King, which is all that matters," grandmother said to Adelina.

Rosa's mother, down the table, said to Miguel de Roca beside her, "From Aragon? You must miss the mountains. As a girl, I climbed in the Sierra Morena, but the mountains here are impenetrable."

Grandmother murmured, "He is an Aragonese. That is not so bad."

Miguel de Roca smiled at Beatris and said in his intimate way, "One day in the snow and amidst glaciers, the next in a valley with the clouds rolling through and thundering. Sometimes, while daydreaming, I am ascending steep paths, the next I am in the city I was born in, and at other periods among the perplexing rocks of the desert. What could have placed them there?"

Beatris nodded. "In summer we ran our horses all the way to the sea. My brother …" she paused. "We are not a wealthy family, Señor de Roca, we do not have your history."

"Señora," he continued—he was a little younger than Beatris; Rosa thought he had not noticed how closely others watched them—"I voyage the world, but nothing is like the sunlight on the cobblestones and the walls and towers of my city. The cathedrals and castles and the universities; the gardens of almonds and olives."

"How long will you be with us?" grandmother intervened from the head of the table.

The Aragonese lifted his head, took in the interest focused on him and Beatris, and smiled. "If it were in my election, if I could have two homes, I would remain as long as possible." He gave a small shrug. "Sadly, I cannot be in two places at once; and I have obligations."

"Of course," grandmother said. "Obligations come in many forms." Something lay within the exchange. Not long ago, Rosa could have asked grandfather, and he would have told her what it was. Miguel dropped his gaze, but merely for an instant.

"In my city, we tell a story of lovers who come from different families," he said, addressing the company at large. "The boy's family is poor, the girl's wealthy. The girl's parents forbid the match but say they will consent if the boy makes his fortune and establishes a name for himself. They give him five years, but when he returns with his riches, fulfilling their conditions, he learns that his lover's family have already forced her into a marriage.

"The tale speaks of our tradition of leaving home but of keeping promises and accepting whatever may occur in one's absence."

"Did they always love each other? Did he find someone else? Have *you* someone to return to?" Rosa could not keep herself from asking.

"Rosa!" grandmother said.

The Aragonese raised his eyebrows but answered gently. "I am a practical man, with his heart and his tasks sewn to the same sleeve. The boy died of a broken heart despite all he had accomplished, and the girl succumbed to despair soon after. They were buried together. Only in death were they permitted their freedom. No, nothing of me is in the story."

Rosa was sure she heard Beatris say under her breath, "It is not true; one does not die of heartbreak."

"But you *will* go home to your family in Aragon and your life there?" grandmother asked, her cheeks flushed.

"I will not go home unchanged." He beamed at the other guests, "I invite you, all of you, to come and visit me if you can. My home is yours."

Grandfather said, "You were telling me today of your work, Señor de Roca. Please, the company would be interested in what you have to say." The conversation turned to Miguel's mapmaking and fieldwork, and his reports to Spain on local conditions: surveys of forests and lumbering activities, with estimated rates for wood; reflections on the advantages and disadvantages of shipyard sites; proposals on fortifications and installations.

"The defensive position of the port of San Blas is weak, its artillery outdated," Miguel said.

Grandfather cleared his throat, and the Aragonese turned to him. "You indicate a future which is no future at all," grandfather said. "Others think differently."

"This evening is for pleasure," grandmother said. "Perhaps we shall speak of these matters another time. Señor de Roca, I look forward to hearing more of your background, your family and homeland."

"If you will permit." The flourish of Miguel de Roca's hand as he surrendered to grandmother's will, drew attention to the gleam of his gold ring with its crest of crown and castle.

"What a funny accent," the Comisario's wife said *sotto voce* to grandmother as the company proceeded to the grand salon, drawn by the music. "Do all Aragonese speak like that?" The older women had paused to wait for a guest who had left her shawl behind. The older men, with apologies, had moved ahead of them. Beatris and the younger women and men, except for Miguel, were already in the salon.

"I trust you have a better ear for music than for speech, Adelina," grandmother said. "The musicians have newly arrived from Spain and may not be what you are used to, either." Adelina did not reply. She hurried to catch up to her husband.

Miguel de Roca's accent, it was true, differed from that of other officers and officials. His voice erased certain sounds, and he spoke with a veiling of intentions that Rosa found intriguing. Grandfather prided himself on speaking his mind—a quality that formerly Rosa had admired. De Roca remained *himself* in company, but without disclosing his secrets. As she and grandmother neared them, grandfather clapped the Aragonese on the shoulder.

"So! What will you report of us to your masters?" Despite the sting in the words, the Commandant's visage glowed with affection, almost as if Miguel could be a son. He had never bestowed such a look on Rosa. Always, there had been a reserve. She bent to adjust a shoe and hide her anger.

"Report? Not at all, Señor Commandant. I will give an account of the scientific projects in which I am engaged. But good harbours on the coast are rare, and harbours close to fertile land for agriculture, and pasture for grazing, and drinking-water and shade, are rarer still. I have not found these here, although I understand that once upon a time, things were different. If I am asked, I will tell the truth."

"You must note our advantages! Safe shelter within easy sailing of the commercial routes: without us, Spain cannot control traffic through the Gulf of California! And our timber! The ships built here for Spain are known throughout the world! But we have been over this before."

"It is not my intention to contradict, but the timber is brought down from further and further away and soon the supply will fail. I observed as much today in our travel upriver."

"Not yet though, we are not done yet." The warmth in grandfather's face remained.

Usually, the hall lay dark and unused except as overflow for storage, its giant beams obscured by the ceiling height, its windows shuttered against the sun, the polished floors covered with planks and sacking. This evening, as happened several times a year, the room was restored to its original purpose. Musicians played from a dais. The lit candles of the chandeliers cast a golden light over tapestries hung on the stone walls. Chairs were grouped at tables along the walls so that while they ate and drank, spectators could inspect the dancers.

Grandfather led grandmother, Rosa, and the Aragonese to the table reserved for them. The Comisario's wife waved and came their way. "I see we will have your friend with us," Grandfather said to his wife. He deposited her, looked for escape, and found it with the officers gathered at the punch bowl. "Are you coming?" he asked the Aragonese.

By the time Rosa noted that grandfather had gone, all the chairs meant for their party were occupied. Adelina had brought companions with her. Rosa leaned against the wall and watched Beatris dance with the Comisario, an old man by anyone's standards. A blue sash crossed his belly, and the gold braid unraveled from one of his sleeves. The colour of the sash exactly matched Beatris's dress. He moved stiffly, but he laughed at whatever Beatris said.

Miguel de Roca brought cups of wine for the women. The Comisario's wife eyed her husband and Beatris. "Tell me the real story," she said to grandmother. The Aragonese had retreated a few steps. "We are old friends: you know me, I never meddle but I have long wanted to know, is it true Beatris arrived on a ship carrying otter pelts and mixed-race servants, and with a horse! So young, and with a child! Your attitude of charity is admirable! I never could have done it."

She was speaking of Beatris and Rosa as if neither were human beings with souls. Rosa smoothed her skirt over the *navaja* on her thigh. It was the Comisario's wife who had no soul: it would take little for Rosa to stoop, raise her petticoats, extract the knife, and release the blade. Rosa would make her suffer for her heartlessness.

The music of the bolero, brought by officers recently arrived from Cadiz, began and Beatris showed the old man the new steps. They told the story of a couple falling in love: two slow steps together to the side to illustrate attraction, and two quicker, rocking beats each way to indicate passion. Rosa glanced to see if Miguel de Roca watched too, but he had gone.

"Rosa will get you something to eat, Adelina, I am sure you long for sweets," grandmother said. "Rosa?" she called over her shoulder. Rosa shrugged away from the wall. Grandmother took Rosa's hand and kissed it. "It was a *coup de foudre*, Adelina, that's all I have to say about my girls." She repeated the sentiment in Spanish so Adelina could not misunderstand, "*Amor a primera vista*. I prayed for children and God sent them."

Beatris smiled as the Comisario strove to follow the bolero pattern. She tried to steady him, but he lurched into her, laughing. His coat and breeches were black velvet; the cummerbund was made of silver and red tissue.

Rosa withdrew to do grandmother's bidding—the old woman's words had surprised and gladdened her—but not before Adelina hissed, "Does your daughter even *know* who the father is?"

Loyalty, not only to Beatris but to grandmother, fanned flames in Rosa's heart. She spun behind the chairs to the wall of tapestries. Everyone was engaged in the dance or conversation; no one noticed her. A sense of purpose, pleasing in its clarity, manifested itself. She crouched to retie the bow of a shoe, her head bent to the brushing wings of the spirit that, as the priest had promised, arrived with the onset of virtuous action. She reached under her skirt for the *navaja*. Rosa stood holding the open knife and took the first step, her mind focused on the gap in the back of the chair on which the Comisario's wife sat. A hand closed over hers so tightly that the blade sliced her fingers, and the knife fell from her grasp. Miguel de Roca caught it and reset the clasp. "A beauty like you will one day break many hearts," he said. Blood dripped from her hand. The Aragonese staunched it with a monogrammed handkerchief. His long face with firm chin and straight mouth, the curved nose no longer arrogant, bent to hers. He held her gaze, his eyes a luminous blue.

"I will fight a duel on your and your mother's behalf, if it is necessary," he said softly, "but I will not fight a woman."

"I fight for myself," Rosa said. "My mother fights, too. Who else will defend us?"

"You have my promise, but would you kill someone for their stupidity?"

"I would kill her."

"You would not be forgiven, not by your grandparents or anyone else. Your future would be forfeit; she is not worth it."

"I don't care," Rosa said. He knotted the handkerchief over her cut fingers; her blood stained his glove.

"Then I will care for you. Come with me. Nod pleasantly as if we are speaking of the garden," he said as they slipped through an open door. "See how simple it is to step outside."

"Someone will see."

"I am trusted, and a friend, it is all right. I will make sure of it."

They crossed the cooling stones of the terrace past the eviscerated carcass of the jaguar and sat beside the reflecting pool. Miguel uncovered Rosa's hand, immersed it in the water and rinsed out the handkerchief.

Rosa wished to hate him for thwarting her attack on the Comisario's wife. She began to tell him so, but what came out instead was the voice of *another* Rosa, one adult enough to ask, "How else can I punish her for the harm she causes, Señor de Roca? How, then, is there justice?"

Her cuts stung but the bleeding had slowed. Miguel gave her his stained, almond-and-honey-scented glove to grip as a bandage.

"Justice is rare, but you can find a way to live the life you choose and be true to your ideals. It does not matter what anyone says. Show them who you are. Let reason be your guide."

"They do not know me. No one does." A ghost of the younger Rosa had intruded, but only for a moment. She added, "But I know myself; truly, I do."

The Aragonese kissed her wrist above the improvised bandage.

A kiss. But what does it mean? Is it, a lover's kiss or a kiss of compassion? How many kisses has Rosa had?

~

Pearl reads over the pages she has written. *SeaPin* rocks a lullaby through the night. Finding a way to live and be true to who you are can be a challenge. She sympathises with Rosa's anger: justice demanded restoration to her grandfather's favour and to meaningful occupation, as well as punishment of Adelina for her gossip. Justice demanded that Rosa's abilities be acknowledged. Since this was unlikely to happen (for reasons her mother had outlined) Rosa must use her mind and instincts to improve her position: she would never win by challenging custom openly, whether by knife or argument. The Aragonese counsels moderation, subtlety, not revenge—good advice, Pearl agrees—but then he kisses Rosa's wrist. Is that fair, is that just? What right does he have to assume any role at all in Rosa's life? That tale about star-crossed lovers? To Pearl, it sounds like an alibi.

Pearl lights the stove, boils water for coffee and goes on deck, leaving the laptop on the galley table under the scrutiny of the Rosa doll on the shelf.

A breeze has scrubbed fog from the stars and revealed Nora's birth sign, Leo, and the Big and Little Bears with the tail of Draco, the Dragon, tucked between them. Pearl and Nora used to make a game of finding constellations. Pearl looks down: beneath the reflection of the stars in the water, other life carries on. Much that Pearl cannot see continues to navigate, fulfill its nature, and make what it can of *SeaPin*'s intrusive hull.

More of the story, from seeds Nora planted in Pearl's childhood, forces a path into the light: Pearl is going to have to finish what she started. Quickly, she drinks the coffee, tosses the dregs overboard, and goes below to resume.

~

Rosa began talking the moment she entered the breakfast room. "I had to leave the ballroom early," she said, indicating her bandage. "A glass broke while I was holding it."

"Señor de Roca told us," grandmother said. "You were fortunate he was nearby."

Grandfather, selecting a pair of boots to wear in search of a mare in foal, repeated the words he had said after the Aragonese's account of Rosa's accident. "A fine young man, and kind with it."

Grandmother gazed into her cup of chocolate.

Grandfather turned to Beatris and said, "Señor de Roca has asked for your company today, yours and Rosa's, on an expedition on *Santa Rosa* to the islands. He wishes to make observations of flora and fauna."

"I must help with the mare," Beatris said. "And Rigel is failing. I need to attend to him."

"I will look after the old horse today," grandfather said. "Nothing is more healthful than a sea voyage: it will do you good."

Grandmother murmured, "He is interested in birds. He collects specimens and catalogues them; surely he will visit longer than he expects."

"Splendid!" grandfather exclaimed. "Grandmother agrees. Señor de Roca will escort you."

"I can do more good here, where I am needed," Beatris said.

"Rosa cannot go without you. *I* cannot sail, the sea makes me ill," grandmother said. "Do you have other offers? Do you never wish to please me?"

Rosa squeezed the injured fingers curled in her lap to quench her feelings. What if her mother refused? More than anything, she wanted to sail with Miguel. Beatris fiddled with cutlery. "All right," she said. She stood and beckoned to her daughter. In their room, Beatris massaged the small of her back.

The *Santa Rosa*—a frigate with Rosa's name!—carried forty eight-pound guns but flew light and fast as it smashed into waves, shuddered, and leapt ahead. Because of her work with grandfather, Rosa knew each line and tackle, the contents of storerooms, and where crewmen slept. From the fo'c'sle, with the Aragonese standing between Rosa and her mother, they watched dolphins criss-cross ahead of the bow and arc away; and Rosa forgot, briefly, about the glove, figured with her dried blood, folded into her bodice.

A wounded booby alighted in the rigging. Rosa itched to climb to it (to show Miguel that she could) but then the ship tacked and heeled, and the women retreated to the captain's cabin at the captain's orders.

The two islands of most interest to the Aragonese were separated from each other by a channel less than sixty feet wide. *Santa Rosa* anchored offshore and let down the lighter. Both islands were marked by tall cliffs and rocky stacks in which caves swallowed ocean waves into green and black depths. Green algae blurred the entrances; guano limed the rocks. Slowly, the lighter travelled round the islets until they found a flat rock outcrop on the larger island on which to land.

They climbed to a treeless plateau thick with grass and sedge. The Aragonese arranged his collecting bags; the sailors spread blankets and cushions, and Beatris took out a sketch pad, settled herself on pillows and began to draw.

Frigate birds nested among groupings of wild pineapples on which they had built platforms of twigs to hold their single eggs. Carcasses of lost hatchlings had caught in the bromeliad spines below some of the nests, the parents wandering nearby, questing, but Rosa found she could approach them without causing alarm.

Behind her, Beatris and Miguel fell into conversation, at ease with each other, their voices carrying with snatches of laughter. The ribbons of Rosa's cap loosened: it blew off and tumbled over the grasses to the brink of the cliff and snared on a patch of cactus. Rosa did not pause to retrieve it.

A little further on, numbers of boobies perched on eggs laid in shallow depressions scraped into the earth through the grass. Their webbed feet tented the shells to warm them. Rosa crouched and tried to imitate the sounds they made—high-pitched whistles and lower-pitched honks.

She glanced over her shoulder to see if anyone observed her, but the two heads, her mother's and Miguel de Roca's, were bent over Beatris's drawings.

A flower trembled between stones at the cliff edge. Rosa moved to pluck it, but it became a butterfly that lifted and fluttered and then flipped sideways and down. She stepped without looking, on to the friable overhang, and fell. Overhead, clouds streaked a promise of evening winds, but Rosa gazed a hundred feet down at the sea, her grip failing on the bush she clung to, her skirt tearing loose from the cacti spines on which it had snagged.

Miguel seized her under the armpits and dragged her to safety. (Of course, he did, of course.) "I will not let you go that easily," he said.

Later, after Rosa had eaten bread and meat, sipped a cup of wine and rested against Beatris's shoulder, Miguel returned from his explorations. "Would you like to see what I have found, Rosa?"

"Go ahead," Beatris said, and smiled. "You will be fine." She spoke as if to a child, but it was Rosa who had been wounded and who possessed the glove of the man who had just saved her life.

He led her through the grass to a rise on the eastern side of the island to view the lighter leaving *Santa Rosa* on its way to fetch them. The oarsmen bent to their work. A fragment of song drifted their way. "*One sweet kiss*," the sailors sang. A flush of faded flame and feathers lay beside Miguel's collecting bag. He spread the bird's wings for her to see. "How has it flown so far from home?" he asked her. "It must have crossed the open sea for many miles without rest."

"Yes, it lives in the forest," she said. "I cannot say what drew it here."

"Too many trees cut down on shore?" he said. "Or to find a mate?"

The lighter approached and they heard more of the song. An oar slipped and splashed: the sailors jeered, ending the singing.

"I will write out their song for you, so you won't forget what you have seen and heard today," Miguel said as he bundled the corpse of the forest bird into his bag. Rosa would have liked one of its green feathers to go with the glove, but he did not suggest it. "The song was composed by the troubadour, Guiliam, an ancestor of mine, who fought against the Moors when he was your age. They say he fell in love and never got over it."

On the night sail home, Miguel taught Rosa and Beatris the words. As he had promised, he wrote a copy for Rosa.

I will die if she won't have me.
If she refuse, my soul will flee.
I pray she give me
One sweet kiss, a key.
I will die if she won't have me.

I am bereft, a barren tree:
If she refuse, my soul shall flee.
If she won't give me
One soft crimson kiss,
I am imperilled, on my knees.

Why would I want a different key?

I will die if she won't have me.

"What does the future hold for you, Rosa? Can you see it?" he asked as they ascended the path to the Commandant's house on the *cerro*. Beatris lagged. At Miguel's urging they waited for her.

"I see myself on a ranch with a thousand head of cattle and many horses, and a herd of donkeys to do the carrying," she said. She had not abandoned her ambition of running the port. Many officials had rancheros *and* held offices. Some regularly sailed between the port and Spain. In Rosa's world, all was possible.

"Where could this be?" He glanced away to check that Beatris was coming. Cool night and stars tingled Rosa's skin, and she shivered.

"Grandfather and I found a place, but I think he has forgotten. It is as you described at dinner: a sheltered anchorage with a beach, a river, arable land, pasturage and shade, and a forest from which one could harvest trees."

"Tell me exactly, please," he said. "I will help you and your mother build a hacienda there. Then I could visit whenever I wanted."

"Do you promise?" Rosa asked. She did not want to include her mother, but it would be kinder to let her come.

"I must complete my surveys, write my report and submit it in Spain," he said, "but after that, I have assured the Commandant that he will hear my conclusions from my own lips."

"How long will this take? When will I see you again?"

Beatris arrived, out of breath.

"I swear to you, both of you, I will come again as soon as I can."

Tides are certain, and the progression of the year with its growth, and then its decay; but the winds are not reliable, and ships lose contact and fail to make port for many reasons; and people can change their minds. Nevertheless, never in the months after Miguel de Roca left did Rosa doubt his word. He would return before long. He had said it, and she would be ready. She no longer accompanied Beatris to watch for ships, although her mother did little else. They did not talk of their future. Beatris had given up riding horses and rarely visited them: it fell to Rosa to take care of old Rigel. As time passed, Beatris stopped going out at all and kept to her room, but Rosa watched for the letters that arrived on grandfather's desk, making sure she was never in the library with him. She saw the seal of the Aragonese frequently, but the letters were unopened and then they were taken away and she had no opportunity to read them. She sorted her belongings for the practicalities of a voyage: she read books on navigation and farming. She studied the history of Aragon. She practised with the *navaja* on her own, since Beatris had lost interest. Beatris, thin-featured and tired, resting all day in their room.

One morning, Rosa woke before dawn to find Beatris sitting up in bed clutching her belly, the soaked folds of her nightdress sticking to her thighs. "Fetch Consuela," Beatris said, naming a servant with whom she was friendly, but Rosa, frightened, ran to her grandmother's room instead. "Go to the Comisario's wife house and wait until I send for you," grandmother said.

Rosa waited outside on the step, but Adelina, the Comisario's wife, wakened by the lights in the Commandant's house, glimpsed her through a window and came outside. "What is it? What is the matter?" she said. She had thrown a shawl over her nightdress. The first rays of the sun tipped the glade where Rosa and her mother used to practise with the *navaja*.

Rosa said nothing.

"You must be brave, Rosa," the Comisario's wife said a short time later. She draped her shawl around Rosa's shoulders. Rosa blinked and followed her gaze to the side door of the Commandant's house. It had swung open. The figures carrying the covered pallet wore dark clothing, but Rosa thought she distinguished the bulk of the priest among them. She leapt to her feet. Before she could run after the procession, she was held from behind. "Let me go! I want my Mama!" she screamed. She twisted and tugged but the Comisario's wife beckoned to one of the soldiers, "Hold her, do not let her go," she said. "This is nothing she should see." Rosa struggled, but the soldier was too strong. The procession carried on while the thin wail of an infant wove into the air. Beatris's changed behaviour and appearance suddenly added up. Why hadn't Rosa's mother said she was having a child? She should have told her! Rosa's stomach churned and she turned her head and vomited. "Please, please," she begged when she could speak, yet the soldier did not release her, and her mother's body and the baby born too soon, a brother or sister for

Rosa, one she had not known she longed for, were taken cruelly away.

"Ah, no," the Comisario said. Rosa felt the tremble of his elderly touch on her arm. "Dear child," he said, and made the soldier let her go. By then grandfather had joined them.

"The next ship to leave port—you will be on it," grandfather said to Rosa without looking at her.

"What ship?" Rosa managed to ask.

"Does it matter? I said the next one, whichever it is." Rosa could not sleep in the bedroom she and her mother had shared. She made herself a lair on the floor of the library with cushions and hangings. "Leave her," Rosa heard grandmother say to grandfather. He had come to the library door, wanting the room for himself. Echoing grandfather's earlier words, grandmother added, "What does it matter now?"

Where *was* her mother? In purgatory if the priest were right? Or, might she be a ghost along with Rosa's father, the father who surely had arrived secretly to make a child with Beatris, only to fade again into the past.

A tiny blue and orange flame; a pitch torch in someone's hand: the Aragonese held a light by the library desk. He bent to examine papers. It was not a ghost—the Aragonese undoubtedly lived; if he did not, Rosa would feel it—but it was an apparition, a sign that Miguel was on his way. It would have been better if he had arrived earlier and helped Rosa put Beatris's mind at rest about a future for her and the baby. It might have made a difference. They would have taken care of them both. Still, the way things were, it could not be helped.

Rosa untangled herself from the bedclothes, lit a lamp and went to the map room. Ships left regularly to take supplies to the colonists of Alta California. It was on one of these that grandfather said she was to go. With ten Franciscan missions established from San Diego to San Francisco, the supply ships strained to fulfill the colonists' needs for food and manufactured articles. Rosa had helped plan the loading of the guns and powder, nails, and fishhooks they carried. She had envisioned going to see for herself one day and learning more of the needs of the province. She had not imagined that the day would come so soon, or amid such shock and sorrow. But surely, as the apparition at grandfather's desk indicated, none of this affected her relationship with Miguel. His spirit dwelled with her although he travelled the coast conducting surveys and writing reports. Whatever Rosa did to solidify the foundations of her calling, could only help their future partnership. What other reason could grandfather have for sending her north (whatever he said in his grief and anger) but to prepare her for more responsibility?

Beatris's death was a cause for heartache, but the Comisario had told her, in a whisper, that the baby boy lived and was fostered amongst the Mexicans. After Rosa and Miguel had built their hacienda, they would bring the baby home to live with them. Rosa: reassembling fragments of the world as it was, to make the world she craved.

Her finger traced north on the mapped seaboard. Her ship would voyage to Santa Barbara, the most recently established of the missions. She had already met many of the naval officers who sailed these trade routes. Grandfather could rely on her for accurate reports.

Rosa sat at grandfather's desk and wrote a letter to Miguel explaining all that had happened; and that she was going to Santa Barbara, and why. She sealed it. Grandfather being grandfather, he would give Miguel the letter upon his arrival. Rosa lay down again to rest. Her heart and mind were at peace as much as they could be within the confusion of loss and change.

In the morning, she went to her grandmother and said, "It is my right to prepare my mother's body; it is my right to see her child before I leave."

"That will not be possible," grandmother said, "but your mother would want you to have these." She went to her bureau and opened a drawer. Consuela and the other servants had packed and disposed of Beatris's belongings in the first hours after her death: nothing was left behind for Rosa, not even Beatris's long knife, the *navaja* brought from Spain that she had used for fighting practice with her daughter. Rosa had looked all through the room they'd shared, but it was as if her mother had never been. The first thing grandfather had done after Beatris's death was to shoot her old horse Rigel.

Rosa began to tremble as grandmother brought out Beatris's dolls. Grandmother's thumb caressed the lace and silk on the doll that Rosa' mother had made of herself and shown her daughter. She'd sewn extra clothes for it and given it a travelling pack. Had her mother wanted her to keep it? Grandmother passed the Beatris doll to Rosa and unwound the covering from another doll. "I saw it coming, I encouraged it, but I never imagined she had no sense," grandmother said.

Sense is for those who have choices. Rosa waited for what would appear. The doll was not, as she had expected, one of her mother's long-ago companions, or the horse that Rosa had seen Beatris begin to construct; neither was it a hoped-for image of her father. This doll, complete to its cutaway coat, glossy black curls, and the tiny book in its hands, was a model of Miguel de Roca. Rosa could read a few lines of the troubadour's song he had taught them, on the book's miniature pages: *I will die if she won't have me*. The doll retained Beatris's scent of oranges. The certainty of the Aragonese's love for her was all she had, so Rosa pushed down a conflicting awareness that threatened to arise. It was for reasons she could not have explained that she left the Aragonese doll behind on the day she set sail.

A few hours after the ship passed the Piedra Blanca, Adelina, the Comisario's wife whom grandfather had assigned to accompany Rosa to her destination, invited Rosa to leave her place at the rail and descend with her to their cabin. Nauseous from the motion of the ship, Adelina lay on her bunk while Rosa arranged their belongings. By dinner time, Adelina's complexion was tinged with green.

"I will fetch bread, water, and wine so you can be comfortable while I am gone," Rosa offered.

"Do not trouble yourself," Adelina said. She moaned.

"You must eat a little if you can but lie quietly. I will not disturb you. After I have eaten, I will return to the deck."

"We are the only women on board. We take our meals in our cabin. It is arranged," Adelina said. She turned her head and vomited into the bowl Rosa had placed beside her.

Before Rosa could access the deck, a sailor posted in the corridor blocked her way, took the bowl from her, and said, "Please remain in your quarters. I will dispose of this and then bring your food."

"My companion is not well and will be content in our cabin, but I prefer to take my dinner with the others. I will speak to the captain about the arrangements." Rosa tried to move past him, but he would not let her.

"Please, Señorita," he said. "My orders are from the captain. He said, if you were to ask, he will not change his mind."

"May I not attend to my personal needs? Is that an order, too?"

The sailor lowered his gaze, but he did not give way. "I will accompany you to ensure your privacy," he said. "You may use the captain's facility on the quarterdeck. Follow me. I will show you."

"I can find it myself. But my stricken companion? What is she to do?"

Despite the dim light, Rosa saw the sailor colour. "There is a chamber pot. I will empty it for her."

Three times a day, the sailor brought meals to Rosa and Adelina. Five times a day, at rising, after each meal and in the evening before bed, he knocked on their door to enquire if they required an escort to the toilet. Rosa always said yes, so at least she could gauge the weather, watch for seabirds, and breathe fresh air. Only the sailor assigned to them responded to her greetings or answered her questions. Others ignored her; a few spat to avert misfortune. Adelina never left their room.

"Are we prisoners?" Rosa asked her escort after the first week.

"You are women on board a ship of men," he replied. "I am responsible for your safety."

In the night, when Adelina slept and their sentry had retired, Rosa slipped out and made her way to the deck. Sheltered by a ship's boat, she could feel the wind yet not be seen. On clear nights, she put her celestial navigation lessons to work to estimate their position. In the daytime, she wrote letters to Miguel and to her grandparents; sometimes she wrote to Beatris's baby son. All these letters she gave to Adelina for safekeeping.

"You will deliver these when you return to San Blas, won't you?" she asked Adelina one afternoon after catching the woman glancing at her with pity as she pleated the latest letter into a growing packet.

"What else would I do with them?" Adelina said.

On days that Adelina was well enough, they sewed the practical wardrobe Rosa would need in her new life. Grandmother had supplied the materials. Most of Rosa's apparel, suitable for the heat and humidity of San Blas, had been left behind. She had packed only a few good costumes and ball gowns for the formal aspects of her new position.

After nearly four weeks at sea, Rosa caught a glimpse of land during an escorted visit to the quarterdeck head. "How long until we arrive?" she asked the sailor.

"Less than a day," he said. "It depends on the speed of that storm." Black lowering clouds blotted the southeastern sky. He hurried away at the call of an officer and Rosa returned to the cabin alone.

"What do you think it will be like at the mission?" Rosa asked Adelina. She opened her trunk to pack stray items inside, looking around to make sure she had left nothing out.

"No doubt it will fit your requirements," Adelina said.

Often unwell and losing weight, Adelina rarely spoke of the future except to say she wanted to go home. Rosa felt sorry for her. They had managed to get along, although each knew the other would be glad for the journey's end.

Nonetheless, Rosa said, "Why don't you stay and explore the town rather than reembarking at once? Surely you may delay. The Franciscans will be hospitable, if not for your sake, then for grandfather's who is well known to them."

"I have a home of my own," Adelina said. "Why would I want to be elsewhere?"

"I am going on deck," Rosa said. "Please do not hinder me. I need to know the approaches to the coast if I am to be of use at the port." She imagined herself studying advanced wayfinding, mathematics, and naval architecture as well as having a role in day-to-day management. Grandfather had said she was gifted. He was sending her to the Mission Santa Barbara to learn.

"Close to port, are we?" Adelina asked. "I do not suppose it will do any harm. I will come too, in case anyone questions our presence."

From the deck, they glimpsed a green and brown coastline, but within minutes, the land was obscured by cloud. Rosa turned to check on the storm. A rain squall raced their way, darkening and ploughing the sea. "Hold on!" she cried to Adelina. A violent wind bowled into the sails and wrung them as the ship pitched and yawed. The women were hurled against a ship's boat and then tossed to the railing. While they clung, the rain laid down a blinding sheet of water, and then it and the wind were gone. Rosa helped the sodden Adelina to her feet.

"Enough!" Adelina cried. She clutched at Rosa's arm. "Help me to our cabin." Nearby islands, looming through mist, added to the confusion of weather, tides and currents that were sweeping them close to shore.

"No! I want to see!" Rosa pulled her arm free. Her hair lay in wet hanks across her cheeks. Adelina's skeletal collar bones and ribs showed through her soaked clothing; her hair sculpted a frail skull.

"What is to see?" the Comisario's wife said. "Why do you contradict me? You might as well get used to doing what you are told."

She tugged at Rosa's arm again, but her shoes slipped, and she fell to the deck. "Look!" she cried. "This is what comes of not obeying me!"

"I will take you below," Rosa said, helping her, "but I *will* come up on deck. There is no reason not to." Once more, Adelina gripped onto her.

"Is there not, is there not?" Adelina shouted into a remnant of the wind. "Who am I to be ordered by a *bastarda*? Do what I say, Rosa, or it will go worse for you!"

"Out of respect for my grandparents, if for no other reason, Adelina, do not insult me."

"Your grandparents have moved to Tepic. Everyone but you understands that the port of San Blas is to close. That means no more ships, and no port to manage. You have nothing to go home to. Forget them, Rosa. They cannot help you. You are sent to be a servant."

Rosa pried herself away. She stumbled to the railing. "What do you mean? I am going to the Mission to study! If what you say is true, how will Miguel find me?"

"You? Study?" Adelina said, choosing at last to say what she meant. "What should you study to scrub floors?" The wind sucked at Adelina's words and swallowed them.

How will you know what is true, Rosa? Truth, when you find it, has a sharp edge. Truth is as much a knife as the navaja. Justice is rare, but you can find a way to live. This is what the Aragonese had told her and in this moment, Rosa felt the deep cut of truth.

The wind dropped further; the ship's progress slowed. They were not far south of the mission. A line of surf broke along a beach. To the west of the ship, waves modelled the shores of Pink Pelican Island.

"Quickly then," Rosa said. She dragged the Comisario's wife to their cabin and sat her on a bunk. She took the bundle of her most precious oilskin-wrapped possessions from the trunk, ran to the deck, stripped off her dress, secured the package to her body with rope taken from a locker, and without more preparation than she used when diving with Beatris through the waves that smashed onto the beach at San Blas, she sprang from the deck into the sea.

Swept into a sea cave, the *navaja* strapped to her thigh, the bundle tied safely, Rosa's arms ached from the long swim. The cave smouldered with colour: red gorgonian and orange and white sea cucumbers, pink, red, and lavender anemones. A seventh wave bore Rosa through a narrow, flooding passage and she came to rest on a crescent of shell and pebble beach, reborn.

"*You do not die of heartbreak*," Beatris had said at dinner with the Aragonese; and it was true.

The Chumash people who found her lived in willow-frame huts constructed in a sheltered hollow of the island from which they hunted for otters and seals. They dried fish and shellfish and collected acorns for meal from the oak scrubland if left in peace to do so by the white otter traders who sometimes landed to burn their canoes and dwellings. During peacetime, Rosa helped the women fill baskets with acorns, and butcher seals, sea lions and sea otters that the men brought them. For this she received a share of the food. When the otter traders came, Rosa kept out of sight with the women and children on a narrow shelf of rock below the lip of a cliff and listened to the raiders moving through the village killing everyone they found.

Mostly, though, she lived apart in a hut she fashioned from whalebone struts covered with hides she had scraped to let in light. From the hut she could easily climb a bluff, watch the ships that plied the channel and never doubt that *Santa Rosa* and the Aragonese would come. For whatever the Comisario's wife had said, Rosa knew that grandfather would convey her letter to Miguel. She pictured the Aragonese arriving in San Blas, learning of Beatris's death, finding grandfather gone, travelling to Tepic, reading the letter, and then embarking on his search for her. As time passed, though, she accepted that she, grandmother, grandfather, and Adelina were links in a chain. If anything happened to any of them, her story would be lost. Unquestionably though, Miguel would never give up trying to find her.

She often swam beyond the waves, dove with the cormorants, and speared fish with the *navaja* strapped to a pole. The villagers had given her a basket and a float. Having filled the basket, she would catch a few more fish and feed them to the birds. Holding on to the basket and its buoy, she rode the breakers in.

One day, a cormorant followed her and let her come close to it on land. A fishing line leashed its throat. As she cut it free, she recalled Miguel de Roca saying that in places he had travelled, men captured these birds and tethered them, let them swim and dive freely but only to haul them in and force them by constricting the throat, to cough up their catch.

"Thus, it is with men," he had said. He had meant that some men held the leash of others. What about women? Did men, including men like grandfather, believe they leashed girls at birth? How remarkable that she had ever considered herself at liberty.

The bird slept on her pallet in the hut and accompanied her into the sea. She kept its dropped feathers and stitched them into a cloak to protect herself from rain. Still, she watched and waited for Miguel. Only death could have kept him from her and if he had died, his soul would tell hers in the night.

~

But Pearl recalls his description of the city he loved in Aragon with its golden stone, its bells that tolled the hours while he read the poems of his ancestor in an almond and olive garden: *I will die if she won't have me.* Had he meant to revisit San Blas and keep his word to Rosa or her mother at all?

~

A daughter born to Rosa, the child who became Nora's great-grandmother, was taken with the rest of the island's Chumash villagers by an expedition of Franciscans and resettled on the mainland. Later, hearing rumours of a woman hermit, the friars revisited the island and located the hut and Rosa and the cormorant cloak and the package of dolls. They would have destroyed all Rosa's belongings, but her Christianised daughter told them: "They are my mother's memories. Please, let her keep them."

After a few weeks indoors at the Mission, Rosa grew ill and died.

~

It is morning. Pearl eats porridge, drinks tea, and scrolls through what she has written. Curiously, the dish of sea turtle at the Commandant's dinner is like a recipe Pearl put on her blog. That post had brought her attention, much of it from people who did not understand that the last thing *she* would do is consume an endangered species. It wasn't her fault, though, if some people didn't get irony.

She scans more pages. As in the Theano tale, puzzles remain. Yet it seems clear to Pearl that Miguel de Roca, the Aragonese, is the father of Beatris's child. He may—to give him credit—have learned of Beatris's death and gone home to Aragon in sorrow with no conception of Rosa's troubles or her love for him, or that Beatris's infant lived. After all, the port was closed, and life as he had experienced it in San Blas no longer existed. If he had happened upon the Comisario's wife, all she could say was that Rosa had been lost from a ship and drowned. Only Beatris had known that Rosa could swim. Pearl doubts that any of Rosa's letters would have survived Adelina's homeward journey. And if they had, Adelina would not have delivered them.

Pearl feels for the girl Rosa had been—marooned and stuck in a longing without resolution—but the story's ending troubles her: Rosa should have done better, been honest with herself instead of indulging in fantasies and wasting time. She might have found a way off the island and made a life for herself.

Sudden fury floods Pearl's body at the realization that she, too, is stuck. She stows the computer and stuffs the Rosa doll and the Theano doll from under the pillow into Nora's workbag along with the furbelows and the diminished box of ashes. Once all is secured, she goes on deck and prepares to haul anchor.

On Pearl's way to the airport with her laptop and little else for luggage but Nora's carryall, the taxi pauses in heavy traffic. While they wait, a black Mazda in the lane beside them rear-ends a yellow Honda Civic. It is a gentle enough bump, but Pearl and the taxi driver expect the two drivers to leap out and confront each other. This is how people get beaten-up or killed. Instead, the drivers' doors remain closed; the Civic inches a few feet forward; the Mazda driver waits two beats, and then he taps the bumper of the Honda with just enough force to move the yellow car with its woman driver, slightly ahead. She puts the Honda in reverse and deftly nudges her bumper into his grille. The woman in the Civic gazes at the man in the Mazda in her mirror. Pearl cannot take her eyes off them. Back and forth they caress each other with their cars, scuffling and courting until the traffic clears.

PART III

GUILIAM & YAMHA: The Troubadour's Tale

Thirty generations have passed since Guiliam was a troubadour apprentice at the siege of Almeria in Spain and met Yamha, a Saracen girl, who was one of the besieged. When you write the stories, Nora wrote, don't forget to put that in.

After his divorce from Pearl's mother, Pearl's father Harry took the proceeds of his prize-winning first novel, moved to Vancouver, purchased a small West Vancouver motel, and found a job with Broadcast News. Since his retirement, Harry and his third wife, Loretta, have taken over management of the motel themselves. The motor inn consists of four two-storey cottages—eight units in all. Two of the cottages have been thoroughly refurbished. The stucco exteriors of the unrenovated buildings are rain stained; mould spackles the interior walls and mushrooms sprout from the carpeting in the bathrooms. The location, though, off a grassy lane populated by a few of the district's left-over, original shack-homes and a scattering of cedar and glass palaces positioned at a distance from the road allowance, is postcard perfect. The air smells green; a hint of creosote and salt suggests the nearby marina with its wharves, cafés, kayaks, sailboats, and floating homes. If he wants to make money, Harry should tear down the motel and sell the property for the millions he could get for it. No matter how many visitors a renewed Casa Rocinante might subsequently attract, it will never make that kind of dough. Instead, Harry holds on and spends his days supervising the motel facelift, and his evenings hosting any guests who turn up, or reading the latest of his ex-wife Sara's books.

Sara's newest work, a thin forty-eight pages, lies open in front of Pearl as she reads at an outdoor umbrella-sheltered table and sips coffee. She arrived late the night before. The housekeeper sweeps pine needles and arbutus leaves from the pool deck. Her son, who looks small for his age—Harry said he was thirteen—trawls the pool waters for debris with a net.

Sara's first story begins: *The serpent has imagination; the woman has nerve. With the serpent she has passion, but she is not loved.* Sara had married the New York editor who edits and promotes her work, but she is restless, always travelling and engaged in research for her writing, an occupation which puzzles Harry who finds nothing in her books that she could not devise on the spot.

"How does she do it?" Harry says, his eyes taking in Sara's slim hardback as he emerges from the office to join his daughter. He pours himself a coffee from the poolside trolley and pulls up a chair across from Pearl. "She gets published, but what does she sell? A few thousand copies? It's a nice-looking product: it's quality," he says, taking the volume from Pearl and leafing through it, "but how does she get by? Collectors, libraries? Do libraries still buy books?"

Harry shakes his head in puzzlement.

"The reviews are good," Pearl says.

"You can't live on reviews," Harry says. After his initial success, Harry had met nothing but failure with his writing. If it were not for Loretta, who doesn't indulge him and helps to pay the bills, he might be bitter at the world's lack of response to his talent. He does not want Pearl to suffer for art like he has.

"Why doesn't Sara write something people can understand?" Harry says. He grimaces and raises his eyebrows at what he finds on Sara's pages. He is tall, grey-haired, and good-looking in a saggy-eyed way; he wears glasses to read. His eyebrows overhang the top of the frames. Harry's pride is a heavier burden than he admits. He places copies of his first novel on the bedside tables in the motel. To guest comments about his authorship he replies, "You've heard of the Pulitzer? Well, I won the Howitzer."

"Come and see this, sweetheart!" Harry calls to Loretta, who is on her way out to work in a gallery in the Kerrisdale district downtown. To Harry's compilation of Mexican folk art at the motel, she has added books of west coast photography, and split-seagrass baskets woven with whale and eagle motifs. Loretta shuts the office door behind her, sits down, and crosses her legs. One of her feet, clad in navy pumps, twirls impatiently. She is dressed in a red suit, her black hair swings to her shoulders. A pair of bright red plastic glasses rest on top of her head.

Harry displays the book. "What do you think?"

Pearl catches Loretta's eye. Neither wants to be the one to tell Harry that, in addition to her literary work, Sara publishes popular historical romance novels under a pseudonym. Pearl believes her mother's literary fables are like logs thrown into the flood of thought to try to slow it down. *Think*, the stories insist. The romance novels are different. In these her mother cries out, *Feel!* Nora's tales are different again: they are trails of bread-crumbs. You follow their lead, hoping they will guide you home, but consume them on the way and then … Pearl's thoughts jam.

Loretta turns a page or two, murmurs, and stands to leave. Harry imprisons her hand and kisses it, reluctant to let her go.

"While you're both here … " Pearl says, her thoughts focused on what is uppermost in her mind.

"Um ... I'm in a hurry," Loretta says.

"Nora's dolls—you can't have forgotten them, Harry—she told stories about them. They should all be in her house, but they're not. Did she bring any of them with her?"

Harry's eyebrows shoot up. "Why would she do that?" He waits, but Pearl doesn't answer. It would mean talking about her refusal of Nora's request, and about the night Nora died, and Pearl's visit to Pink Pelican Island; and she *can't*.

"I remember them," Harry says after a pause, "but if she had them with her, she didn't tell me." He looks at Loretta. "What about you, honey?" Loretta tilts her head to one side and purses her lips.

"I'm supposed to find them and summon up their stories and write them down," Pearl says. These are not easy words for her, but she withstands her father's scrutiny.

"Supposed to? How did you get that idea?" He seems interested, but again Pearl can't answer.

Loretta says, "I really must go."

"Okay," Harry says, but he doesn't release her.

"Uh, Pearl," he says, "I had this friend, and after his mother died he took care of the estate, cleared out the house, but he told me that he checked her answering machine every day to see if she had left a message for him."

"Had she?" Loretta says.

"Well, no. It's a natural human impulse, though: we can't believe people leave like that without getting in touch again." Harry kisses his wife's hand once more and lets it go. "Be patient, Pearl. It takes time to heal."

Loretta's heels click on the pool deck tiles. She speaks to the housekeeper as she goes by, and to the housekeeper's son who jumps down from the diving board on which he has been balancing. He throws his arms around Loretta, and Loretta hugs him. Until this moment, Pearl has not thought of Loretta as liking kids or them liking her, or that she and Harry might one day want a family.

The garden, half an acre of established intertwined roses, lilac, and rhododendron, overwhelms a slumping wooden fence. The pool is functional and clean, but the whale mosaics on the bottom need restoring. The fractured tiles catch tiny parcels of light, split them into fragments and bounce them to the surface of the water. Pearl blinks and refocuses her gaze on her father.

"Who are they, Harry?" Pearl says, indicating the sweeper and the boy, who is staring into the pool.

"Friends of Nora's," he says. "I thought I told you. She brought them to us when she closed down Refuge House." He is about to say more but Loretta calls "Bye!" as she climbs into the car, and Harry turns to blow her a kiss. Loretta drives off down the lane. Harry resumes reading Sara's book, and Pearl returns to her coffee and her thoughts.

In the public pool near their house, Nora had taken little Pearl to the shallow end and held her under the belly while she kicked. Pearl in a yellow swimsuit, sculling the water with turtle-like arms and legs. Later, Nora taught her to put her face in the water and blow bubbles, and float. Later still, Pearl took swimming lessons and went to swim club practices. She competed for her school and was good enough that her coaches encouraged her to swim in statewide competitions: but Pearl wasn't the best at sprints, and she wasn't interested in the endurance abilities that had made her a candidate for long-distance meets. She wanted to be a thoroughbred, not a workhorse; and so, she quit.

These days, Pearl prefers to swim in the ocean, but the squeak on tile as a swimmer jumps into a pool is distinctive and she swivels her head to the splash of the fully dressed boy entering the water. Pearl leaps to her feet as the housekeeper screams. She waits for the boy to lift his head, kick, and stop giving them a scare; instead, he hangs facedown, underwater. He will be drowning in twenty seconds.

Pearl scans the pool area for equipment, but all she finds is the pool rake the boy had used. Where are the flotation tubes and the liferings? Dimly she hears Harry say, "He can't swim, Pearl. Do something."

She grabs a cushion off a lounge chair and jumps into the water. It takes moments to reach him—it isn't a big pool. She slips the cushion under his chest, pushes him to the surface, grasps him under the armpits, and flips him upwards. He is heavy, his slack limbs deadweight, but she tows him to the side of the pool. Harry helps to pull him out.

"Call the ambulance," she says. She kneels, turns the boy's head to the side, releases his jaw to clear his tongue from his airway, listens for his breathing, and checks for a pulse. She can't find one. His skin is blue and cold. She tilts his head, lifts his chin, breathes into him four times to make sure the air is moving in and out. She repeats this, looking for signs of life. Finding none, she pinpoints the centre of his thin chest and initiates compressions.

Pearl has taken classes; she is trained in what to do, but suddenly Maria pushes her aside.

"Let me, let me!" his mother cries. She is flushed but calm as she hunches close to her son and whispers into an ear, "Listen, Joachim. You have done well. Everything is all right. You are safe. You do not need to hold your breath. Open your mouth and breathe." Gently she eases him into the fetal position.

To Pearl's amazement, the boy does what his mother says. The pinched furl of his mouth blooms: a dribble of water runs down his chin and falls onto the tiles; he coughs, takes a gasping breath, and sits up with his mother's help. She strips off his wet shirt and pants. Shiny puckered pink welts cover much of his body. "Thank the lady for helping you," she says. He has not quite found his way from wherever he has been, but he murmurs, "Thank you."

The episode is chilling. Pearl recalls nights at Nora's house, trying not to hear people talking in the kitchen downstairs; people whom she'd seen while she awaited her turn, as they came and went to the bathroom in shorts and singlets that revealed scarred flesh.

After she has changed into dry clothes, Pearl finds Harry in the motel lounge, an untouched drink in front of him. Loretta's taste is evident in a wash of green forested hills, blue sky and sea that calms the walls, and canoes, brave in fingers of mist, making way wall by wall through the four directions.

Pearl sits across from her father.

"His mother said he was safe around water," Harry says.

"His mother! She told me he wasn't drowning; he was holding his breath! Did you ask him? Did you *think* to ask him if he could swim?"

"There's more to this than you realize, Pearl."

"It looks like he's been burned intentionally!" Pearl waits for her father to say she is mistaken, but instead he turns his glass round and round on its coaster.

"What's going on, Harry. Who are these people?"

"Nora went to San Blas looking for them," Harry says. "She found them and applied for their papers. When they had their documents, she brought them to Refuge House. The boy went to school. They were fine. But she had to close the house, so Nora asked if Maria and Joachim could live with us, like I said."

This time the name sinks in. "*He* is Joachim. The one in Nora's will? What else did you forget to tell me, Harry? Tell me! Tell me what I need to know."

"Joachim's father was a fisherman," Harry begins. "He and his friend left to catch sharks, but they had trouble with the boat's engine. They rigged a sail with a blanket and worked their way down the coast until they could make it into a beach. They hiked to a road. Several people saw them thumbing for home. At some point, Joachim's father called Maria and told her what had happened. He said not to tell anyone he'd called, and to give his love to Joachim. The boat was found later, but neither of the men was seen again.

"Maria thinks they stumbled across something they shouldn't have, maybe drugs. The next day, two men came to the house and asked for the boy. They said they were from his school. Maria didn't believe them—she knew Joachim's teachers—but Joachim ran in from the kitchen before she could get rid of them.

"They burned Joachim in front of her with cigarettes to make her say what her husband had told her. She said he'd told her nothing. Then, they held the boy down in a tub of water. Why do you think he learned to hold his breath? It's a miracle he *wants* to work near the pool. He seems all right but if you see any of those baby wipes—the disinfecting ones, in squares, leave them alone. He lays trails. You can get him to clean up most of them, but he won't move the ones in front of their door. He tells his mother they scare bugs away. Oh, and he sleepwalks.

"So, you see ..." Harry offers his palms in resignation. "What would you have had me do?"

Pearl is awakened at 3:00 a.m. by a noise outside. She dons the Egyptian cotton bathrobe the motel supplies in the upgraded rooms and goes out onto the balcony. The damp night air makes her shiver: she has been dreaming about her grandmother and the cave on Pink Pelican Island. Nora in dust motes, Nora's molecules reconfiguring from her ashes under the spell of the cave drawings.

Joachim slumps in one of the deck chairs beside the pool. White and pink garden lights outline the courtyard; their light glazes his skin. His thin frame is swathed in a towel. The air is motionless, but dank odours of seaweed and washed-in logs trickle from undercut mudbanks a few blocks away. Pearl watches Joachim for a few moments then goes indoors and puts on her bathing suit.

"Hey, Joachim," she says, pulling up a deck chair beside him. "Nice night, eh? Mind if I sit with you?"

Joachim shrugs.

"Does your mother know you've gone out?" He does not answer, but Pearl notices that he scans the window of the suite opposite. Pale baby-wipe squares chart steps to the door. Just like Harry had told her, it is a trail that Joachim lays to avert a world of harm.

"If I can't sleep, I count stars," she says. She goes on talking into his silence. "It's not hard to learn to swim, but somebody has to show you how. Nora taught me. I could teach you if you wanted.

"In fact," she continues—the tension in his profile shows he's listening—"I might go for a swim now. Do you want to join me?" Pearl slips off her robe and eases herself over the side of the pool. It is pleasant in the water, warmer than the air. She floats, chin up, as if her head is resting on a pillow. She begins to name the constellations she can see.

"Ursa Minor, that's the Little Bear or Little Dipper. It's got seven stars, four in the dipper bowl, the rest in its tail or handle. The other clear one is Boötes. It has five stars. The brightest is Arcturus. It's supposed to be a ploughman, but Nora said just call it 'Boo!' In between them, kind of faint, is the Dragon, Draco. It's really a huge snake, or a kite with a long tail."

She runs through the ones she has memorized, and is considering inventing names when he says, "Could I do what you're doing?"

"Float? Sure." She lets her feet drop, paddles to the side.

"I'm not afraid," he says.

"Of course not!"

"I can hold my breath."

"Yeah, you're good at it, but you could swim *and* breathe."

Their session in the pool doesn't last long. Joachim is apprehensive, and Pearl asks him repeatedly to hold his chin up and take in air. She shows him how to scull his hands underwater and wiggle his toes whenever he feels he might sink: her arm beneath him won't let him, anyway.

"Look at the sky. How many stars are there?" she asks. "Can you count them?"

He is at twenty before he realizes he is floating by himself, her forearm barely supporting his head. Pearl pulls him to her before he can go under.

While they're drying off, she says, "I could teach you a little every day."

"If you want. Sure."

"Joachim, will you tell me something?" His shoulders tense under the towel. "Why did you jump in the pool today? You went in on purpose."

His mother opens the door of her suite and assesses them.

"To see the whales," he says. "What they look like up close."

"The whales? The mosaics on the bottom?"

"My father saw whales from his boat. He said next time he'd take me with him."

Pearl understands. The leap into the pool is the logic of loss. In a weird way, it brought his father alive. "Well, don't do it by yourself again until you're a better swimmer. It's all right if I'm with you. In a few weeks, you won't need me at all."

Maria takes him in her arms and Joachim shivers, pinned to the pain of his younger self.

"Whales don't spend all their time under water, Joachim," Pearl says. "They're mammals, they have to come up for air."

"I'm not stupid!" he says and pulls away from his mother.

Pearl takes a breath and decides to risk it. "I read an article on the plane," she says. "One of the whales at the aquarium is expected to give birth soon." She looks at Maria who nods. "Do you want to come with me and see how the mother whale is doing?"

"Okay," he says.

Pearl's heart lurches. What if Nora had not made her continue lessons after she had cut her bathing suit into strips so she would have to quit? She'd hated how she'd looked in that swimsuit, how she wasn't as skinny as her friends, or as fast a swimmer. She closes her eyes. What if she hadn't known how to save Joachim from drowning? The bonds that tie Nora to the world are multitudinous. Theano was right: those you love and remember are never absent.

On her way to her morning workout, Loretta drops Pearl and Joachim off at the Stanley Park Aquarium.

It is 7:30 a.m. A thin veil of rain releases grey light through the trees, enough for Pearl to see that the entrance beyond a large black sculpture of a whale, is open. They had planned to breakfast first at a nearby café, but the Aquarium issued a birth alert online just before they left home.

Clusters of adults and children are passing under coloured banners on their way into the enclosure. Pearl and Joachim follow them, and soon they are standing quietly behind a rope barrier with the others. Across the pool, on a flat section of landscaping rocks, attendants in red rain jackets, black track pants, and bare feet scrutinize the water. Two divers suit up in scuba gear, and a small band of men and women in dark clothing squat beside white equipment boxes, looking intently at something Pearl and Joachim can't see; and then the pale curve of a beluga breaks the surface. Pearl stands on tiptoe, but Joachim pulls her out of the crowd to tuck in behind two women descending a flight of concrete steps to the blue light of an underground gallery. The turquoise water shimmers against floor-to-ceiling glass, so clear that it seems to disappear as they stare into it.

One of the women spots them. "What are you doing here?" she says. But the other woman says, "It doesn't matter. Let's go or we'll miss it," and they exit through a door marked "No Admittance" that clicks shut behind them.

The beluga bends and bows underwater. Scuba divers tread nearby. In the Arctic and sub-Arctic, the whale's home, its ice-pale colour protects it from predators; but in the lights of the aquarium, the whale is fluorescent, safe from all but humans. The beluga's tail waves, its body arches; its head and tail clench, and a dark-bodied calf emerges tail first from its mother's ventral opening. She twists to expel the rest of its body, and the baby drops out in a rush of blood. Cheers from the spectators above filter down to Pearl and Joachim in the underground hush.

Red water foams around the little whale. It swims upwards, drops down, swims again, sinking and rising until the mother manoeuvres beneath it, and supports and lifts it on her spine into the air.

Pearl's face is wet. She wipes it with her sleeve. The mother whale comes and presses her nose to the glass where they stand. She waits until Pearl and Joachim flatten their palms to the glass, and then goes to her calf and raises it once more so it can breathe.

We need to protect these great mammals, but we shouldn't turn aside if we chance upon a beached whale—most of them have died of starvation, not disease, Pearl had written in a SaveOurSouls cooking blog. *Have the meat tested, to be safe; but don't forget that one slice from a whale's flank can make a meal for four. Splash the meat with red wine, rub it with butter, wrap it in seaweed, fix it to a seasoned plank and turn it to face the fire.*

She did not mention that the whales were starving because of human-caused destruction of the marine environment, from plankton on up.

Pearl and Joachim stand beside each other, watching the mother and calf until the aquarium bosses turn off the lights in the tank to give the whales some privacy.

After Joachim's swimming lesson at Casa Rocinante, during which he behaves like a whale calf learning to sink and rise on its own, Harry brings out the chessboard, and he and Joachim set the pieces for a match. Almost immediately Joachim says, "No, Harry, no! I'll show you."

Loretta, who is home early, joins Pearl at the poolside. Harry mugs and slaps his head at his losses. "He would make a good father," Pearl says.

"He *is* a good father," Loretta says. "You don't need to worry, Pearl. Not everyone needs their own babies. I come from a family of eight, and I have dozens of nephews and nieces. That's more than enough for me." She places her briefcase on her lap.

"I've got something for you," she says. She opens the case, brings out a small cloth-covered object and unrolls the packaging. Pearl holds her breath. It is one of the dolls Nora had brought to the café.

"You said none of them were here!" Pearl exclaimed.

"No, I didn't," Loretta says. "Look at this." She flips the doll upside down to reveal a second doll beneath the first doll's garment, this one a boy. She flips it right side again. "It's called a topsy-turvy: two dolls in one. Nora said you should tell their story to Joachim."

Pearl doesn't like Loretta as an intermediary. The dolls are hers from Nora, not Loretta's. Had Nora really suggested she tell this story to Joachim? The tale that goes with the double-doll is not suitable, it really isn't.

Loretta puts the doll in Pearl's lap. "The girl doll's name is Yamha," she says.

"I know." The black hair glued to the doll's head sticks out in tufts. The painted dark eyes are shiny black gobbets; a tiny green bird dangles from a length of string that's wound around one of its pale bone arms. For as long as Yamha had sat on Pearl's shelf, the doll had worn a red and violet woven vest as a finishing layer to an indigo shirt and skirt. The only clothing the doll has on now though, is a dirty, yellowed underdress. The unbleached cotton is streaked with rust-coloured stains.

"What happened?" Pearl says pointing at the discolourations. Loretta shrugs, takes the doll from Pearl, and turns it the other way. Yamha's shift reverses to become the boy doll's grubby fawn tunic. Dimly, Pearl recalls that the *boy* side of the vest was green: you had to switch it yourself from one doll to the other. Elegant red leather shoes dangle from his belt, and a diminutive lute is slung on a strap tacked to his shoulder. His hair is long and fair, and whoever made him gave him blue glass eyes. Loretta taps the lute, and it rattles.

"I was going to give the doll to Joachim, since this way it's a boy. Joachim was close to Nora, Pearl. He was so distressed at her death—but I thought I should wait and see if you showed up."

Showed up? Pearl takes a steadying breath. She does not want a fight. If only someone, even if it were Loretta, had told her that Nora was ill! *If only*, Pearl's inner voice admonishes, *you had listened to your grandmother when she needed you.*

"The boy doll's name is Guiliam," Loretta says. "You do remember him, don't you?"

As a child, Pearl had not been interested in the boy beneath Yamha's skirts. It has taken her a moment to recall him. "Sure, of course I do."

Loretta looks at her doubtfully. "His mother came from Castile, and his father was Aragonese, in the Middle Ages."

"*The* Aragonese? But not in the Middle Ages! *The* Aragonese lived in the late eighteenth century, in Rosa's time!" Pearl cries before she can check herself.

But Miguel de Roca *had* mentioned an ancestor, the troubadour who wrote *I will die if she won't have me.* Was that Guiliam? The Middle Ages, of course, during which hunger and warfare drove people onto the roads, and often far from their birthplaces. It is all coming back.

"How should I know?" Loretta says. "I only know what Nora told me, and she said you knew your stuff." Loretta sighs. "I hope she was right. Anyway, the story belongs to them both, to Yamha and to Guiliam in Spain. Does that ring a bell?"

She squints at the chessboard—checkmate is not far off—and relinquishes the doll to Pearl. Pearl fingers the minuscule lute. It rattles again, but it does not appear to be broken.

"They have their own doll," Loretta says.

"What? Who?"

"Joachim and Maria. Ask them."

This is such an absurd notion that Pearl instantly rejects it. If it were so, Nora would have told her.

"Honey?" Harry calls. "Did you see that?" He overturns his King and surrenders. "I can't take the punishment! Time for a drink."

Loretta's chair scrapes back, and Harry and Loretta depart, arms linked. Joachim stays to run through chess strategies on his own.

In her room, Pearl tosses the Yamha-Guiliam doll on a chair and lies down on the bed to rest. She closes her eyes as a vision of the mother whale comes to her, its nose to the glass, teaching the calf to breathe, to follow her, to nurse, the baby's eyes like lacquered buttons. Then Joachim is in the tank with the whales, his body stuck to the aquarium wall, mouth agape, scars luminescent on his chest and belly.

Pearl's eyelids fly open.

She fetches the doll and runs her fingers along the seams of Yamha's dress, upends the doll and rustles through the boy's clothing. Surely Nora has left instructions with this doll as she has with the others: but no matter how diligently Pearl searches, she cannot find anything.

She takes several deep breaths to relax. She will do it without help. The memories are inside her, after all. The door creaks open and Joachim's long face pokes round the frame.

"Loretta said she forgot this," he says. Pearl takes the slip of paper from him. It is torn from a pocket datebook. The handwriting is Nora's. *Thirty generations have passed since Guiliam was a troubadour apprentice at the siege of Almeria in Spain and met Yamha, a Saracen girl, who was one of the besieged. When you write the story, don't forget to put that in.*

Pearl rereads the note after Joachim leaves, arranges herself at her laptop, and stares into the pool in which the stories swim.

~

The Troubadour's Tale

Almeria, Spain, 1147 ACE

The towered city of Almeria sat on a stony hill above the sea, so rich that its streets were made of pearl, its dust of gold, and its gardens were images of paradise. Twelve-year-old Guiliam, a troubadour apprentice, did not know this for himself, but the soldiers who were promised its spoils said so. Guiliam and his master Marcabru had accompanied King Alfonso VII, Emperor of All Spain, to the siege of Almeria on behalf of Pope Eugene III's Second Crusade.

Marcabru laughed when Guiliam raised the subject of Almeria's treasure.

"The city is rich in mulberry trees and silkworms. Ten thousand silk looms, Guiliam. Silk and trade; that should tell you enough. What matters to *us* is that it is a city rich in poets. The poet Almotacin used to be its emir. My master took me there to see him. Almotacin was old but still handsome in those days; not as good-looking as I am, though." The troubadour chuckled. Guiliam disliked his master's attempts at humour. He preferred him brusque, difficult. Himself.

"*The white dawn spreads over thou its delightful wing*," Marcabru quoted. He ruffled Guiliam's hair. The boy twisted his neck away. "With these words, the poet welcomed me under *his* wing with all poets who have gone before. I was honoured. The wing is the spirit poetry shares with Nature—and with God, of course."

"Tell me what the city is like!" Guiliam interrupted. Marcabru's evasions annoyed him; he did not understand why his master spoke admiringly of a Mohammedan emir.

"See for yourself," Marcabru said. He gestured at the fortress and its environs. "The landscape is hot and dry, yet they grow many crops on the hillsides. They have the secret of conducting water." He pointed to Almeria's walls and towers. "It is a city built of stone like any other, but its name means *watchtower*. From the battlements, they can see for miles in this direction and southwards out to sea. When the walls are lit by sun or moonlight, the stone shines like gold and becomes a mirror that reflects the nature of the onlooker. Some find wonder in it, others only greed." His master sighed. "We must look like insects to those in the towers as we polish our weapons down on the plain."

"I see no mirror," Guiliam said. "I feel no wonder! We should have come earlier! The Venetians and Genoese fought the Moors before we arrived. You've heard what they say about us—that we were late on purpose; that we are cowards!"

"Hold your tongue, Guiliam, or it will have you in trouble again. Do you mean to insult the King?" The troubadour raised his hand as if to strike his apprentice.

"No!" Guiliam said, horrified. "No one is braver than he!"

Marcabru glared but withheld the blow. For days he had been slipping into the city and bringing out manuscripts for safekeeping. His apprentice had not approved. "They are our enemies. The King would not like it if he knew," the boy had said.

"The King ordered it be done," Marcabru replied, but he knew the boy did not believe him. He would have taken Guiliam into the besieged city along with him, but he wished to spare him the pain of knowing more sharply than he must, what was about to be destroyed. The King had promised to exact revenge for all Christians killed or imprisoned in the name of Mahomet.

Marcabru gripped the boy's shoulder. "Do not worry. There will be more than enough opportunities to meet the Saracens in battle. We will not shy from any fight ordained by God."

"No, never!" Guiliam cried.

"And *you* may not shy from what I've asked you to do." The troubadour pinched the muscle between Guiliam's neck and shoulder. Marcabru had told Guilliam to prepare a story of the crusade now underway that would inspire the soldiers and knights in the coming fray.

"I won't shy away!" the boy said, trying not to flinch. "But how may I work? There is no quiet anywhere!" Around them swirled the chaos of tent building, weapons practice and of troops and cavalry wheeling in formation.

"Find some place, Guiliam! It must be done by tonight." The troubadour moved away, calling over his shoulder, "See me when it is ready, but do not disturb me needlessly."

The apprentice noted the effort in his master's steps. He might still be straight and brown-haired, but Marcabru was no longer young.

The boy smiled to himself as he made his way south from the camp, passing through groves of small dry pines, kicking their dropped cones ahead of him. He walked all the way to the coastline crags below which the Genovese galleys had mustered for battle. He had not needed Marcabru to tell him that a successful rooting out of this den of Saracens would mean remission of sins and, if God willed they died in the undertaking, a smooth entry into Heaven. To those who lived, it would bring a large reward. He had heard the Genovese envoy declare they were not interested in plunder, but the envoy also made clear that Christian control of the city would allow Genovese merchants access to new commercial markets. If there was one thing Guiliam had learned since the day Marcabru took him in, it was that one purpose nests within another. *What is your purpose Guiliam*? he asked himself. Firstly, to honour the King; secondly to follow his master; and thirdly to become a richer and better poet than Marcabru.

Guiliam loved the King. If it were not for him, Guiliam would have died in Oreja along with his parents and hundreds of other captives held by Oreja's Muslim ruler. They had been taken from their fields along the Tagus River.

With food and water running out, his mother had hidden him in a dry cistern with the last of her drinking water. His parents, like most of the other captives, had died of hunger and thirst before King Alfonso's forces had broken through the city's walls in an attempt to free them. Marcabru had heard Guiliam's cries and extracted him from the empty reservoir.

"Weren't *you* found abandoned and squalling?" the King had said glimpsing the boy in the troubadour's arms. "Does he have your lungs. Will you teach him to sing?"

"I found him in a Mohammedan pit of bones, not on a riverbank as I was," Marcabru said. "We will need to wait until he is fed and watered to hear what he has to say, or sing."

"Water him and feed him, then, troubadour. See that he is useful."

Each time Guiliam heard the story, he renewed his vow to serve.

The cliffs were jagged, the trail was dry and dusty and wound close to the verge of steep drop-offs: if Guiliam fell, he would impale himself on rocks. The boy bent to brush dirt from his red leather shoes: these were new, a gift from his master in anticipation of the verses Guiliam would write, and for which Marcabru would—if they were good enough—take credit. Fair was fair. Marcabru had taken blame for a verse Guiliam made about one of the court ladies in Zaragoza. She deserved it, but he would have been beaten for it and possibly dismissed if his authorship had been suspected, while from Marcabru rough satire was expected.

The cat and the dog only know of one thing,
*To fight and to f*** and to do it again.*
I'll never be able to tell you my pain,
For nothing could loosen the clutch of Elaine.

Marcabru had sniggered on hearing it and then cuffed Guiliam's ear. To atone, Guiliam had been forced to write a love song. Love! What could he, an orphan, tell of love? He had done his best, and the court lady made sure that the flattering song circulated with whispered suggestions as to who was behind it and who it was for. Guiliam longed for the day that he, like his master, could write what he liked about anyone other than the King.

He stood at a rock fringe of myrtle. Below him, white cliffs plunged in deep folds to the sea. A rose twinkling of foam softened the waterline. The pale sand and green water were entrancing, and Guiliam savoured the mesmerizing measures of the waves; but he had come in order to work. After he had fixed the story the Genovese told of their part in the opening battle into a serviceable order in his memory, he would use it to shape a poem which would be called for within a very few hours.

He began by constructing an outline of "The Tale of the Battle":

Fifteen Genovese galleys, their sails like the wings of doves, set out at dawn from the sea and proceeded into the mouth of the river below the city of Almeria's walls. Also, at first light, the noble Count of Barcelona and his knights slipped into the hills above the city and hid. The Saracens spied from their towers as the galleys arrived and discharged their fighters onto the beaches; but before leaving safety and committing themselves to clash with what appeared to be a manageable force, the Saracens sent reconnoitring soldiers into their surroundings to make certain no trap had been set. God being on the side of the Christians, the Saracen soldiers, one White and one Black, were blinded and did not find the lurking Spanish knights.

The Saracens came down from the battlements, opened the city gates and engaged with the Genovese; but instead of standing their ground, the Genovese warriors withdrew to their waiting galleys with only a few men slain. Then, the signal was given and the Count's forces in concealment descended the slopes, tearing, trampling, and slicing all in their path. They were like wolves, the Saracens their natural prey, and they slew by the thousands while the men in the galleys leaned over the hulls and slaughtered those Muslims who had fled to the water.

Under the swords of the Christians, both river and sea turned scarlet.

Guiliam was beginning to see how the tale might be configured as poetry. He would have to be careful; sure to record sufficient details but not so many as to overpraise the Genovese and the Count of Barcelona and anger the King. His task was to rouse the Spanish army, not undermine the alliance. In any event, the Moslems had retreated inside the city and still held it. It would not be easy to break in. The walls were thick, and from the towers and battlements on the hill, as Marcabru had pointed out, the enemy could scrutinize the besiegers' preparations. On his way to the cliffs, Guiliam had viewed his side readying siege towers and catapults, and the King's soldiers (having left camp at last) setting fires against the city walls to weaken them.

The sea today was a wind-ruffled meadow on which light crackled. Guiliam had to struggle to imagine men within its crystalline depths, dying with the thrust of weapons. He thought of what his master had said about the city, the poets in it, better poets than Marcabru; and the meaning of the city's name. Once the work of the siege engines began, it would not be "the watchtower," more like "the shattered tower"; less like "the mirror," more like "the broken mirror." He wanted to laugh about it, but a pang of regret ratcheted his guts instead. He had taught himself to ignore such feelings, however, and instead of thinking further, he fumbled in the bag he carried and brought out dried figs and ate them.

Cloud had blown in; high puffs that sapped colour from the sky and the ocean. The sea no longer glittered; it was a warped cloth of beige and olive. Guiliam's foot dislodged a stone. It clattered from the height to the sands below. He shied in case anyone should look up and disturb his solitude. He could see along the coastline to the galleys beached near the city, and to the men installing the machinery of assault. The Crusaders—the Genovese and Catalans along with the King—had control of the river entrance and port: no Saracens would be escaping that way. In their walled safety, the Saracens had placed themselves in a prison. Perhaps Guiliam would stroll that way later and have a look. For now, though, he was in search of a place of *re*pose in which to *com*pose.

He resettled the lute across his shoulders, set his course and climbed, making his way over piles of boulders and along faint tracks, and by holding onto cracks and fissures in the steeper crags. He mulled over ideas for verses, but he was stuck on lines like those that had nearly ended his career, or on fragments of chiming doggerel. Marcabru would thrash him if he had nothing but *Christ's blood, as it must / Guiding Knights and Kings to dust* for his day's work, which was all he had come up with so far.

At the foot of a great tumble of rock, he rested and shook out the pebbles and grit that had infiltrated the red shoes. Such fine leather deserved better treatment than this rough ground, but Guiliam could not reappear in camp without a finished poem. He'd hoped observations on the walk would inspire him, but all he could recall of note since leaving camp, other than the sea itself, were bloody Moorish heads mounted on posts in the sand, the eyes picked out by birds.

As he bent to the task of wrestling his shoes on, Guiliam caught sight of a spark of colour in the grey palate of dirt and rock; a late flower sheltering in a straggle of bushes. He pushed the bush aside and found himself looking into a small cave. Taking this as a sign, he crept inside where he saw a tunnel and propelled himself along it. He was drawn by the tunnel's glow, and then later, he realized he could no longer turn around. He was sweating, half-convinced he would be trapped without hope of rescue, until the burrow swelled into a cavity. He could stand and touch its sides and ceiling. Light and air entered through fissures: the air swirled and dried his sweat. Thin beams of light blazed off sharply faceted crystals embedded in the walls. Guiliam had not cried since Marcabru had found him in the reservoir, but he sat on the smooth stone floor here and wept. Water dripped from the ceiling into pools of green algae. He dried his eyes, plucked the strings of his lute, and listened to the crystals sing. He was inside the heart of a jewel. The lines he needed were here.

Afterwards, he went out into the world, blinking at the harsh light, his ears assaulted by a cacophony rising from the beaches. He scooted down the way he had come and pelted for the conflict without thought. He ran in leaps and with giant steps: the period spent in the cave had made him invincible. In his exalted state, Guiliam flew past fires around which men had been working moments before; and found himself hurdling heaps of what he took to be tangled wood strewn along the strand, before the smell of death revealed them as the limbs and torsos of slaughtered men.

A phalanx of the King's mounted knights rode by, coming from their camp. Behind them followed the infantry, heading for the river and cutting into Saracen sorties as they advanced in the direction of the beached galleys. Guiliam was caught in the flow of soldiery and turned like a pebble in a stream, turned and turned, scarcely able to maintain his footing; deafened and disoriented by the noise of sword fighting and the smashing of catapult stones into the city walls—he could see the gaps the stones made—and by the screams and the stink of blood and shit and death. While he had been playing and singing in the cave, the battle had opened. From the ramparts, the Saracens hurled down fire.

"Ho! Little poet!" It was Marcabru's man, joined to the King's forces in restitution for his sins. "You! Boy! Up with you!" The valet swept Guiliam onto the horse behind him. Guiliam clung, too shocked to make a sound. They rode close enough to the city walls to crush Saracen corpses underfoot, and for the screams of those alive and half-buried in the sand to penetrate his senses: but the encounter was almost over, and his master's man found no more killing to do.

They wheeled round, and the valet, lightly armoured in leather, steered the horse knee-deep into the river. He twisted in the saddle and gave Guiliam a push and tumbled him off. "You've fouled my horse!" he shouted. "Clean yourself! Next time stay in camp and stick to your poetry."

It was so: Guiliam's breeches ran with excrement. He stripped them off. Trembling, mortified, terrified, he sat in the river and let the water rinse him. No one took any notice, and why would they? The dying did not care, nor did the women weeping from behind the walls. He listened to the curiously clear voice of a girl singing a song in a language he did not understand. Everyone who mattered had left.

Half-naked and cold, he slipped into camp, pulled on a spare breech cloth and his good woolen hose, and slung a cloak over his shoulders to cover his dirty tunic. Leaving the ruined red shoes to dry, he put on an old pair of leather slippers and joined the supper fires, ready to contribute his poem at the King's request.

The King sighted him and called out, "Boy poet, I have been hearing about you. You went into battle unarmed."

Guiliam flushed, stepped forward and bowed. "Armed with my verses, Sire."

"In tribute, the men have given you a new name," the King said.

Guiliam's heart throbbed. His stomach, sick from the day's jolts, cramped at the odours of roasting meat and unwashed bodies and the overhanging stench of wounds, but he managed to swallow his nausea. Soldiers crowded round: many were injured and in pain, but no one complained of their suffering at this fire.

The King drew his damascened sword, and an aide traded it for a flat wooden blade with a wooden hilt and pommel. The King flourished it at Guiliam. "This shall be your weapon. Care well for it, boy poet; it is firewood we can scarcely spare!" At this, the others shouted out and laughed. Then the King said,

"In memory of your actions this day, I name you Sir Brown-Stain! This shit stained cloth is your flag!" The aide handed him Guiliam's filth-soaked trousers, retrieved from where he had dropped them, and tied to a pole. The King grinned, and the soldiers shouted approval of the joke.

"As well, boy poet, so you shall never have to go into battle on foot again, you have your own nag," the King said. A set of reins was draped round Guiliam's neck from behind. He knew what was expected so he pranced, neighed, and pawed the air.

"No, no, boy poet, you are meant to ride!" the King said. His grin broadened: which, Guiliam understood, was a good thing.

Guiliam beamed, waved the wooden sword and staggered into the sagging-bodied nag they had fetched for him. He climbed onto it and received the flagpole that was offered.

"Sir Brown-Stain! Sir Brown-Stain!" the men shouted. Somebody slapped the horse's rump and sent Guiliam and his steed rocking into the night.

He was a boy, a poet: after everything done and witnessed that day it was a gentle enough prank; loss of bowel control was no real disgrace amongst soldiers, but to be shamed and scorned by his King! If he'd had the courage, Guiliam would have killed himself. Instead, tending his rage, he endeavoured to control the broken-down mount before it swayed him all the way to the besieged city. Pride kept him in the saddle until he was certain no one was near enough to witness, and then he slid from the horse to lie curled on the ground, his face squashed into the soil, wetting the earth with tears and snot and saliva. The ground was peppered with bitter herbs. Their pungent flavours scoured his taste buds.

He may have slept a little in retreat from his ignominy: he awoke stiff and cold, realizing he was no longer alone. Tear-damp earth had dried in his nostrils, but he pinched them quickly and did not sneeze. He lay under his cloak next to a clump of brush. That, and moonless darkness, sheltered him from the muffled men who hailed each other only yards away. The distant campfires had diminished to embers, but Guiliam could smell their smoke and the food he had been denied. Two of the voices belonged to allies of the King from Navarre and Urgell. The others he could not identify, but by their accents, he could tell they were Saracen. Guiliam thanked God for the disloyalty of the nag which had wandered off to browse for its supper.

"We do not see the need for further loss of life," a Saracen said. Several of their towers had been captured by the Genoese, and eighteen yards of the wall destroyed. "If the King will retire from the ground and his support of the Genovese, we will pay him with hostages and a hundred thousand gold *marabotini*. We will make a treaty with him for control of the city's trade. Why would he want these interlopers in a land we have shared with him with little trouble?"

"The King has given his pledge to the Pope," the Navarro said, "but he does not necessarily share the urgency of his allies. Why destroy what he will have to rebuild? Why should there be but one way to secure a desirable result? We will take your offer to the King."

"What time will we have our answer? The Genovese are an impatient people; they launch endless attacks against the city walls."

"You will have a reply by dawn," the Urgellian answered. "A message may be on its way from Zaragoza even now which will require the King's immediate recall on urgent business." Guiliam imagined the wink that accompanied the statement.

"Until dawn, then," the Saracen said. "We will bring half the money with us."

After the men were gone, Guiliam blew his nostrils clear on one sleeve, then washed the grime from his face with the other sleeve moistened in spit. God had leaked the plan into Guiliam's ears, but the boy poet alone had to decide what to do with it. If he did nothing, the King, his troops and Guiliam with them, would return to Zaragoza and the life of the court without achieving their great purpose. Not only were the so-called allies proposing the King's dishonour, but Marcabru would hear of "Sir Brown-Stain" and enshrine the worst day of Guiliam's life in a song bound to be repeated for the remainder of Guiliam's life. He did not think he could endure it. "Sir Brown-Stain" could only be expunged by a victory so great it would be all the King wanted to hear of the Crusade. All thoughts of "Sir Brown-Stain" would be eclipsed and Marcabru, along with Guiliam, would write great songs about the Spanish triumph. One purpose nested within the other.

It was not for him to consider those Spanish, Genovese, Catalans, and Saracens whose lives might be saved if he kept his eavesdropping to himself; or what those so spared might go on to do with their lives. It was not for a boy like him to unravel God's purposes. He had heard what he had heard.

And so Guiliam, a miniature cog in the wheel of circumstance, retrieved the disgraceful horse, took the wooden sword, and with grim satisfaction left for the beached Genovese galleys.

"Why have you come to us?" asked the Genovese consuls, shaken from sleep.

"I am certain the King knows nothing of what is being done in his name by traitors," Guiliam said. "He has sworn to kill Moslems and would not be foresworn. I am but a boy and a poet: how can I approach him on my own? The conspirators will deny it and say I bear a grudge against them."

One of the younger consuls leapt to his feet. "The Saracens show no mercy to us! They attack our ships and kill our men and make slaves of our women and children. They undermine our commerce. The evil they do must not go unpunished! Not one of them shall escape!"

While the stars paled in the sky and Guiliam could taste the sea moisture, soon to evaporate under a stinging October sun, he joined one of the Genovese companies ready to attack the city at dawn. Thousands of men set out that morning because of the troubadour apprentice in as much silence as they could manage, and listened for the trumpet signal at which they would storm the gaps made by the catapulted stones in the city walls. With the attack underway, a messenger rode to inform the King that the battle had begun and ask if he and his knights would care to join in the shedding of faithless Saracen blood.

Trumpets pealed, and the first rays of the sun pierced the mist stringing the horizon and struck the city walls with mirrored gold. The armed companies responded and clambered over the broken stones of the breaches. It was not long before King Alfonso's forces joined them. Most carried sacks and bags to take away the rumoured treasure from Almeria's streets and citadel.

Guiliam had planned to join in the hunt for prizes, but he was only armed with the wooden sword, and, on reflection, he couldn't see logic in risking his life unarmed. Not with his whole life ahead of him. He and the swaybacked horse skirted the breaks in the wall and veered north and east until they found themselves among tall reeds on a relatively dry portion of the riverbank. The steed grazed, and Guiliam hunkered in the reeds. While twenty-thousand and more of the city dwellers found paradise with the help of the invaders, and countless others were captured as slaves, he concentrated on a poem.

It was not Guiliam's fault. Of course it wasn't. The killings would have happened anyway, if not that day then another. All he had done—*all* he had done—was allow his feelings to play a small role in the timing. He, Guiliam, had no say, none of them had any say in the outcome, only God did.

Accordingly:

Blow trumpet blow!
Drum strike hard!
We won't grow old.

The blood of Christ
Flows from a spring eternal.
But that noble
Holding an offended nose,

That Knight—he'd better run!
He won't have heirs;
God does not reward his type
With a red rose.

And I, Sir Brown-Stain, I won't care . . .

He kept his head down, palms to his ears, counted syllables and juggled lines; he sniffled into his dirty sleeve and committed phrases to memory. He would take out the reference to Sir Brown-Stain, unless its presence in the satire might please the soldiers enough to turn it to his advantage; he would leave it in for now.

He was on the riverbank, not in the thick of the battle, but even here, despite muffling his hearing, he could hear the howls of people in the citadel as their throats were cut, and the clang of steel that signalled a sword miss-hit striking pavement: yes, that made a terrible ringing. But the discipline of the attackers was formidable, and they prosecuted their work with efficiency. In time, the din abated, and he un-clapped his hands from his ears to listen. No birds, winging their way to winter havens, disturbed with their calls; no insects wove among the bolting herbs in the gardens that greened the city perimeter. The air held its breath. Shortly, though, as the smell of blood carried, the flies would come.

A sudden thump on the Earth made him look up at the city's northeast tower and the people flooding its height. *Thump*. It happened again. *Thump*. And again. And again. He crawled, taking care to screen himself in the reeds, until he had a view of the tower's east wall. One after another, women threw children from the ramparts and leapt after them. The gowns of the plummeting children belled and flapped as they dropped; and the women's heads and extended limbs made the ragged points of stars. Most died on impact, but not all. Straightaway—it was like viewing dogs sniffing out wounded game—the soldiers with little left to do came striding through the grasses and swished their swords, striking and stabbing at what they found.

Guiliam inched in reverse and let himself sink into the river mud. Black muck smeared his clothing and one of his shoes came off. He thought of his good shoes, left behind in camp to dry. Would he see them again? He was frightened of being found. He did not think a self-imposed task of composing poetry would exempt him from a soldier's judgment. As he considered whether to risk a break for a faint path that threaded through tumbling gardens into the hills behind the city, a movement with a difference caught his eye. A figure on the tower separated itself from the others and lowered a large basket on a rope down the tower's east face. The basket met the ground, and an arm stretched from inside and unknotted the rope that was holding it. The rope was retracted without delay. A child of about eight emerged. Cautiously, bent low, she examined her surroundings. Believing she was alone, she turned to retrieve her belongings and quickly tied them into a bundle. At the same moment, a King's soldier appeared. From his desultory progress, he was no enthusiast, or perhaps he was tired. For those fighting it had been a long day. He let her nearly make the apparent safety of the thick reeds in which Guiliam cowered, before he moved.

She heard his steps; she tried to run, but she was slow. The soldier tackled her, and she fell into the hump of reed-covered earth behind which Guiliam was sheltering. Their eyes met and he saw himself reflected in her pupils. He feared betrayal, but the child withstood in silence. If it were him, he would have screamed. The soldier grabbed her feet and hitched her towards him, away from the bushes and Guiliam; and then, as if performing a necessary duty, he flipped her over, lifted her skirts and kicked her legs apart. Guiliam could not move—to do so would mean his death—but he closed his eyes against an image that threatened to superimpose itself upon all his notions of love.

"Christ's blood," the soldier muttered, "it is hardly worth my dart." Guiliam opened his eyes to see the soldier tuck away a deflated penis. He closed his eyes again: he had no wish to witness the child's murder; but his eyelids reopened against his will. The man was slow in lifting his sword. Despite himself, and fully against his resolve, Guiliam sprang forth and waved his wooden weapon.

"Look out, soldier!" he cried. "My sword is Tizona, my horse Babieca; and mine is this radiant charmer!"

The soldier whirled round, swung, and braked his sword a hair's breadth from Guiliam's neck. "Brother," the startled soldier cried, "you have come within an inch of dying, Sir Brown-Stain!" He grinned then, as if finding Guiliam in front of him gave him great pleasure.

"Sir Brown-Stain, Sir Brown-Stain that is me!" Guiliam shouted. "Happy as an owl, busy as a bee." He bared his teeth in an attempt at a smile. His legs could not hold him and as he collapsed to the ground, he felt his traitorous bowels give way.

"Sir Knight," he yelled at the soldier, "best stand clear of Sir Brown-Stain whose stink brings no glee! You will not like the entrance fee." He hauled himself to his knees, fumbled with the ties of his breech-cloth and yanked it down from his dripping bum.

The soldier lowered his sword, laughing.

Guiliam shouted, "In good warm-farted friendship, Sir!" The lines had arisen of themselves. From nowhere, from Marcabru's teaching, from his own propensity for crude verses. Guiliam risked a glance at the girl who lay as the soldier had left her, skirts tangled above the waist, her face wiped of expression.

"Have her if you wish, young poet," the soldier said, "but you will not like the terms. Make me a hero in one of your songs and I will forget I saw you here. Do not neglect it: you have been paid." He moved off, whistling. Guiliam's last sight of him was of his curved spine as he recommenced scything through the reeds and grasses.

From behind the citadel wall came cheers—the final surrender of the Saracens, or the divvying of plunder. Guiliam was not interested. He fought the urge to sleep. He was odorous; and he felt depressed even though the Christians were victorious and with relatively few losses, as God intended.

He wiped himself with grass, rinsed the breech-cloth as best he could, put it on anyway and retied his stockings. He searched for and found his missing shoe. This time, he'd leave none of his clothing behind. The girl. Oh yes: what to do about her? If he left her there, someone else would come along to rape and kill her. He approached and grimaced at his view of what had ended the soldier's assault. The immature genitals had been cut and the vaginal lips stitched together. To penetrate here would require more gusto than most men possessed. Blood oozed from the coarse stitches. He lifted the girl in his arms. Her breath huffed: she was wounded in her side. Her eyes closed, but her rapid breathing divulged her fear. Why hadn't she been pushed to her death from the tower like the others? It would have saved everyone, including her, not to mention himself, a lot of trouble.

He found his meandering horse, draped the child across its neck and climbed on behind. Encountering a knot of soldiers, he flourished his wooden sword and cried out, "Sir Brown-Stain rides in triumph!"

He passed near the King's fire on his way to fetch a store of supplies and felt a pang of worry in case his role in inciting the battle had been discovered and misinterpreted. A few men shouted for him to give them verses, that was all. He responded, "*Here goes the poet and his whore / I ride to swive her with my sword*!" He was nodded past even as the priests were calling everyone to prayer: the compendium of rags and black hair across his saddle was his passport to go where he liked.

He found the entrance to the cave without difficulty and made the child go ahead of him. She did not question but gave one quick glance round before she drew herself inside on knees and elbows, dragging the bundle of her belongings with her. At length, they squeezed into the haven of the hollow crystal. She lay down with her eyes shut before he could place his cloak for her. He sat beside her, his mind empty, and listened for her breathing. He found it and dipped his sleeve into the water he had brought with him. She suckled the cloth like an infant. The body did things on its own that you did not mean it to; it acted without permission. He had not wanted to shit in fear, and he had not intended to help this girl. It did not matter why he had; it was done. He could watch over her for the night in the after-triumph chaos, but then he would have to return to the camp, or hazard death for desertion.

The girl pulled at his clothing and then at her own. Weakly, she tried to open her garments. He was mindful of what was beneath them—it was a wounding that would haunt him always—but the child was urgent and there was that gouge in her side to contend with. He removed the vest she wore and the shirt and skirt beneath it and the shift beneath that. There, strapped around the girl's waist and chest were leaves of parchment, and tucked inside the leaves, a set of small dolls. It was these that had prevented the weapon from penetrating deeply into her body. He gave the dolls to her. She held them while he poured the *aguardiente* that he carried, over the injury, then bound it with strips from his shirt. He thought she had fainted from the pain, but her eyes opened, caught his again and flicked to the bundle at her side.

He pulled it over, and checking from the packet to her for agreement, he opened it and found a dress, a small knife, a few dates, some seeds, and a little bag. It was the bag she wanted. It surprised him with its warmth. He eased open the drawstring, touched his finger to a round feathered head and scooped out a bird. It was small with a greenish grey front, striping on its wings, and a beak like an almond. It gave a "cheep," and he laughed, and it flew from his hand to the girl and perched on her fist.

What is happiness, Guiliam, but the revelation of the unexpected? What is beauty, but the astonishment of life? And sound! The bird trilled. The notes thrilled along his spine and echoed round the walls of the gem cave. Then he realized it would die here in the glittering cave without food or water.

"What is your name?" he asked the child. It was foolish to ask, but a longing to hear it had seized him. "Please," he said, putting his lips to her ear, "please tell me your name." He repeated the request without hope, in the languages he knew. He said his own name, "Guiliam," and touched his chest. She showed him by signs that she could not speak and grasped his hand. Her fingers drew shapes on his palm. One by one the symbols burned there and left behind them a shape and sound he recognized from Marcabru's teachings of Mohammedan poetry. Her name was Yamha. He said the name aloud and was rewarded by a glance and a nod. The name meant *dove*.

Over the hours, as the cave darkened, she traced words for him, and he did his best to expand his understanding of what she wanted him to know. Her ancestors had crossed deserts and seas, outlasted wars, and famine to settle in Almeria. She thanked him for what he had done: she wanted to live for the sake of her family. He told her his stories as he knew them: of going with his parents and the horses into the fields; of the look of the river at dawn, its mist a shelter for animals as they bent their necks to drink; of how his father had come to sit with him on the riverbank and given him a small lute he had made; and of how his mother sang him to sleep at night. His stories were like mirages, but he did not think they were untrue. He sorrowed that she could not speak or sing. He was a troubadour: he could not have lived without his voice. Finally, they were quiet. All of time had conspired towards this meeting; they were always meant to find each other.

In the deepest part of the night, he sang her a song that came from nowhere, from the instruction of Marcabru, from the hollow part in him that the girl, Yamha, had revealed and filled.

I will die if she won't have me,

If she refuse, my soul will flee.

I pray she give me

One sweet kiss, a key.

I will die if she won't have me.

Verse after verse came to him, each one filled with the knowledge that in a few more hours, he would leave her.

Guiliam lay beside her and kept her warm. In the morning, he made sure she ate and drank. He gave her his own sack to carry the dolls and the pages of vellum and left the cloak with her. He placed food and water nearby and prayed to the only god he trusted, the god of beautiful words, that she would live and heal and find a safe future. The little bird hopped onto a gem facet and shook out its wings. Then Guiliam had to go. Before stooping for the tunnel, he looked behind at Yamha. Her hands lay relaxed and open, cup-like, near her hips, and her chest rose and fell gently with her breath.

He had reached the bottom of the hill that held the cave, his thoughts tuning to what he would say in camp. He must tell a story of celebration, a story that others would accept. Suddenly, he felt a brushing of his shoulder and glimpsed a small, green-bellied bird swoop past and alight on a branch. It sang to him briefly, and then fled into the sky that held the home of everything lovely.

~

Pearl stops typing. She is tired, and the tale has left her unsettled. Guiliam was dependent on his teacher and on his King; he could not have remained any longer with Yamha. Nonetheless, he abandoned the girl without knowing what would happen to her. The story said they were meant to find each other. They *had* found each other, but then what? Nothing? The boy did his best to save her life, but his disclosure of the Saracen attempt at peace-making led to *countless* innocents killed or captured. Imagine if an agreement between the King and the Saracens had been made and the Genovese and Catalans had withdrawn in exchange for a share of Almeria's trade.

Then Marcabru could have taken Guiliam to the city of golden towers to talk with poets. He could have met Yamha there, fallen in love with her, composed a song for her and lived happily ever after. But you cannot reshape the past to your preferences.

When Pearl was little, she'd been interested in Yamha's muteness. She had practised *talking* to Nora using signs, making Nora shut her eyes, drawing them on her grandmother's palm until Nora guessed correctly what she wanted to say; and for a reason that has become obscure, Pearl printed messages to Nora in lemon-juice ink and posted them on the fridge. Messages on blank squares of white paper that could only be revealed by the heat of a match. Not unlike, in its way, the baby wipe squares Joachim sets out. Could these be messages too, waiting for someone to decode them?

Pearl has much to think about, too much for one evening. Her thoughts return to the song for which Guiliam is known, *I will die if she won't have me.* A song that entered the later lives of the Aragonese and Beatris and Rosa, and which Pearl may pass on to others. Guiliam must have written many songs, but only this one, composed during a war, has survived. Before she closes the laptop, Pearl holds the story in her mind and writes lines that Guiliam will sing on his own:

A soldier weeps, the enemy is levelled.
But the road home is long,
And at every turn,
Only the birds of the sky and field
Fly free.

As she gets into bed, Pearl flips the doll from Yamha to Guiliam and back several times. She turns it over and gives it a shake. A tiny plastic chess piece, a white pawn, plops out of Guiliam's lute and onto the floor.

In the morning, Pearl waits beside the pool for Joachim to arrive for his swimming lesson. She dandles her feet in the water. Rhododendron petals float on the water's surface. Joachim should be scooping them out with the net, but he isn't. A mat of leaves on the pool deck underlines the additional absence of his mother and her broom. A glance around shows a baby wipe square pinned with pebbles in front of Joachim's door: other squares, dried out, have blown away and caught on various plants.

It has, officially, been summer for more than a week, but the wind, slopping over the hedge from a skim up the lane from the sea, makes her shiver. A few frail late lilac blossoms shred; rose canes shoot out new buds, blooms open. Dog roses (wild roses) vaunt red *hips* and tussle with blackberry canes in the ditches; scotch broom flaunts invasion from every neglected corner.

At 9:30 a.m. Harry shuffles from the office with a cup of coffee. "What are you doing here so early by yourself? Want some company?" He slips off his flip-flops and splashes his feet into the water beside hers.

"I thought I *had* company, but Joachim didn't show. We were supposed to meet for a swimming lesson. Where is everybody?"

"It's a holiday, Pearl! July 1st. Loretta's gone to the airport. We're going sailing later, want to come?"

"What's she doing at the airport?"

"Taking Maria and Joachim." Noticing Pearl's expression, he asks, "What? Did you forget?"

"Forget what, Harry? I don't live here, remember!"

"Joachim was invited by the Continental Chess Association to a tournament in New York City. They pay his expenses; and he goes to a chess camp afterwards. His mother is with him because he is a little young to be on his own."

"He's older than he looks," Pearl says. Her eyes stray to the mute contrary of the weighted baby wipe square. "He should have said something to me."

"He's incredibly good for his age! He could have a future in chess! What is wrong with you?"

Pearl takes her feet from the water and dries them vigorously on a towel. If she doesn't blink hard, she will cry. For a few hours she'd thought she had found a role, an opportunity to be useful; but she hadn't. It had never existed.

Harry stands and wiggles his feet into his flip-flops. "His father taught him to play chess. Joachim and his mother kept it up to remember something good, I suppose. After Nora saw Joachim play, she made sure he got the best instruction."

"Yes, she would."

"Pearl! We'll talk when you're in a better mood."

Pearl studies Harry's stiff-legged gait as he makes his way to reception. She had assumed that Joachim needed her, and that the chess pawn in the lute was confirmation from Nora that she was on the right track. Saving a child in need, as Nora did, only (absurdly) in Pearl's case with swimming lessons. What had she been thinking, relying on signals from the dead? She'd had all the guidance she needed from Nora in her lifetime.

It is late at night. Pearl, who can't sleep, sits by the pool. Harry has gone to bed, but Loretta still labours in the office. Her shadow, head bent over the desk, unreels a torpid film against the blinds. With Joachim away, Harry drained the pool to repair the mosaics. Tools and sacks of ceramic tiles and grouting are heaped beneath a blue tarp. Mice scuttle around its periphery and tickle the cover into motion, and the mound of supplies seems to undulate under the starlight. The trees quiver from top to bottom. The scent of roses mingles with that of the sea. Pearl holds out her arms: if anything lives in the dark tonight, she would like to welcome it, so she won't feel so lonely; but willing as she is, her arms remain empty.

"What are you doing?" asks Loretta, who has padded from the office in soft shoes to sit beside her.

"Me? Nothing. I was stretching."

"Were you?" Loretta waits while Pearl puts her head and neck through a series of nods and circles, demonstration exercises. "I am not unsympathetic, Pearl," she says at the conclusion of Pearl's efforts. "It can't be easy." Loretta's dangling foot, her legs crossed at the knee, rotates one way and then the other. "Nora had high standards. They must be hard to live with."

What is Pearl to say to this? She settles on the truth. "I miss her more than I thought I would."

"I miss her, too. She was friends with my mother. Judy—my mother—looks after Nora's cabin. It was through her that I met Harry. I knew Nora long before I met him."

"What cabin?"

"On Nootka Island where my family lives. Harry told you."

"Did he? I don't remember."

"Well, remember now." Loretta extracts a piece of paper from her pocket with a flourish and gives it to Pearl.

"What is this?"

"Your instructions. Make sure you book a flight as soon as possible; they sell out quickly."

Pearl gazes at Loretta's writing, but it is too dark to read.

"You need this," Loretta says. She turns on a tiny flashlight attached to her key ring so that Pearl can view the list of websites and telephone numbers she has prepared. Loretta has also drawn a map of the island. "My mother will meet you on the ferry."

"Ferry?"

"It's in the paper you're holding."

"But Loretta, I don't understand!"

"For heaven's sake, Pearl. You said you wanted to go where Nora went, and she went straight from here to see my mother on Nootka Island!" Loretta stands, yawns, and looks at her watch. "I'd better get some sleep."

"Oh," she says as she turns to go, having repossessed the key-light, "I meant to ask, did you finish the story for Joachim? You aren't keeping the doll for yourself, are you?"

In her room, Pearl books the flight and the ferry she will need and leaves a message for Loretta's mother about the cabin. A few minutes later she is outside. All is quiet. Gripping the cardboard container of Nora's ashes, she sprinkles a little of what is left of her grandmother in each corner of Harry and Loretta's property. Then she offers a scant teaspoonful to the whales at the bottom of the drained pool and goes to her room to pack.

Before she leaves next day, dressed in tight jeans, boots, and a smart leather jacket, Pearl finds Loretta and Harry in the reception area installing the aquarium they had promised Joachim after he and Pearl had witnessed the birth of the baby beluga. The tank stands in what used to be a planter. Its water bubbles soothingly.

Harry beckons her over. "Come and see this, Pearl. We've got goldfish and guppies. It's not like having a dog or a cat. If one dies, it won't be so bad, and we can have a fish funeral."

"Or replace the fish before he finds out," Loretta adds.

"By the time chess camp is over, we'll know what we're doing. With luck we'll only have killed a few of them." Harry playfully punches Loretta's arm.

Pearl touches the glass: the fish zoom over to butt against the splotch of her fingers.

"Sorry! I didn't mean to scare them." She retreats. The fish disengage from the glass and swim in and out of variegated plastic fronds.

"Ah," Harry says, so close behind her he could rest his chin on her shoulder, "so you've still got it. Nora wondered if you'd lost it for good. 'Buried her gift,' she said. But you haven't, have you. I'd give my eye-teeth for something like that. Have you any idea what it's for?"

Pearl steps away. "I'm sorry about yesterday, Harry. I *am* happy for Joachim, and for his mother. I'm glad he is so good at chess. I guess I was feeling a little …"

"Jealous?" Loretta says. She adjusts her reading glasses to check the fine print on a fish food label.

"I came to say goodbye."

"You don't have to go, Pearl. We're glad to have you for as long as you want to stay. Agreed Loretta?"

"Pearl is on a mission," Loretta says.

"Well, yes, I suppose," Harry says. "But Pearl, I *am* a little worried by how hard you're taking Nora's passing."

"You two are busy with the renovations and everything," Pearl says. "I'm in the way."

Loretta steps forward and gives Pearl her cheek to kiss. "You are going to love it, Pearl. Believe me. It might change your life. What time are you going?"

"Right away. I was about to call a taxi."

"Why don't you take my car to the airport? You can park it, leave the ticket in the glove compartment and text me the location. One of the gallery staff will get it."

"Okay. Thanks!" Pearl says.

On this petal-green morning, pale sun suffuses the windows of Loretta's Volkswagen as Pearl drives from narrow West Van lanes bubbled with paved-over tree roots onto the slick, wide asphalt of the main road, where post-holiday traffic bleeds onto the Lion's Gate Bridge. Despite two lanes having been opened into the city, cyclists and motorcyclists zigzag between the slow-moving cars, pedestrians outpace the traffic on the walkway, and Pearl idles behind a stalled BMW long enough to watch a tug escort a container ship between the bridge pylons and into the mists of the Salish Sea. The shoreline greys into the strait, but sheens of colour glimmer where the sun highlights glass or oil. The world as it is this morning has more to offer than old stories.

In the deeps, below what's available to the eye, myriad life fulfills its purpose. The inlet is a bed of propagation from spore-shedding phytoplankton to the eelgrass beds where herring spawn in spring. The BMW belches smoke and moves ahead, and then the traffic halts again.

In fall, salmon navigate tidal currents to the streams at the head of the inlet. They spawn and die; and their offspring emerge from silt redoubts to gorge on herring larvae, and then tail-and-fin to open waters. In time, those that survive return. The herring, in the meantime, attract whales, which use sonar to corral them in a purse of bubbles. All egg and sperm, all the mechanics of reproduction, rely in the end, on numbers. If there are not enough, the species perishes.

It feels good to be out in the world, away from the confines of her family, with the opportunity to think through a proposal she is constructing for *Findable Feast Magazine*. When she told them she was going to the west coast of Vancouver Island, they suggested she pitch an article about salmon (thus the current run of her thoughts) to help their readers make responsible consumption decisions. Pearl needs the work. Nora's house and boat became hers through Transfer on Death deeds the moment Nora died, but Pearl has little cash to live on, let alone to maintain Nora's property, and she is nearing the limits of her credit cards.

The traffic squeezes from the bridge, and travels bumper to bumper until Pearl crosses another bridge to join the airport road, its environs pebbled with industrial bunkers despoiling the delta lands that used to produce crops of spinach, kale, carrots, squash, and berries, and once grew grass and corn in rich greens and yellows for dairy herds and horses. The ghost life below the asphalt acres resolves into the airport's landing strips, glass towers, and concrete hives for parking. The terminal, against the drop cloth of mountains, is a statement of Coastal First Nations' artforms in cement, steel, wood, and glass: ovoid eyes, fins, beaks, and tongues that can only be appreciated by aircraft, or spacecraft, or by trickster figures reincarnated as constellations. Pearl parks Loretta's VW in one of the concrete hives and enters the *Departures* concourse.

PART IV

BEATRIS: The Stowaway's Tale

Rosa's mother, Beatris, born in the mountains of Spain seven generations before you, ran away to sea, Nora wrote. She voyaged the west coast of North America to Nootka Island before making her way to Mexico with her daughter. When you write the stories, don't forget to put that in.

The passenger turboprop flies through a cloud-soaked sky from the Vancouver airport over the skipping-stone islands of Haro Strait on its way to Vancouver Island. The sea is steel, the islands are green, and the sky is a puff of white and grey etched with light. It is a view Nora will have seen when she travelled to the cabin on Nootka Island off Vancouver Island's central west coast; a place, according to Loretta, that Nora often visited. Pearl had to consult a map to find it. The same map made it plain that Nora's Refuge House, which Pearl had thought of vaguely as *in the north*, was sixteen hundred kilometres away. She places her forehead against the cool window to help herself stay awake. Pearl had hoped for breakfast and cups of coffee, but this is a no-frills flight.

An hour later, the plane sweeps through a series of turns and lowers over a patch of brown earth scraped from forest and lands on a tarmac strip. Following Loretta's instructions, Pearl locates the yellow school bus for Gold River idling outside the small wood and glass airport terminal. A knot of workmen carrying duffle bags boards the bus with her into a fug of tuna fish and apple juice lunches. Pearl's stomach gurgles. She settles in on one side of the bus, the workmen take seats on the other. A buxom woman in a blue baseball cap perched on a frizz of short red hair takes an empty seat in front of her.

After a few kilometres of scattered settlement, Pearl is dozing as the bus turns inland for the drive west. She blinks herself awake and opens her laptop to record details for the article she plans to write. Tall cedars and Sitka spruce spike through dense undergrowth along the roadside, then the bus crosses a series of narrow wooden bridges over creeks that boil around rocks embedded midstream. The road coils on through forest hung with moss, and soon the bus is putting along the rim of a tea-coloured lake strewn with skeletons of drowned trees.

Camper trucks and trailers towed by four-cylinder vehicles slow their progress. Logging trucks scrape by on the corners of a looping mountainside climb. Even steep slopes are stippled with stumps and strewn with slash piles. Pearl forsakes notetaking. She clasps the metal rail of the seat in front of her, and glances from the scenery to the men. Their bodies sway easily with the turns. They ride, well-muscled or packing beer guts, dressed in thick jeans and flannel jackets, their hands splayed on their knees. One after the other they note her attention and turn their tanned regard her way. She tries a smile, and an older man winks. The woman in the seat in front of Pearl, whom Pearl has glimpsed applying pink nail polish, turns around, waving her drying nails in greeting.

"Hi! I'm Sheila," the woman says across the seat rail. She casts an eye over Pearl's leather jacket and Levis. The spaghetti straps of Sheila's orange tank top cut into her shoulders. The ballcap's logo of a white lab flask enclosing a red fish is outlined in silver thread. "You're visiting? Hard at it, though, eh," she says with a glance at Pearl's open laptop. "All on your own?"

"Sort of. I'm Pearl." Pearl smiles and folds the laptop away. "My stepmother's mother, Judy, lives at Friendly Cove."

"Hey, I know her!" Sheila says. "Is Judy's daughter Loretta your stepmother? I heard she married an older guy in the Big Smoke."

"My father."

"Well, then. You looking for work?"

"I could be," Pearl says cautiously. "But I'm not sure how long I'll be staying."

"If you're still here in twenty-four hours, give me a call, or tell Judy I could use someone for a few days. I'd dig out a card, but I don't want to ruin the manicure." Sheila proffers a daytimer with a clear plastic pocket on the front of it. "Go ahead, take one." Pearl extracts a card with yellow lettering on it and tucks it into her bag. "I won't hold my breath, though; a lot of city people blow in, but after a day without cellphone coverage, they're cut off at the knees. You don't see them for dust."

During the conversation, Pearl feels the men staring at her, but when she finds the nerve to look, the only eyes turned her way belong to a gangly young man who swallows and blushes. His thatch of light brown hair stands on end, but she can't tell if this is artful or accidental. She smiles and he smiles back at her. He has pale blue eyes. There's a thin blanched strip at his hairline from a hat of some kind. Good shoulders, from what she can tell from the drape of a plaid shirt and an unfastened oilskin jacket. Not a runner, not gaunt, and not with that squat neck they get from too much time in the gym, either. She looks away. Suddenly she wants it over—the intensity of too-close mountains, the hostility of the clouds, the gendered division of the seating. The vibrations of the bus's engine clatter through her, chattering her teeth. Then the vehicle pops out of the forest-green gloom to a wide ocean view beyond a precipitous drop and built-up seafront. Pearl flips open the laptop and finds a passage she copied before she left Harry's motel. She hopes to mine it for the magazine piece once she's had an opportunity to look around for herself. If the place is still anything like it describes.

> *A stretch of inlets and headlands, mountain walls, treacherous shoals, unnamed islands, unmarked reefs, mudflats and salt marshes, river mouths, reversing tides, glass surfaces beneath which currents boil; and storms that pound in from a thousand miles of nowhere against which the navigator can do nothing but run: a coast that ties its features into a negotiation between sea and land, air and water, birds and fish, humans and animals: a compass of direction with no apparent end to its possibilities.*

The small coastal ferry from Gold River to Friendly Cove on Nootka Island is not a pretty vessel like Nora's *SeaPin*, or purpose-built like ferries Pearl has come across before. *Uchuck III* is a madeover minesweeper. Its funnels and the eyelet portholes in the horseshoe upper cabin give it the look of a rough-hewn toy. Half the host waiting to board rushes for the forward deck towards the tiny galley selling coffee and snacks; others mill around with backpacks and suitcases and grocery bags. The more knowledgeable passengers stack their belongings under a set of stairs before powering their way to the on-deck seating at the stern.

From the forward rail, Pearl inspects the pallets, fuel barrels, coils of rope, and block and tackle piled on the wharf. Popcorn clouds stipple the sky; log booms lace the opposite foreshore. The hills are scraped with clearcuts.

"Yoo-hoo, Pearl, I'm here!" The woman who calls from the deck above is compact, with a smooth rosy visage and black short hair that tinsels silver strands. "Come and take a seat!"

When Pearl reaches her, the woman pats a space beside her on the bench. "Take the weight off." Pearl sits down. "So, you made it!"

"Judy?"

"Who else?"

"Thanks for meeting me!"

"Look, Loretta told me what you're doing for Nora, and I'm happy to help. Fred and I and the kids … we're going to miss her."

"Loretta said you and Nora were old friends."

"Yeah. She leased the cabin for her foundation and got in touch a bit later with some questions about family history. So, yeah, we were real old friends."

"How did Loretta …"

"Meet your father? He stayed at the cabin for a while after his divorce. The second one, I think. Then Loretta headed south for university, and after that, well … Who can say what brings two people together?" Pearl, herself, has long wondered about the age difference between her father and stepmother.

"I guess it's just the way it is," Judy says.

Uchuck III casts off, the benches filled with families and groups of middle-aged women. Young lovers and teenagers lean against the rails. Across from Pearl and Judy, two women are unpacking baskets and a cooler, disgorging potato chips, nuts, apples, and grape juice tetra-packs into their laps.

"I met this lady," Pearl says when they have finished with family matters. "She gave me her card. She said she might have a job."

Judy takes the card. "Oh, yeah, that's Sheila. She manages one of the fish farms. You were on the company bus."

"I was?"

"You should take her up on it. What else are you gonna do? I'll give her a call."

Uchuck III's egg-white wake churns back towards the dock and the heavy machinery and the beige buildings around the beach logdump. Ahead, the waters of the inlet converge between vees of adjoining hills. Clearcut scars funnel into log chutes that plummet down the hillsides to the sea. Small logging camp settlements sit precariously on stilts above coastal rocks, looking as if a gentle shake of the landscape could shed them. The mountains sift, one behind the other, until their greenery fades to the same shapeshift colours as the watery world.

"Is that a fish farm?" Pearl asks, pointing northwards at a green multilevel shed anchored in hill-shaded waters. Beside it, a series of buoyed pens link it to another similar structure.

"One of them. Sheila's *SoliSunny* is that one." Judy points to a tight complex of float sheds along the southern shoreline. Whatever else she says is obliterated by the snarl of a speedboat that catches *Uchuck III* from behind. The men on board give the ferry a wave as they shoot past.

Judy waves in return and yells into Pearl's ear, "That's Sheila's crew!"

"Oh!" Pearl says. "The men from the bus!" They look happier in the open air.

Near the entrance to Friendly Cove, *Uchuck III* slows to let a float plane finish its landing run across their bow. The seaplane taxis to a dock below a collection of pagoda-like wooden buildings joined by walkways above a rocky seafront.

"Fishing lodge. Swish, eh?" Judy says, following Pearl's gaze. "We get doctors, lawyers, celebrities, film crews. You wouldn't believe it. Every one of them 'God's gift.'"

The ferry nestles into the wharf at Friendly Cove and unleashes a flurry of passengers. Piled supplies, towers of backpacks, and a bevy of children diving from the wharf have turned the pier into uproar. Judy guides Pearl through the chaos to a boardwalk and onto the island. A lighthouse candles on a nearby islet. Ahead of them, a wide meadow is mushroomed with tents. Beyond the campers, a white wooden church lofts its steeple.

They pack Pearl's gear and Judy's groceries onto an ATV parked at the end of the boardwalk. Judy pilots it through the meadow where she and her family are camping for the summer food harvest, and up a trail through a spruce wood to Nora's one-room cabin overlooking a small lake.

"This is it, Pearl," Judy says. She grabs a bag and strides up a ramp onto a narrow deck. The cabin is supported on posts at waterside, across from a small island.

At the far end of the lake the hills display gentle curves; in the water below the balcony, a shoal of trout fingerlings sparkles in the green shallows. Two children are skipping stones from a curve of gravel beach.

"It's not really safe for swimming," Judy says, following Pearl's gaze to the water. "You should use the beach shower further down the trail to wash."

"Okay, I'll find it."

"Come on inside and I'll show you how to work the propane. Then I need to get back to the campsite. You've got enough supplies for tonight."

"Judy, I wanted to ask about Nora."

"I don't have time. Sorry Pearl, I've got to get the kids' dinner."

"Nora was here, though, wasn't she? Did she leave anything for me?"

"We'll talk later, eh? Oh, and you are clear that Nora only leased this cabin? I promised her we'd let family keep on using it, though, and she left some funds for maintenance. I would have done it anyway. I really loved her, Pearl."

Sweating, tormented by mosquitoes, Pearl awakens every half-hour throughout the night to swat at them and spray repellent. Something is rustling in the kitchen alcove, rummaging beneath the sink. Pearl hears teeth crunching through bone, gets out of bed and takes the broom to deal with it, but finds nothing behind the bead curtain, although the front door is open and she's certain she closed it after her trip to the outhouse. Pearl likes nature, wants to preserve it, but this place makes her think that nature might have plans of its own.

At 5:00 a.m. Judy bangs on the door. She has brought the quad with provisions: drinking water, fuel, vegetables, tea, coffee, tinned milk, and fruit. She heaves sacks onto the porch and comes inside. Pearl is half-asleep in her sleeping bag. Judy plunks an insulated cup of hot coffee down beside her. "Wakey, wakey Pearl. I radioed Sheila last night. You begin work this morning; the shuttle won't wait for you."

"The shuttle?" Pearl sits and fumbles for the coffee. Judy is wearing a bright pink shirt with the turquoise jacket. The early sun lights the silver in her hair.

"How else will you get to the fish farm?"

Pearl yanks on jeans, a shirt, and a pair of sandals, and takes the coffee onto the balcony. A ruby-throated hummingbird zips by to check out the red underpants she'd rinsed and hung to dry over the railing before going to bed. Its jewel-flash blurs towards a bank of wild rose. A different kind of flash—sun reflected off a discarded tin or cigarette foil or a shard of glass—glints among the brush on the lake's little island.

"What's over there?"

"Nothing. Maybe at one time, long ago," Judy says and scans the lake, which is bruised with shadow. "Now hurry up! You'll need a fleece." She clatters down the ramp in heavy boots and starts the quad.

Pearl climbs on board. "You're in luck, Pearl," Judy says, dipping into a jacket pocket, "I saved you a bacon and egg sandwich."

The others on the *SoliSunny* zodiac shuttle speeding through salt spray and pink early rays of the sun, are napping. Only one of them—the younger man Pearl had noticed on the bus—is awake enough to say hello. His hair still prickles in tufts, although the wind is doing its best to flatten it. Pearl leans from her seat, touches the cold rushing water with her fingertips, flinching when it splashes her face. Friendly Cove drops behind. The zodiac is an arrow in the watery shadow of Nootka Sound hills, hurtling towards *SoliSunny*'s metal-roofed sheds, and weather-bleached wharves, piers, and walkways.

Sheila, dressed much as she was on the bus, but wearing a different baseball cap over her red hair, beckons them in. She ties the lines and gives Pearl a hoist from the shuttle. At the office, Sheila says, "Before we get into this, I should tell you that I don't care if you've got a degree, and I don't need your résumé. What I need from you is common sense and hard work, and that you do whatever Cliff asks. Can you do that?"

Pearl nods. "Who's Cliff?" she asks as she signs the papers Sheila puts in front of her.

"You're on his pilot project. He saw you on the bus, and you were on the shuttle with him this morning. He says he can tell you're the type with patience. *He's* the type who knows what he wants."

"What do you mean?"

"Instinctive, intuitive, whatever you call it. He'll do things before he sees why, but then he'll work to collect sound data." She taps her temple. "That's why he's a good scientist. And he's not afraid to admit it if he's wrong."

Sheila opens a locker and furnishes Pearl with overalls, gloves, boots, a hairnet, and a floater jacket. She makes Pearl put it all on, then sits her down in the equipment room for a ten-minute video about the dangerous chemicals used on site.

The planks beneath Pearl's feet lift and fall gently on their moorings. She has to concentrate to remember that she is not on board *SeaPin* on a perfect sailing day with the open ocean all around, and nothing to do but chat to Nora and adjust the sails or take a turn at the helm, but instead is learning to be an employee. It's funny how the past seeps into the present these days, for although her life feels different, it is still on hold. She focusses her attention to learn about respiratory problems associated with fish meal, and the risk of leptospirosis that is always a concern at fish dumps like the ones on land behind *SoliSunny*. The dumps attract rats, yet not far from the fish farm floats, the sea is deep enough to bury cities.

Sheila reappears.

"Just so you know, I don't eat farmed salmon," Pearl says. Her bootlaces are still undone, the gloves clumped in her pocket.

"Of course, you don't," Sheila says, looking her over. "You hire a private plane, and fish in an untouched stream. You cook what you catch over an open fire and play at *wilderness* while the world starves."

Pearl's cheeks grow pink. "That's not what I meant. But I do have the right to choose, don't I?"

"Sure, you do, if you can afford it." She pauses.

"Look, Pearl, we've got problems in this industry, but they're not the ones most people think. Really, give me a break! We have no fish; not like we used to. This farm is the result, not the cause. We give people jobs, and you'd better keep that in mind, or you won't make friends, however much I admired Nora." Sheila opens the office door. Low sunlight frosts the waves and highlights the pink glitter on her boots.

Pearl's boots are oversized, plain leather; she bends to tie the laces. "What about sea lice?" she says, thinking of the article she is going to write for *Findable Feast* and the angle she plans to take with it.

"Jesus H. Christ, Pearl. Do you want this job or not? Come! Take a look!" Sheila seizes her arm, pulls her to her feet and slides open a door to a room in the big shed. At the far end, a conveyer belt relays fish through an opening and drops them, alive, onto blocks of ice. Two women are sorting them into cold-bins.

"We select for quality," Sheila says. "The best—that's Fran's job, she's the one in glasses—end up on your table, the others we turn into cat food, or fishmeal that we recycle as feed." Sheila drags Pearl to the women.

Close to, it is apparent that some of the fish have fin and tail injuries, and others have growths. Some of them are deformed. The eyes of the dying fish turn dull, and then opaque.

"It's all food, and we don't waste it," Sheila says. "The planet is crowded, Pearl; and then you dam enough rivers, spoil enough streams, pollute the water systems, run pipelines through water sheds, and what's left? My dad was a fisherman. I grew up on the water. There was fish for everyone, we knew how to share." She yanks off her hat and screws the brim. "I saw what happened! Fucking trawlers! Fucking cannery ships! They vacuumed the oceans near-empty, and then we did our best to poison the rest and wreck the habitat.

"I'm happy to explain, but I'm running a business. Yeah, we get sea lice, but the cleaner the operation, the fewer. So, I test for salinity, oxygen levels, temperature, turbidity, and plankton levels every day, at three different depths, and we don't cram the fish in the tanks like some do. I'm constantly looking for a better way, and that's why I support what Cliff does. He intends to improve the world for fish, and you can help him if you want to."

Pearl is listening: what Sheila says isn't new—Pearl has done her research—but what are those chemicals again? And don't farmed fish harm native stocks? Without thinking, she touches a dying fish on the ice block. Its skin is rough, cool silk, and she feels the ebb of its life. The base of her spine stirs with sadness. It's a grey wave that washes into green water where plankton outlines a webbing of her fingers and she flutter kicks after Nora who is swimming ahead with the storytellers. It reminds her that she has brought the dolls—Theano, Rosa, and Guiliam / Yamha—with her to the cabin. They will stay with her until the end of whatever it is that Nora left for her to do. But what is she doing *at this moment*, witnessing the slow death of fish?

"Most of what comes out of the oceans is hatchery spawned. You get a boat and go out with your rod and reel to *source* your own food and what do you catch? Some fish that is hardly aware it's a fish.

"Or you go to the store and see this great display in a glass case, but—hold this thought—just about everything in it—not ours, not *SoliSunny*'s—is processed in China and that's okay, but you might want to get tested for heavy metals if you're going to get pregnant.

"Pearl," Sheila says into a silence broken only by the slap of fish on fish as the women shunt them into the bins, "did you hear anything I had to say?"

"Yes, yes, of course, I was thinking …"

Sheila sighs. "Let's go outside, we're done here. If anyone gives a rat's ass for the future."

A line of narrow waves, kicked in by a passing Coast Guard patrol, rolls and tumbles a filigree of seaweed over the gravel and rock of the foreshore.

"I'm sorry, Sheila," Pearl says. "You're trying to do me a favour."

Sheila lights a cigarette. "Not you, Pearl, but Nora, and Judy. It's all right, maybe you'll learn something. You're entitled to an opinion, and I'm sorry for the sermon, but you can't get me going on this stuff. It's simple: if Nature's finished with us, *anyhoo*, it's about over. I'm only trying to buy some time."

A metal-roofed open shed shelters half a dozen chest-high turquoise tubs, each about four feet in diameter, and one smaller grey one. It also gives refuge to a man in shorts and a floater jacket who balances on a stepped platform, leaning over one of the tubs. He's the younger, lanky one from the bus and the shuttle.

"Brought you a helper," Sheila says. "Pearl, this is Cliff; Cliff meet Pearl."

He straightens. A net like Pearl's squashes his hair into a thick brown pad, its band likely responsible for the tan line she'd noticed on the bus. His eyes meet hers, and she is swimming with the storytellers again, but in clear aqua seas and not thinking about Nora, only that he is familiar, and it isn't from the shuttle and the bus. People do remind others of others. But who else has she met that tall, with distinct cheek bones and bony wrists?

Sheila winks at Pearl, butts out her cigarette in a tin can, and leaves.

"Come on up," Cliff says. "I'll show you what I'm doing. I take it Sheila gave you the tour?" He peels off a latex glove and offers her his hand.

"She said you're making the world a better place for fish," Pearl says, as he steps aside to make room for her on the platform.

"Do you find that strange?" he says, not looking at her, putting the glove back on. "Some people do."

"No!" she says. "No, I don't. How are you doing with it?"

"Have a look."

The fish in the tub are big and silvery, with dark spots on the flanks and tails; most of them have a reddish stripe along the spine. They move gently, turning, sliding under and over each other.

"They're beautiful! Can I touch them?"

"No, not yet, not without gloves. I'll have to show you."

She leans closer, watching them.

"These are steelhead, Pearl. They're not like other salmon. They don't die after they spawn. Typically, they survive a number of spawning runs, returning over and over to the sea."

"But they come from hatcheries. Sheila said most fish do."

"I wouldn't have said *most*, not yet. Not for all species." He pauses and looks out over waters that not long ago teemed with wild fish. He returns his gaze to the tub. "Just those with the pink fin-tag are hatchery fish. The others are wild born and bred. I've put an acoustic tracker down the gullets of those ones. For the purpose of the experiment, all the fish, wild and hatchery, swim together as much as possible. The idea is to see if the hatchery fish and their hatchlings can learn real fish behaviour from the wild ones.

"I milk and strip hatchery fish. *Only* the hatchery fish," he emphasizes. "And then I mix the eggs and sperm. I make nests, *redds*, for the fertilized eggs in the home spawning bed of the wild fish I'm tracking. But before that, I'll have put all the fish into the ocean to make their own way to the wild fishes' natal streams, if they can."

"The hatchery fish too?"

"Some will follow the wild fish: that's what interests me. A number of the hatchery fish respond to the stock-specific pheromones emitted from the wild fish and their waste. There's also site-specific imprinting early in the fish lifecycle, so I monitor the hatchlings from the redds I've made, to see if they'll adapt to the local environment and imprint on the odours in the water the way wild fish do."

He grins. "It must sound complicated."

"Not really: you're testing a theory that hatchery fish can learn from fish that smell right and know how to behave; and you've focused on their homing behaviour and site imprinting."

"You've done your research," he says.

"I'm writing an article, so I've read a little, that's all." They're both smiling.

The roiling fish have wedged against Pearl's section of the tub. Cliff gently paddles the water and shoos them away. "We must have disturbed them. It's not good for them to be so crowded together." He and Pearl step down to the deck.

"We're a long way from understanding all this, Pearl, and I don't want to overestimate the likelihood of success, but I've had enough of it to believe it's worth keeping on with.

"Speaking of which," he says, pointing to a band of cloud that cuts the hills on the far side of the Sound, "we need to get to work. If the weather changes before we're finished, I could be stuck for days. I have to fly them north as quickly as possible. So, let me show you what to do."

At his instruction, she washes at a hose. "No perfumes or creams from here on, and don't use a deodorant," he says. He takes off his floater jacket, hangs it on a hook, and drops his pullover on the decking. In his T-shirt, he smells of salt and cedar.

"Can I take my jacket off too?" Pearl asks.

"Go ahead but put it on if you see Sheila coming; she won't like it if you fall in and drown. You can swim, I take it?"

Pearl nods and hangs her floater jacket beside his; she is down to overalls, boots, and hairnet.

"Ready? Then get the gloves on and watch closely."

Cliff unlocks a cabinet on one wall and retrieves a plastic container and a measuring cup. He motions Pearl over to one of the tubs of fish. When they are standing together on its platform, he turns the label of the container so she can read it. “It’s a special anesthetic for fish,” he explains, “the safest I could find.” He pours a small quantity of liquid from the container into the cup and empties it into the water.

“One of the first things I learned was not to stress them. If you do, you can affect the learning prospects of their offspring. In brood farms, they make a slit in the female with a knife and use a mechanical squeeze for the male. Instead, once the fish are numbed, I do it like this.” Cliff extends his long arms, his big hands deft, and lifts out one of the tagged fish. He holds it over a pan, grips its belly between his thumb and forefinger and strokes towards the tail. A necklace of coral-coloured eggs slides from the fish’s vent. He repeats the stroking, talking softly under his breath. When the store of eggs is empty, he slips the fish into the recovery tub nearby.

“This is what I need help with, Pearl. Not everyone can do it, so don’t worry if you can’t: I’ll find something else for you to do, but I would like you to try.”

“Why do you have to anaesthetize them all? Why not just the ones you need?”

“Separation distresses them most, so I have to sedate them together and limit their time apart. Once I’ve milked or stripped the tagged fish, I replace them in the tub with the wild ones and move on to a new set.”

Pearl understands the stress of separation—it has been a factor her whole life. At least Nora hadn’t pretended it didn’t matter that Pearl had longed for a blonde or dark-haired mother instead of a grey-haired grandmother to fetch her from school. “Living things adapt,” she had said, “but one living thing can’t truly replace another.”

Not long before Pearl moved in with Gerry-David, she’d spent a few days by herself in the flooded Sacramento Valley rice fields watching short-legged bitterns and pale, long-legged egrets wade through shallow wetland marshes. Then the ibis flew in, calling to find their mates. The ibis touched each other’s necks with their bills, surveyed the waterlogged land, and bent to drink. After more intense bill rubbing, the male approached the female and alighted on her from the rear. He did not stay long, but a lengthy period of self-grooming followed in which the movements of the male and female ibis coordinated.

“They build a nest, she lays the eggs, and they take turns incubating them. Depending on the species, they may mate for life,” Nora had told her. Pearl’s parents hadn’t mated for life nor had Nora herself who’d gone through two husbands before Pearl was born. Had they meant to? You had to try, didn’t you? You had to consider the possibility. For a long time, Pearl had wanted to tell this to someone.

“Don’t be nervous,” Cliff says, mistaking her inaction. “Remember you have to be gentle. If you break the skin, the fish will die.”

Pearl leans over the water, and the fish glide near. She selects the first tagged one to bump against her fingers and lifts it out, keeping it close to her body for fear of dropping it.

“Okay, hold it close to the pan, then stroke it. If it’s a ripe female, the belly will be soft. You’ll feel the eggs roll.”

Pearl mimics what Cliff had done, but nothing happens. "More firmly," he says. She rubs the belly forcefully.

"Not that hard, Christ!"

Shutting out Cliff's alarm, Pearl closes her eyes until she feels the life of the fish flowing along its spinal column. She caresses its belly, murmurs reassurance, tries not to think about what it is she is doing, and coaxes out a few drops of pearly milt to mix with the eggs.

"A male. Great! That's good!"

At lunchtime, Pearl dangles her legs over the side of the walkway and eats the sandwich Judy made for her. Cliff is in the shed, preparing tanks and nest boxes for their journey. He has estimated that the remainder of the milking and stripping will take two to three days, in spite of the fact that Pearl is more relaxed and quicker to relieve the fish of reproductive material than he expected. Nevertheless, each passing hour degrades the fertilized eggs, and he is anxious about time.

Pearl brushes crumbs from her overalls. "Ready," she calls.

Cliff emerges from the shed with pen and logbook. "Can you work on your own for a while?" Pearl nods. "Let's check the water temperatures first, then you can go ahead. I'll be nearby if you need anything."

Soon, Pearl is into a rhythm: anaesthetise, lift out a fish, milk or strip it, place it in the recovery tank, stir the mixture of eggs and milt, and add a little water. Once she has finished an entire tub, she places the recovered, tagged fish in with the others.

Cliff checks in with her from time to time, compliments her on her progress, clatters through his lists, leaves, and reappears to discuss weather and schedules over the satellite phone with the pilot, but for several hours, Pearl is alone.

By late afternoon, shadow seeps from the mountains, muting the metal roofs and walkways. Mosquitoes buzz Pearl's nostrils and eyelids. She pauses to swat them away, conscious of the conversations of men and women finishing their day's work at the pens and in the sheds.

"Nearly done," she calls to Cliff.

"Be right over," he replies, his voice muffled by the walls of a storage cabinet.

Pearl soaks in the paling sky, pulse of waves, forested mountains, and reaches into a tub for a tagged fish. She lifts it, strips the eggs into the collecting pan, and within moments observes the fish swimming briskly in the recovery tank. Soon, she will be able to reunite it with its wild-fish mates.

Cliff arrives and inspects the turquoise tub she has been working from; he looks into the other tubs before frowning at the recovery tank. The fish are zooming and swirling, tangling and diving.

"These fish weren't anesthetized, Pearl. I know how long it takes them to recover and look at them! What have you been doing? I don't understand." His face is a plane of disappointment.

"I thought you wanted me to work quickly," she says. She rinses off at the hose, shakes her hands dry, and joins him at the recovery tank. Cliff contemplates the full collecting pan and turns to face her.

"If you didn't use anesthetic, how did you manage them?" He stares at the tank again.

"I forgot to do it one time. It didn't make any difference, so I stopped. *Don't separate them longer than you have to.* Isn't that what you said you wanted?"

She bends over the turquoise tub containing the final few intact, tagged fish, "See? I've only got these ones left."

"You stripped and milked the tagged fish without sedation? Is that what you're telling me?"

"Not all of them. Not the ones we did together and until what I said happened."

"Show me."

Cliff, so near that they meet at shoulder and hip, feels it as soon as her hands enter the water: the tagged fish swim over to her as if pulled by wires. Pearl passes a fish to him. "Feel how calm it is," she says.

"Have you hypnotized it? I've heard it can be done."

"I'm not sure. Maybe." She guides Cliff's touch along the fish's stomach, and they milk it together. They finish and carry the fish to the recovery tank where it immediately flicks its tail and swims. Never has Pearl felt so close to anyone.

"I didn't mean to upset you," she says.

"I'm surprised, not upset. You *know* it's a gift, don't you?"

She shakes her head.

"How could anyone not realize they have such a gift? You draw them to you, Pearl. They come and they're not afraid." He pauses and grins. "Is it only with fish?"

When you fall in love, Nora had told her, the heart wakes from its long sleep and finds itself at home. Pearl's heart stirs from its hibernation. Involuntarily, she touches Cliff's arm. He puts his hand on hers, and she waits.

"Give me a minute, Pearl," Cliff says, "I have to make a call."

Pearl deals with the final few fish, places them briefly in the recovery tank and then adds all the recovered, tagged fish to the turquoise holding tub. A few minutes later, Cliff reappears to cover the tubs and pour the pan of eggs and milt into a container and seal it.

"I'm impressed," Sheila says sauntering up to them. "You two deserve a beer. Want to get a couple for us, Cliff? Bring the chips, too."

With Cliff out of hearing, Sheila says, "What did you do to him? Did he tell you who he talked to?"

"No. Is everything all right?"

"Yeah. Sure, terrific!" Sheila scrapes a flake of pink polish from a fingernail, her face softened by the west light. "Better than I could have hoped. He said he could fly out with the fish tomorrow, and asked if it was okay with me if you went with him. I said, fine, so he's going to ask you. He's on the radio with the pilot, changing the schedule. But before that, he called that girlfriend of his—what's her name—in Vancouver. She's been to visit once or twice, and I have to say she is pretty, but she likes to stand around and be admired. He told her he'd found somebody else, isn't that something? I wonder, how could that have happened since this morning? Anything you want to tell me?"

If ghosts can be anywhere, they should be here at Friendly Cove, puzzling through vanished layers of habitation from

Mowachaht plank houses to the storehouses and barracks of an eighteenth-century Spanish settlement and on to rows of beachfront cannery workers' shacks. The few structures—a house, a church, the lighthouse—do what they can to pin this history for the cameras of the tourists the ferry brings on day trips, but it's the summer campground of traditional food gatherers that attracts familiars.

Pearl sniffs the wind, ripe with the scent of salmonberries and late wild rose, as the last shuttle of the day, carrying her and Cliff and the remaining crew, nears the landing. Suddenly, the driver throttles down and shouts, "Hold on!"

A large twin-engine craft runs straight at their bow from its trajectory at the Fishing Lodge, swerves, and tosses them in its wash. Blue smoke from the diesel engines hazes the air.

The helmsman is drained of colour.

"Assholes," someone says.

"Probably tracking a whale, eh?"

"Nah, going fishing with lights."

Hoots and yells are heard from the retreating craft. It yaws, then super-speeds for the open ocean.

At the wharf where they moor, the smell of seaweed that has baked on hot sand all day wafts from the beach. Waves ripple silver in the late light, and roll many-coloured stones (grey, green, ochre, purple, and the black and white of basalt and quartz) in the undertow. The beach is a ruin of dried out sea wrack: shells, broken wood, and lengths of sea-bleached rope. Sand fleas and flies swarm the debris and vanish the moment the wind rustles through. A little girl gathers pebbles and rains them onto her toes. An eagle flies over the waves, swoops, and rises with a fish in its talons; a little boy with glasses, wearing a blue T-shirt, wades through the long grass of the meadow to the boardwalk, trudges along it, and hops off into the field of tents.

Cliff and Pearl are close behind the boy. They have hardly said ten words to each other since they left *SoliSunny*, but they step off the boardwalk together and pass through its fringe of wild rose and bramble to follow the child across the field.

"I stay at the church," Cliff says, pointing to the little bell tower that pokes above a stand of spruce trees. "It's deconsecrated. Judy lets me sleep there. She has an office downstairs, but because of the artefacts in the main part, she's happy to have someone stay over. No one uses it for anything much, but soon they'll be holding conferences in it, and I'll be homeless." He shrugs.

"Where do you live usually?"

"Vancouver. Until I finish my post-grad anyway. Then north, probably."

"With the fish?"

"As long as possible, Pearl. It's what I'm good at."

"*You* have a gift," she says.

He grins. "I'm a scientist who likes his work."

They brush against each other, and then they are arm in arm, and he adjusts his step to hers.

"I'm staying at my grandmother's cabin."

"I know. I asked Judy about you after I saw you on the bus." The little boy joins other children at a picnic table.

"Did you know my grandmother?" Pearl asks. "Nora didn't tell me about her life here. I only learned what it meant to her after she died."

"No, I never met her, but Sheila told me stories."

What stories? Pearl is about to ask, but Judy calls from her tent. "Hey, you two, you're coming for supper. I won't take no. The girls have been picking mussels all afternoon. If you see them, tell them it's time to come home. I have to help Fred with the barbecue."

"Are you sure?" Pearl says.

"You're family Pearl, and Cliff's the next best thing. Anyway, Sheila radioed you had quite the day at *SoliSunny*, and I want to hear it from you. She says you're both flying out tomorrow with the fish." Judy raises an eyebrow at Pearl. "Nora did say you were a fast learner." She turns to Cliff, "Why don't you show Pearl the church until we're ready? When I need you for dinner, you'll know it."

The church is white clapboard, stark against the twilight, with a peaked roof below a bell tower: scaled down wooden flying buttresses strain from its sides like trimmed wings. The basement windows are partially obscured by grass that has grown high around the sunken foundations. The interior is dark, but as Cliff and Pearl approach, a light flickers across the stained-glass windows.

"Somebody's inside," Cliff says. "I'll check it out. It's supposed to be locked."

He vaults the steps. The front door lock has been forced, but before he gets inside, the sound of breaking glass and splintering wood shakes the walls. "They've gone out the back!" he yells, jumps from the steps, and sprints past Pearl.

Beyond the church, the ground gives way to an eroded bank. Against the glare of the sinking sun, they make out a pair of figures down on the beach, leaping across the gravel and splashing into an inflatable. While Cliff and Pearl scramble down the slope, the intruders fire up the engine and speed off.

"I wonder what they wanted?" Pearl says, her eyes on the spatter trail of the inflatable's wake.

"Carvings, candlesticks. Whatever they thought they could sell. It isn't the first time it's been tried, but they weren't carrying anything as far as I could tell."

He takes Pearl's hand, and they go through the main church entrance into its murky foyer. Cliff tries several light switches, but nothing happens. "Too bad. I wanted to show you the stained-glass windows and the photographs that were taken of the whaling shrine over a hundred years ago before it was dismantled and shipped to a museum. Judy said it wasn't too far from your grandmother's cabin. Most people here want to get it back."

"A shrine?"

"The Mowachaht hunters prepared for weeks before they went out whaling in their canoes, nearly always successfully. It was like they'd reached an agreement between species. Maybe it makes sense to me because I spend so much time around fish, but this was a relationship on a scale I can barely imagine."

Pearl recalls standing with Joachim in the gallery of the whale tank, the baby beluga dropping from its mother's vent, the mother nosing it upwards for its first taste of air. "They grieve at the deaths of each other. Do you make room for that in your kind of writing?" Nora had asked after Pearl posted a whale meat blog for SaveOurSouls cooking. Yes, Nora read her work online. How had Pearl forgotten? Remembering brings with it a flush of shame.

Cliff takes a flashlight from his backpack. As they pass into the nave, he plays the light over the church walls. In place of an altar, carved poles depict humanoid figures, animals, and birds. He turns around and aims the beam back at the doorway which is surmounted and framed by more carvings and poles. A giant bird supports a disc bracketed by serpents. "Thunderbird, sun and lightning snakes," Cliff says.

Pearl guesses at the identity of the other carved figures—more birds, a long-nosed wolf, and a bear—but as on Pink Pelican Island, in the cave where she could not read the symbols on the walls, the figures tell her little beyond the reality of their power.

"Everything seems okay," Cliff says as they proceed down the nave. "I guess they'd just broken in."

He moves off to examine the rest of the interior. Sheila had called him intuitive, but he is painstaking as he checks for signs of damage. "They loosened the putty at the bottom of this window," he says, shining the light around a small pane of stained glass. "I'll fix it in the morning." Then the light disappears, and he calls out from some hollow, "I'm going into the basement to see if I can find the circuit breakers. I want to look at the office, too."

Pearl is not afraid of the dark, but she does not like being on her own without light in an unfamiliar place.

It's like being shut in a closet, something she did to herself as a child to see if she could stand it, and if anyone would come to look for her. She *had* stood it, because she had the dolls with her, and Nora had searched until she'd found her.

"Still okay, Pearl?" Cliff calls from downstairs.

No wonder Nora had worried about her, although the most she ever said in criticism was, "I don't always understand your decisions, Pearl." Even when Pearl moved in with Gerry-David she had not said more than, "Are you sure it's what you want?"

Yes, Pearl is okay, but she would like Cliff to be quick. Because if she has too much vacant time, it balloons with her mistakes. Her chest tightens. Mistakes like that time with Gerry-David at the beach. She'd had her shoes off, her toes massaging the sand. "Walk into the shallows, and I'll make a video for your website," he'd said. He'd squeezed her elbow, then fiddled with the settings on the video camera. A handful of beachcombers with shoulder bags meandered over the sands, but they were not close by.

"I thought we were going for a walk?"

"We are, we are. Come on, Pearl, put your feet in the water, let me do you a favour!"

When Pearl was in water, things happened. Mostly it was nice—a few fish swimming alongside her—but it could be unpredictable, and she hated it if anyone noticed and she had to explain. Gerry-David knew this, but since this was the two of them by themselves, why shouldn't she try to please him when he was trying to be helpful? She let a wave wash over her feet. Crabs scuttled over her toes, which was nothing unusual, but moments later a splash of silver grunions—dozens of them, each five or six inches in length—washed in and around her legs. "Wait," she'd said to them. "It isn't safe for you yet!" They needed a full moon, or a new moon and a high tide, and hundreds of companions, not this suicidal rally in twilight. But the females dug in the sand to spawn anyway, and the males flopped to wrap around them. The blue-green highlights along their scales were beautiful: it was impossible for her not to watch them.

"Perfect!" Gerry-David had shouted. "Don't move!" She'd turned to see him train the camera on the grunions in the sand at her feet, then pan up to her face. Behind him, half a dozen other people, the strollers, were filming, too, giving Gerry-D the thumbs up. Local KeyTV and the Comedy Network, and the Cook-Off channel: all of them.

Wing beats, rafts of gulls dropping from on high, dipping to land and feed on the breeding fish. *What had she done?* Pearl retreated quickly from the frenzy.

Her photo with grunions was Gerry-David's new advertising feature, winged predators filling the space above her head. "Everyone flocks to Gerry-D for real estate," he captioned it. Nora must have seen it on the billboard at the shopping centre. How could she miss it? Nora gunning the RAV to get out of the billboard's range.

Pearl is having trouble breathing. What must Nora have thought of her?

"Pearl needs to make her own decisions," Nora had told Harry and Loretta on her last visit; and Pearl had.

The aisle lights come on. "Sorry to be so long, but it took me a while to find the electrical box. It's in a cupboard in the office," Cliff says as he comes towards her. "Judy keeps the side entrance bolted. The radio and all her records are inside. Thank god they didn't get that far."

Pearl coughs as she tries to speak. "Cliff? Can we go somewhere? I can't breathe in here."

"Is it an allergy? The dust? The bastards who broke in will have stirred it up. Let's get you upstairs. I can open a window in the loft, or do you want to go outside? We don't have to stay."

"No, I'll be fine." She climbs the stairs ahead of him, her chest already easing. Honestly! The only real allergy she had was to herself and her thoughts.

A large cupboard off the landing houses statues of Christ, the Virgin Mary, and Saint Francis, their polychrome faces fixed, polished, and patient. Cliff's room below the belfry is sparsely furnished with a table holding a kettle and cups and dishes, a pew he steps on to open the clerestory window, an inflatable mattress on the floor, and a chair he uses as a bedside stand. His belongings lie folded by his backpack. His sleeping bag and pillow are rolled together at one end of the mattress.

"Sit down and take slow deep breaths, Pearl." She sits, her breathing better with the window open. "I'll make a tea that should help." He rummages in his pack and pulls out a pair of socks, plucks a knife and an empty plastic jug from the table, and seizes the flashlight. "I won't be long."

She hears him sprinting down the stairs and out the door. Several minutes later, he re-enters holding the filled jug and a bunch of leaves in his sock-gloved hands. He holds the leaves up to show her. “Stinging nettles!” Still gloved, he pours water into the kettle, plugs it in, and shreds the leaves into a cup. “Keep doing that slow breathing.”

When the water boils, handsocks off, he pours it over the leaves and covers the cup with a plate. A few minutes later, he spoons out the leaves. “Drink this.”

The room settles into peace. Maybe it is because of the medicinal properties of the tea or because of the saints next door, or the stained glass and the bright carvings of birds, the sun, sea serpents, whales, people, and animals below. Whatever it is, Pearl’s tight chest clears.

She turns to thank him and finds him looking at her. “Okay?” he says.

“Yes. Thank you. How did you know to do that?” She leans in to kiss him on the cheek, but instead, her mouth finds his. Too few moments later, the throb of a drumbeat reaches them from the meadow.

“That will be Judy’s dinner call,” Cliff says.

“We’d better go,” she says.

“Yes.”

But he doesn’t move. Instead, he places his palm against her palm and spreads his fingers. A transparent webbing unfolds between the base of his middle and his ring finger. He closes the fingers and the webbed skin packs itself away. “It’s a genetic anomaly. We are closer to other species than we think, Pearl. It’s a matter of degree.”

Pearl spreads her fingers too, but the webbing between her fingers is of no account.

"It isn't useful. It doesn't help me swim," he says. "I'm an evolutionary dead end."

He grins. "I learned about stinging nettles from a book."

"Don't worry about it. I'll fix the lock and glass tomorrow," Fred says when they join him and Judy at the tents. "They won't be back tonight, not in the dark by boat. I've got an idea who it is, anyway."

"Who, Fred? Who would do a thing like that?" Judy asks.

"Most of the people from the lodge are okay; they want to fish. But these two guys. They asked me, '*What's in the church*?' So I said, 'It's locked, you can't go in without permission.'

"'*You got a key?'* one guy asked.

"'I'm the caretaker,' I told them.

"'*So, open it*!'

"'Not without permission, like I said.'

"'*Okay, so where do we get permission?'* the other guy said.

"'From me,' I said. You should have seen their faces. I bet they saw pictures on the Internet, got an idea of value, and decided a light-fingered viewing on their own was worth the risk. Every carving in there belongs to a family, Pearl. You don't sell things like that. And the old priest, what would I tell him about his statues if something happened?"

Judy bangs the drum again, and the family congregates near the barbecue pit. Eight-year-old Sandra and her friend Tanya hover by the sacks of mussels they collected; the older boys stack wood near the fire, and two toddlers fold paper napkins at the picnic table. Judy scoops the baby from where he's dozing in a carrier.

"We never used to lock the church." She passes the baby to Pearl who buries her nose in the fine hair of the baby's scalp and inhales.

"Where did you put the doll Nora gave you for Auntie Pearl?" Judy calls to Sandra, but the girls are busy talking, and Sandra doesn't appear to hear. "Sandra? Are you listening? Where are your glasses!"

"What is this, Judy? Nora gave you a doll for me? She told you I would come?"

"Sure, why not, Pearl? You're here, aren't you?"

Sandra takes a pair of wire spectacles from Tanya who has been wearing them, puts them on and whispers in her mother's ear. Judy rolls her eyes. "She's not sure where she put it, she'll look for it tomorrow."

"But I'm flying out with Cliff first thing in the morning!"

"Then you'll come back, won't you." Judy smiles. "We're family, and you have to hear my stories."

Pearl is going to ask which stories Judy means, but Judy says, "Looks like the baby is wet from what I can see of your shirt, Pearl. One of us better change him."

Fred spreads seaweed over the coals. He and Cliff scatter mussels onto a metal grill and set it on the seaweed bed. The fire smokes and recovers. In a minute or two the mussels open, spilling their juices over the crisping seaweed. The orange meat shines wet within the charred blue, black, and white shells. Fred darts in with tongs to fill the plates. Pearl pries a mussel open, burning her fingers, and scoops out the hot salty meat with her teeth. Mussel liquor runs down her chin.

Judy puts the freshly changed baby beside the girls in his carrier and gets the boys to pull baked potatoes out of the fire while the toddlers run to Cliff and embrace his knees.

After supper, the children play catch. Cliff clicks the flashlight on and off the ball, the children shouting, "That's not fair!" and laughing. The boys pile pine brush onto the fire to awaken the enveloping shadows, and the girls withdraw to private consultations. The moon spotlights the coastal mountains. What is happiness, Pearl, if not a night like this?

"Well," Cliff says. "We should get going."

"Hey, Auntie Pearl," Sandra says as Pearl turns to go. "Me and Tanya want you to try this. We got it for you." Pearl strains to penetrate the liquid density of the pail Sandra is holding.

Sandra picks out something that looks like a miniature armadillo. It fits easily in Pearl's palm.

"What do you do with it?"

"Peel off the shell and scrape out the insides. The thick part is what you eat."

Pearl does as Sandra commands: the meat is chewy and bland, and difficult to swallow.

"You have to blanch them first, Sandra," Judy says. "You know that. Why did you make Auntie Pearl try a raw chiton?"

"So she could eat them if she gets lost," Sandra says. "What if she starves before I give her the doll?"

"Sandra? Sandra, do I need to talk to you?" Judy says.

Enfolded in the bell tower room, with waves cresting onto the beach below the church to a card shuffle of wind, Cliff and Pearl make love. They have weeks ahead of them. They are in no hurry, the evening with Judy's family a blessing on the day; learning each other's shape and texture, limbs intertwined, testing for consent and pleasure, reading the dimmed, softened gaze of each other's eyes. They hold to each other with all the time in the world.

In the morning, Cliff lends Pearl socks, underwear, and a T-shirt. He packs his possessions, and after a brief look at the whale shrine display in the foyer, they set off for Pearl's cabin so she can pack her things as well. Dragonflies dust the plate glass of the lake, and the green forest perimeter ascends to pale misted hills in the distance.

Cliff makes coffee while Pearl organizes her gear for the next few weeks. They are in a rush now, mindful that they can't miss the shuttle. Before the float-plane lands at *SoliSunny*, they must prepare for a quick loading-in of fish, fertilized eggs, and nest materials to limit their degradation.

Fred is out on the fishing boat with the older boys by the time they reach the meadow. The other children are asleep. Judy gives Cliff a hug and says, "Pearl, somebody radioed for you last night. He wouldn't say who he was, so I said I'd never heard of you. He said he'd try again."

The news is disturbing, but they can hear the shuttle coming and so Pearl merely says, "Can you tell Harry where I've gone?"

"Sure," Judy says. "Your dad worries, eh? I am happy for you two, but you'd better look after each other or Fred will be upset, and you don't want that."

"I'll see you soon," Pearl says, and they dash across the field and down to the dock.

It's not until Pearl is passing her backpack to Cliff onboard the shuttle with the creosoted wharf planks adjusting under her weight, that she registers the white pleasure craft tied at the end of the pier. Its twin diesel engines are idling, the passengers drinking orange juice under a blue awning.

A man steps to the rail. "Hey!" he calls. "Hey you!"

Pearl has never seen him before, but this person dressed in white trousers, white deck shoes, and a black collarless shirt, is calling to her. He jumps onto the dock. Pearl's foot slips between the zodiac and dock, and Cliff steadies her by the elbow.

"Pearl Rosa Narvaez Smith," the man says confronting her. Sunglasses blank his eyes. Diamond studs gleam in his earlobes.

"Yes?" No one ever uses her full name.

He holds out a large envelope.

"For me? What is it?" Pearl asks.

"Open it and see."

The moment she has it, he adds, "You're a hard lady to get hold of, and you're lucky I'm the one who found you. Some of my colleagues aren't so understanding.

"Smile," he says, and he snaps her photo with his cell phone.

The men in the shuttle gaze out to sea; the shuttle driver revs the engine in neutral. Someone has cast off the lines, but Cliff's foot hooks the zodiac to the side of the wharf. "Pearl? We have to go. Can it wait?"

Slowly, Pearl opens the envelope, pulls out a sheaf of papers and leafs through them. Some are for loans she does not recollect; others are private mortgages on properties in which Gerry-David had invested her money, she and Gerry-D jointly responsible to repay them. The penultimate document is Gerry-D's declaration of bankruptcy. The ultimate is a lien on Nora's house. The papers drop from her clasp. She brushes by the man in the white shoes, walks calmly down the dock, past the white boat at the end, and dives into the sea.

Mountains ripple like a Chinese painting against a sketch of high cloud; green shrubbery and wild rose fold into the fall line of a forest. Pearl lies in the field, soaking wet, coddled in a nest of blankets, insects strolling the angles of her face. A blade of grass tickles her forehead.

"Mom said I should wake you." Sandra drops the blade of grass and stoops close, ponytail tied with a pink ribbon, silk and gold complexion, wire spectacles at the end of her nose. She pushes them up with a finger. "Tanya's here, too. She's my friend."

"Yes."

"Mom says she's sorry. She didn't know who they were, or she wouldn't have let them land. Dad says if he ever sees them here again, they'll have to deal with him.

Mom says she is sure you didn't mean to lose Granny Nora's house; you wouldn't have done it on purpose."

"She knows about the house?"

"You wouldn't stop talking after Cliff pulled you out of the water. Cliff's gone, too. He couldn't wait because of the seaplane. He asked mom to look after you. He said he would call from *SoliSunny* before he left."

"Okay," Pearl says.

"Mom says he'd be here in a flash, if he could."

"Sure," she says. "Sure, he would."

"Why did you jump off the dock, Auntie Pearl? Me and Tanya would like you to tell us."

Pearl closes her eyes. She had surprised herself with her leap into the water, but for a brief period swimming had brought her calm. While swimming, she had no questions, nothing to explain to herself or anyone else. Minutes before, Cliff was waiting and a future was about to unfold, one in which her gift—if that is what it is—might find a use; then suddenly all she hoped for was annihilated. By debt. And guilt. And shame. How could she have trusted Gerry-David? Why had she been so stupid? If she were Cliff, she would leave, too. He wasn't going to call, he wasn't.

Pearl's guts squeeze: she turns her head to the side and vomits.

"Okay," Sandra says, "you don't have to say why you did it, but I am supposed to give you this." Sandra undoes a sling made from a sweater tied around her waist. Nora had knitted the sweater for Pearl years ago. Wrapped in it is one of Nora's dolls.

"I said I couldn't find it when mommy asked. I could but I didn't want to." Sandra places the doll on Pearl's chest. Pearl lifts it so she can see it more clearly: the doll is Beatris, Rosa's mother, the doll that Beatris had made of herself for her daughter. Pearl sits, pulling the blankets with her. The eyes she had repainted on the doll under Nora's guidance have faded from green to dull olive, but the cedar-wood body has recently been polished. Pearl's thumb finds the score that represents a scar, under the doll's chin.

"That's okay, Sandra. I'm glad you're giving it to me today."

Instead of the indigo satin and lace gown Pearl had last seen the doll wearing, it is dressed in what she had considered to be its undergarments of loose cotton trousers and a long-sleeved shirt. Beatris's curly dark hair has loosened from its pins to make an aureole around her smiling face. The embroidery on the shirt is faded, but Pearl makes out the minuscule stitching of a tiny horse.

"I tucked everything else in, too," Sandra says, passing over the little pack that came with the doll. "She takes it travelling."

The pack contains a miniature sailing ship, a twig doll with a leather hat, and a diminutive *navaja* with a broken strap. Pearl had been the one to break the strap.

"I didn't put the dress on her," Sandra says. "That's not for every day."

"It doesn't matter about the dress."

"Can I play with her again?"

"Yes."

"I can?"

"Can I, too?" Tanya asks. She pokes her head over Sandra's shoulder. She has been listening behind Sandra, biting the ends of her hair.

"You'll have to take turns after me," Pearl says. "I need a long one."

"I had a long one," Sandra says.

Pearl is shivering.

"Don't let the doll get wet, Auntie Pearl." Sandra retrieves the Beatris doll and re-wraps it in the sweater. "You have to be careful. She belonged to Granny Nora."

"Pearl!" Judy yells from halfway down the slope between the church and her tent. "Put some clothes on and come to the office. You missed a call."

In the tent, Pearl pulls on the sweatshirt and sweatpants Judy left for her, and her running shoes, wet as they are. Her good boots are in Nora's cabin and her new work boots are in her locker at *SoliSunny*. Pearl takes a breath and walks up the hill. She won't know what to say to Cliff until she hears his voice.

"Have a coffee. You'll need to like it black," Judy says as Pearl enters the office. She points to a chair next to hers at the radio desk. "Take a seat, I'll show you what to do."

Pearl sits.

"Hey, you're shaking," Judy says. "No need for that, Pearl. I'm not going to say anything except you gave us a scare. Lucky Cliff grabbed that tourist's kayak and went after you. He can paddle, eh? Were you going to Japan?

Like stories say people did from here in canoes in the old days? Crossing the ocean as easy as *we* go shopping to Gold River.

"Just in case you're wondering," Judy adds, as she unhooks the microphone from its holder next to the transmitter, "it wasn't Cliff who radioed for you, it was Sheila." She glances at Pearl again, then lays the microphone down. "Just a minute." She rummages in the first-aid cabinet and brings out a bottle of brandy. She pours some of the spirit into Pearl's coffee, screws the cap on the bottle, places it beside Pearl, and settles in her chair.

"Sheila said Cliff wanted to talk to you, but as soon as the plane was loaded, they had to take off. The weather is changing. Look for yourself. They had to get ahead of it." Judy gestures to indicate the view out the open door. Pearl swivels round: a black thicket of cloud is rapidly advancing from the south-west.

"What's been going on, Pearl?" Sheila asks from her *SoliSunny* office. "No one will tell me anything, but I've had comings and goings all morning. Care to enlighten me?" Into Pearl's silence, Sheila says, "Okay, you can fill me in later, but you've got to give it to what's-her-name—she doesn't let go easily."

"What do you mean?" Pearl takes the sweater-wrapped Beatris doll from her lap and lays it next to the bottle.

"Cliff's girlfriend, the one he dumped yesterday, she flew in early and then flew out with him. She must have paid an arm and a leg to charter that seaplane. You should have been here, Pearl, you really should. So . . . are you coming in to work? Do I tell the shuttle to go and get you or not? Cliff left a hell of a mess behind, and

I could do with your help. Tanks unsterilized, equipment all over the decks, half the storage cupboards open. It isn't like him."

Pearl can't speak, she can scarcely breathe.

"Say something, Pearl, don't leave me hanging. Can I count on you?"

"No. I'm sorry, Sheila."

"That right? You're breaking your word? You're sure?"

"I have some business to attend to."

"Business, eh? Well, I am disappointed. I had hoped Nora was right about you."

"What did she say?"

"Never gives up, that girl, once she gets her head on straight. You could stick her in the middle of a desert in a sandstorm, and she would find her way."

"Nora said that?"

"She did."

Pearl takes a moment to swallow her coffee and adds an extra slug of brandy from the bottle. "I've made a mess of everything, Sheila. I need to fix what I can. I didn't mean to let you down."

Sheila sighs. In the silence between them, Pearl believes she can hear the lift and fall of the fish-farm floats and the stir of fish in their pens.

"Do what you have to Pearl," Sheila says. "But try to do it quickly and get over it. Your boots will be waiting. Hope it all works out for you."

"Sheila? Was there any message for me?"

"Message? Oh, you mean from Cliff. No, no more than I said. You want me to ask the crew?"

"No, no, it's okay. Look, thanks for everything."

"Take it easy, Pearl. I mean it."

Pearl clips the microphone into the holder. Judy shoots a box of tissues across the desk.

"You going to the cabin?"

"Yeah."

"Wipe your face before you do. Jeez, Pearl, the kids will see you."

Pearl rubs her face with her sleeve, but the tears persist.

"Oh, for Heaven's sake, Pearl!" Judy wraps Pearl's fingers around the bottle of brandy. "Take all the kleenex. Take the brandy. Just don't drink it all."

Pearl sits on the deck of the cabin on the lake, wrapped in her sleeping bag. She has slept for an hour or two and is on her second pot of coffee and sixth glass of water. Enough brandy is left to get her to sleep again if she needs some help. The sun is high in a clear sky, the lake transparent to the bottom. It is perfect flying weather.

She opens the envelope the man on the dock gave her and carefully goes over each document. Her signature on some of the recent loans is obviously forged—she is sure her lawyer can have them dismissed; but the mortgages are genuine. She remembers signing them, and that she had believed they were to briefly bridge the buying and selling of properties she was investing in with Gerry-David. He had told her he'd paid them, and she'd believed him. She had asked for proof for her records, but he'd put her off so many times, that in due course it slipped her mind. She'd had no idea she could be held solely responsible if he neglected to make payments and went into bankruptcy.

The question was, what should she do about it? She might win damages if she took him to court over the forgeries, but she wouldn't recover her savings or escape the mortgages and the lien. To pay them off, she would have to sell Nora's house anyway. The lenders, judging from what she had seen of the man on the dock, were not going to wait quietly for their money. She needed to talk to her lawyer.

Pearl's eyes follow the play of light and cloud shadow across the water.

The plane with Cliff, his girlfriend, and the fish must have arrived at its destination by now. As Pearl writes the note she will leave with young Sandra to keep for Cliff, she tries not to think about this too much, or about what is going to happen to Nora's legacy.

Judy will tell you how to get in touch with me, if you want to, she writes. She pauses and bites the end of the pen. *I would like it if you did.* She takes another moment and adds, *A long time ago, a boy and girl lost each other. I hope, sometime, to tell you their story. "The road home is long, / And at every turn, / Only the birds of the sky and field / Fly free."*

She signs it, *Love, Pearl* (*poem by Guiliam*).

That finished, Pearl checks the ferry schedule she'd saved on her laptop. She'll take the boat to Gold River and find a place to scan documents and phone her lawyer.

She'll talk to Harry, too—he *is* Nora's executor—and see if the estate can give her an advance on what is likely to be left after the dust settles. More than ever, it matters that she complete what her grandmother had asked of her.

At dusk, Pearl gathers her belongings, tidies up the cabin, and unwraps the doll Sandra had parcelled in the sweater sling. As she does, she catches a finger in a loose loop of the sweater's pink and green wool. The sleeves are overlong. Nora has had to roll and tack them into double cuffs. Thoughtfully, Pearl runs a finger inside one of the cuffs and teases out a slip of paper. It is a note from Nora:

Rosa's mother, Beatris, born in the mountains of Spain seven generations before you, ran away to sea. She voyaged the west coast of North America to Nootka Island before making her way to Mexico with her daughter. When you write the stories, don't forget to put that in.

Pearl blinks back a surge of tears. So much could have gone wrong with the delivery of Nora's note, but Nora had trusted that Sandra's pride would guarantee she'd bestow the doll with its accessories intact, including the improvised sling. Pearl lights a kerosene lamp against the rolling in of the dark, and while moths swirl around the chimney glass, she summons the pool of stories afresh, more than willing to welcome thoughts that can distract her from her misery.

~

The Stowaway's Tale

South Sierra Morena, Spain, c. 1776

They were left, infants Beatris and her twin brother Baruk, on a hillside under a bush on a ledge. Their mother Inés scanned the path that led past the cave in which she lived, to see who might climb it and find them. When, years later, Frey Tomas at Friendly Cove said to Bee, scandalized at how little she knew of Church matters, '*Were you born in a ditch*? *Were your parents heretics or plain ignorant*?' she could honestly answer (if only to herself), 'Yes.'

Her mother and stepfather *were* heretics, if that meant they objected to such cruelty as priests practised, and yes, the rock shelf on the hill (horses grazing on sweet grass in nearby pastures) where she and Baruk were left, served the same purpose as a ditch. In a ditch or on a ledge, planning and fortune determined survival.

A shepherd heard the babies cry and found them and carried them down the footpath.

"What have you got there?" Inés said from the cave entrance as he passed by with the mewling infants.

He stopped and showed her. "Let me see if I can quiet them," Inés, their secret mother, said. She held out her arms. "Poor things." She stroked the smoky amber of the babies' limbs. They blinked black-lashed eyes and fell quiet.

"They might be mixed blood," the shepherd said. "You can never tell." They were near trade routes through the mountains used by merchants and travellers. He stared, not unkindly, into her face. Her parents had died during the months of her absence in the wars of King Charles III. They had been his family's friends; and before she left, Inés had safely midwifed the birth of his son. Both Beatris and her husband Dario were from families long-established in the area.

"My wife won't like it if I bring them home," the shepherd said. "It's hard enough to feed our own, the way things are." He meant the tithes of crops and other goods he had to pay to maintain the priest, and the tax they paid to support the King's army. "But I could not leave them there to die! I have spent my life saving newborns, carrying wet lambs around my neck down the hill. You comfort them well. Perhaps *you* should keep them since you and Dario have no children."

"How would I feed them?" Inés said. Her swollen breasts leaked into a layer of thick wool padding beneath her blouse. She moved as if to return the babies, but the shepherd stepped away.

"I doubt they will trouble you. One of our goats has kidded, but its kid died. I will send it over for as long as you need the milk. We'll take some of the cheese you make from what's left over." He did not look back as he continued down the hillside nor did they speak further of the matter, just as they did not speak of the handsome horses Inés had brought home with her after the period of her captivity, or of what had happened to her during that time.

Thus, Beatris and Baruk became orphans, but only as Moses was left for the Pharaoh's daughter to discover in the bulrushes while his family waited nearby.

Dario, who loved their mother, joined her from within the cave. He had watched over the infants from the hillside. At dawn, a wolf slunk down the ridge and he had set the horses running to drive it off. Good Moorish horses that they were, they could kill a wolf with their hooves: they grazed the upper pasture in tranquility.

"Did he believe you?" Dario asked. "Does he suspect who they belong to?"

"What does it matter as long as we can raise the babies as our own?"

It was their real father, not Dario, who occupied the thoughts of Beatris and Baruk as they grew. He dusted their imaginations with desert and horses and blood. "Didn't our father want to keep us?" they asked their mother. They took the care and protection of Dario for granted.

"Yes, but he knew I was unhappy away from my home," Inés said.

"Tell us the story again," they said, and settled in between Inés and Dario at the evening's fire.

Dario and Inés were childhood friends who had left for Cartagena to join King Charles III's army in an expedition to occupy Algiers. Many untrained fighters, scores of women among them, enlisted in that raid across the Mediterranean, their families' income taken in rent and other payments to landowners and to the Church. It went without question that the Spanish invasion would be victorious: they hoped to make their fortunes with the spoils. But Moorish merchants from Marseille had watched the Spanish military preparations for months and sent word ahead of the invasion. The Spanish ships, carrying thousands of combatants, sailed into the Bay of Algiers and put the troops ashore where they were met with veteran Algerian fighters. As the Spanish force advanced, the Moorish troops feigned a retreat. With the aid of warrior tribesmen from the interior, they encircled Charles's army, inflicting heavy casualties. Dario and other survivors fled to the ships, but many were cut off from retreat. Inés, one of the wounded, was left behind on the battlefield.

"What did you do then?" Baruk asked his mother.

"She was brave!" Beatris said.

"She was a rose among the dead. They saw her, and …"

"Let *her* tell the story, Baruk," Beatris said.

"The victors went through the battlefield, killing the injured," Inés said. "When it came to me, the Algerian soldier finding me alive called to his commander, 'Please do not kill this one, it is a woman!'

"The commander came to look. Already, he had killed many of us. 'She fought against us, she deserves to die,' he said.

"'Ask her which of us to spare and which to kill,' the soldier said. 'If she tells you to kill me, not her, do so. At least she will think of me as I die.'"

"The soldier was our father!" Beatris said. Dario put his hand on her shoulder to calm her.

Inés continued her tale, "'Who should I let live?' the commander asked me. 'You, a woman but my enemy, or my own soldier?'

"'For his sake do not kill me,' I said, 'and because he is brave, don't kill this soldier.' The soldier said to his leader, 'If you want her, you will have to fight me, for I shall never give her up.'"

"But he did!" Beatris said.

"Not at first. Not for a while."

"He might have killed you, but he didn't!" Baruk said, imagining himself as a soldier.

"He risked his life for you," Beatris said. Would anyone risk his life for her?

Inés had learned to swim after her capture. She was young, younger than Pearl is today, a girl who was also a woman. Her captor feared drowning. He had all his wives taught to swim in hopes that one of them would save him.

"I'd stand near the water and watch ships passing—fishing vessels, pirate ships, traders of all kinds. Once I thought I glimpsed a Spanish vessel in the distance, so I leapt into the sea. I kept on swimming, I would not have given up, but my husband, your father, sent a boat to fetch me."

"You could not have reached the ship," Baruk said. "It was too far. You would have drowned. If you had drowned, we would not be here."

~

Pearl suspends her writing to adjust the lamp. Her face reflects in the window. Many of the refugees Nora helped had escaped danger on land only to meet it at sea. All their money taken, overloaded into boats, cast adrift, some had clung to ropes and supported those who could not swim. Untold numbers drowned. Many were saved too, but only those lucky enough to have had a rescuer on watch for them.

~

"I did not think about drowning," his mother said to Baruk. "I knew you and Beatris were coming, and I wanted to go home. After they brought me back, I wept so bitterly the women thought I would lose you. It was then that your father decided to free me."

"He gave you the horses to take home as a gift," Beatris said.

Dario stirred the fire with a stick. Sparks flew into the night.

"He gave me these as well," Inés said, bringing out the package of dolls she kept with her most precious possessions. "Each comes with a story. He said I should tell them to you. He said, 'Spain was our home, too, but they drove us out. There is cruelty and kindness in the tales, you must tell the children of both.'"

"Look, it is written down," Dario said, and he showed the children a parchment with their names on it written in Moorish script. He put his arms around them and their mother. "You must be proud of this heritage, but it is also a secret. Not everyone will understand." He looked at Inés intently. He had not forgiven himself for allowing her to be taken prisoner.

Their mother's story lit coals of fervour within the twins. Distances called. If they were to be anything like her, the flames of their innermost lives would blaze only if they left their homes.

The little family lived above a valley fed by springs. In winter, the pine forests on the lower slopes of the mountain offered firewood and shelter for them and the animals they husbanded. In summer, the family made a pilgrimage to the sea to collect salt, and to ride on horseback into the water.

Their mother pushed the twins off their horses into the sea. They popped to the surface, buoyant as the pig bladder floatation devices she'd tied to their arms when they were infants to keep them safe around water. Laughing, spluttering, they always came to the surface. They were born to the sea as much as to the air.

Inés had just the two children, Beatris and Baruk. Beatris was the one who loved horses. At her whistle, they ran to her; and when the mares were in foal and began their birth pangs, they allowed her near to assist them. Baruk and Beatris were part Moslem, part Christian; half their lives were kept from view. They were two peas in one pod and shared everything. Yet, at thirteen years of age, Baruk left on his own.

"Your father is dead," their mother had said a few days earlier. They had been busy with the animals before Inés had called them in. The hooves of a departing messenger's horse puffed dust down the track. Baruk watched it longingly, while Beatris carried on to the stables.

He left without farewell, returned six months later and told Beatris that in the world beyond the mountains, girls did no more than what men said they could. She did not believe him. She had never asked permission for anything.

"Girls are not clever; they cannot learn and be scholars." This he said to Beatris, although their mother spoke Arabic as well as French and Spanish and had taught them these languages. "Girls are not strong enough to handle horses," he said. His gaze slid sideways, as if he could no longer fix it on his sister. Beatris had ridden horses from the time she walked and had not needed to be taught how to train them.

"Girls cannot travel on their own. They can never go to sea like I can."

"What do you mean?" Beatris said. "You're not a sailor any more than I am!"

Baruk contemplated the family's simple stone house, the cave where they lived before they built the house, and the barn, corrals, and gardens in which he had toiled.

"Who told you these lies?" Beatris said. She knew someone had come between them. "What do they want from you?"

"I have a friend," Baruk said, his cheeks flushing. "Ignacio has signed on with an expedition ship sailing from Cadiz. I have done the same. It may be that I will never see you or our home and parents again. It is your duty to stay with them."

While he spoke words designed to shut her from his life, Beatris understood that he was lost without her. "If you think I will assent to this, you are a fool," she said. The horses whinnied from the hillside, but they no longer took her attention. The keeper of half his soul, she *would* accompany him. Nothing was too hard for Beatris, except for being without her brother.

Both brother and sister were tall and thin with chin-length curly black hair, perfectly alike in speech and manner. Gender was not strong in them. No one who did not know them well could tell them apart. Beatris trailed Baruk along the valley until he made camp in a grove of oaks and swam in the river.

Early the next morning, Beatris packed the little she could not do without, said farewell to the horses and to her parents and said, with kindly-meant deceit, that she was going to visit a friend in the next village. Inés and Dario, aware of the bond between the twins, knew they could not keep her home without Baruk against her will.

The ashes of the fire at the campsite were warm. Indolent Baruk, who never stirred if he could help it until the sun was well risen, had left a trail of scuffed earth and breadcrumbs at his halts along the valley to the west. From there, he had climbed a goat path through rubble and up carved rock steps, to a trail that skirted caves. The way wound to the summit of the mountain around tall blocks of limestone. On the far side of the crag, the path tracked through hills, each with a village on its lower slopes. Beatris had been to the first of these before. She and Baruk had accompanied their mother and Dario there, summoned with the whole of the populace by the priest. At a further village, she asked at an inn for water and the proprietor addressed her saying, "I hadn't thought to see you back so soon; did you change your mind about your journey?" He mistook her for her brother.

The vista widened, sparse brush over dry rocky soil gave way to stands of pine and gall oak trees that provided good shelter. Beatris was not lonely: Baruk was never far away. But one day, a boy she did not recognize stepped out of the grove in which he had been camping and ran towards her brother. "Baruk!" the boy cried. "What has taken so long? I waited and did not follow, as I promised!" He was thick-set and muscular, with lank dark hair, his buttery features pale beside Baruk's. "I was afraid you'd changed your mind."

Beatris's brother glanced around, but Beatris was well screened by the forest. "I will not leave you, Ignacio," he said. "I gave my promise, too." Baruk held the boy by the shoulders and kissed him. It was the first time Baruk had had a friend of his own.

Chestnut trees and fungi, and grain and vegetables stolen from farms supplied her food, but Beatris was often hungry. Sometimes, she earned a meal by cutting wood or hauling water. At these holdings too, she was occasionally assumed to be her brother. "What happened to the other one? Gone ahead, has he?" one man asked. "You are better off without him. I didn't like his looks."

Beatris had nodded. How could she disagree?

The nights were warm and the days not yet too hot for travel. A few cattle and a small herd of donkeys kept her company until she reached the cork groves and smelled the sea in the dusty wind that blew across the straits from Africa. The cutters saw her with the donkeys and believed that she had deliberately brought them with her. "Welcome, boy! Our thanks. You have saved us the trouble of going after them ourselves. What can we give you in exchange?"

"I will work for food, if you will have me," she said.

She toiled with the cork workers for several weeks and learned to strip bark with the sharp thin blades they used, without wounding the trees. The harvesting over, they loaded the bundles onto the recaptured donkeys and set out for the city.

The cork woods thinned to widely spaced pines, and the land flattened into a wedge of spongy delta. Beatris and the cork-cutters arrived at the beach at nightfall. Dozens of small boats rocked at anchor. Others were drawn up onto the sands. The cutters rested in the long grass of a sea bank and watched the moon climb as bonfires flared along the coastline while fishermen mended their nets. Later, while the travellers ate the fish they had bought and cooked at their fire, they talked of the expedition that was soon to sail from Cadiz, and the money to be made from its provisioning. It was to be the greatest scientific enterprise Spain had engaged in, a product of King Charles III of Spain's enthusiasm for learning.

Some of the men had friends who worked at the shipyard and naval base, the Arsenal de la Carraca, on an island southeast of the city. Several had laboured building docks, warehouses, offices, workshops, and homes. "They finished the dry docks a year ago and the new ships were quickly built and launched," one man said.

"What ships are these?" Beatris asked.

"Two corvettes, large enough to voyage safely to the New World and beyond—if they are lucky—each carrying a hundred souls." They named the ships. One was *Descubierta*, the ship Baruk had spoken of, the one he had signed on to with Ignacio.

"Good seamen, most of them, I hope?" she said.

"Not all, though.. Some are boys no older than you."

At dawn, in the first glitter of rose and gold, Beatris and the cutters set out with their loads in hired boats to cross the water to the port. She helped with the unloading at the docks and then combed the waterfront until she found *Descubierta* lying at anchor alongside its companion, *Atrevida*. Lighters sped to and fro stacked with sacks and barrels. Several carried well-dressed civilians and officers out to the ships.

"Who are they, where are they going?" Beatris asked a passing porter, pointing at one of the lighters which was transferring its passengers onto rope ladders that hung from *Descubierta*'s side.

"They go to hell, as far as I can tell," he said. He set down his burden gladly. "You young ones call it a voyage of discovery, but I am too old for any thought but of heaven."

"How long till they finish loading?"

He shook his head. "Not soon enough for me. They sail on the morning tide."

"I could take your job for a few hours, if you wanted," she said.

"Why would you do that?"

"I have never been on board a ship. Tomorrow I must return to the mountains."

"I won't pay you," he said.

"No matter. I will do it once, for the adventure."

On board *Descubierta*, with a load of glassware balanced on her shoulders, Beatris explored the officers' quarters and the cook's stores. She left the glassware in the galley and followed other porters below decks. Fifteen minutes and a look-in at the bunks, shops, and lockers gave her the ship's layout. It was not difficult to gather what she needed—water, a blanket, biscuits, and a bucket for a latrine—and find a place to hide, jammed in with the supplies. The officers never imagined a stowaway: the lookouts watched solely for deserters. At night, while much of the crew slept and groaned in their hammocks, she slipped out to renew necessities and drink in fresh air on deck. She knew the stars, and watched the constellations turn through time. If she was seen, she stood politely aside. If asked, she gave her name as the boy sailor, Baruk, and said she was unable to sleep, and offered to assist with the ropes or other tasks. It was not difficult to be useful since in these early days she was not expected to have any skills, only to be able to obey; and it was an enlightened ship, not cruelly run.

Then, once the ship sailed too far out in the Atlantic to return to port, Beatris revealed herself to her brother. He was alone in a forward locker mending sails.

All worlds are intelligible to those with the patience to read them: the ship was the weather, and the bells that rang the watches; the dividing of cooked beans and salt pork and hard tack; it was the cooperative mechanisms of its operations. Yet the ship was still part of the single inhabited world of Beatris and her brother.

"You should not have come!" he cried. Tears stood in his eyes. "I saw you in the forest, but I thought you were a ghost!" The awl slipped from his grip, and she jumped from a pile of sacking to retrieve it.

"You are not dead?" he said.

"As much and as little as you."

"What will happen when you are exposed?" he said. "You have put us both in danger!"

"Nothing will happen. You are tired, that is all. I can do your work and let you rest. No one will see the difference."

"Except for Ignacio," he said.

"What have you said of our family?"

"Nothing. I've said nothing. Why would I? I have a new life."

He had her hold the sail and showed her what to do: in the half of a heart that was his, Baruk was soft as a peach. Beatris was the lion. "But what will you eat?" he said after she had finished repairing the first sail and they had folded it so that it might be unfurled in a moment.

"I have foraged in the night; I have survived on scraps. I can do that still; I will thrive, you will see."

Beatris kept watch. By the time Ignacio came looking for Baruk, their story was ready. Beatris (a boy called Bee) and Baruk were brothers who *would not* be parted. Bee had followed Baruk and stowed away. Ignacio, in on the secret, was gleeful. "A brother! Why didn't you tell me! Am I the only one you've told?" Baruk took Ignacio's hand and placed it over his heart. "Swear to me you will not tell."

"I swear on my life and yours," Ignacio said. Then, "What kind of brothers are you? Jacob and Esau? Cain and Abel? Are you rivals?" He laughed and Baruk told him, "Hush!"

Over the next weeks, while Baruk slept, his head cushioned on the wrapped packet of dolls Beatris had brought with her, she learned to repair broken instruments and cared for the goats in the hold and milked them and walked them on deck; she climbed in the rigging and served in the captain's cabin if the cabin boy was ill. In all this time, not one of the crew or officers appeared to notice the difference. It was too small a community for surprises. The sea and sky set the mood; the captain and the officers did the thinking. The men followed their trades, and the boys were well looked after if they were not troublesome. "We will make a sailor of you yet!" a trained seaman said to one of them. Then it would be the other's turn, and the bosun or second mate would cry, "Have you forgotten what I told you?" Nothing was expected but duty. No food went missing and only one hammock was slept in. If anyone thought there might be two boys instead of one, Ignacio was ready to deflect attention with his sharp fists and anger from identical, curly-headed, Baruk or Bee.

They arrived at Montevideo at the end of September and passed two months while the ships' crews, scientists, and artists were set to tasks, each in their own field or in support of the experts. *Descubierta*'s Captain Malaspina made mapping expeditions in a smaller vessel along the coast; the botanists and naturalists went on excursions for specimens; and researches were made into the material and economic resources of the region. Since Baruk had disclosed that he could read and write, he was sent to local archives and government offices to help catalogue and transport historic records selected by officers to be taken to Spain for study. Ignacio, who could not read, carried the packages, and protected his friend from the local gangs. Beatris, a ghost, slipped along behind them and made plans.

The ships were overhauled, and fresh supplies taken aboard. With the voyage set to resume, Beatris signed on as one of several local replacements for crew who had deserted. She had altered her appearance by shaving her head and donning local clothing stolen from the markets. She had starved herself until her cheekbones were chisel heads. Baruk, to help with the deception, let his hair grow puffed and tangled, and stuffed himself with fresh butter and meat, eating until his skin shone with grease. He was teased for the padding over his belly, but it made him more cheerful, and the sailors liked him the better for it. Fatty, dark Baruk, and Ignacio his sallow companion. It made crewmen smile to see them together. With Bee (as she was called) on board with a real job to do, and Baruk engaged in regular duties. Ignacio had no respite if he were to keep an eye on them both. Baruk and Ignacio muttered between hammocks, Ignacio sobbing or angry. He and Baruk were exhausted: Baruk, rarely allowed to sleep through the night; Ignacio, running himself down. Only Bee, nearby in a blanket and dreaming, slept well.

They rounded Cape Horn and worked their way up the west coast of South America to the harbour at Callao and paused to wait for the end of the rainy season. Both expedition ships required serious maintenance, and since they were to be in port for four months, the expedition commander, their own Captain Malaspina, obtained lodging for the crews on an isolated farm run by friars, away from the temptations of the settlement. This suited Bee, who worked in the gardens and was commended for it and was let off the more unpleasant jobs on ship. Thus, she was not present for the fire that broke out on a vessel anchored next to *Descubierta* close to where Baruk was working from a sling, making repairs to the ship's hull. The fire quickly took hold. Its flames leapt the gap between the ships and engulfed him; the ropes attaching the sling to the ship burned through and Baruk dropped on fire, into the sea.

Ignacio, as always nearby, plunged into the water, and swept Baruk into his arms.

"I cradled his head so he could breathe," Ignacio told Bee afterwards, "but his skin came away in sheets; he had no voice; he spoke to me with his eyes, and I held his head under the water until he died."

Ignacio was the only witness to the accident and the extent of Baruk's injuries, and so Beatris could not blame him. Moreover, Baruk was a good swimmer and strong, and could have escaped from Ignacio if he had wanted to. She took the news and went into the fields to be with the imported Andalusian horses that ambled and fed. They turned to look at her, and in that moment, she felt that she could summon whatever endured of her brother through the air so she would not be alone.

When they were children, Beatris, Baruk, their mother, and Dario were compelled, with others from the mountains and farms, to climb to the closest village not only to pay their tithes and taxes, but to watch a woman burned alive for witchcraft. Priests, officials, and soldiers made a ring around the summoned witnesses. "Let this be a lesson," the priest said signalling to the soldiers to light the pyre; and it was. Their mother, Inés, said to her children, "Count the number of sticks in the pile and tell me how many, and then commit the faces of the inquisitors to memory so you may find them again in the afterlife." Their mother did not believe in an afterlife and only spoke this way for whoever might happen to eavesdrop. Then she said, "Imagine you are looking from above, as from heaven, and that the woman's soul is leaving her body. Imagine that you can perceive its nature and follow it to its destination. The example of this soul will help you choose a wise way always." They did as they were told, and the rush of the woman's life sprang into the air as sweetly and as unlike as could be to the terror in the woman's screams.

Bee hoped this might have helped Baruk with his own sufferings. She raised her head and looked for him.

Instead, Ignacio, who had followed her, burst from his hiding place, took her in his arms and forced his leg between hers. "I am sure you wish to comfort me, Ignacio," she said and pulled away, "but this loss will not be allayed by you."

"Even a horse likes a dry stable in the rain," he said. She pushed him off with all her strength. He staggered and wept and shook but she ignored him. Bee was not to be the same to him as Baruk.

She did not cry at Baruk's funeral. "Do you not miss your friend and shipmate?" Frey Thomas asked. "Is your heart so hard at your young age that death cannot soften it? God will find a way to break you, Bee." The other young sailors sniffled and wiped away tears and took glances at each other to see who cried most. They peeped through spread fingers at Ignacio, Baruk's best friend. They only thought of themselves and of the gossip later, and not of Beatris's brother. In the mess that evening, one of the boys looked at Bee's softened, grief-fattened face, and saw its repertoire of emotions paint familiar expressions. "He has swallowed Baruk's ghost," the boy said aloud. But only that once because Ignacio slashed the speaker's cheek with his knife.

They left Callao behind and sailed north towards New Spain. On the way, Beatris, who missed her mountain home, began to find things to like about the ocean; and when she was not busy, she stood at the rails. The colour of the water changed from grey to green to dark turquoise. Golden serpents propelled their muscular bodies through the currents; shining green turtles paddled and lagged. Every day, the ship was joined by pods of whales or dolphins which raced alongside or in front of the bow. Sea birds lodged in the rigging and watched and commentated. One day, as Bee worked on deck polishing brass fittings, the ship's naturalist, Tadeo, set his drawing board and paper on his knees and began to sketch the birds in graphite. He drew a petrel, one wing dipped, in flight.

"The head is too small and the tail's not right," Bee said impulsively. Tadeo covered the drawing with his arm. "Oh no!" she cried. "You will smudge it!"

"It is only a sketch. You know something about birds, do you?" He said it nicely, as if he thought Bee might. His brown hair, stringy from salt, straggled and blew over his collar from beneath a leather hat. He had tied the hat down under his chin with a string. His narrow cheeks flushed to his sideburns. She stooped, embarrassed to have spoken, and resumed her task of polishing the rails, but he insisted. "Please, I am interested."

"Not birds," she said and shook her head. "I claim no knowledge of them."

"What then," he asked, "Wherein lies your expertise?"

"Horses," she said, "but I am good at noticing, and I have excellent eyesight."

"Well then, tell me what else I have got wrong."

She checked his expression before answering. "You have missed the fork in its tail and the legs tucked against the body—you can hardly see them as it dives."

"No doubt that must be true," he murmured.

She put out her hand for the drawing tool. "May I?" With the graphite holder in her fingers, she made a quick sketch of the petrel in one corner of Tadeo's paper. "Like that."

He assessed it. "You are no artist, but you have caught the details." He rubbed his chin. "I wonder."

"Sir?"

"Would you help me? Be my eyes? I have no problem close to, but at a distance … I miss things. I could ask the captain."

"Yes sir, I would like that very much," Bee said.

"Have I seen you before? I am not sure."

"I signed on at Montevideo. The boy who died at Callao," she said, "he came from the same part of Spain. I have been told of a resemblance."

"Yes," Tadeo said. "That must be it. I was sorry to hear of his death. We lose too many." He would have asked a question, but she said, "Begging your pardon, sir, I had best get to work."

"I will not keep you from your duties; thank you for your interest in my drawing. I will speak to the captain this evening."

With Tadeo gone, Ignacio stepped from behind a ship's boat that was tied on deck. "I will not let anything happen to you," he said.

"What could happen?"

But Ignacio simply shook his head and smiled.

At Acapulco, the expedition commander received instructions compelling him to alter plans. Instead of heading west for the Hawaiian Islands, he was to sail north to search for the Strait of Anian, the passage said to have been used by Maldonado two hundred years earlier, to voyage between the Pacific and Atlantic oceans. Russian, British, and American activity in the North Pacific threatened Spain's control: if such a passage existed, it was essential that Spain find it first. Consequently, the two ships reprovisioned and sailed the coast to Maldonado's co-ordinates, contending with many squalls and much wind, or else completely becalmed. They explored a coast of ice bordered with dense pine forests and snowcapped mountains and ventured into icebound cul-de-sacs where they met glaciers plunging to the sea. Failing to find anything but a massive wall of ice-covered rock at the terminus of the most promising channel, they buried a bottle containing a record of their survey, to mark possession of the coast in the name of the King of Spain. The captain named the island "Tadeo" after the expedition naturalist. After a further evaluation of the region, they turned southeast and set sail for the newly re-established Spanish settlement at Nootka Sound.

During this part of the voyage, Beatris began her first bleeding. It was brought on by the fresh fish and meat the crew consumed, and the wine given to help them withstand the cold. In the wine, Beatris tasted the salt marshes and sea urchins of the Spanish coastal river mouths, as well as an echo of the womanly smell that clung to her. To mask the odour, she dressed in filthy clothing left behind by a crewman who'd deserted in Acapulco, and threw her own overboard, claiming they carried the miasma of fever. If she had to accompany a party to gather wood or water, she kept to herself, and undertook small tasks for Tadeo so she could secretly bury her bloody rags and gather animal dung. She stored the droppings wrapped in a pouch of possessions she wore around her waist. She starved herself—privation was not difficult for her—and with the lessening of fat, she became, once more, like a child.

At one of their landings, they blundered upon a place where bodies of the dead were confined in decorated boxes. Ignacio hissed at her to help him and his party with the lifting of a sarcophagus to be taken on board. He was eager, always eager, to engage in whispers, but she turned aside, disturbed by the idea that anyone might be treated after death in this way. (Baruk was ash and bone in the sea, safe from plunderers.)

Among the trees, in the undergrowth, wild celery and chamomile grew along with some other plants she thought might be medicinal. She took samples of these for the naturalist. Tucked among the rocks and near the deer paths, she found patches of wild strawberries. She picked as many as she could carry in the folds of her shirt and took them to the sailors in the wood party. They helped themselves and thanked her, but one tapped her on the shoulder and said, "These are small but sweet. You had best be careful who you give your presents to."

Ignacio was in the ship's boat with several others returning to land after having stored the coffin onboard ship. She dumped the balance of the strawberries into the water, and they swirled and dispersed.

The ships neared an area of scattered islands in the vicinity of Nootka Sound. The sea was green, the mountain chain it bordered was tall, forbidding, and shadowy. Wherever an inlet opened to the waves, surf crashed onto the beaches. Bee's eyes were in demand: she scanned for reefs and shoals and helped the naturalist identify and describe the life that swam or flew near them.

"You must understand," Frey Thomas said as he joined them at the rail, "God has designed the universe for a purpose; the Earth is a mirror of the human body. The hard places such as these mountains you see, replicate the bones; further south with less rock and more earth, the landscape imitates flesh."

"Why would this be?" Tadeo asked.

"The reasons are God's alone," Frey Thomas said, "but the order of things in evidence over unnumbered leagues is witness to Creation, not accident. It is the work and wisdom of Divine Providence."

He left them; his long skirt pasted to his fat legs by the wind.

Tadeo smiled at Bee. "What do you think about what you see around you?" he said. "What part of the body are these islands of such various sizes?"

Bee said, thinking of the landscape in which she had grown, "The islands seem to be mountain peaks with the rest below the waves. This is how they look from above, their tops poking through clouds."

"From above?" the naturalist asked. "I suppose … from the highest peaks you must look down at the clouds? I have never seen this for myself."

"Sunshine and clear skies are the hallmarks of summits. The clouds mask what is below."

Frey Thomas had circled the deck.

"I believe an earthquake submerged the land," Tadeo said—he could not see the approaching friar—"and that the land once ran a greater distance out to sea, even as far as Asia."

The priest clapped Tadeo's shoulder and spun him around. "Only the earthquake that occurred at the death of Our Lord Jesus Christ could have been of such force as to separate continents," he said. "If it did so in this forsaken land, it was God's judgment on the inhabitants."

"Sir, look!" Bee cried and pointed out to sea. In the distance were many whales—more than they had seen together before—blowing, breaching, and diving.

"We had best tell the captain," Tadeo said. "Such unrest amongst whales is often the precursor to storms."

While they waited for the weather to change, they crossed a thick swath of an unusual orange plant. After the naturalist had some of it drawn aboard to preserve, the wind blew in from the southeast bringing heavy rainfall. The roaring of the wind grew stronger; waves boiled higher and higher until the ship had to run with only the foresail. For three whole days they were buffeted and swamped. Then, as suddenly as it had arisen the wind abated, and the sky cleared of clouds and fog: the world was clean and new.

Many of the sailors, wet and cold and shaken, knelt with Frey Thomas on deck and thanked God for their deliverance: but not the naturalist or the captain, and not Bee who busied herself helping the carpenter with repairs. She noted, and thought it would have made Baruk laugh to see, that the same sailors who had cursed and blasphemed during the storm were those who scraped their knees on the boards and prayed loudly in safety.

They approached the coastline of islands, islets, inlets, and channels anew. Pines covered outcrops and low-lying points of land. The sea was flecked with foam. White birds flew from it like spray, and eagles hunted the waters and flung wide silhouettes over the ship. Late in the afternoon, Bee stood lookout at the bow and watched for the navigation point where they would set a bearing for the settlement at Nootka.

She was about to call out when she noticed an object on their portside, nearly lost in the buffeting waves. She could not make out what it was, but since it splashed in circles it was clearly alive. It was too small for a whale but larger than the seals and sea lions they often encountered. She puzzled over it, alerted the naturalist who looked at it in his turn, and he sped to ask the captain for permission to launch a boat and investigate. The boat was let down, and half a dozen crewmen, including Ignacio along with Tadeo and Bee, rowed towards the swimming animal. By now, Beatris knew what it was; soon they drew near, and all could see for themselves that—improbably far from shore—it was a horse.

Green and white foam blew from the top of the waves. The horse's nostrils rose with the crests and fell in the troughs, flecked with bloody pink foam. Its long cream neck stretched like a serpent's; its eyes rolled in terror. Without a moment's thought, Bee stood up in the longboat and dove into the water. She heard a shout from the others and then the cold slammed her chest, and she sank into a closed and dark world. Baruk was there, *Beatris*, he said. He tried to embrace her, but the horse's legs thrashed in the way. Her head broke free of the swells and she was at the animal's side. She grabbed its mane and let the horse feel the drag of her weight. One of its wild watery blue eyes caught sight of her, and she spoke to it softly of the green pastures she would take it to if only it would trust her. She felt its exhaustion and pitied its struggle, although the numbness in her body told her that she, too, was running out of strength.

"A rope! Throw a rope!" she called to the men in the boat. In a moment, one was flung. She slipped the loop over the horse's head and around its neck, hauled herself onto its back, held on and waved the longboat onward to a beach on which waves were breaking in a low white line. The men rowed, the horse with Bee on it swimming behind. The animal listened to her despite its fear, following the lead of her body; but she felt its life-force ebb. There was no telling how long it had been in the water. But it caught the scent of grass and forest and renewed its efforts until Bee cast it free of the rope and swam with the horse into the shallows.

"We come to an open door," Beatris's mother had told her. "If we pass through, we cannot change our minds." Her mother had stood at the door on the battlefield and turned aside. Beatris lay on the sand, sensible of the animal gasping for breath beside her. Through the open door, she could see a fire burning in a grate and its reflection flickering on the presences convened around it: if any had beckoned to her, she would have joined them, but they would not look her way. She took a second to search among them for Baruk and for her father—the man who had given her curled black hair and slender limbs—but could find neither of them, their spirits too restless, perhaps for such idleness. She opened her eyes and rested, shivering, a tumble of coin-sized clouds overhead.

The longboat, which had not been able to land, swept on.

Beyond a stretch of sand and shell and small stones, a band of tall grass strewn with bleached wood extended into an open forest of pine and cedar. The horse staggered to its feet, went to the grass, put its head down and ate.

The sky was streaked red and navy, and the sea had turned purple by the time a woman wearing a bark robe emerged from the trees and came towards her. She helped Bee up and spoke to her. She gave her water. Bee did not understand although Spanish words glittered like gold coins, like *reales*, in her speech. Beatris thought of the wet shirt and trousers she wore—the woman undoubtedly knew what she was—but as it dried the cloth fell in such thick folds, Bee believed she could keep her secret secure from those who knew her as a boy. The woman (little more than a girl, like Bee) helped her onto the horse and stayed beside her, the sea a constant on their right, and in the sky a glimpse of stars, until they could see the little Spanish settlement. Then she slipped away. Both expedition ships lay at anchor with only the lookouts' lanterns showing. The longboat was beached above the tide line. The instant Bee and the horse were noticed, men ran from their dwellings with lamps to guide them, and soon Bee, fainting, was in their charge.

Ignacio jostled with the rest calling, "What's wrong with him? What is it, is he dying?"

But Tadeo had arrived to ease Bee down from the horse and warm her in a blanket. "He cannot walk, I will carry him," he said, and shouldered the others away.

Bee's head lolled in weakness, and Ignacio said again, his voice thick with excitement, "Is he dying?"

"He's not going to die," Tadeo said. Ignacio kept pace alongside.

"The other one died," Ignacio said.

The naturalist said more, firmly, "He will be all right, he is young."

They tried to take Bee indoors and undress her, but she fought and said she would not be separated from the horse. "He is given to me," she cried, "I must take care of him!"

"It is a soul horse," someone said. "It comes from the drowned."

"That is contrary to reason," Tadeo said. "It broke free from the hold of a ship damaged in the storm."

"What ship? We saw no ship," someone said.

"An American ship most likely, since they recently traded here."

"And had no horses with them, either!"

"Then it was another! A Russian ship. The Russians have horses on this coast. The horse could have come from anywhere."

"The boy may harm himself if he is not given his way," said the settlement doctor, who had bustled his way to them. "The cold water has affected his brain; I have seen this before. The trouble will ease if he is treated kindly and not held responsible for anything he might say in his delirium."

It was mid-August. Star candles fell from the Pleiades, and the air was warm, and Bee was permitted, at last, to lie in the open.

"I will sit with him," Tadeo said.

"No, I will," Ignacio said, but Tadeo sent him away.

Bee awoke at dawn, shed the blanket, and quickly tugged her damp clothing into order. The horse was on its feet, staked loosely nearby. She felt for injuries and swellings in its legs and feet.

Tadeo had slept on the ground nearby. He braced himself on an elbow. "You will have to name him," he said.

Bee stroked the horse's neck. "His name is Rigel." It was the name of Baruk's horse. She turned to the naturalist. "I must thank you for your help. I am sorry I caused you trouble."

Tadeo yawned and folded his blanket. "We had only just organized a search party and held out little hope for your rescue. You were seen in the waves; your head went under." He paused. "I would have been sorry to lose you, Bee. You show promise and are quick to learn. Those waves, and the currents—we were told that all who are taken by them perish. It is not common for sailors to swim." He looked at Bee with questions he did not voice.

"Today you must rest, but you will soon be restored to health and duties," he said. "When you are well, you can help with the collection of plants. You will surely find some I may miss." He smiled. "We need to dry a good quantity to add to our stores and those of the garrison that must spend the winter here. Heavy rains destroyed their work on the vegetable gardens last season, and their dry food was devoured by rats. If it had not been for the Mowachaht people's gifts of deer meat and fish, more than the nine who died would have perished. Fortunately," Tadeo gestured to land that was recently cleared and planted, "the new gardens flourish."

Bee looked at the plots of beans, peas, potatoes, lettuces, radishes, and maize. Several hens wandered nearby.

"They are building storehouses to protect against the rats, and houses for the men; the hospital is finished. So, you see ..."

What else she was to see was not evident, other than Tadeo's habitual optimism.

The settlement stirred. Parties rowed in from the anchored ships on which most of the company of several hundred were bivouacked. Doors opened in the soldiers' barracks.

The thirty or so men who lived in them, the remnant after the illnesses and deaths of the winter (the sick had been sent to Monterey; others were absent on exploratory voyages), came and went to the latrines, and to and from the mess. A party under the supervision of the expedition commander began to erect an observatory tent and a viewing platform on the beach, and to install the pendulums, barometer, and other instruments necessary for the recording of weather and celestial conditions. Ignacio went with another group, overseen by the ships' carpenters, to cut a new mast for the longboat. Its mast had cracked from the strain of the tow rope tied to the horse and Beatris during the attempted rescue.

"I have yet to make my report," Tadeo said, "but I have noted the good local timber the soldiers use." He was one of the younger officers, but he looked tired and worn. "You should attend to Rigel. Go past the gardens and you'll find the well. Beyond it is a meadow where he can graze while I see if there is hay. I'll ask the blacksmith for materials to make a harness. I assume you know what to do?"

Bee nodded.

"We will need a place to stable him. I'll see to that, too." He paused. "What you did yesterday was foolish, but brave. Well …" He brushed sand and earth from his clothing and put on the battered leather hat he habitually wore and walked away.

After Rigel drank his fill, Bee took him to the meadow and hobbled him. She skittered down a bank to a west-facing beach of pale sand and shells with a littering of driftwood. Sea wrack popped in the sun. Tiny green and gold, black, white, and purple stones shone where the waves lapped. Obsidian black nearby islets were ribboned with the white lace of breaking waves: beyond these swept the unbroken line of the horizon that cut the world. She lay on the sand and listened to the calls of sea birds.

Bee heard footsteps, lifted her head and watched Frey Tomas make his way across the seashore. Behind him, a boy of nine or ten jogged along the beach, challenging the waves. Bee waited.

"Bee!" the priest called as he huffed up. "God has seen fit to restore you to life. Let us give thanks to Him!" Bee scrambled to her feet, but Frey Tomas sank to his knees and pulled her down beside him. He finished praying and leveraged himself to his feet using her shoulder for support. The boy approached and tugged at the priest's robes: the priest smiled down at him.

Then he glanced at Rigel in the field at the top of the bank. "We were told of your mysterious sea-beast, Bee. May we come near the creature?" The priest climbed the slope without waiting for her answer. Bee followed. "A gift from God, or the Devil?" He reached for the horse, but Rigel backed and tossed his head. "Ah ha," the priest said to the horse, "even the Devil won't get far on you with your legs tied!"

The boy approached, too, and before Bee could deter him, he stepped forward and leaned into Rigel's flank. Bee feared for him: the horse was trembling. She touched the boy's shoulder; it too was shaking. The foolhardy child was living on his nerves. She calmed the horse and held onto the boy and spoke to him softly and eased him away from the animal.

"What is the boy's name?" she asked the priest.

"Someone brought him here, and the men took him in. They call him Primo." A silence stretched between them. Before they left Mexico, the commander had made clear to the priests, and to everyone else, that he disliked the practice of removing children from their families. A number of girls and boys had already been sent from the island to San Blas and more to Monterey, each acquired for a shotgun or musket or a few sheets of copper. Bee recalled the commander saying, "Most of them die within months."

"Has he no family?" The boy wore a European shirt with sleeves cut short; the shirt tails dragged between his bare legs. "Surely, he must be restored to them."

"The men say they paid for him," the priest said. "If we did not take him, he would be a slave or killed or worse." He leaned close and hissed into her ear. "He has seen terrible things."

"What things?" Bee asked.

The priest shook his head. "It is a charity to take them."

Bee bent down to the child. "Are you thirsty?" She mimed drinking. He nodded. She left the priest with the horse and took the boy to the well, drew water and gave him a drink. He gulped it quickly, but when the cup was nearly empty, he spilled water on her and placed his thin-fleshed hand on her damp breast.

Over the next weeks, the commander sent out mapping parties which were to try to contact the Mowachaht. Except for the few who were employed at the settlement, they had absented themselves to villages scattered along the Sound, although this meant relinquishing their summer village and principal food source at Friendly Cove. Traditionally, they had built racks to dry salmon on the beaches close to their most important fishing grounds, but now the Spanish had constructed their naval base in this place. Two years previously, a Spanish officer had killed the chief's brother in an episode never adequately explained and which had fractured the relationship between Mowachaht and Spanish. Part of the expedition remit Tadeo explained, while he and Bee collected spruce tips and needles to make a beer to treat settlement men ill with rheumatism and scurvy (their bent bodies and disfigured joints aroused everyone's pity), was to mend the trading relationship between Spain and the Mowachaht people. Spain's security on the coast lay in it. The Spanish intended to stay.

The arrival of English, American, and other foreign fur trading vessels a few years earlier had resulted in bloody conflicts with the Mowachaht and considerable loss of life. And there persisted a longstanding history of violent molestation of Mowachaht women by sailors of every nation. All this Tadeo reported to Bee as they combed the fringes of beaches and boundaries of thick forest and noted plants distinct from European species.

The days were hot and windless; mosquitoes and flies plagued their eyes and nostrils. Bee worried about Rigel who she often left tethered on his own. Only at night, having shut him into a hut they'd enlarged into a stable at the margin of the gardens, did she not worry he'd be attacked by wild animals. The men spoke of bears, wolves, and pumas.

"Did you know, Bee," Tadeo said as they continued cutting branches, "one of the Mowachaht men told us to wrap the pelts we buy from them with wild rosemary. If we do, they will be better preserved for the markets in Canton. We have much to learn from these people. I intend to ask them about their medicines."

"You would trust them, sir?"

"They live and thrive and do not suffer as we do in this climate: do you not think they have something to teach us? The commander has urged them to live near the settlement. He promised it would be forbidden for sailors to go to their homes. But the chief said he feared the soldiers would solicit their women, and he preferred the discomfort and privation of their present existence even though it meant they could not prepare enough food for the winter. Hunger was better than the depredations inflicted by our men.

"It is a terrible thing to believe we could behave like animals to those for whom we are obliged to care."

Tadeo transferred cut branches into large canvas bags. "We Europeans have spread syphilis among them, Bee. It was unknown before our arrival. Many have died of it, and many more will. These people may have different customs to us, but I am sorry to think any Spaniard, even of the lowest class, could harm any woman."

Oh Tadeo, Bee thought, *how can I tell you anything*?

In the mess, Bee had listened as crews spoke of what had been done to Mowachaht women by sailors from visiting ships. Within the hearing of the officers, the settlement soldiers asserted that they had never taken part in anything similar, but afterwards, Primo led Bee to the blacksmith's workshop and simulated pulling her inside and shutting the door and burning her with red-hot tongs. He touched the wad of leather she wore under her breeches to suggest manhood and shook his head. "*Madre*," he said. She pushed him away. Clearly, *he* knew she was a woman, but Primo lived in the settlement on sufferance, dependent on the goodwill of others for every morsel. No one need take him seriously. Bee's experience on the ship had taught her that sailors ignored suggestions of trouble as long as they could. Besides, Primo would soon be leaving with other purchased children for Monterey or San Blas. Whatever the commander had to say about the practice of acquiring children, the priests were a law unto themselves.

Bee and Tadeo carried the bags of branches to the beach, and Tadeo supervised the organization of vats in which to simmer the cuttings for brewing. The fires needed to be kept burning day and night. They took first watch. While doing so, Tadeo asked Bee to label the specimens they had gathered earlier and dried.

"You write well," he said while reviewing her work. "Few of the other boys are literate."

"It was my mother's doing," she said. To say this, risked questions. Literacy was rare in ordinary Christian homes; it was primarily a Moorish practice. What Beatris's mother knew, she'd learned while in captivity and passed on to her children; but Tadeo simply nodded. His hands were blistered, and his arms were scratched from toiling in thick vegetation. He went to the shore and washed his hurts in the sea. "To prevent infection," he said shaking his hands dry. "You must do the same." He spoke as if to a friend.

"I believe that you will understand, Bee, why I say we have a duty to bring peace, civilization, and prosperity with us. The commander directs that nothing can be allowed which would contradict the inalienable rights of any of those we encounter whether Mowachaht or others. Inalienable rights, Bee. The same as belong to you and me and to every man."

But not to women, Tadeo, she longed to say; but only harm could come from speaking the truth.

"Cruelty may live in everyone, as we too often see, but we do not need to nurture it. I abhor cruelty above all else." Tadeo paused and brushed sand from his clothing. "We are adjured to meet higher principles. Is that not also what the priests preach?"

After she had finished the labelling, placed the specimens in dry storage, and Tadeo had gone, Beatris fed the fire and maintained an eye on the level of water in the vats until a boy arrived to relieve her. By then it was night. The others were in the mess or on board the ships. Taking all the time she could, her face lifted to the rain of the stars, she walked to the field to fetch Rigel and then stabled and fed him. Not everyone approved of the time she spent with the horse or that she was permitted to sleep in the stable. She had overheard a sailor comment as she passed by with Rigel, "The spirit horse has possessed him; he lives in another world; it would be well to be rid of it before it infects us all." The sailor spat on the ground behind them.

A few days later, they finished distilling the spruce liquor, ladled the vats of its essence into casks, and carried them to a storeroom to ferment. "With luck," Tadeo said, "that will see the soldiers through the winter without a reoccurrence of scurvy. Still, I do not envy them the coming months." He secured the door, and they stepped out into the noon sun.

The day was hot. Tadeo removed his hat and wiped his forehead. He looked tired and thin. Did he have worries he kept to himself? She left him resting in the shade of a tree while she drew water, first for Rigel and then filled cups for Tadeo and herself.

"Why did you join the expedition, Bee?" Tadeo asked. "Will you tell me?" He drank the water she had brought him and leaned against the tree-trunk with his eyes closed. She sat nearby.

"There was nothing for me at home," she said after a moment's thought.

"Many voyage because of poverty or other reasons," he said, "and yet good may come of it."

He told her that he had trained in medicine, natural history, geography, art, anthropology, and volcanology, but that he was a scholar who had grown restless. "For me as well," he said, "home offered few opportunities." He paused, "Or those I had, were not what I wanted."

"Perhaps some are born restless," Bee said.

"Do you think so? Unless it is selfishness." He opened his eyes. "We leave friends and family, sometimes never to see them again. Most often it is they who pay the price. What about your family?"

Since Baruk's death, and the impossibility of her returning to her old life in Spain—where would she go, what would she do, who could she be?—she considered herself to be alone. "I have none, sir," she said. Tadeo nodded. Loneliness as well as poverty drove many boys into a career at sea.

"To this date, I have catalogued several thousand botanical specimens on my journeys. Each is neatly, if not artistically," he smiled, "drawn and carefully housed, along with its seeds and flowers. You have seen my sketches of birds and mammals and of the local people. I could never have accomplished this work on my own without the help and teaching of others.

"You have promise in this field, Bee. Your eyesight, memory, and powers of observation are unusual. I could train you, formally, as my assistant if you so wished."

"Sir!" Bee exclaimed. Bee did so wish; that is, the boy, Bee, wished. For Beatris, the girl, such training would not be possible.

"Shortly before joining the expedition, I was shipwrecked and cast onto an island where I survived until a passing ship rescued me," he told her. "Before it came, if it had not been for my training, I might easily have given way to despair.

"I tell you these things about myself, young Bee, to point to my good fortune. God has preserved me, certainly." He glanced at Frey Tomas passing by with Primo. "Yet, I also believe that in some part, we mould our own fate. Fate includes study and hard work and the help of those who can gauge our potential. I have offered to help you. However, you must be careful. Your ordeal in the sea may have affected your brain. This is due to no weakness of yours, but your brain, like all brains, is malleable and subject to external influences. You must try not to let your thoughts darken. I have spoken to the commander. If all is well, you will commence your apprenticeship with me in Mexico."

"Sir!" she said again. He stood.

"We must continue our work: we have little time left and much to do." He replaced his hat on his head. "One further piece of advice, if you will permit me.

Just as we find happiness in belonging to a family, and take pleasure in enterprises that benefit that family, so in this period of separation from home, your shipmates become your family. You must endeavour not to be too much on your own, regardless of its being for the sake of the horse. Have in mind that we are engaged in an enterprise which may enlighten the world and that the wellbeing of all depends on the wellbeing of every one of us."

The naturalist spoke sincerely. Beatris looked into his eyes and believed him. It was not good for her to be alone; she needed to be part of a family; and yet it was not possible. Her safety depended on her ability to keep herself at a distance. A slip in attendance to her monthly needs; a few extra pounds that filled out her breasts; an occasion when Ignacio dug at her soul, and she could not deflect him; or an accident that resulted in the removal of her clothing—and her secret would be revealed. Disaster had already come breathtakingly close. Sooner or later, Beatris would have to live as herself, and it could not be as Tadeo's apprentice. He was too straightforward in nature to understand what she had done. She needed to hold out long enough for the ship to reach California where she would find a way to disappear. Yet, the place in which love could reside in Bee, vacant since Baruk's death, yearned emptily. If she were not careful, she would ask Tadeo to fill it anyway. Beatris lowered her gaze.

"Well, think over what I have said, Bee. I will not try to persuade you."

Ignacio was often away with the exploratory parties. It was a relief to Beatris who had begun to dream about his drowning of Baruk and to imagine in daylight, his breath on the nape of her neck only to turn and find no one. She did not invent his interest in her. He left signs—the letter B laid out in stones on her blanket, or a feather in the folds of her spare shirt that matched a feather he wore tucked into his belt. Ignacio: catching her eye and conveying a message she did not want to receive.

Those left behind while the rest ventured afield, carried out projects of mutual assistance between the settlement men and the visitors. In gratitude for the expedition's gift of a Reaumur scale thermometer to assist with accurate meteorological measurements, the settlement men dug new wells and filled the expedition ships' water barrels, drawing heavily on one of their scarcest resources, fresh water. As the time of departure neared, goods that the expedition ships could spare were unloaded and put into settlement warehouses: vital supplies such as broth tablets and flour and medicines and wine; also cloth, utensils, cigarette papers, and gun parts. No one in the expedition begrudged these gifts; they had only pity in their hearts for those they would leave behind to face cold and loneliness when the ships' companies were safe and warm in Mexico.

Bee stood at the door of the mess as darkness fell and inspected the activity on the beach. A vat of boiling pitch was being used to waterproof planking. Primo, the priest, and Ignacio were in attendance. Ignacio, newly returned from an exploratory party, saw her and hurried up the path. She could have slipped away, eluding him for the moment, but they were bound to meet occasionally, and it was unlikely he would trouble her in the open.

"I brought this for you," he said, catching his breath. He unwrapped a stick-like grey object from a cloth. He watched her expectantly.

She turned it over. "What is it?"

"I took it from a pile of bones in the chief's village."

"Then it doesn't belong to you, and I don't want it." She tried to give it back, but he would not take it.

"I risked my life for you. Don't you see? I was lucky no one saw me."

She turned and entered the mess, but he followed her.

"I want to make things easier; let me help you with the horse. It's what Baruk would want!"

"You have too much to do as it is, Ignacio." She sat on a bench with the sailors and placed the bone to one side where she thought it was unobserved. But the sailmaker, a red-faced Basque, saw, picked it up, and flourished it.

"It is as I told you." He pointed to the roughly cut end of what Bee realized, too late, was a human bone. "You can tell it has been hacked off. Take care or we will end the same!" The object passed from man to man with growing murmurs. She looked for Ignacio, but he had fled. Before Beatris, too, could leave, Primo climbed onto her lap and settled against her breasts.

She stood so quickly that he fell to the floor. Primo blinked through his tears. He got to his knees, smiled at her and began the repertoire he had learned to please the men, crossing his eyes and trying to talk like the foreign traders. The men, their attention diverted by his antics, laughed and clapped and whistled. Primo spotted the bone where it lay on the table and dropped it onto Bee's plate.

Thus, it is that one misunderstanding leads to another.

Tadeo came into the room, attracted by the noise. He observed the plate and the bone, and in the silence that fell, said to Bee, "I cannot conceive how you came by this, but it belonged to a human being. I ask you, in all decency, to return it to its place of origin. Its possession will give offence to those to whom we should be friends. We have spoken of this." He regarded Bee sadly.

He looked round at the others, last of all the priest, who had also entered. In the candlelight, the naturalist's eyes were sunken and dark; his profile fell along the wall. "We are all—all of us in this company—men committed to science: do you think the commander and I and the other officers have not investigated the rumoured charge of cannibalism?

"We did not find that people here conduct themselves any more improperly than our troops who take trophies in battle. Which among you, who have fought against the Moors have not kept a blackened finger or ear in their kit for good luck?" Such a prize, as Beatris knew, might have come from her own father. Tadeo enclosed the bone in his handkerchief. "I will see to this myself," he said, "and I will tell the commander who is responsible."

The night burned raw with scent: the bushes around the camp were heavy with berries; to this was added the tang of salt and pitch. As Bee reached the perimeter of the gardens and Rigel's stable, the odour of rotted meat that characterized the human waste from the latrines, joined the mix.

She had just reached the horse when a noise behind her made her turn. Ignacio stood so near that within the darkness she could see his grin. He said to her, as he had frequently, "Before he died, Baruk asked me to take care of you. Why won't you listen?"

"You are a liar," she said this time, wretched at what Tadeo must think of her, angry at Ignacio for giving her the bone in the first place, and unwilling to indulge him further. "Baruk would never have said that. My brother hated you. He told me over and over. It was a joke between us. I am still his brother, and you—you are nothing." Ignacio leapt back as if she had struck him. She pushed past and jumped onto Rigel with only a rope for a halter and kicked the horse into motion. She should not have said what she did: doing so took away what was best in Ignacio—the belief that he had been loved. But Bee did not care about Ignacio and his countenance damaged with pain. She only cared for her wounded feelings.

Beatris had ridden Rigel along the shore and scrambled him through the beach grass and into the periphery of the pine forest regularly, always taking care not to penetrate too far inland and into the territory of wild animals. This evening, she gave Rigel free rein. He galloped the length of the beach until spooked by a wave that crashed against his legs, he veered into the forest. She clung to him and kept her head down; the pines gave way to a dead zone of moss-hung hemlock, followed by widely spaced cedars. Ridges of bark and low branches scraped her skin as he charged ahead, and then the undergrowth thinned and Rigel pelted through a wall of thick bush, his hooves picking a trail she could not see. She smelled fresh water, the tang of old copper, and a moment later they burst through the brush and onto the verge of a small lake.

In this season—the end of summer and before the fall rains—fresh water was hauled bucket by bucket from the wells. The men drank what they needed, washed with the balance, and poured the filthy dregs into irrigation ditches for the gardens. If they bathed at all, it was in the sea, but this was pure lake water at no great distance! Were the troubles of transporting it insurmountable? Or could such a resource have been kept from them? It would not be difficult. Near as the lake was, the settlement soldiers' routine was to watch over the trading practices of the nations which sailed into the territory, and to occupy themselves with wood cutting, gardening, ship repair, and building for their own needs. They had constructed lines and squares and circles in the landscape to correspond to these pursuits—paths to the wood cutting areas, the squares of the houses and gardens, the circle inhabited by the range of the guns on the rocks at the harbour's entrance. For the most part, they ignored the thickly wooded inland, and travelled by sea. The interior of the island was thought to be impenetrable, of no interest beyond the supply of timber on its fringes.

Bee slipped from the horse and waited at the water's edge while the horse bent its neck and drank. If she announced the news of this finding at the settlement, might Tadeo forgive her? No, his opinion of her was altered forever. He believed her to be callous, heartless towards those for whom, as he'd told her, they were accountable, his disappointment magnified by the high opinion he'd formerly had of her. It would have been better if he had never singled her out.

The days were long, and full nightfall was slow to arrive. The lake lay spread between forests and ended at a low line of hills to the west. Pale water shimmered around Rigel's legs and shaded into indigo and violet. Slowly, light sieved from the sky and a pointed dullness lengthened into the depths as the air stilled. A few dragonflies paddled the lake's calm. Beatris was conscious of the gravel underfoot, deer stepping from the undergrowth to drink, gnats seeking the warmth of her skin, and black flies biting the horse's neck. But on the helter-skelter ride, she'd left thought and worry and constant vigilance behind.

It was a trick of the hour and of disorientation and emotional tumult, doubtless, but as a mist thickened over the water, she felt it did so for her. She sluffed off her clothes and the pouch she wore beneath them, piled stones over it all and waded into the water until the vapour reached her shoulders and she could surrender to its cool silk. The horse swam with her. She felt light, in her own skin for the first time since leaving home masquerading as a boy.

Good swimmer that she was, she retained a perception of her surroundings although she could not see them and was always aware of the nearness of the horse. That is, until she reached for it, and it had gone.

She pivoted her body, creating a swirl of ripples, thinking that the horse would sense what she did and find her; but it did not, and so she swam in and lay in the muddy shallows and listened. All was quiet, but as she watched she noticed movement in the brush nearest the water's edge. She slithered into deep water and pulled the white blanket of mist over her. She was far out in the lake, as far as she had ever swum alone anywhere, when she heard Ignacio cry, "Bee! Come back! Bee!" Her heart was beating so strongly that it pulsed the water at her neck. Then a piping voice, mimicking, rang out. "Bee! Bee!" It was Primo.

The idea of their joined forces sickened her. It was unlikely the first time the two spies had tracked her—Bee had been alone less often than she'd imagined. She let her legs drop, trod water, and willed herself not to fear the unknown in the depths below. Primo on his own was no danger, she could manage him, was already doing so. Ignacio was a different matter. In his anger at learning the truth that she and Baruk had kept from him, he would make sure she was punished and exiled; or, if not that, relish the power he had over her. Either way, the prospect was unbearable.

But was it certain he had divined her secret?

He could have watched her enter the water, but she'd been shielded by mist and darkness. Was it possible he was merely worried because she'd been in the water for some time? That he had no idea she was a woman? If she waited until he and Primo believed her drowned, all might yet be well. Once they left, she would retrieve her garments, find Rigel, and vanish. A search might be made for her, but Ignacio would say little if anything about the circumstances of her disappearance in case it raised questions. Like, why had he followed her? And had he harmed her himself?

What she needed was patience.

The commander had orders to sail as soon as possible. He could not long delay, whoever went missing. The approaching change of season would bring high winds and danger to his ships and crews. Thus, if she concealed her whereabouts until the ships went, she could stumble into the settlement afterwards with a story of being lost. She had no doubt that she and the horse would survive; best of all, she need never see Primo or Ignacio again.

Her thoughts ran on. Tadeo might grieve if he thought she was dead, but his grief would be mixed with relief that she had revealed her true nature—over the matter of the bone—before she became his apprentice. *She* could be grateful that she no longer needed to maintain a life of lies in front of him. He deserved better; he had believed in her abilities. That treasure she could always cherish.

Beatris floated and listened and tried to recollect the shape of the lake as she had seen it at twilight, and to hear where water touched land, and gauge where she was. The clock of the sky ticked past. She idled until a breeze swept the mist away and raised waves that splashed and faltered. By the time she reached the cover of vegetation at the limit of the slough, the mist was banished, and waves and wind had declined. She hauled herself behind a fallen log and lay still.

Ignacio gazed lakeward; Primo played with stones. Then, from the slate depths of the water, the horse reared up, snorted, blew foam from its mouth and nostrils, churned froth and debris, and climbed onto land. It shook itself free of the wet.

Beatris's cry of shock was smothered by the shouts of Primo and Ignacio, and by the slowing engine of Rigel's fiery breathing as the horse calmed. It was a moment's work for Ignacio to grab hold of the rope looped over the horse's neck and lead Rigel away with Primo trotting after. Ignacio's glance over his shoulder to where Bee thought herself concealed was a spear to its target. Even with that—the worst she had imagined—she had never considered they would take the horse from her. It was a lesser surprise, in its way, to find that her possessions no longer lay under the rocks where she had hidden them. They had been found and taken.

She slipped into the water and swam, then turned onto her back to rest. The moon gave shape to the clouds; and when the clouds cleared, it illuminated a view of a nearby landmass. Thick brush grew to the island's rim, but as Bee paddled in place, unsure of what to do, she saw an opening in the wall of bush and pulled herself onto a strip of stony beach. For a few moments she thought she glimpsed another world through a moon-lit gap, but the branches shifted, and the otherworldly window closed.

Above her, the sky shed stars that her mother Inès said were the fiery tears of the martyred San Lorenzo. He had died of his burns like her brother, Baruk. She wished to find her brother again and so she closed her eyes.

As in a story that finds its own direction, the world became cold, the mountains and the waterways froze, people abandoned their settlements, and only those who made their way to outermost islands—the tips of mountains as she and Tadeo had once discussed—survived to hope that others might be left alive elsewhere to share the world with them.

Bee awakened, naked and shivering. She was not at the lake any longer but in a wood of fir and cedar and hemlock and yew at a site from which she could hear the wash of waves onto a beach. Primo squatted beside her. She tried to sit, but he pushed her down and covered her mouth to silence her. Tendrils of a sea fog slipped through the trees in the dawning sun. A party passed nearby, speaking in Spanish, footsteps crunching on gravel. A wooden hull scraped over the stones; a boat splashed into the water.

Only then did Bee notice that her clothes and the pouch containing the other possessions she'd had with her, were arranged nearby. "You brought them for me?"

Primo nodded.

"What about Ignacio? Did he not try to stop you?" she whispered.

"After he left this morning, I took them."

"Ignacio is gone?" she asked. Primo nodded again and gestured at the just-launched craft they could now glimpse through the trees. They listened to the soft splashing of its oars and the low voices of its crew. "Many boats leave today," he said. "Ignacio went first."

It made sense, the commander mounting excursions to the Mowachaht before the expedition departed, his final opportunity to dispense goods and affirm a Spanish claim to the territory while recording local habits and customs. Ignacio usually went with them and would have no reason to change that practice today. But could Bee re-enter the settlement as if nothing had happened? Given how she had fled the mess after the confrontation with Tadeo, and that Rigel, as Primo affirmed, was safely returned to his stable where she often spent the night, and that it was still early, she doubted anyone but Ignacio and Primo would have concerned themselves with her whereabouts. Ignacio would not want to be the one to bring a problem to the commander. He would let someone else—Tadeo if he bothered to look for her—report her absence. Tadeo and the horse had long composed the elements of Bee's days.

"Rigel?" she said to Primo, to be certain, "You are sure he is all right?"

"I am sure," Primo said, and then he rested his head against her breast as he had done before. "*Madre*," he said, and this time she understood, and pulled him to her, and held him while he wept, a boy with sorrows like any other.

"Where is your mother?" she asked. He grew quiet. He held up seven fingers and pointed northeastwards. "Seven days," he said.

"Seven days distance? But that is over the mountains! Did someone take you from her? What happened?" She recalled what the priest had told her of terrible things the boy had seen, and what Tadeo had said in the mess, of all of them in battle, Spanish and Mowachaht and their enemies, everyone engaged in the same practices.

"Tell me about your mother," Bee said.

But Primo would say no more.

~

Not every story can be told, Pearl writing, reminds herself; most are stored forever within those who lived them, and not everyone can bear their telling. Fortunate are those who *can* tell, and who have someone who will listen. More so are those who have someone who will listen and remember. Pearl thinks of the storytellers, and the deep pool they gaze into and how it must be bottomless; and of all that has not yet been related, and of her own story in the midst of its making.

~

Bee's body ached. Blood had pooled in her limbs from the cold, and her stomach and thighs were blotched and bruised. Tadeo had told her, "Do not let the balance of your mind suffer. Do not be too much alone." Well, she was alone now, except for Primo.

It hurt to twist her arms into the shirt, and to lift her legs to pull on the deceitful, padded breeches. She tied her pouch of belongings around her waist, felt its unaccustomed lightness, and looked inside. One of them, either Primo or Ignacio—and she did not believe it was Primo—had taken her knife, the *navaja* she had brought with her from Spain. No second knife like it existed in the settlement or on the ships: Ignacio could not secrete it forever. One day, she would get it back. Primo tugged at her, and when she was standing, moved off, beckoning her to follow.

They followed the shore and dipped into the trees when there was danger of being observed. The sea was calm; the fog had cleared, and sunshine lit the cool shallows. The forest sewed itself to the waters with a green stitching of roots. They skirted the meadow and went into the gardens near the well. Bee bent as if picking vegetables, giving herself and Primo a reason to be on the fringes, and all the time she was thinking, *Ignacio will say nothing, and I must endure until I can leave the ship, with Primo, at Monterey. It will be easy; I have done much harder things than this.*

A few men came and went, but the settlement was mostly quiet. Tadeo, too, had gone with the longboats that morning, leaving written instructions in his workshop for Bee to finish all outstanding sketching and labelling. As soon as she had seen to Rigel, given him hay and fresh water, cleaned his stall, brushed his coat, led him into the field and hobbled him to browse, she set to work on the drawings, determined to complete them. Not since they had arrived at Friendly Cove—until today—had Tadeo failed to take her with him. But it was better this way, better that he did not learn of her overnight absence; and that she need not face his disillusionment until she felt stronger.

Primo came and went on errands for the priest, soliciting discarded clothing for the children who would travel on the ship to California with him, and begging for stale bread from the baker. He did not glance through the open door at Bee working at Tadeo's table in Tadeo's hut, but when he passed by, she felt the pull of his need.

In the evening, Bee led Rigel to the stable as she did normally. It was growing dark, only a crescent of blood-red sun touched the horizon. Cooking odours wafted across the gardens from the mess. Soon, she would have to acknowledge both Tadeo and Ignacio and pretend all was as usual. She fetched water from the well and poured it into a trough for the horse. After that, she moved to the rear of the hut to gather hay from the shadows. Rigel pawed the earthen floor impatiently. Suddenly, Bee caught the stink of bodily sweat and rancid hair oil and remembered she no longer carried the *navaja*. She turned quickly but was too slow to avoid the knife Ignacio pressed to her throat, opening a point of blood beneath her chin. It was her knife, her *navaja*. Ignacio shoved her against the wall. Blood dripped from the cut and down her neck.

"You should not have lied to me," Ignacio said. "I loved you like a brother.

"Be still, and let me," he said. He tugged at her shirt. "Do not think to make a noise. If someone comes you will be dead, and I will not be here. I will be with Primo." His knee pushed her thighs apart. He opened her breeches with his free hand. The knife point drove more deeply, and Bee felt the growing yaw of the wound at the same time as his thickened penis wedged into her genitals. Outside, the door of the mess opened, spilling light and laughter into the clotted dark, but everyone was too far away. No one would come to rescue Bee.

"It does not matter that you think you do not want me," he said. "It does not matter that you have forgotten who you are. I will not betray you. We will live together in New Spain as Baruk and I had planned.

"Why did you have to spoil it?" He grunted, and his penis tore the tissue at her vagina, and he thrust inside her, and split her body from herself.

"Bee, Bee, Bee," he said, shoving and tearing, "I will always be your first."

She prayed for her brother to come and take her, and she tried to drive her neck into the blade to kill herself, but she could not move against Ignacio's strength and weight. It was not her death Ignacio wanted, anyway. When he came, he cried her brother's name, and for a moment, his grip on the knife eased. In that second, she drove the sliver of wood she'd scrabbled from the planks at her back, into the softness below his eye. As it struck, it broke in her hand.

He bellowed in shock. Someone carrying a lamp opened the stable door from outside.

Our ancestors come to aid us if we need their help, her mother had told her. And it was true: a stream of women, men, children, all in the same river; and a bridge of words across the world; and a woman who sat at a window with a view of the sea and wrote down everything. All of them came to witness. But the one who mattered *now* was Tadeo, who swung the light to see where the cry had come from. "Bee?" he said, "Are you in here, Bee?"

"Stop!" he yelled, for he saw that Ignacio held a woman against the wall. "You should be ashamed of yourself!" He grabbed Ignacio by the shoulder, but Ignacio had repositioned the knife at Beatris's throat. "Get back or I will kill her," he said.

Tadeo retreated a step but raised the lamp to find out who it was that Ignacio threatened. His eyes met Bee's: hers blurred with tears and his with disbelief.

Truth, as Nora had often told Pearl, has a hard edge, that is how you know it; and this was Tadeo's moment to feel it.

"You should not have done that," Ignacio said to Bee, ignoring Tadeo. Blood streamed down his cheek. "You may have wounded me, but we will always be together."

A certain moment comes, and the soul decides to cut its strings from the body. Bee looked down from above, but instead of watching herself die, as she expected, she saw flame splash onto Ignacio from Tadeo's hurled lamp. Before the flaming oil could reach her, Tadeo dragged her away. Still, she hovered and gazed at Ignacio as his madness faded and a lost intelligence arrived in its place, apologized, and ebbed. So too must Baruk have bloomed and paled when Ignacio held her brother down and drowned him.

"I knew, I knew," Tadeo sobbed and held her. "I came last night to look for you, but you and the horse were gone." He pulled her to her feet. "We must leave quickly." The hay was alight around them. Rigel screamed in his stall, but Ignacio made no noise, and Beatris watched the tiny double of Ignacio emerge from his skull, and dissolve.

Then, Tadeo pulled her clothes together, pocketed the *navaja* and kicked the rest of the hay over Ignacio's body. The hair on Bee's head and on Tadeo's smoked and singed and for a second Rigel's tail was on fire. Tadeo crushed the flames with his hands, and they wrestled the horse outside.

"Fire, Fire!" Tadeo shouted. "Fire, Fire! Oh, help us!" The stable transformed to a searing tower that sparked the beach grass ablaze. The grass burned and fizzed to the waterside. Only the damp earth of the gardens halted its march to the forest.

"I did not know he was in the stable," Bee said when the charred sticks of Ignacio's body were found in the ruins. "I fed Rigel and shut him in, as always. It was only because I happened to look over my shoulder that I saw the fire and ran to free the horse."

"Why was Ignacio in the stall?" the commander asked.

"I do not know," she said.

"He was jealous," one of the sailors listening said. "He begged to help with the horse although he had no skill."

"And the lamp, you didn't light it?"

"No," she said. "I had no need of a lamp for a few moments' work in a place I know so well."

"Ignacio must have set the fire by accident," the commander said. "Was he acquainted with the arrangement of the stable?"

"No," she said. "He took no part in caring for the animal."

"You were fortunate the naturalist came along when he did," the commander said, "or you, too, might have died." Briefly, he clasped Bee's shoulder. "I have heard the full story of the bone Ignacio gave to you, from several witnesses. You were not to blame. If he had lived, he would have been disciplined. He was a troubled soul." And that was that. Ignacio was smoke and ash: they buried what was left of him in the Spanish graveyard.

The first night after they sailed from the settlement, Baruk came to Bee. He smiled at Primo beside her—they slept in the hold with the horse as Bee had no more work to do for Tadeo, even though his burned hands made writing and drawing difficult. He had come to the stable the night of the fire to tell her how well she had done with the drawings; he had come to say he was sorry for what he had said in the mess, that others had told him the truth after she'd left.

Baruk smiled at her, as well as at Primo, but Bee could see that he held fast to someone behind him. It was Ignacio. If Beatris were to be honest, she would say she knew the truth of Baruk and Ignacio's love all along. How could she not? She and Baruk were two halves of the same being.

At Monterey, she and Tadeo left the ship, taking Rigel with them to escort the purchased children down the road to the mission. Part way along, they bought a dress for Beatris from a market. They planned for the sailor Bee to be counted with the deserters, of whom there were often several at most ports of call. Few onboard the expedition ship would care. The death of Ignacio had tainted her. "Two friends dead, yet this one lives," Bee heard several times as she passed by. When she and Tadeo knocked at the mission gates for entry, Bee, apparelled as a woman, was holding onto Primo. Around her waist, she wore a pouch with her few belongings.

The friars made Primo go with the other children. All the children were hungry. They went happily. They could not guess what was coming. Primo left without looking back.

"This can be a home for you," Tadeo said to Beatris. "The friars will look after you until I return."

He smiled, but he had not looked into her eyes since he had killed Ignacio and saved her life.

"Give me Rigel," she said, taking Rigel's lead.

"No," the friar waiting for her said. "You will have no time for a horse. This is not a work horse. We have no need of any creature that cannot earn its keep."

"The horse will be no trouble," Beatris said. "I am used to it, and I am good with horses. I could work in the stables. Rigel and I could carry messages for the fathers."

"It would not be fitting."

"Horses are in the blood of Spanish women!" Beatris protested.

"Do not argue with me, girl. Be silent."

"I beg you to reconsider," Tadeo said. "The animal is her only companion." These were the kindest words Tadeo had spoken in some time, and yet they chilled Beatris to the heart.

"She will find companionship with us if she surrenders her own ideas and learns humility," the friar said. "You are free to go your own way and keep the horse," he said to Beatris, "but you may not have it here."

"I can do no more," Tadeo said to her. "I will see that Rigel is looked after. What else would you have me do?" He met her eyes unwillingly, and she searched them.

She would not give the friar the pleasure of her tears. "Tadeo?" she said and drew him aside. "Is this truly what you want?"

"Peace is what I want for both of us, Beatris, and to find a way to carry on with life. The boy relies on you. Would you leave *him* utterly friendless?"

All winter, she scrubbed floors and cooked the corn and barley mush the mission fed its residents; and she kept a lookout for Primo. But the boys worked long hours in the fields except on Sundays, and she only glimpsed him a few times, at meals. At night, soldiers locked the women in crammed *monjerias* that lacked light and air and had only buckets to hold their waste. Tuberculosis, cholera, and pneumonia killed many in these stifling quarters. Beatris had her own room (a cell) and sufficient space and time to pray if she wanted. How could she complain? She saw Primo face-to-face just once: it was at the lessons in Spanish she gave to new Indigenous converts. By then, her belly had popped out round and compact from her frame. "*Madre*," he mouthed to her. "*Madre*." She saw him again from a distance when he was flogged for falling asleep during mass. Each day, the bells for mass were rung and the overseers policed the church with prods and whips to harass laggards.

"Primo was given to me to care for," she said to the friar who reluctantly agreed to see her. "I gave my word to watch over him. I swore it on God's Holy Book. He is a child; he could sleep in the room with me."

"You are too young to care for such a boy. You swore out of ignorance. God will forgive you. You are released from your vow regardless since the boy is dead."

"When?" she asked him, surprised she was able to voice the question.

"Only a few hours ago," he said. Perhaps the news scoured her feelings, for she felt nothing: grief had gone to wait for her elsewhere with its companions; guilt, regret, and despair.

"Did he ask for me?"

"I would not know, and it does not matter," the friar said. "What matters is that he was baptized. He sleeps in Christ, now." The friar had more to say, but Beatris did not hear it: how could she? Her senses had vitrified. *Most of them die within months*, the commander had said of the transport of Indigenous children.

"How will I manage once the child in my belly is born?" she asked. "I have seen no infants, and no place for them at the mission."

"Every child has a place with God," he told her, "How long until your husband returns?"

He meant Tadeo, but Tadeo would not arrive until several months after Rosa's birth. He had not known what he would find when he next saw Beatris.

"I will give you bread and pork and tomatoes and beans and wine one day," Beatris promised her daughter while she waited, and tried to shut out the sounds—the shouts and cries and falling blows, and the thud of fist on bone—that flew to her from the dormitories of the men and boys as she swept the courtyard each day.

"It does not matter who your father was or what he did, or what I did, you have come to the world for yourself," she said to Rosa. Nothing was as important as this child: how Baruk would have loved her.

~

Did Tadeo ever hold the baby? Pearl, writing, tries to remember. Yes, he did, but he did not find what Beatris found in Rosa's innocence. He saw only a resemblance to Ignacio and a rape, and a death of which he was the unwilling instrument.

~

"I have made an arrangement," Tadeo said to Beatris as he handed the baby back. "The governor at San Blas requires help with his horses, and his wife has wished for a child. You will go tomorrow on a ship that is leaving for Mexico. I have brought Rigel: you can take him with you."

"And you?" Beatris asked him. "What will you do?"

"As I have always done," he said. "I will collect plants and label them." He twisted the brim of his leather hat.

"And then?"

"After that, I will have to see." For an instant, he risked an unguarded look into her eyes. How green they were. As green as deep reaches of the ocean.

"It is too bad," he said. "But how could I?"

"Yes, how," she said, and put the infant to her breast.

"I have acknowledged the child," he said. "The friars have the paper. Do not forget to take the document with you."

He turned and passed through the side door in the mission wall. It was the door through which they had taken Primo's body. Beatris had asked to follow it, but they would not let her, and they would not tell her where he was buried.

Beatris was just sixteen years of age. She ran to the door and looked out. The road was dusty, framed with groves of pines and oaks. Only Tadeo was on it; cicadas sang in the grass. Tadeo bent as he walked and took samples of plants from the verges and put them into his pockets. He turned around, he waved, and the youthful heart of Beatris burned with hope, but he was only signalling that he had reached the tied-up horse so she would know where to find it.

~

Pearl awakens with her head on the table and the laptop in power save mode. Wisps of Beatris's tale persist in the morning mist over the lake in which Beatris had shed her clothes and swum with the horse, her nakedness revealing her secret to her enemy.

Pearl closes the laptop and puts it away.

Everyone's path winds through the dark, one time or another. Tale after tale is written in deserted streets or in cars, in the presence of strangers and acquaintances, some with weapons and others wearing masks of greed or indifference. The story of the rape and murder was always in Beatris's tale, but young Pearl had only considered Beatris's daring in running away disguised as a boy. She had not been aware of a shadow within the bond between the brother and sister, or of Beatris's near-miss with love. She and Tadeo had come so close. Had he lacked the courage to choose? Had she?

After she has cleared out the cabin, Pearl surveys the lake from the ramp. Without Beatris's suffering, without Rosa's abandonment, there would be no Pearl: but how is she to judge the cost of her existence? And should she? How can anyone?

At the lakeside below the cabin, with the note for Cliff she will give to Sandra in her pocket, Pearl takes a scoop of Nora's ashes from the grey cardboard container and dusts them on the water. The ashes drift, filaments of bone sift and settle. The veneer of the surface puckers with gulping tiny fish that rise to the disturbance, and insects stride the resolving tension of the surface.

It is not quite dark when Pearl finishes dealing with documents and phone calls at the Ridgeway motel in Gold River. The pub parking lot below her window is a stir of motorcycles and trucks and taxis, coming and going. The pub door pushes open, and springs shut, only the smokers loiter longer than a few seconds on the steps. One sees her looking out and waves a greeting: he is grey-bristled, his wrists knobbed as tree roots; he wears old jeans and a faded *SoliSunny* T-shirt. He was on the shuttle. He grinds the cigarette end under his heel and re-enters the pub. For a few minutes it is quiet.

Pearl sips a cup of in-room coffee, shuts her eyes and imagines Cliff pouring fish from the tanks into the ocean: his work, their work, and all their hopes flow seaward as he leans out of the open door of the low-flying airplane. In the afternoon light, the spilling fish are silver and diamond. She has mapped the contours of their bellies with her hands, her spirit swims with them. Unbidden, two sets of manicured female fingernails enter the picture and grip Cliff's jacket. "Don't fall out, honey," the unnamed woman says.

Pearl has no need to fill in more. The plane flies on to the steelheads' natal stream in which Cliff will seed the redds. She hadn't thought to ask him exactly where it was, hadn't thought it necessary. They were supposed to go together. She and he. Not the way it has become.

At the sound of cheers and clapping, she opens her eyes. A group of kids are playing playing basketball under the parking lot lights, using portable hoops. The ball hits a vehicle and sets off an alarm. A man runs out of the pub, yells at the kids who keep on playing, and resets the car's system.

Pearl's cellphone rings on the dresser she is using as a desk. Above it, a print replicates the view from the window, its scenery daylit, whereas in the real world, the mountains form a wall of night and mosquitoes.

"Hello, Harry?"

"Everything go okay with the lawyer?" he asks.

"Yeah, all fine. She'll meet with the mortgage holders in the morning. The house should be listed for sale within the week. Nora left it in good shape. The housekeeper should be able to manage—I've sent her a to-do list. She'll put everything in storage. I can deal with it later. Or maybe you would like to? Just to get it done?"

"I'm sorry about this, Pearl."

"Yeah, me too."

"No rush, though. Take your time."

Pearl stands at the window. A girl is practising free throws, her ponytail bouncing. The others are counting her successes. They're at ten, eleven, twelve. It looks like nothing can stop her.

"The money will be okay if you're careful," Harry says. "You can go north, have a look around, wrap up whatever you wanted to do, but you'll have to …"

"I'll have to get a job. I'm on it, Harry." Pearl glances at the list of freelance contacts on her laptop screen.

"Look, Pearl, we've been thinking, Loretta and I. Something has to be done with Refuge House. Nora willed it to her foundation, so either we sell it and figure out how best to use whatever we get for it or take on a new manager who can fundraise. You interested?"

"Me? Fundraise?" Pearl is sitting in the scoop of an orange plastic chair. Shouts and groans ripple from the parking lot: the girl free-thrower has missed a basket.

"You could make sure the place is warm and dry over the winter, see how it goes. Think of it more as caretaker-manager. That way you can supervise Joachim while he's in school. Find out if the thing is viable. Make an assessment; write a report. We can decide then."

"What do you mean? Joachim's at chess camp with his mother for the rest of the holidays. Why wouldn't he go to school in Vancouver? You're not making sense."

"He ran away from camp, twice," Loretta pipes up via speaker phone. "His mother can't deal with him. He wants his life to be like it was before. Refuge House and the school and the town are familiar. He can't take on anything new."

"But his mother!"

"Maria needs medical tests and not to worry," Harry says, "and the good thing is …"

"Joachim wants to be with you, Pearl," Loretta says. "The swimming, he thinks you meant it. You promised to teach him. Youngsters get attached. He trusts you. You don't make promises you're not willing to keep, do you?

"So, I've booked him on the flight from Vancouver. Your route's more roundabout but you'll be in time to meet him at the White Lake airport. You'll have to drive from there. I'll leave directions with the lease company.

Joachim will have everything with him," Loretta says. Pearl pictures Loretta's red-framed plastic glasses pushed on top of her head, a wing of glossy black hair tucked behind her ear. In the motel vanity mirror, Pearl is hollow-eyed, her hair on end.

"It's what's best until his mother is well," Harry says.

"Nora would have approved, Pearl. That house, it isn't big, but the people who have gone through—mothers, fathers, children, grandparents—it gave them a safe place to start over."

"Do I have a choice?" Pearl says.

"Of course," Harry says. "Say no if you want to. A brief visit to Refuge House might be enough. Any idea where you'd go next? You'll always have a home with us if you want it."

"But you're going anyway," Loretta says. "It was Nora's last call, so what's the problem? What if it takes a little extra time; what else have you got to do?"

Before she shelters under the faded blues and greens of the Ridgeway bedspread, Pearl glances at the article she is writing for *Findable Feast*. Quickly, she types a few more paragraphs about the effects on salmon of silage and fertilizer entering the water system, clear-cuts eroding the hillsides, and the silt from the resulting runoff that chokes the streams. As Sheila pointed out, when the streams and rivers die, fish no longer spawn in them; and if they somehow do, the drug and hormone laden products that have leached into the water damage their DNA and their ability to reproduce. Human beings, like all jawed vertebrates, share a fish-like precursor, so what on earth is the human species up to? Contemporary *and* antecedent suicide?

It would explain some things … what if her dive from the dock was more than a desire to flee? What if it was an instinctive need to revert to *before* life-on-land? As if the evolutionary time bomb of human presence could be disarmed bit by bit, one person at a time.

Pearl crawls into bed, her thoughts thick. The dolls' stories flip through her mind, each one illuminating the others. The most recent, Beatris's tale, gave context to the story of young Rosa and the handsome Aragonese; and through the Aragonese to Guiliam and his troubadour song for Yamha; and through Yamha, the wounded child and her dolls, it touched the tale of Beatris's mother, Inés, and the Moorish soldier who found her on a battlefield. The dolls were like footprints, like breadcrumbs or still-life objects stored in a palace of memory, a palace that Nora said contained the rooms of your life. All you knew and learned and all you had inherited was stored in them, but you had to make a map to find your way through, like the storytellers did.

Nora and dolls and stories. Nora who not only dragged Pearl in and out of bookstores and galleries but took her to Pink Pelican Island as often as she could. If she could have one more conversation with Nora, Pearl would ask her, *What about the plants and animals you showed me, what about the nature of everything alive—are these not also houses for stories? What is DNA but memory of the texture of loss and discovery*?

So much *texture* has occurred to Pearl on Nootka Island that she can scarcely take it in. She fluffs her pillow, punches it, and tries to get comfortable. Much happened at Nootka to Beatris too, but did that signify a connection, or was it simply Nora's engineering? Is Pearl truly in the same circle as the storytellers? Could Cliff (for whom she aches) be inside the circle with her?

Right to the end, Beatris had hoped that Tadeo was a permanent part of *her* story, but despite his kindness, he could not cope with her reality. Tadeo's problem, in Pearl's opinion, was that he asked himself, "What will people think?" and "How will I handle my emotions?" Although the only question that mattered was the one posed by the girl in Theano's tale, "How will I get through the coming days and nights without the companionship of those I love?"

Why not think about that for a minute, *Tadeo!*

Pearl punches her pillow once more.

The little girl who made dolls resemble her lost family in Theano's tale had done her best to keep her loved ones with her. And Beatris had followed her brother onto his ship because of her love for him. *Virtue is to choose*, Theano had said. People choose: they have that power. Theano's poet, as woolly as he was, had made a choice. On the brink of disappointment in love—would Theano have left her husband for him?—he had chosen hope. *To raise a child is to hope*, he had said.

The bedside lamp fizzes and slowly fizzles out completely. Bats wing into the trees surrounding the parking lot, and raccoons set out on their confident patrol of the Ridgeway garbage cans. After her thoughts calm and she is on the verge of sleep, Pearl finds herself at *SoliSunny* with Cliff at the holding tanks, their joined hands gently stroking the belly of a steelhead until it releases its eggs. What had the fish hoped for? Did it possess choice? Shall we be fish or birds like those we see, or will we be new versions of ourselves? What of the future? What tale has hope to tell *her*?

Time is the future. Things will settle and we will see. All this, the storytellers had already said.

PART V

RIB: The Orphan's Tale

The scribe and dancer, Arishat, lived one hundred and twelve generations before you, Nora wrote. Her foster brother, Rib, was your ancestor. The tale includes a cat. When you write the story, don't forget to put that in.

Hydro crews, construction workers, truck drivers, and labourers flown in from Germany, Mexico, and China to work the gas fields, the fracking fields, and the dam and mining projects, spill over lands which have been home to First Nations including Treaty 8's Blueberry River, Doig River, Fort Nelson, Halfway River, McLeod Lake, Prophet River, Saulteau, and West Moberly, for thousands of years. They pass through northern towns leaving behind a spoor of company-paid motels and restaurants, and ditches littered with condoms and coffee cups. Other than the temporary strain on the walk-in clinics, nothing else shows they have been there. The show moves on, northward and westward, and dissipates in gulag-like settlements of industrial achievement and environmental poisoning, aided and abetted by online porn, travelling evangelists, musicians, and comedians, and the hope that all that money will mean something to someone at home.

To this is added a population of long-stay trappers, farmers (some the descendants of remittance men and hippies), and the lost and lonely who find they can exist in a one room shack if there's wood to get through the winter.

Where all these congregate, so gather the professionals: government workers, police, medical staff, and teachers who cycle through on two-year contracts. A year to live in an overheated apartment, socialize at the Legion, watch videos in the school gymnasium, and cheer community basketball teams at the tournaments. Another year to cope with colleagues who get sick or have breakdowns because of the long dark nights, the kids who live on soft drinks and chips, the drinking that never ceases, the drivers on Benzedrine eliminating the idea of curves from the roads, and the wives and husbands who run off leaving no forwarding address. Fragile souls, those who sense but fail to make peace with the progenitors of snow and ice, the spirit callers in mastodon boneyards and those long turned to stone who awaken in the fractured, blasted geology of shale, have nightmares in which their flesh burns like gas flames. They become wraiths on the skirts of housing tracts that slither into the tailings. No one cares what they do, as long as they make room for a new wave of dreamers and the needy and greedy.

Pearl knew the lore from her father and from Nora: the desire and despair of those who search for fortune anywhere other than where they are. Which is precisely what Pearl is doing now, isn't it?

In the silence Pearl and Joachim have maintained since exchanging brief hellos at the White Lake airport and leasing a four by four to take them to Saint Francis where Refuge House is, Pearl's thoughts are her own. Her worries for the future diminish as they drive through a landscape of serried spruce, bog willow, barrens punctuated with shed moose antlers, and snow-tipped storybook mountains inviting them onwards—although she is a little concerned about Joachim.

He is taller, paler than she recalls, and too thin. His shrunken long-sleeved T-shirt draws his shoulders together, flaps the bottom of his ribcage, and exposes his wrists. He wears sunglasses taped at the temples. If he has brought a jacket with him, he has left it on the plane. He leans against the vehicle window and hugs a duffle bag to his chest.

After an hour or so, the road grows narrow and follows a deep canyon with a fast, green river scouring its bottom.

"I take it you didn't like chess camp?" she says, thinking it only courteous to try for conversation.

He shrugs.

"How's your mother?"

He shrugs again, but says into the car window, "She's all right."

They pass over a rock bridge between two rivers and the road launches into a climb. They meet an oncoming truck. Pearl reverses to a pull-out area and the truck squeezes by with its wheels on the precipice. When she is breathing again, Pearl tries anew.

"I suppose it will rain soon. It looks so dry, but Harry says it always rains by the end of the month."

"You won't be able to drive out," Joachim says without turning his head. "There's mud, then it freezes, and then it snows and melts. The slush is over the wheels."

"Okay, and?"

"We'll be trapped." He detaches the sunglasses and smiles tightly. The glasses go back on.

Aside from a pebbling of wooden houses, Saint Francis Bywater consists of a church, an elementary to middle school, a general store, and one or two official looking buildings encrusted on a stepped slope above the river.

"You should get groceries if you want to eat," Joachim says as they near the store.

Pearl bites back a sharp reply. *What is wrong with him*? But she asks, instead, "Are you glad to be here?"

"I didn't want to leave in the first place. Nora said we had to."

Pearl parks the four by four beside an ATV in front of the General Store. Under its low front windows, dried-out geraniums nest in a wooden planter.

She puts the keys in her pocket. "I need to talk to you, Joachim, and I can't when you've got those glasses on, so will you please take them off?"

He obeys and chews the end of one of the arms. The lift of his chin is in keeping with his flared nostrils and indifference, but there is pain in the bared eyes.

"Okay, I get it. People change your life without asking you and that's not fair, but Nora didn't want to close the house down, either. So, let's be honest. Harry said you wanted to live with me, is that true, or isn't it?"

Joachim fiddles with the straps of his duffle bag. "Sure," he says, "but you said I could swim, and I couldn't. They made me take off my shirt. All I could do was float."

"At the chess camp?"

"There were girls."

Pearl's throat constricts. "I'm sorry," but sorry doesn't help with his having to expose his failure *and* the scars on his body to young women his own age in the pool. "We haven't had enough time to work on it, that's all."

"It doesn't matter."

"Sure, it does," she says. "Do you want to come inside with me? Help pick out what we need?"

"No, I'll stay in the car."

The shelves are stocked with oil lamps, mosquito repellent, and shotgun shells as well as toothpaste, deodorant, and a full wall of tinned fruit and vegetables. Tea is in a corner cabinet above a freezer, next to a cooler.

Before she can tell the storekeeper what she wants, he reaches below the counter and pulls out a stack of mail. "You're Nora's granddaughter," he says. "These will be for you. Nora said you'd come."

He tweaks the brim of his Husqvarna cap. "I'm Bob. Open that one first." He points to an envelope from a barge-tow company. "Last thing she did before she left, Nora. I've got the spare key."

Pearl lays aside the rest of the mail—all bills as far as she can tell—and opens the barge-tow dispatch of an invoice for two thousand dollars' worth of supplies procured by Nora on behalf of Refuge House. Pearl scans the list: flour, salt, sugar, tea, coffee, oil, dried fruit, nuts, rice, beans, spices, tins of vegetables and fruit, powdered milk, canned fish, toilet paper, and a wheel of cheddar cheese. With a sigh of relief, she sees, at the bottom, that the invoice is marked paid.

"Get someone to shoot you a deer, and it should do the winter," Bob says. He has come out from behind the counter to read over her shoulder. "They haul it upriver on the barge all the way from the coast. Cheap at the price.

"I've got the cheese in the cooler, and you'll want fresh milk and eggs for the boy. I'll scoot the truck over later. You'll need candles. Phone once you see what's left in the garden. Get the leaks fixed. You'll need more firewood soon. I'll see to both.

"And *he'll* have to register for school; you're late arrivals," Bob adds. He thumbs outside at Joachim who has left the car and is looking at the gun case on the ATV. "His winter clothes fit? Doubt it, from what I can see."

"What about Internet?" she says, but her mind isn't on the question, let alone on why Bob thinks he can tell her what to do although she'll have to pay for it. Joachim is strolling in the direction of a ramp, down to the river docks.

"In the school library. My wife's the principal. Ask her."

Joachim has reached the dock. Runabouts and zodiacs slap against the wharfside—it is late in the season and runoff from mountain rains clots the river with debris and speeds the currents. Joachim leans forward and stares into the water.

"Tell my wife, 'Bob says you need a job to pay for the extras,'" he continues, but Pearl is out the door and running past the parked vehicles, yelling so Joachim will hear her. He does, but after a glance her way, he looks at the river again, puts his hands together above his head as she taught him to and prepares to dive.

"No!" she shouts. His arms drop to his sides.

"I wasn't going to, Pearl, don't be stupid," he says when she reaches him. Yet as they walk to the four by four, he swivels towards the watercourse as if he can't help it.

Pearl waits for him to buckle in beside her. "Okay," she says, "it'll be swimming lessons right away if I can find a decent pool, but you'd better take it seriously. I'm tired of worrying about you."

"Refuge House has a pool."

"It does? But I thought …"

"Not that kind of pool, Pearl, a real one, outside. Nora showed me."

The house is a kilometre beyond the village, down a rutted road between sheltering trees. Its metal roof is new but the board and batten walls, ancient, warped and damp-stained, will have to be rebuilt. A leaning two-by-four supports one end of a gutter: the other end drips water onto the steps. Someone has painted the name *Refuge House* onto a shingle beneath a set of moose antlers nailed to a post. A stream burbles and woofs from the bottom of a path enmeshed in the tripwires of berry bushes. Joachim leaves the four by four and pivots towards it, but Pearl grabs his sleeve and tows him after her into the house.

They eat canned soup and toasted cheese at a wide plank table in front of the living room window. Joachim is anxious to go outdoors. Late light tips dry leaves and grasses with gold. Apple branches scrape the windowpanes, the fruit small, and red and yellow. "The pool's in the creek," he says, "I'll show you. I'll get my stuff."

"It's getting cold," she calls, but he has raced up the ladder to the loft. Doors slam, drawers hauled open and banged shut. "Where are my swim trunks?" he shouts, as if she might have hidden them.

Pearl is tired, and the place needs cleaning. Spiders nest in hanks of herbs suspended from nails in the kitchen, and the shelves and dishes are dusty. On one of them, hunters passing through have left half-full coffee mugs, an inch of a bottle of rye and spent shells. No doubt Bob let them in. Before she can do much about any of it, she needs to find out how to turn on the hot water. She climbs to the loft. "Joachim," she calls, "where did Nora keep the towels?"

"In the linen closet in front of you," he says from his room. "Aren't you ready?"

No, she isn't ready. When she opens the closet door, she smells lavender and sandalwood. Nora's embroidered sheets and pillowcases, along with quilts and towels, are zipped into mothproof bags. Pearl unfolds and shakes out the sheets. Lavender sachets and blocks of sandalwood drop to the floor. Something else, not very big, and wrapped in muslin, falls from the heaps of bedding. Quickly, she puts it in her hoody pocket.

"I can go by myself. You don't have to come," Joachim calls, heading for the ladder. Pearl grabs two towels from a bag and empties the contents of her backpack onto the floor in the room that will be hers, and scrabbles for her swimsuit.

"No, wait! Just a minute!"

Finally, swimsuit on, running shoes half tied, towels under an arm, she descends the ladder in his wake, loses her footing and scrapes her belly on the rungs.

Black cottonwoods snake into the creek bank, their leaves a rustle of pale green and yellow, their trunks inking the path of the water course. Pearl looks from trees to bush to water and rocks—but no Joachim. The clouds are on the boil again—or it could be fog, a moving froth that flows between water and sky. A figure breaks from it, splashing from the stream, darkening rocks, distributing whitewater. "I can't find the pool! It's gone!"

What choice does she have but to ignore his banged and bloody shins from tripping over rocks, and his shivering in wet trunks, and carry on? "Show me what you found, Joachim. Joachim? Look at me. I need you to tell me what you saw."

He wipes his nose on his forearm. "Over there. We made steps down the bank, see?" The light is fading. Beneath the overhanging trees, Pearl makes out a set of neatly cut descending steps, inset with pebbles. There's a Department of Fisheries sign posted on a tree above them. The steps end at a distinct lap line in the bank. At its new level, the creek is shallow, and foams over uneven bedrock, but it is limpid at its flanks. Despite the encroaching veils of fog and darkness, she discerns several salmon idling on the bottom with noses to the current.

"I'll show you," Joachim says, calmly. He points out the broken concrete of the small dam that had made the pool. "Somebody wrecked it."

"Tomorrow after school, we'll have a look and see what we can do," Pearl says, watching the salmon.

He splashes to the middle of the creek, hoists stones and deposits them, one onto another, to create a new barrier. He bends for more.

"It's getting dark, Joachim, we need to go indoors." She is cold, but he is cold and wet: he must be freezing.

Joachim drags over more stones and piles them on top of the others.

"If you come here," Pearl says, "I'll show you something interesting." As she speaks, the rocks Joachim has stacked topple over. Before he has time to react, Pearl steps into the creek and hauls him out of the water to squat beside her on the bank. "Look—see those shadows? Keep watching." She keeps a tight hold on him with one hand and immerses her free hand in the stream. A salmon promptly sways its tail and moves to rest against her fingers. Slowly, she lets go of Joachim and strokes the fish along its length.

"Can I try?"

"Put your fingers on mine, gently now." Pearl eases out of the way, and Joachim's fingers graze the salmon's flank. It is only for a moment, but he is ecstatic. "It let me touch it, Pearl! It let me!"

After he is in bed and asleep, Pearl gathers Joachim's clothes and looks for something clean for him to wear to school. He'd indicated he had left clothing in his room, but the belongings in the garbage bag in his closet smell musty and look small. She sits on the floor, leans against the cupboard door, and rolls her shoulders to release her neck. Pearl is responsible for feeding and clothing them both for the time being, and she must settle Nora's bills. The money Harry advanced won't go far if the prices at Bob's general store are anything to go by. However, the blaze in the airtight downstairs makes the house dry and cozy. The hunters had compensated for their mess by leaving the kindling box full and splitting a pile of firewood which they had stored under a tarp beside the porch.

"I can do that," Joachim said after Pearl built the fire. "Nora showed me."

"Okay, so next time it's your turn, and I get to supervise, right?"

Joachim nodded and almost smiled.

Pearl listens to his breathing, salvages the chess book he'd been reading from the floor, and places it on the bedside table. Joachim's forehead is damp, but he is sleeping easily so she tiptoes out and closes the door.

A baby wipe brightens the dim hallway; another one glows softly in front of her bedroom door. Pearl steps around them and descends the ladder. Refuge House's main windows view west to the barrier of mountains between the village and the sea several hundred kilometres away. Pearl snubs her nose to the glass and tries to peer through the trees to the creek. Cliff had told her about dismantling dams for fish recolonization, and if that's what's going on here, she and Joachim won't be able to restore the pool as Joachim hoped. A dam is dismantled, Cliff had said, so that strays as well as introduced fish can expand spawning territory into a new or former habitat. Biologists trace this behaviour from the time of the retreat of the glaciers that covered much of the northwest coastal salmon range. But for the colonization to work, the colonists, however introduced, must produce offspring that will return to the new area to spawn; and this requires fish with developed instincts. Pearl's thoughts linger on Cliff's passion for his project, his belief that what he does can affect the future; that lost instincts can be restored.

She leans back in the chair, reflected in a window square, lamp-lit highlights on her forehead, nose, and chin.

No ghosts or presences intrude the way they did in Nora's house the night she died, but the potential for something like it passes through Pearl's mind as she takes the well-wrapped muslin package from her fleece pocket. This doll's body is formed simply, with unbleached cotton stuffed with straw and tied into sections. It is the oldest of the dolls, the one from the earliest of the stories, distinguished by little more than a sketch of sloe eyes, a line for a mouth, and squiggles for curling hair. Pearl had played with it under Nora's close supervision. She had liked to rearrange its exotic costume, but it wears no outfit now. Attached to the doll, though, are several tiny objects sewn to the knobs of its palms: a scroll, a reed pen, and a minuscule, inflated bladder. Pearl squeezes the bladder between her thumb and forefinger until an air bubble bulges one end. It isn't a wineskin—her first thought—but she can't think what else it might be.

A different texture in the folds of the muslin wrapping draws Pearl's attention. She explores it and finds a silk square enclosing a net-and-sequin dress with a veil, flimsy undergarments, and a set of tiny ankle bells. This doll—Arishat is its name—is a dancer, and Pearl has uncovered its missing regalia.

Thoughtfully, Pearl brings the doll to her chest: each time she had been allowed to sleep with it at Nora's house, it had made her dream.

Pearl awakens, the fire is out, and her back is stiff. In the fragment of dream she remembers, a female scribe in a mudwalled workroom brandishes a reed pen and turns to look at her. Outside the window, above the scribe's desk, a green sea plashes onto pink sands.

She is about to haul herself out of the chair and go to bed, but a figure passes by the window and into the trees.

It is Joachim in the T-shirt and sweatpants in which he'd been sleeping. She races to the door and outside, and down to the creek-bank to find him stalled on the path, turning his head one way and then the other. She won't call him, even though he appears to stare right at her, because he is sleepwalking, hunting perhaps, in the only way he can, for all that he is missing.

In the morning, Joachim is achingly slow. Pearl must climb the ladder twice to coax him down to breakfast. At the school—a concrete one-storey in an L-shape beside a fenced playing field—they hear that the class he should be in is full.

"Full?" Pearl says to the office receptionist. "His mother told you he was coming!"

"You are late registering; there is no room," the receptionist reiterates. She smiles at her computer screen. Her bobbed grey hair matches her gunmetal suit.

"That's fine, Mavis," a voice from behind them interrupts. Another woman, broad-shouldered and substantial in a long skirt, colourful blouse and work boots, glides out of an adjoining office. Her thick hair falls in a plait. "Welcome, Joachim. We *were* expecting you." To Mavis she says, glancing over the woman's shoulder at the screen, "Joachim's in eight-nine, Miss Wanda's class, not seven-eight." She tugs her skirt straight. "I am Principal Padma. You're Nora's granddaughter."

"Yes, I'm Pearl. I met your husband, Bob, at the grocery store."

"Ex-husband. He told me you'd been in."

A surge of students passes the office door, "Here's Miss Wanda, taking the class for gym." Principal Padma urges Joachim forward and calls into the hallway, "Look who I've got with me!"

The teacher steps aside from the chatter. Joachim, who Pearl expects to be shy, rushes to her and high-fives. "You're back!" Miss Wanda says. "Good! We need you for the chess club!"

"Henry!" she calls to a lagging student. "Run ahead and get out the dodge balls."

"Bob tells me you need a job," the principal says when Joachim and his class have gone. "Let's go to the teacher's lounge and have a coffee, and you can tell me what it is you do."

Later, using one of the computers in the library, Pearl prepares a résumé and a model lesson plan for teaching basic computing skills and social media safety to Grade Threes. Padma has offered her a two-week tryout, and if her credentials check out and the kids make progress, they will see if they can give her regular hours on an emergency-contract basis. The computer teacher they'd hired hadn't turned up and they are scrambling. "He got a better offer at the last minute. We're too isolated for some and they think they'll get stuck, and it will hurt their careers; but lots of experienced teachers are looking for jobs and we have advertised again. If anyone more qualified applies, I might have to let you go. But as far as I'm concerned, it's all about the kids."

Fair enough. Although Pearl thinks the school is lovely and would be a good place for her to work. Drawings and posters, books and rocks and plants enliven the rooms she has peeked into. Joachim's classroom is decorated with outer space photos and star maps, the bookshelves overflow with chemistry, poetry, and history books. Chessboards and chess pieces occupy a shelf of their own. On a corner of Miss Wanda's desk, a small, framed photo of an orange-robed saint beams goodwill.

After Pearl has printed out the documents she needs, she finds the Fisheries website. It takes a while to negotiate its pages, but eventually she traces the creek dam project near Refuge House. Since the dam is no longer needed for a local water supply, Fisheries has demolished it to see that if, in a free-running stream, fish will spawn in historical locations. There is no premeditated recolonization plan, but a Fisheries officer checks the site biweekly. Pearl scrolls through the reports: they have found no more than a few fish. At least she can tell Joachim *why* they won't be able to rebuild the dam.

Before she logs out, Pearl scans the school's home page. Upcoming fall events include the Welcome Potluck, Tahltan Day, Outfitters Training, and a prize for the student who collects the most sponsorship pledges for the paddle course. For this, students row or kayak laps in a boomed-off area of the river. The money they raise goes to the school band and the library. Then comes Thanksgiving and Halloween: if Pearl and Joachim have made it that far, Joachim will need a costume for the middle school party. Remembrance Day and Christmas (the school play, the mini cantata) take them to the end of the year. Valentine's Day, Saint Patrick's Day, Easter, etcetera follow in the new year—special days celebrated with something to look forward to beyond the humiliation of passing time. At the commencement of summer holidays, Pearl will be twenty-eight years old.

This time, Pearl finds Joachim half a kilometre upstream in the middle of the night. Moonlight flattens the brush on the opposite bank of the creek, where a deer stands watching. She was sure she had locked the front door. She had made herself a bed downstairs so she would hear Joachim if he went outside. But she hadn't heard. She had slept. Observing the tension in that gaunt, child-adult, her heart aches so acutely that she can hardly breathe.

What is the meaning of life but the care of this child? What is this child, but all of life?

The next morning, after dropping Joachim at school—Pearl doesn't teach the computer class until the following day—she visits the Outfitter's shack attached to the boathouse at the dock. The door is open, but no one is in. A shipshape range of kayaks, paddles, fishing rods, nets, and other equipment, plus a variety of camping gear, is suspended from the ceiling, packed on shelves, or arranged in tidy displays. A counter holds catalogues and an order book. A pass-through leads to an addition that contains clothing. Since it is the end of the season—the Outfitter's will close in a few weeks—bargains proliferate. Pearl selects a warm jacket, three shirts, five pairs of socks, two pairs of jeans, and lined rubber boots for Joachim. With her arms full she re-enters the main room, places the goods on the counter and takes a stroll to an uninvestigated corner which contains consignment goods. These are mostly complicated camping stoves and flimsy alpine tents: but Pearl uproots a stash of diving gear from the bottom of a pile. Wetsuit socks, gloves, hoods, and full suits. Could it be? Yes—one of them might fit her, and another is ideal for Joachim.

Finally, she finds a notice on one side of the door which tells customers to ring a bell to summon assistance. She rings it. Moments later, Bob from the general store jogs in, wheezing.

"Oh," she says. "Sorry! Is this your store? I'd have called at the other one first if I'd known. Hope it's okay—I've picked out what I want. The door was unlocked."

"Why would I lock it? I'd only have to unlock it and then wait around for people to make up their minds."

"Yes, but …"

"Are you planning to run off with that?" He indicates the pile of Pearl's selections.

"No, of course not!"

"You see!" Bob says. His eyebrows twitch rapidly.

Pearl looks at her watch. She needs to mind her schedule. "Right then, Bob," she says, "just put this on my tab."

The afternoon light is golden, but in the shadow of branches, frost grips the leaves. The creek ripples and bubbles, but within its pleasantries a few fish are swimming. Putting aside her intention to explore the path to a pool she had found on the map, Pearl turns in the opposite direction, following the flow of the creek past the concrete vestiges of the reservoir dam. Cottonwoods, birch, alder, and scrub birch surmount bushes that look like azaleas. Green, yellow, and red foliage flashes in the wind, the stream running beside her like a thread of music. It is exhilarating, she could be the first human to pass this way, although the path *is* well-worn. It does not occur to her to wonder why this is until she climbs to the top of the rocky bank where the creek meets the river. A grizzly stands below with its snout angling, sniffing the air. Pearl backs off—she is fairly sure she is downwind and that the bear is too short-sighted to have seen her, or so she hopes. When it lowers its head and splashes into the river to swat up a fish, it seems so. Pearl takes a shuddering breath and beats a retreat, but not before she has noticed that a section of the fish-run in the river has veered to enter the creek.

Retracing the path but maintaining a lookout, banging rocks together, singing, moving at a steady pace, not too quickly—whatever must be done to let Nature understand she is harmless—Pearl passes the demolished dam again, and follows the trail onwards. A splish-splash makes her glance at the creek: but it is only a unit of fish, red and silver, travelling at her heels.

The pool is bigger than she'd anticipated. Reeds prickle its circumference, the marshy edge a conglomerate of mud, waste wood, and stones. Water spills over a weir at the downstream end. As she stands contemplating, a salmon leaps upstream over the weir. At the far end of the pool, the water resolves into a bed of gravel and what may be the creek's source in a spring. Pearl takes in the landscape—a muddy path emerging from the woods, the scent of smoke in the air—until a black pup with white patches on its head advances through the trees wriggling its rear. "Hey, you, gorgeous," she says, and squats to let it nibble her fingers. Its short bushy tail window-wipes. Pointed muzzle and ears, thick glossy coat.

"What are you doing?"

Pearl leaps to her feet. An old man with a white-bristled face, scraggy and dressed in stained trousers and lumberjack shirt, is glowering at her. "Is this your pup?" she says.

He studies her, taking a moment to reply. There is a shotgun, broken from the stock and angled downwards, in his arms. "The pup is mine, and so is this land."

A blush brightens Pearl's complexion. "I'll go then. Sorry. I was hoping … I thought the pond would be public." A few more fish leap the weir, and splash.

"You're from Refuge House," he says.

More fish jump over the weir into the pool. "What the hell is going on?" he says, scowling at the water. "They don't come up this far."

"The Fisheries project took out the dam," Pearl says.

He moves closer. "I saw you the other night with the boy."

"If you did, then *you* were trespassing."

He grins and steps back. "Heard some noise, smelled smoke; I keep an eye out for Nora's place if she's away."

"My grandmother," Pearl says, and she tells him that Nora is dead.

"Ah." He looks away. "I knew she was sick, but I never … She never said."

"You were friends?"

"She didn't mention me, eh? Walter? Well, why should she?" He bends and pats the pup, tickles its ears, straightens, and wipes his sleeve across his eyes. He looks tired.

"What was it you wanted again?" he asks, and listens as Pearl asks if she and Joachim can use the pool for swimming lessons.

"I bought wetsuits today," she says.

"Don't care if you bought wedding gowns," he says, but not unkindly. More fish plop into the pool. Walter's pause as he watches them is long and speculative. He says, "Use the road, don't walk in the way you did, it can be dangerous."

"I'm not frightened," Pearl says, pretending she is simply fine with bears.

"You should be—that pup you like's got parents."

In the quiet after Joachim is in bed, tired from their cold swim, and with a sprinkle of rain rapping the window, a cup of chocolate at her elbow, and her amorphous features distorted in the glass, Pearl unwraps the Arishat doll for the second time. Its aspect is smeared, the body damp and disordered. She smells the straw figure, then opens the drawer in which she'd stored it: a wet patch has darkened the wood. Pulling the drawer right out of the dresser, she spies droppings and a small hole through the end of the drawer and into the wall. Mice. In her care, the doll is being tenanted. Troubling too, is that Pearl has scrutinized the doll and its belongings every which way and found no note from Nora. Refuge House was Nora's final stop; and Arishat is the last of the dolls Nora brought with her to the café, the one remaining signpost to what her grandmother had wanted Pearl to know.

Pearl powers up her computer; her wrists rest on the keyboard. Traces of Arishat's tale stir among the oldest stories in the silt-laden depths of the pool. Arishat, both scribe and dancer, with her see-through dress and an ancient pen. In the dream Pearl had that first night at Refuge House, just before she rushed out to look for Joachim, a scribe in her workroom had lifted her reed pen and looked at her. Was that scribe Arishat?

She turns the image over in her mind, examines the doll and breaks the thread that tacks the tiny pen to the doll's hand. She hunts out a sewing needle from a kit in the kitchen junk drawer, and ferrets inside the reed until she extracts the slip of paper lodged in it. Yes: a note from Nora. *The scribe and dancer, Arishat, lived one hundred and twelve generations before you. Her foster brother, Rib, was your ancestor. The tale includes a cat. When you write the story, don't forget to put that in.*

Was a cat in this tale? The only cat Pearl recalls immediately is the tabby, Grim, that Harry had brought to his marriage with Sara. Pearl had smuggled it into Nora's several times after her parents' separation, but each time the cat escaped and went to its former home. "Too old to change," Harry had said.

"Too dumb," was his ex-wife's verdict.

Pearl sits at the desk and holds the doll, hoping it might give her a clue about how to start. It is only as she touches the tiny, inflated pig bladder again that she understands it is a float—a rudimentary water wing. Soon the characters, including the cat, bubble up from below: Arishat, and her sister Arinna, and their foster brother Rib, and the cat Buto, and others. A little girl Rib loved, an old warrior, and a King.

~

The Orphan's Tale

Sierra Morena, Spain c.950 BCE

If you can find the beginning, it will be inside a cave across a mineral-dusted floor from a small blue pond. At night, moonlight or starlight glides down a shaft of laddered rock and makes the water shine. Moth-currents of air flutter the pond's surface, and in this place of rock and ash, and the massive bones of bears, the cave walls are painted with deer, goats, fish, and ochre-dabbed discs.

Thus far, one daughter, Arishat, has left the hunger that dominates their days and followed her desire to be a dancer; another daughter waits for her parents and foster brother to sleep so she can go too, although hers is a different ambition. A fire burns low, surrounded by stones, and the stones radiate heat. Everyone in the story this night is warm and their stomachs gurgle with soup made from fresh spring greens: but not everyone is content.

"If only I'd been born in a city," the girl said to herself, arguing for what she has already decided. "Then I would be rich and not have to slave for my family. Why should I have to run barefoot over mountains chasing after goats?" This image of her servitude saddened her; tears fell from her eyes. "I have worked hard picking grasses and herbs for others to eat, and my hands are cut and swollen. Who will love me now?" If she was vain, it was not her fault. Arinna was spoiled because she had lovely thick hair and eyes that changed from grey to green; she laughed easily, and people felt happy around her. If she were not honest—did she not eat, too, did not others hunt for her?—it was because she knew that what she was about to do would grieve her family.

Arinna was like a reservoir swollen not by frequent rains but by imagined injustices: it was inevitable that sooner or later the reservoir walls would give way. The danger had been noticed. This was why her brother (an orphan foster brother called Rib) was not asleep. When Arishat left, she'd made Rib promise to be their younger sister's protector. "Arinna is not like us, she doesn't think, she cannot be on her own."

Hearing nothing but silence and snuffles around her, Arinna shifted aside the bear hide that covered her and quietly gathered clothing, murmuring all the while as if she almost wished her sleeping parents to hear her. "My mother says, *Why can't you be like your sister*? My father says, *Say something nice for a change.* Rib says, *Why do you complain? You always get what you want.* It is not true. Nobody in the family cares about me but *someone else* does."

She jumped down from the sleeping platform, dislodging several stones: the sleepers slept on. She hesitated, but time was passing, and although she wanted *him* to wait a little, she did not want *him* to tire of waiting for *her*.

Arinna shut the wooden door that barred the cave behind her. Moonlight patterned the pine and scrub brush in the valley below. It was cold. The mountain-side path was made of broken rock, and it was up that difficult way she was pledged to climb. Arinna said to herself, "*I am not appreciated here. I won't look back*"; but as she climbed, she glanced over her shoulder and saw the heavy door open and Rib slip out like a wraith.

He was thirteen years of age to Arinna's twelve and a half. He would give his life for her if necessary, whether she wanted him to or not. She certainly did not want him coming after her and thwarting her plans.

A long walk brought her past the barking dogs at the herders' huts to an icy field of snow from which she skidded down through scree to a forest. Fir trees gave way to oaks and laurels and then to ash. Owls tidied the flesh and bones of prey and retreated to their dens as Arinna set foot on a riverbank, with Rib lurking, darting from tree trunk to tree trunk after her. Dawn tipped the upper branches of the trees and sent lances of light into the water. Rib squirmed to get a better look but Arinna, mysteriously, was removing her clothing. Rib closed his eyes: she *was* his sister.

A bird sang; the forest shivered and erupted with insects. Something splashed into the water. Rib opened his eyes, could not see Arinna, and bounded from behind the trees. She was gone! He looked around and discovered her folded cloak on the ground beside the river. "Arinna! Arinna!" he screamed. Seconds passed while his mind researched the possibilities, each worse than the other. That splash! The cloak! Together they meant that his volatile sister was attempting to drown herself: Rib jumped into the river to save her.

The rain-swollen waterway ran deep and fast: Rib did not know how to swim. It turned and tumbled and held him under until he finally bobbed up and managed to clutch a broken-off branch of a tree as it passed him. At length—scrubbed bloody by rocks and battered by debris—the river released him and his spar, and he twirled in a quiet eddy next to a dead fawn with never a glimpse of Arinna.

Far upriver, the sun climbed, wildflowers grew beside verges, and the runaway youngsters, Arinna and her love, the son of a wealthy farmer, jogged along in the goat cart he'd pilfered from his father to fetch her. They were pleased with themselves and with the trick Arinna had played on Rib, who was only a foster brother. But the fate of the boy occupied little room in their feelings or plans to live on the carob and olive farm that the young man's father tended. If they gave no thought to those who would suffer from their actions, it did not seem so to them because they were young and unacquainted with pain.

Rib dragged himself from the water and lay gasping in the mud, heartbroken because his sister had drowned. He had promised to look after Arinna and had not kept his promise. He'd failed his foster family, just as when only a small boy, he had failed his own parents after a great wave flooded the land. He had fled into the mountains without waiting for them, while they had delayed to look for him.

He could never return to the cave, to the fire, to the paintings on the walls, to his foster parents. The loss of Arinna was not like the loss of a flower, to be replaced in a season: this loss was forever.

The way ahead was marshy and reed-mapped. Ibis and egrets waded in pursuit of the tiny fish that splashed from his footsteps. Only his foster parents could have told him that the river had brought him to the place he had come from, and that the sand dunes and half-buried relics of laurel and pine he passed were configured upon bones. More than once in this region that shadowed the coast, the sea had retreated in a breath after an earthquake, then swept in at the speed of a galloping horse.

After two days of walking, he arrived as he'd hoped, at the road south to Gadir, the road his older sister Arishat had taken when she left home. Seaward, the dunes were stable, underpinned by deposits left behind when a covering of ice and snow had melted into the sea. Landward lay a widely spaced pine forest. On its fringes, Rib found evidence of camp sites—charred grass within circles of flat stones, broken pottery, and shreds of worn clothing. At every curve of the way, he expected to meet merchants or entertainers or others who might give him food in exchange for some service—travelling as he was to the city of commerce; but all he came upon before the sun touched the sea's horizon, was a white cat that stepped in and out of the trees and kept pace with him.

His foster mother, who had been out in the wide world before her marriage, said that cats came on ships from lands in which they were privileged companions, but in the city of Gadir they were kept in order to kill rats. If true, it was an honourable living, for Rib had seen rats destroy his foster family's crops and had watched helplessly when horses he had tamed and loved and ridden had starved because of this over a long winter.

He called to the cat to see if it would come to him, but the animal ran off.

With the sun dying to his right, the moon rising over a cork forest to his left, and the city straight ahead, Rib approached a crossroads. To go on in the dark would not be wise. He was not frightened of wild animals—he had preserved horses from wolves with clubs and stones and chased bears from caves with lit torches—but he was cautious. The unknown was a window which once opened, was difficult to close. He withdrew into the corkwood, and after a scrabble for mushrooms at the base of trees, he rolled into the cover of low brush and dry grasses and tried to rest.

Gadir, the city to which Rib journeyed, was built on an island which all but closed off a bay not far to the west of the Gates of Hercules. It was a centre for trade under the protection of temples established on nearby islands. Rib's foster sister, Arishat, lived on one of them, the dancers' island. Rib's plan was to speak to her about Arinna's death and ask her to tell their parents what had happened, for he did not have the courage. *Look how he had repaid them for all they had done!* He did not hope for forgiveness, but perhaps Arishat, initiated into the cult of the Goddess, creator of all, would tell him how to make what recompense he could. Images of Arinna undressing at the river, him shutting his eyes, the sound of the splash, her cloak on the riverbank, and his unpardonable indecision while his sister swallowed water and sank into darkness, tormented him unrelentingly.

Moonlight illuminated each scar the cutters had made in the bark of the cork trees. He blinked at this until exhaustion overcame his hunger and distress, and he slept; and since a dream can be what is and what is not, Rib dreamed of a bridge with a leather sack in the middle of it. Each time he tried to cross to Arishat at the far end, he delayed to open the sack, but before he could look inside, the dream restarted. Eventually managing to traverse the bridge without halting, and with Arishat in sight, Rib jolted awake to the sound of breaking branches. A man shouted, "Come here you brat!" Speeding footsteps thudded towards him.

"I'll teach you to run from me!" the man cried. Rib crawled deeper into the undergrowth. "You won't escape for long! You are silent now, but I'll soon have you yelling!" the man roared.

Suddenly, a girl of five or six years of age scrambled in beside him. Their eyes met and he saw that she held the white cat. The pulse in the girl's neck was beating violently. Her pale grey eyes recorded his appearance. She breathed, "*Look after him!*" He put his finger to his lips to warn her to shush, but she thrust the cat at him and darted into the open like a flushed quail. Rib's gasp as the cat clawed his arms was covered by her scream as the man stepped into her path and seized her. The moon washed the scene with blue light: the blue dress of the child, her red hair drained to ash, the violet of her skin, the blue-black of the man's beard. The swing of his fist to her head. Could Rib not help anyone? He let go of the cat and rushed as the girl had, into the open. Only the Goddess that his sister served, knew who he thought he could save—this strange child, or drowned Arinna, or perhaps himself. Although the man was fat-bellied, when he saw Rib he pivoted quickly, jammed the stunned girl under an arm, and grabbed Rib's throat.

It could have been the end, so early in Rib's story, but this was not the time.

A merchant, neither kind nor unkind, but who did not want his merchandise stolen, was also sheltering in the wood, and hearing the commotion, woke his sleeping sentry. The sentry hauled up, clattered his sword, and swept all before him. The little girl escaped from her attacker and vanished as if she had been a butterfly.

Rib lay on the cork forest floor. He was a heap of cuts and bruises held together by skin. He was young, on the cusp of manhood, but in his humiliation, his childhood leaked from his eyes.

Myron, the merchant, said politely, "What sorrow has brought you to me?" before attending to the boy. He rubbed ointment into Rib's wounds, wrapped him in a blanket and gave him a piece of bread dipped in wine to gnaw. Then, Myron checked over his goods, made certain the sentry was awake, and rolled himself in his blanket. Rest eluded him. By the look of the boy, the rags he wore, his calluses, and his neck—unspeakable—no family would come looking for him; but bravery counted, and what the boy had done by intervening against a grown man, a notorious slaver, was valorous. What to do?

He looked at Rib's swollen countenance in the moonlight. If the boy's arrival had a beneficent purpose and the Goddess had an ear tuned to his prayers, it would show itself. If not, well then.

Rib woke early, and while the guard lay abed scratching his groin, he folded the blanket into a neat square, rolled it and tucked it behind Myron's donkey's saddle. He combed his hair with his fingers, inspected the camp site to see what else he could do, and saw Myron assembling packages. "Can I help?" he asked. Myron paused. The guard wandered off to relieve himself. A horse, not too distant, neighed, conveying the presence of others along with a question about its breakfast. Rib angled his head to listen to it, but then Myron said, "Where have you come from? You are not from here. Come, eat, and tell me."

Rib squatted to eat the bread Myron cut from a loaf. The white cat dashed from between the donkey's legs to gobble the crumbs. The cat's left ear flopped, half torn off. Rib glanced round to see if the little girl were with it, but she was not.

"Well?" Myron said. The guard sat near them. The cat scooted away. Rib said nothing and they ate in silence, for he did not want to tell the story of his shame. The donkey jangled its harness. Myron sighed.

"Go on, get on with it, go home," he said at last to the guard. "You know the way, and what will happen if anything goes missing." Then Myron turned to Rib. "I could use your help today, if you are willing.

With Rib's assistance, the merchant gathered a variety of collection bags, nets, and bird cages, and they followed a path out of the wood to a rocky coast on a large bay, the sea a polished flexible sheet of marbled stone.

Women and children were bent to the work of salt gathering on rock platforms pocked with hollows in which salt had crystallized. The rock pans were blue and pink at their rims, sugary in appearance. Some of the labourers glanced at them, but the wind blurred any greeting they may have shouted. Rib gawped, but Myron tugged at the rope that linked them together in case of a fall from the rocks. "Mind your feet, boy, mind the nets and cages." By now, Rib had an inkling of what they would be doing, but he knew not to rush in with questions. They turned inland, proceeding through soft sand to a clump of pines where they stopped to rest and eat. A song sparrow warbled, and the merchant nodded with satisfaction.

"Come," he said, and gave Rib a bag of seed. Rib followed Myron's example and scattered the kernels on the ground, then helped him unroll and string fine-meshed netting over the baited earth and through the trees. Myron fished a soft bag from a pocket, undid its strings and took a live bird from it which he placed on a branch. It was a sparrow, fitted with a harness, a ring, and a tether. The little bird launched itself from the branch only to fall when it came to the end of its leash. It sang and sang, and soon other birds—finches, swallows, thrushes, and waxwings—flew in to feed and were caught in the net where they beat their wings in frenzy.

"Such good companions for women, my customers love them," Myron said. He took another bird from a bag. "Pay attention, boy! Hold this while I am collecting." *This* was a bird with a white stripe on its head and dull brown feathers frazzled over its wings. It carolled sharply, beautifully. "Hold it like this," Myron said, putting the twig on which the bird perched between Rib's fingers. He straightened it so that the wood crossed Rib's palm, but the bird's quaking body tipped and fell against Rib's wrist and Rib realized that its feet were glued to the stick. Any attempt to release it (he was tempted, of course he was) would cripple and kill it; but left as it was, it would break its heart in song and lure more and more birds to Myron's traps. Rib righted the bird, and it sang.

The city's harbour lay tucked close beneath the city walls. The boat-master navigated in with the last of the day's sun and helped them onto the shadowed pier with their bags and parcels and cages. Since the fate of animals is tied in with that of human beings, Rib was not surprised that the white cat with the torn ear jumped ashore when Myron's back was turned, or that the little girl from the wood emerged from beneath a pile of sacking in front of the tiller. The boatmaster ruffled her tangled hair as she dashed by onto the quay and into the arms of a tall foreigner. Rib caught a glimpse of the man's grizzled locks and woven cap within the hood of his calf-length robe. The man swung the girl up, lightly stroked her facial bruises. "You should not run off like that, Margetta! Not even for Buto! What would I do without you?" he said. He did not plague her with questions.

The child twisted round to stare at Rib, then squirrelled her head into the man's shoulder. "If you cannot find Buto, come and tell me. You know what he's like; he runs away but he always returns." He carried the child to a waiting horse, placed her astride it and climbed on behind. Rib knew something of horses from working the herd in the mountains with his foster father. Those horses were small and sturdy, with large heads and erect manes. But this horse was different: it was tall, with a long neck and elegant head. Its mane and tail were woven in intricate patterns.

Myron, busy snapping the necks of birds with broken wings, glanced over. "You want to steer clear of those people," he said.

"That horse—it is unusual."

"If you say so."

"I have never seen anything like it."

"Why would you? It's a battle horse. They do not tie them to haystacks. But I mean it, you should stay away."

"Who are *they*?"

"Does it matter?"

Rib, armed with bags and cages, waited. Although Myron liked collecting information, he also liked to show it off. Rib had learned much of the habits of Myron's customers, what they ordered, and from whom they hid their purchases.

The merchant killed more wounded birds. "He is a mercenary—he hires himself out for money."

"The horse, too?"

Myron gave Rib a sharp look. "He trains them for whoever leases them. Someone like that will do anything if it pays."

"And the girl?"

Myron shrugged. "A stray he took in with the cat."

"You can sleep here tonight," Myron said after they'd transported the captive birds to a storeroom in Myron's house and filled the cage trays with seed and water. He took Rib into the kitchen. "First, of course, you must eat." He assembled bread and cheese and wine, told the guard to stand at the outer door, and steered Rib up the stairs to the roof.

They made themselves comfortable on cushions and rugs, and ate. The moon ascended into the darkening sky and Myron lit a lamp. He waved a smoking pot of frankincense to perfume the air, set it down and said to Rib, "So, if you please, your tale?"

Pain suffused the boy who had been relishing these comforts and forgetting to think of Arinna. The weight of his failings, freshly evoked, threatened to crush him. Yet, a bargain was a bargain, albeit unspoken, and the price of the meal and a bed was this task. He protested anyway, "I am too young to have a story."

"Surely not," Myron said. "No one is too young." He smiled, patted Rib's foot and settled in for whatever entertainment would unfold beneath the clock of the constellations. The silence expanded. Myron hummed a little and said, "Tell me about your home. Let us open your story with that."

Rib began. He told of the mountains and his work with his foster father.

"What more? What made you journey so far from those who love you?" Love was Myron's subject; or he would like it to be. Until recently he had been happy counting his money, but in the market weeks earlier, a girl had come to his stall.

She was a young dancer, making public entry into service of the Goddess. In the market, she had spread the oil and spikenard she had purchased from him through her hair: then the drumming began, people arrived, the wind blew, and the sun climbed. A pipe joined in. The girl rang her finger bells, and someone began clapping rhythmically. The spell of the spikenard took hold, and she kissed Myron on the mouth. Whatever spices lay within Myron began to flow, too. The girl swirled into a group of women and was gone. The next thing Myron knew, the sail of the boat carrying her cut the sky on its way to the dancers' island.

"Please," Myron said, "you must tell me all you can. Little on this Earth occurs by coincidence. Have you come to Gadir with a purpose?"

"I am looking for my sister," Rib said reluctantly.

"A sister! Here, in Gadir! Why didn't you say so? I will take you to her."

"She does not live in the city, exactly, but nearby," Rib said.

"Not in the city, but . . ."

"On the dancers' island. I have news for her. Family news," he added in a strained voice. "A report only I can deliver."

"A temple dancer?" Rib nodded and Myron hummed again. "Is she older or younger?"

"Older," Rib said.

"Not a new dancer, then."

"She is a scribe and a scholar."

Myron tapped his cheeks with his fingers to help him concentrate. The humming and tapping frayed Rib's stretched nerves.

"No men are permitted on the island, except for certain purposes, for which you are too young, and I am not likely to be invited."

"I am her brother," Rib said. "Foster brother," he amended.

"No matter. A man is a man, unfortunately."

Rib stood. "What will I do? I must see her!" He thought of their parents, alone in the mountains with no idea of what had happened to him or their youngest daughter. He wished himself asleep in the cave, too lazy to have followed Arinna. But no: she would have taken the path on which she had determined anyway, but without a witness to tell the tale. Young women were not like other persons, he reminded himself. They were driven by baffling passions.

"Despair is for the old or the very young: you are quite the wrong age," Myron said. "Let me give the problem some thought, I may be able to help you."

They arrived at the docks early the next morning to find that many of the market traders had arrived ahead of them, their goods already arranged in the best spots. Larger crowds than usual were expected. As well as housewives, maids, and factotums (typical market-goers), many relatives and the curious would be at the docks to bid farewell to the party of gifted children and dancers, an annual tribute, who were being sent by ship to the court of the King of Jerusalem. Some of the dancers were trained scribes and accountants, wise in the ways of business as well as the Goddess: some would warm the King's bed. The children were budding magicians, tumblers, and musicians. While the children waited, they showed off their skills to spectators, little thinking they would never see their families again.

The wind blew and stirred the pot of the harbour, lapped waves against ship-sides, rattled ropes, fluttered robes and loose belts and unbound hair, snapped the shutters of the sun open and closed. Portside was a flurry of porters, donkey-drawn carts, and oxen pulling heavy loads of timbers. Crates of fish, jars of honey, heaped sacks of barley, wheat and spelt, great baskets of dates, figs, pomegranates, and pears formed obstacles to the passage of the crowds. And then came a rush of livestock—goats and sheep and the famous Gadir cattle clearing a path by their numbers.

A white cat, one ear cut at an angle, jumped onto Myron's goods bench, and buried its nose in a facial treatment of ants' eggs. It was Buto—Margetta's cat! Rib spun, cast around for the girl and spotted her by the flare of her hair amid a flock of sheep. He scanned the throng for her mercenary friend and spied him on the battle horse, twisting his head in quest of his charge. Like Arinna, Margetta only did what she wanted.

The dancers entered the precinct led by drum and flute, the older ones in heavy dress robes, the younger with coverings so light the wind wrapped them to their bodies. "You can see everything!" a woman near Rib exclaimed, but any hint of censure vanished in the joyful lift of the music and the step of the dancers' feet. Rib climbed onto the bench to look for his sister. Earlier that morning, after confiding his passion for a young dancer, Myron had told him, "They'll all come to honour those who sail with the children, every single one of them, your sister and the girl I love with them."

The gangplank slithered and met its block. The departing children and dancers split off from the others and ascended it. The sailors lining the sheer strake, blinked against the slanting light. The oars groaned into position. As drum and flute fell silent, Myron eased into the company of dancers left on the dock. He bowed, he smiled, and he bestowed on his beloved a basket of oils, cosmetics, and perfumes. The pack flowed around them as if they were stones in a stream. Rib stretched taller to look, but his sister was not with them. Was that her onboard the ship? He raised himself on his toes. Yes, that was Arishat, wasn't it? He lost sight of her. The girl opened another of Myron's packages and slung a rope of amber beads over her head. It settled around her neck and drew eyes to her bosom.

"Come with us and you'll pick jewels like that from trees!" a sailor shouted at her from the ship. It was one bellowed remark, that was all, but it made Rib recall the slaver's shouts and the flash of Margetta's heels as she ran in terror. His head snapped round. "Margetta, Margetta!" he cried, suddenly anxious. The horse and rider had shifted station, and he could not find them. He jumped down and pushed through the mass of people to where he'd last seen the child. He heard her yelp, elbowed those in his way aside and arrived at the feet of the black-robed slaver who had wrapped the girl in his cloak. Rib dove and wrenched Margetta from his clutch. She fell, the cloak opened, Margetta raised the dazed dish of her face to acknowledge Rib, and then she was up and gone.

The slaver caught Rib by the throat. "Once is too much, twice means you die," he said. Rib had an instant to inhale the man's stench and register deep stinging as the slaver drew a blade under Rib's chin. Blood sheeted from the opened flap and drenched the boy's clothing. He kept his footing, but his life was an ebbing wave as the slaver walked calmly away.

As the withdrawing gangplank shrieked, Rib blinked, swivelled his head, and saw the cat with the torn ear hanging from the footway's underside. "Oh, a ratter, let it come!" someone cried from onboard. In that instant

Margetta, tiny and determined, sprang from the dock with her arms out: she took flight for the ship, and a hand snaked from the sheer strake and grabbed her.

"Let the tumbler come too," a woman said. The sailor hauled Margetta over the railing.

A swirl of seabirds lofted from the water at the splash of the departing ship's oars; and then the sails elevated, and the tides and currents closed. Air bubbled in the blood from Rib's slit throat. He slid to the ground. All was lost. First Arinna, and this day Margetta, and lastly Arishat, the wise counsellor he had counted on: for the voice welcoming the tumbler was hers.

Rib woke to find himself on a cot, with a bandage around his throat, in a little room built over stalls in the horse trainer's quarter. A cool, dust-laden wind, all the way from Africa, blew through the window. A smell of horses wafted from below and settled over him as lightly as a feather blanket.

"Do not touch the wound. I have put an ointment on it I use for the horses, you will be better in no time." It was the mercenary—the man he had seen with Margetta. Rib tried to speak.

"No, do not talk; you need the gash to close. He had not the skill to sever a throat, the butcher, but he did make you bleed. If I had not got to you, you would have drained your life while others dithered. Maybe that's what he wanted. That style of cut is the way to leech a pig and not taint the meat."

"Mar …" Rib tried again to speak. Tears welled in his eyes. The man studied him.

"Do not doubt yourself. You saved Margetta. If it had not been for you the slaver would have taken her." His eyes glistened, too. "It is not the first time you have come to her rescue; she told me what you did for her before.

"At least she is free," the mercenary said and wiped his nose on a cloth square. "He would have made her suffer; he does not like to be balked. I have seen his work before."

"Who?" Rib managed.

"Do not talk. A cut throat is a cut throat; it must be rested. You will wear the scar for life, but you will not end up like me." He leaned close. One side of the man's visage, normally obscured by his hood, was a web of raised welts that pulled at an eye and continued down his cheek to the side of his mouth. Combat scars, honourable wounds doubtless, not like Rib's from his futile bumbling.

The man raised Rib's head and dribbled liquid between his lips. "You have to drink or die. You must not die. You must help me. The merchant said your sister, the dancer you search for, was on that ship with Margetta. We will go after them both."

"Father?" Rib managed.

"Do not speak!" But the mercenary knew what Rib asked. "Margetta is an orphan. I will tell you how we met if it makes you hold your tongue." He poured more liquid into Rib's maw and looked to see if it soaked the bandage around his throat from inside. "Better. The binding holds," he said.

A horse whinnied in the stable below and was answered by another several lanes away. Outside, women busied themselves with water and brooms and brushes, undoing the dust wind's work.

"My name is Vethur. I was horse-master to the brother of the King of Jerusalem. They fell out over the succession and the King had him killed. I was threatened with death, too, and so I fled.

"Since then, I have trained battle horses and fought in conflicts in every part of the world. After the fight that did this to me,"—he indicated his scarred cheek and damage to his arm and side—"I came to Gadir. They say I train with magic; it is not magic, but it is costly." Vethur smiled.

"Your merchant friend told me you are handy with horses and might be useful. I hope that is true. I have no employment for the ignorant." He settled Rib on the pillows.

"If you remain quiet, I will tell you about Margetta. You are in her room, as you see."

Rib shifted his gaze and spotted a small robe on a hook, and a pair of slippers on the floor. An assortment of pebbles on a table was arranged as the rooms of a house—with pottery fragments, feathers, sticks of wood, and other scraps standing in for furniture. He had not thought of Margetta as a child who played.

"Her parents were foreigners. I learned how they died because I made enquiries; but what is done is done. In the poorest of neighbourhoods, like anywhere else, some people have what others want." Vethur sighed. The hood filled with deeper shadows, but Vethur shook them off.

"After the slaughter, Margetta—four years old, no more—followed the cat away from the blood in that house. She took nothing with her but this doll." He delved into his sash and brought out a small paddle-shaped object that he set beside Rib on the bed. "The cat spotted a place to sleep beneath a fisherman's boat and Margetta crawled in with it. I upturned the craft, looking for an acquaintance of mine who sometimes slept outdoors, and instead I found them: Margetta and Buto. She would not come with me unless I let her bring the cat. It was both or none, you see. We have been together since. If you look at the pillow beside you, Rib, you will observe that the cat slept with her." Rib looked: short tufts of white cat hair clung to the pillow's fabric.

"Having found Margetta, I was not sure what to do. But she was safer sleeping in the horses' quarter than on the seashore where wild dogs roam. Buto was safer, too. He ate scraps and paid his way by catching the mice that live in the hay. Margetta was not afraid of the horses; I caught her climbing the leg of a stallion and pulled her down. 'Let me go!' she cried—you have seen what she is like—so I let her do what she wanted. She hiked herself up by means of horsehair and skin and lay across the animal's back. She fell asleep as if she'd found the lap of her mother. Buto leapt up to accompany her. The horse stood for it, I don't know why, only a tremour in his hide revealing the strain. If you want magic, there it is!

"I took Margetta with me outside the city to train my band of horses for combat. I work them through a string of trotting, cantering, and swimming until they can trot twenty-five miles and canter a mile and a half without resting. Their legs grow strong, their hearts improve. Seven months of training; seven months without break. I feed them four times a day. Margetta gave them salt and a meal of vetch after they swam. She helped wash and brush and rub them down. She became my good right arm." Vethur opened his palms, gazed into them, and folded his hands in his lap.

He re-checked Rib's bandages, and finding them satisfactory, he went on. "After one of those long training days, a troupe of travellers camped nearby. They had horses, too. Their animals were short and stocky—yellow, with dark legs and a streak down the spine. Their children vaulted over the horses' croups, rode backwards, stood on their heads, and somersaulted, all while the horses cantered. I had seen it before—riders' stunts are no use to my horses—but it was new to Margetta. I found her trying these tricks herself, the cat leaping and jumping with her, too, although the most patient warhorse of all will not permit it for long.

"You saw how she sprang after Buto at the departing ship, without a thought that she could miss or fail. Her confidence is her strength and her weakness."

The mercenary took a deep breath. Rib thought it must be rare he had anyone to talk to.

Rib struggled to speak. "Me!" he said, but Vethur's glare silenced him. He wanted to say that he had done similar feats with horses at home. He was not afraid of anything Vethur might ask him to do.

"Hush! Just listen.

"It was only after the mice were gone that Buto began to go out on his own. I would have fed him meat from my plate if it could have kept him home and eased Margetta's mind. Something drew him—we know little about what a cat wants, and the cat does not say.

"What more could I have done? She *had* to follow the cat: where Buto went Margetta went. Blame me for not being able to rein her in if you like. But, why, *why* did she have to?"

If Rib could have answered he would have said, *Because she thinks the cat will lead her to the home she lost.* Not to have a home at all—that was hard. The cat and Margetta would never stop looking.

"Well," said Vethur, lifting his chin, "we have to bring them back, so I will tell you the rest.

"Before coming to Gadir, I'd had a year of swimming for my life after shipwreck, of entering villages on outermost coasts where, at sight of me people threw bricks and sticks and stones, whatever they had. At the Gadir city gate, I drew my hood close about my head, lowered my eyes and expected to be challenged and chased. Instead, the soldier at the gate only said, 'Profession?'"

"'Horse trainer,' I said, and he pointed the way to the stables. It was not long before my skills were sought after. You will see what they are if you work with me.

"I am strong, notwithstanding my injury. I help the fishermen haul their boats; and if the fish fail and the fishermen starve, I take them west to new fishing grounds, beyond their fear that the Earth is a saucer from which they will spill. North from there, you reach the Tin Islands; south and you find the coast of Africa; follow it round and across to Arabia and there is gold so pure it does not need smelting, and incense and perfumes and precious spices, all traded without licence or tolls. We are at the close of a horse-training period. I am telling you Rib, because we must leave soon and take the horses with us to sell. You will need to conquer your fear about such travel—for who am I to contradict the certainty of our betters who assure me it cannot be done, although I have done it! Yes, that is the way I came!" He laughed, and the scarred half of his aspect produced a grimace.

"I had promised Margetta she would be safe. I want you to help me with that promise. I believe you care for her, and you have your own motive for the journey. From Arabia, if you are as brave as I think, we will make our way along the trade routes to the King of Jerusalem—the same to whom Margetta and your sister are bound, and the same who threatened me with death. By then, we will have money. Gold in sacks, and profits from goods sent back here to Gadir that the merchant will sell for us.

"Our only means to success is to act in secret and with surprise, and with plenty of money for bribery. And by keeping far from the King's spies who will wish to kill me."

Rib imagined the journey: he would be fine with the horses, and the mercenary would conclude he was indispensable. There was no other purpose to his life anyway but to find his sister and the child who voyaged with her. He held out his hand in promise, but the man's attention was on the sky beyond the window, not on him.

"I think of my own childhood, its winter cold, and loneliness. I have seen the look in Margetta's eyes as her memories come. Maybe they are not memories but the paler impressions of infancy. Whatever they are, may there be good in them as well as the evil she witnessed. I will not abandon her: I am all the family she has."

Rib struggled out, “Me!” This time Vethur saw and grasped his hand.

Before he left Rib alone to rest, Vethur retrieved Margetta’s doll from where it lay. He tucked it into his sash. There was little to it, a rectangular wooden form with a face and a dress painted on; and hair made of twine strung with clay beads.

“When I was transporting horses, I saw dolls like this in a country at the confluence of three rivers on the Nile. Its rulers wanted small fast horses to invade their neighbours. If that is where Margetta’s parents came from, they had travelled a long way to get here. I am sorry for what was done to them. She will be sad without her only treasure; we will take it to her.”

Even before Rib sighted the coastline of southern Arabia, he smelled frankincense, myrrh, and cinnamon on the wind. Soon, they were docked in the country of the Sabeans, just as Vethur had promised, selling the battle horses that despite the long voyage, had arrived fit and well. Vethur had used his relationship with the fishermen to hire a crew and captain willing to overcome their doubts about the route for a share in the profits, and now they were eager to return to Gadir with the cargo of perfumes, spices, and gold bullion Vethur had purchased for Myron to sell in the Gadir market. After bidding the ship farewell, Rib and the mercenary signed on to a caravan travelling the spice route northwards. Concealed in their belongings was enough gold to finance the venture and to pay any bribes or ransom needed once they found Margetta and Arishat in

Jerusalem. From Rib's point of view, they'd faced down one impossibility and were ready to take on another. In the meantime, Rib's new world began to display its wonders.

In the grey desert, stone columns cast shadows over the sand, and stone cities lay sweating next to wadis that conveyed water in the wet season into the desert for irrigation. Seeds slumbered in the sand, ready to bloom at the first touch of rain, but for now the exhausted sky was hot and white.

At oases with date palms, wells, and cisterns, they harnessed camels to wheel shafts to draw buckets of water; and went on to cross fields of pink stone over which the camels had to pick their way. Filigreed cities retreated and became sandstone cliffs, and there were hills with green in the clefts between them. Mountains inscribed with catchment ridges stored rainwater that seeped through pinprick holes into massive chambers where the water slept, ready to be tapped and spilled down steps that had been carved by slaves in the stone, to disperse intruders.

A day from the crossroads that would take them off the northward route and east to Jerusalem, a soldier summoned them to his captain, and the captain to the steward, while the others in the party (drivers and traders and cooks) unloaded camels and prepared to eat and rest, and the soldiers to set pickets.

The steward lounged on cushions inside his tent but kept them standing. "We have seen you before, but not for some years. Vethur," he said to the mercenary. "It took time for us to remember you. We never thought to see you again. Why are you here?"

Vethur caught the captain's eye. These two were battle mates from long ago clashes. The captain looked away. The steward stroked his beard and waited.

"My child was taken," Vethur began.

The steward waved him to silence. "No woman would have you with those scars. You are running from something, or you have come to make trouble. You should have been put to death on sight, but the King has granted amnesty to his foes. I wonder, though, does it extend to one who served his greatest enemy?"

"I did nothing deserving of exile."

"The King ordered your banishment."

"The King killed my master."

The steward shook his head. Rib, who had followed only a little of the exchange in a language new to him, watched a cat creep into the tent and snatch roasted meat from a platter.

"However, we cannot foresee a King's wishes, and it is better to be cautious, to let things lie if we can." The steward tented his fingers and tapped them against his chin. "Yes, that would be best, but you have made me unhappy by making yourself my problem. I believe you and your young friend would do well in the northern territories. There is always a need for fighters at the borders."

"I will consider the offer."

"It is not an offer."

"The boy is an apprentice; he grooms horses; he is no fighter. He can make himself useful here."

"Unhardened in combat, is he? He is young, yes, but he is also a keen rider who has trained under you. He bears his own scars." The steward gestured to the captain who tilted Rib's head back and exposed his scored neck. "Is he a thief? Did you save him from execution? It shows heart, Vethur, I will give you that, if you have taken in a thief to reform. Unless you are a thief too?"

"Secure them," the steward ordered and dismissed them, but not before murmuring, "Of course, if you could pay," he rubbed his thumb and index fingers together, "we might find another way."

The fall of the tent flap as they left cut off the steward's laughter.

Night-time: the stars in a brilliant sky were a scrip of silver. Rib lay, bound, on the ground and listened to the dark-muted sounds around him. "Old friend," the captain had muttered to Vethur, "they have found your gold, I am sorry," and then he tied ropes around Vethur and Rib himself. With the nearby world asleep, Vethur kicked Rib's foot and Rib slipped off his bindings. The caravan breathed deeply. Its chimeras configured the air like wavering candles. Rib did not say of the easy escape, "Could it be a trick?" but he thought the words of a prayer to his lost parents and his grieving step-parents and to drowned Arinna before he crawled after Vethur into the darkness. Campfires snoozed behind them, watch-soldiers snored, sodden with drink. The captain would be punished for his largesse with wine as well as for their flight, it went without saying. Or did it? His sword was sharp; his men were his own more than anyone's. Blood and danger form ties of which the steward was ignorant. Not all men can be governed by fear.

"Be merciful, be kind, have tenderness towards us." Vethur's prayers winged to his own gods.

They had travelled deep into the hills by late morning and come to a town encompassed by a thick wall of dried brick. On a heap of rubble at the base of this wall, a batch of old men swatted flies and warmed themselves in the sunshine.

"Brothers," Vethur said to them, "we greet you."

"Brothers," the men responded.

"May we trouble you for a cup of water?"

"All are welcome to drink from our well," an old man said. An attentive child drew water, filled a jug, and poured out two cups. Vethur and Rib seated themselves and drank the cold water thankfully.

"Whence have you come and where are you going?" the old man said. "What is your purpose while you are here?"

Vethur was about to reply according to the formula, *From my old home to my new home, and to be of service to you*, when a white cat sunning with the ancients glided off a stone and jumped into his lap. He gasped, but no words came. He felt its jagged left ear and then over its head and body. "It cannot be!" he cried. But there it was: not only the damaged ear, but a dent in the skull and certain marks on the paws that both Rib and Vethur knew. Tears rinsed the mercenary's eyes. "Rib, can you believe it. It is Buto!" Vethur buried his face in the animal's fur. The cat bristled, moved off, and rubbed against Rib's ankles. The elders tapped sticks on the ground and laughed.

Rib had *thought* it was Buto in the steward's tent but had not believed it possible. Yet, here was the cat again! If it *were* Buto. The world was awash in cats. All night long, in any street, you heard them wailing, smacking into walls, toppling garbage. It could be another like him.

Rib considered the bleached stony ground, the few dusty trees, the knots of sheep and goats. He bent and stroked the cat which purred as it brushed his shins. "Where Buto goes, there goes Margetta," he muttered to himself, but before he could decide what to do, the cat stretched and loped off. Vethur stood to follow.

For days, they trekked the ravine the old men had shown them, then journeyed into a land of open chalky soil, no springs, and few wells. Wherever they found water, Buto appeared, drank his fill, and slipped away. They climbed from the flat into sunburnt hills, passing flocks and herds and stone villages on ridges. For a while, there were enough coins in the pouch Vethur wore and never took off (if only the steward had known!) to buy bread and cheese and barley and give something to the cat when it turned up. But autumn advanced and winter surged into the hills through which they wandered. Lightning crackled the ceramic sky, and rainwater gushed through gullies and shifted boulders to block their way. In the higher hills, crystalline limestone paths cut through the worn soles of their shoes to tear at their feet, and they made slow progress.

They were thin and weak from hunger after Vethur's coins ran out. They spoke the names Margetta and Arishat and went over their plans to reach them; but these, like the destination of Jerusalem itself, became like a well-chewed, flavourless bone that offered little sustenance.

Late one afternoon, after a bitter fall of hail, they halted to wash their feet and apply a salve that Rib made from herbs and a little oil. Rib had used the ointment for his stepfather's horses, and it seemed to help their own sores and blisters. They bound their feet with rags, tied on what was left of their shoes and climbed a little higher to a sheepfold. To the west, cloud and mist lay over the sea like a stack of white dishes. To the north, torches lit the thick stone walls of a city at the end of a long valley.

"We will have to risk going there," Vethur said. "We cannot survive like this much longer." He was practised at building fires that smouldered all night, and he could guide them to paths few others travelled. Rib could always boil a meal from frosted herbs and tubers: but, if they were not to die before they reached their goal, they needed to find better shelter and food.

"There will be a price on our heads. What will happen if we are discovered?"

"We will not be," Vethur said. "But if so, you will run at my signal and find Margetta and your sister."

"Me?" Rib croaked, as if his throat were still wounded. "We do this together. That's what you said."

Vethur shook his head and went off with his knife to cut fuel.

The flames of campfires sprang up all along the valley. The smell of roasting meat climbed from the nearest fires and mingled with the sweet scent of the thyme branches Vethur had found to burn. The cat materialized, paced the sheepfold walls, caught a rodent among the stones, and crunched its way through the minute bones while Rib and Vethur ate their mess of herbs and grains.

Next day, after continuing despite sleet and wind until they were not far from the city walls, a man at a camp site called out, "Come and join us. Come! Tonight, we feast!"

Vethur halted, turned aside, and said over his shoulder to Rib, "It will do us good to talk with others and remember we are not the only unlucky travellers in the world."

Rib wanted to say, "No." He was afraid of distractions; fearful he would lose the will to continue. He hesitated, but before he could speak, Vethur saw his reluctance and said, "Would you have us insult those who offer what little they have out of kindness? But look! The weather is clearing; we do not need to reach the city tonight."

"All right, but we cannot stay long," Rib said, thinking how much time had passed since his friend had enjoyed a conversation. The road had taken a heavy toll. Vethur's weary eyes brightened. He waved agreement to the strangers. As he and Rib drew closer, they saw that the women's clothes although well-worn, were sewn with gold thread, and the men's vests displayed beautifully embroidered birds. Rib brushed dust from his ragged tunic and straightened his shoulders.

Inside a skin tent, a circle of men sat on the ground around a cloth spread with dishes of olives, melons, and dates. A woman brought bowls of water, and towels. "Eat something please, and then we will talk," the man said. "Later, there will be meat."

They ate sparingly, aware that women and children would not yet have been fed. Rib listened to Vethur and their host converse in a dialect he could not understand. After a time, Rib tired of pretending to be part of the conversation and fell silent, his facial muscles stiff from grinning. He tugged at the hem of his shirt and yanked down its sleeves. Despite the poor diet, he had grown, and the shirt no longer fitted him.

"Ah," the new friend said to Vethur, noting Rib's discomfiture. "It is a shame he does not understand. He is not your son, not of your people?"

"Like a son," Vethur replied.

"He must go outside and be with those his own age," the man said. "We are too dull for youngsters."

Outdoors in the shortening day, with the wind knifing down the valley, Rib neared a group of youths at the cooking fires. One of the boys beckoned him to help shift a beheaded, skinned camel onto the burning coals of a cooking pit. With the help of three others, they lifted and arranged the carcass as the women directed. It was a poor camp, with no stock except for a hobbled, flea-plagued donkey and an old horse chewing at the thin grazing. He shrugged away the puzzle of the origin of the slaughtered animal (was it a stray, a payment, a gift?) and stood near the donkey. He watched hungrily as the roasting carcass spat fat, and shrivelled. The camel's legs drew in. As the slit stomach crisped, curled, and parted, it revealed the tucked head, nested limbs and blackening backbone of a calfling. Rib crouched, retched, and vomited, not caring who saw him.

At home in the mountains, Rib helped to birth the foals. He had witnessed the pain of mares in long labour and intervened to turn the foals in the womb and unhook their stuck hooves. He had seen the mothers sniff and lick the newborns and rejoiced with them to see the babies wobble to their feet and suckle. He had watched other mares refuse to leave their dead young. It was unthinkable to kill a pregnant animal for its meat.

He straightened and met the gaze of a boy. Rib stared back, tears unashamedly on his cheeks. The child shifted a water jug to his hip and proceeded on his way.

One by one, and then a million stars pebbled the sky. Rib returned to the tent where the men drank and sang, their eye sockets deep craters in the lamplight. Vethur held forth, swung an imaginary sword, gloated over enemies, and roared with laughter. Women arrived with trays of roasted meat and shooed Rib to a place beside the mercenary. Rib smiled and patted his stomach to indicate he was full; he could not touch the meat, but did not want to spoil the night for his friend. Unease walked his spine and whispered just beyond hearing. *If only*, Rib thought, but his thoughts went no further as he caught the eye of the boy who had watched him vomit, and who now stood at the door ready with a water jug. A woman scolded and slapped the child; and he was gone.

So it is that a life is snatched from an oncoming wave.

Rib stretched out on the ground near Vethur who snored in such peace that his scars ironed smooth. What is happiness, Vethur, but oblivion; what is contentment but the erasure of memory? Rib dropped weightlessly into bottomless absence and let its depths take him.

He awakened to shouts and dust and men on horse-back riding through the camp and slashing at the sleepers with their swords. Rib curled to protect his head and throat. He felt the ground shake and heard cooking vessels break, tent poles crack, and the stomp of horses' hooves striking soft flesh. Most of the sleepers never knew what happened. The unfortunate few who did, screamed. He smelled sharp sweat as a rider leapt from his horse and loomed over him. He closed his eyes and waited. Nothing happened, so he opened his eyes and saw the unprepossessing boy who had watched him on and off all evening. The child shouted to the others, hauled himself onto the horse and rode away. They all rode away. The attack ended as quickly as it began, the camp in ruins and in silence except for the groans of the injured.

In the brief shocked dream into which he plunged, Rib saw his parents sitting at a fire that snapped golden fingers into the night. The sound of waves rinsed the distance. Only he knew that they would not escape the coming cataclysm. He awoke for the second time. Vethur lay nearby, alive, but with half his skull staved in. Everyone was gone except for a man left behind to bury the dead.

Inside Arishat and Margetta's rooms, in a small, enamelled palace of the King of Jerusalem, Margetta waited impatiently. She trained with the tumblers, leapt on and off horses, and performed acts of balance to entertain the court. Arishat, who was teaching her to read and write and who was always short of time, was late.

While she waited, Margetta wrote a letter to Vethur so he would not forget her, and to Rib because twice he had rescued her; and to the cat for the future pleasure of reading it aloud to him. She was too old—more than seven—to run after Buto anymore, but she worried each time he left. This time the cat had been gone longer than ever before.

Margetta paused—were those the dancer's footsteps approaching?—but whoever it was passed on. She put the letters away and brought out the dolls she had made from twine, straw, paint, and pieces of wood the carpenter had given her. She had cried on the ship when she realized she had left behind the doll that belonged to her mother. Fingering the beads in its hair, smoothing them between thumb and forefinger, had helped her fall asleep without the murmur of her mother's voice and the warm scent of her skin. Those tears on the ship, however, had brought Arishat to ask what was wrong, and through the telling of the story of the doll, Arishat learned about Vethur and about Rib, Ari's own foster brother, and his role in Margetta's life.

"Why did he leave home?" Arishat had asked, but Margetta did not know. "Did you see what happened to him in the crowd before we sailed?" Margetta had not. The dancer did not tell her that in the glimpse she'd had of Rib on the dock as their vessel pulled away, he was soaked in blood.

Margetta stirred restlessly and tried to be understanding of Arishat's delay. "You cannot hurry a King," Arishat had told her. "Sometimes the stories he tells are very long."

One of the long stories Margetta liked was of a boy a little older than Rib, who was taken by his brothers, dropped into a hole, and abandoned. She'd made a doll of him to help herself retain the story. Before bringing him out, she examined the other dolls she'd made, to make sure all was well with each of them. She rearranged

Vethur's hood to drape his forehead, and darkened Rib's eyebrows with charcoal to make him look fiercer. Margetta had asked for scraps to sew a dancer's costume for her doll of Arishat but had not yet begun to make it. She wanted a doll of Buto too, but no shape she tried looked anything like the cat. She needed glass for its eyes, scraps of white fur for the body and a bit of red leather to stick on for a tongue. Not that she needed help to remember him, for he slept on her pillow and did not require imagining. She frowned, recalling once more that the cat was too-long absent.

Margetta picked up the doll from the King's story, measured it with her fingers and cut a square of cloth which she decorated using Arishat's cosmetic box. Murmuring the tale to herself, she tied the fabric around the doll's shoulders and dropped it into a pottery jar. "I will buy him," she said in a deep voice and sold him to some passing slavers. She removed the doll from the jar, took off its little coat, and closed the doll inside a chest as Arishat came in.

The dancer put her scrolls and writing materials away, sat down on the divan and patted a space beside her. "Come and tell me what you've been doing."

"Well," Margetta said, "I'm in the middle of a story." She opened the chest and showed Arishat the new doll.

Arishat noticed the tiny, coloured cloak discarded on the floor. "That one's a long story, isn't it?" she said inferring the cloak's significance to the King's story of Joseph and his brothers. It was a family drama of jealousy, betrayal, bravery, and forgiveness. "Can you finish the story later? I have honey cakes for us to eat while you have your writing lesson."

"No," Margetta said, "He has to go to prison, make friends with the King, and meet his family again.

"Or," she said, reconsidering, reluctant to waste any of her time with Arishat, "I could skip to the end. Let me try." Margetta closed her eyes. "I am shutting my eyes for the parts I miss out. When I open my eyes, we will be at the end. I don't have time to explain, so you must pay attention. The lost boy's brothers have turned up. He is important now and they don't know who he is. He knows who they are, though. Look, he's gone into hiding." She put the doll behind her. "He can still hear everything."

"I see."

"I'm pretending to be a soldier now, Ari." Margetta spoke forcefully, "'That one—the youngest of you—has stolen a costly cup from my master. I will have to arrest him.'

"Now I will be another brother, "Margetta said. "'No, no, it was me, blame me!'" she said and hissed, "Say it, Ari, you say it. Everyone in the family has to say it."

"It was my fault, punish me," Arishat said. Tears pooled in her eyes because of all the blame there was to be had in the world, none of it belonged to Margetta, and yet here she was, an orphan far from home.

"'Look at me!'" Margetta said as she brought the new doll out of hiding. "'Don't you know who I am? I am the brother you cruelly abandoned, but I forgive you. I can see that you have changed!'

"Now I am the family again," Margetta said. "'We thought you were dead!' You say it Ari, say it!"

"'We thought you were dead, but you are alive, after all!'" Arishat said weeping.

"Don't cry, Ari. People don't always stay dead." Margetta placed the new doll with the others. "Sometimes they do, but sometimes they don't."

Arishat wiped her eyes and unwrapped the cakes from a napkin. "Sit beside me, Margetta, and help me eat these. We deserve a treat. It was a difficult story, but in the end, the family were together."

Margetta sat beside her and drew her knees up. Her grey eyes glittered as she slipped the cakes into a pocket to save for her friends Rib, Vethur, and Buto.

When the water in a basin in their rooms froze, Buto slept beside Margetta on her pillow. When the cat left again, it was spring.

There was always a need for a boy to do the dirty work of mucking out stalls, carrying feed and water, and polishing harnesses as barter for a meal and a place to sleep; and it was fine to let the stable boy's older broken companion live there too, as long as he kept to his corner.

Over the months that Rib bathed, brushed, combed, and curried the horses, he grew tall and very thin, his hair leached by weather to the colour of dry leaves. He whispered endearments into the animals' ears so that the cold wind and barking dogs would not bother them. He did much the same for Vethur who hunkered unmoving all day. Vethur had recovered from his physical injuries, but full use of his mind eluded him. Rib fed him with a spoon and aired him twice a day to the latrines and for exercise around the yard. Morning and night, he repeated to Vethur, as Vethur used to say to him,

"We will find Margetta and my sister Arishat; it is only a matter of time."

The morning the first spring sunshine warmed the yard, Rib took his friend to spend the daylight hours outside; at lunchtime with no one around to witness, he hoisted Vethur onto a horse. Vethur slumped, but suddenly, as if a key clicked in a rusted lock, he straightened, gripped the neck straps, and kicked the horse with his heels. Rib yelped and ran after them, but Vethur wasn't trying to go anywhere; he was putting the horse through its paces. He walked and trotted and galloped the animal as far as an abandoned watchtower in a disused field where the horse stopped to graze. Rib caught the reins. Dead sycamores and fractured house walls signalled they were at an abandoned settlement. More watchtowers in the distance testified to what once were numerous and widely scattered flocks. The flocks were gone, and the people, too, except for the remnant in the village near the stable in which Rib laboured.

Rib helped Vethur, who had lapsed into his usual apathy, dismount. Inside the modest lookout, Rib cleared a place for the mercenary to rest. It was dry and peaceful and free of the smell of dung. Rib made him comfortable with a piece of bread and a skin of water. He returned on foot that evening after his work was finished, lit a candle, and saw that the place had been swept and that Vethur nodded over a besom of thyme. Clean water brimmed a half-broken cup by his side. Outdoors, Rib discovered a cleared wellhead and a chipped jug with a length of rope tied to its handle for drawing-up water. Overhead, stars leaked light as if through a parchment shade.

Indoors again, Rib discovered Vethur and the cat nibbling a heel of bread. The cat! Not seen since before the terrible night of the assault on the nomad's camp! Buto swivelled his head to groom a shoulder and Rib caught sight of an object tied to a cord around the cat's neck. He approached and bent to look more closely: with a lightning swipe of its paw, the cat clawed him.

He jumped back, "Dung heap!"

"Dung heap!" Vethur echoed. For the first time since the incident in which he'd been wounded, he laughed. He scrubbed at the downy grey fuzz that covered the dent in his skull with one hand and installed the cat on his lap with the other. "Look!" he said. He held the wooden rectangle that dangled from the cat's collar between his fingers. A face and a dress were scratched into the grain.

"Did you make it for Margetta?" Rib asked. Vethur shook his head and pulled Margetta's doll from within the band he wore around his waist. "*This* is for Margetta." He put the doll down, hugged the cat to his chest and touched the neck emblem again. "*This* is for Buto."

When the mercenary could wash and feed himself, and he had acquired sufficient endurance, and the weather had brightened and settled, Rib marshalled their scant belongings, bade farewell to the horses, and collected a few loaves of bread from his master in lieu of wages.

At first, others on the way were as scarce as raindrops in a drought, but slowly they trickled together until group encountering group, path meeting lane meeting road, the travellers combined in an unending flow on its way to Jerusalem. Procession after procession, caravan after caravan of camels and mules and asses, carried spices and ivory, gold, and perfumes. At the head of each convoy rode notables attended by slaves; at the end a knot of beggars appealed for charity, and in the middle, the soldiers and the tradesmen and the cooks kicked the emaciated boy and the ugly simpleton at each opportunity until a horse master noticed that his animals were soothed with these two near, and called, "Hey, you! Bring that bucket! Hey, you, the other one, get on over and hold that rope!" They were useful enough that they were fed. Buto was welcomed too, for chasing vermin from the cook's supplies.

Once inside the city walls, the caravans broke apart—merchants to the trading quarters, slaves to the King's endless building projects, notables to scramble for places in court. Rib and Vethur, and the cat, a familiar on Vethur's shoulder, followed dust and drums and flutes past gardens to the royal precincts. They no longer feared recognition. Vethur, stooped and gray-haired, gazed vacantly, looking nothing like the warrior he'd been. Blunt-boned Rib was no longer a smooth-complexioned boy, but a sharp-cheeked youth with a skull shaved clear of vermin, and with half a dozen new scars to join the one under his chin. People swarmed in and out of the King's palaces. Servants carried plates of fruits and sweets; butcher boys and game providers hastened to the kitchens.

They paused within a complex of hastily constructed tents and outbuildings to get their bearings. As they did, Rib detected a pocket of birdsong within the din. The sound came from behind a terrace wall. "Wait here; don't move," he said to Vethur. The slope dropped away behind the terrace to a grassy level. A net imprisoning many songbirds lay tangled there. Most of the birds were stunned and silent, or dead, but one of them sang. Rib climbed down and eased the birds which breathed from the net and carried them to a tree where he hoped they would recover, and fly flee. When he returned to where he'd left Vethur and Buto, they were gone.

Inside the second-best of the palaces, in a hall of cedar beams and pillars, a troupe of tumblers performed for the King and his companion, the scribe and dancer Arishat. The King's fingers drummed the arm of a throne gilded with palm trees. More than once his gaze wandered in Arishat's direction. She bent close and spoke in his ear, and he exhaled and straightened to pay attention to those who worked so hard to please him as they cartwheeled and somersaulted, climbed pillars, dangled from ropes, and built human pyramids up to the beams.

Margetta spun from the troupe, and in time to lyre, drum, and cymbal, took a feather from a basket, balanced it on one end of a pole, added a stick, and another pole and stick, length after length, weight on weight of poles and sticks until she had built a cage held together only by the precision of her placements. She tipped up a stripped curved branch and set it in the centre of the network like a pin and lifted the structure over her head. It was not possible that the structure could hold. The King leaned forward. Margetta revolved slowly—all eyes on her, the courtiers holding their breaths—and made an orbit around the room. Just then, Buto slid from behind a curtain and wrapped himself round her ankles. In and out Buto slithered, silky, chaffing, crafty, a wooden ornament at his neck tapping against her shins. Margetta paled, and her ears reddened. In the time it took for the company to grasp what had happened, the cat abandoned the girl and sprang between the hangings. The structure collapsed with a clatter as Margetta fled after him.

"If you will excuse me, Sire," Arishat said, bowed, and followed them. And then with the courtiers agape, the King moved fluently off between the blue and purple curtain folds as well.

Rib tracked Vethur to a stable where he stood with his arms around the neck of a stallion. Vethur knew this horse. Its scream had summoned him. He had trained it for the King's renegade brother, although he did not *know* this as well as he recognized the sound which had brought him, and the horse's smell, and the place deep within himself where his art and craft lay sequestered. A white rag blown by the wind into the animal's feed box had frightened it. He pocketed the cloth and coaxed the stallion out of the stall. Strain raised ropes of tendons along the stallion's neck, but its legs held steady as Vethur grasped its mane. He wiped his tears on his sleeve when Rib approached, but kept firm hold of the horse. Rib took a step closer, and the stallion shuddered.

"Don't," Vethur said. "He doesn't know you."

The cat flowed in from a gap between boards and took residence below the table of the stallion's belly, and a girl cried, "Buto! I have found you!"

Quick as the cat, she flashed past Rib and scuffled over the straw on her knees to join it beneath the horse.

"Naughty Buto, come here!" she demanded. The cat yawned and displayed its pink tongue. Margetta folded Buto into her arms.

Rib stifled a cry. "Margetta, please Margetta, it is I, Rib," he said softly. "We have been looking for you, please come away from there, it's dangerous!"

A stableman approached slowly with a rope. "Old man," he said to Vethur, "do not press your luck for all our sakes." He proffered the rope to the mercenary who took it, and soothing the animal and stroking its head, placed the rope around its neck.

The stableman passed another rope and Vethur eased it around the stallion's tail and legs, all the while clucking to the horse.

The cat squeezed from Margetta's embrace and spurted from under the stallion and between Vethur's legs. Margetta followed, caught Buto again, and untied his collar.

"Why are you crying," she said to Rib, at whose feet she had arrived. She held out the collar with its tiny dangling doll. "Did you make this?"

Rib shook his head. "We thought we had lost you."

"Naughty Buto," Margetta said to the cat. "I won't let you run away ever again." She stood, met Rib's eyes, squinted at the details of his face and bearing, gave him Buto to hold and went to Vethur who continued to calm the horse.

"I know the other one, but do I know you?" She peered at him as if at a smudged mirror.

"This is Buto's," he said and took the collar from her.

"Of course, it is, but what did you bring for me?" she asked. Vethur boosted her onto the quivering horse. Neither Rib nor the stableman, nor Arishat and the King who had entered behind her, dared breathe.

The mercenary undid his sash and brought out the little girl's doll. "This is for you," he said. She took the doll and felt the beads in its hair. Then she reached out and her fingers traced the scars from Vethur's eye to his mouth. Margetta slid off the stallion and landed on her feet. "It is all right," she said to Vethur. "Buto and I will take care of you." She turned to Rib. "You, too."

"Sire," the King's guardsman said, after puzzling over Vethur's appearance and watching him work deftly with the horse, "we believe we know that man! Shall I arrest him?" The stallion backed against the stable wall and trembled.

The King glanced at Arishat before he answered, "God is the keeper of identity, not I. He is not a threat as he is."

Arishat kissed the King's cheek. "When justice is forgiveness," she said.

At her voice, Rib, who'd had eyes only for Margetta, turned and saw his sister. He let go of the cat which fell and ran straight to the girl. Rib's legs failed. He dropped to his knees and cried, "I am sorry, so sorry, Ari! What can I do? How can I tell our mother? How can I tell our father?"

His sobs were those of a child. Arishat knelt beside him, stroked his head and murmured, "Tell me."

His words came so haltingly that everyone except Arishat gave up listening and watched Vethur and the stableman return the stallion peacefully to its stall. Rib wept and stammered out the series of events: Arinna running away, the walk in the dark, the river in spate, the splash in the water and Arinna gone, her old cloak folded on the riverbank. "I tried, I tried," Rib said to Arishat, "but I have never learned to swim!"

"Are you saying Arinna drowned?"

"Yes," he sobbed. "I was supposed to watch over her—you told me to, and I promised. We knew what she was like, and I failed, how will I ever … "

"Arinna's oldest cloak, you say?" Arishat said.

"Ye-ees," Rib stuttered, "it bore marks of our mother's mending."

"Not the new cloak, not the one I sent her?"

"No, no, she would never leave that one." He frowned, knitting his brow.

Arishat helped him to his feet. "You are right, dear brother, Arinna would never have left her new cloak behind. There is more to this than you realize. A letter has come from our mother telling of Arinna's marriage."

"Her marriage?"

"With a babe on the way," Arishat said.

Rib's mouth dropped open. "It cannot be, the dead do not live again, how can I believe it?"

She pinched him so hard on the arm that he yelped. "You will believe it because it is true."

The King advanced and said, "Who is this young person? What is wrong with him?"

"He is my brother," Arishat said.

"You have not spoken of a brother."

"My foster brother. Reared with me in a cave."

"In a cave! Why have you never told me?"

"Would that there were time for every tale," she said. She gestured to Vethur for Buto's collar. "May I have it? Now that we are together and Margetta has her doll, perhaps Buto doesn't need it any longer?" With sudden shrewdness, Vethur glanced from her to the King and relinquished the collar.

Arishat presented it to the King. "Summon me with this when you are ready to hear *my* story," she said.

"Why this?" the King said, dandling the rough wooden charm by its string. He inspected it more closely. "Is it old, is it valuable?"

"Perhaps not in your terms, Sire."

"I am too busy for trifles."

"I am busy with *your* work," she said. "Stories of your god and his people."

"That is different. You are a scribe."

"And you are wise, my King."

He grimaced in annoyance. "Well, if not valuable, what is it for?" The ends of the collar had tangled round his fingers; impatiently he shook them loose and tried to return the object to Arishat, but her hands were tucked into her sleeves.

"It is for remembrance," Arishat said. "It cannot restore the dead to life, but there is a restoration. Shall I describe it for you?"

The King looked from the emblem to Margetta cradling her doll; and from her to Rib and Vethur who were watching the child, all tension eased from their damaged faces. "I see for myself that people suffer, and that love is remembered and endures," he said.

He removed a gold ring from his finger. "A memento in exchange. I will hear your story and all else you wish to tell me. If there is time."

"That is wise, my King," she said, although the scribe and dancer knew no time could be sufficient to tell it all. She twisted the King's ring onto a thumb to keep it safe.

"Until then, you will record the stories *I* give you." He smiled and left, twirling the cat's collar.

Margetta tugged at Rib's tunic, "Tell me about your sister, the one who drowned."

"She didn't drown," Arishat said.

Rib, plucked from his reverie, began to speak, more coherently this time, his voice stronger. "One night I lay awake, thinking of Arinna, you understand what she is like (or perhaps you do not), how impulsive she is, a little like you, Margetta, although her hair is light coloured, dusted with ashes, and yours is a wildfire. When you meet her, you will see; still, it is all my fault as I must tell you, although I am wondering if I might have missed anything?"

~

The story is at an end. It has spilled onto the page throughout the night like grain from a pierced sack. The sack is empty. Yet Pearl remains at the keyboard. In some ways, what Arishat says supports Theano's belief that ordinary stories matter: but the scale of Rib's quest to do what is right, and the scope of his journey suggests a myth, or in the poet's construct, the eternal stories of the gods. Perhaps less difference exists between the two than Theano and the poet thought? Is it not human experience that makes the tales of the gods relevant?

At least those who should, have found each other and no one was punished unfairly. Pearl likes, as well, the suggestion of an affinity between Rib and Margetta. Together they could be the source of the dolls and the stories, an inheritance migrating through centuries of dislocation until it arrives at the edge of the western hemisphere and *her*.

There must be innumerable such migrations west to east, east to west, north to south and vice versa, just as countless stories never leave home. Stories that linger on tongues and in memories; and in people whose job it is to remember, and people whose task it is to listen.

Be that as it may, Pearl has no more dolls, nothing else from Nora to guide her on her way. She is as she is with what she has learned, and with what she can make of her life. She types a final line, an instruction to herself, and stares at it, *The story you will write is the one you will live with this boy.*

A sound behind her makes Pearl turn. Joachim stands a few steps away, his new-chopped hair on end, sleep marks on his face. His feet are bare; he is in his pyjamas.

"Did I wake you?" she says.

"It's time to get up, Pearl!" A crumpled baby wipe protrudes from his fist. He catches Pearl's glance at it, drops it on the floor and propels it under the table with his foot.

Outside, the sky is white, the trees dark. The sound of the creek mingles with a wind that pushes mist through cracks in the window frame. Pearl stirs, stiff from hours of sitting.

Joachim removes the Arishat doll from the work-top and tucks the straw that has fallen out, back into its body.

"Did Nora show you that doll?" she asks. "Maybe when you were here at Refuge House before?"

He nods.

"Did she tell you the story?"

He nods again. "She said *you* would tell it so I could remember." He turns the doll over. Several thumb-sized mice tumble out onto the makeshift desk. They are pink, their eyes sealed shut. "Whoa! Pearl! Can I have them?" He lifts them gently and replaces them in their nest.

"They're too young; they need their mother. Let's put all this in the drawer and see if she comes for them."

He leaves to get dressed and Pearl closes the story file. With each of Nora's notes and the tales Pearl pens, she has learned a little more of what makes up Nora's legacy. In narratives that knit kingdoms and centuries and cross oceans, each story with echoes in it of the others, it is as if, as Theano said, time *could* bring renewed chances, reunite lovers and facilitate forgiveness, and yet leave room for what is new.

"I'm hungry!" Joachim calls from upstairs. "What's for breakfast?"

"Okay, just a minute, almost done!" By this point Pearl is thinking about the Grade Three class she is to teach this morning. She opens a file and makes some notes. Then she writes what she hopes is the end of the article for *Findable Feast*:

> *Done properly, when the fish dissolves in your mouth, you taste the salmon's journey. If it's not a wild fish, but the red-dyed mush of a farmed fish, or a hatchery product uncertain of its ancestry, the flavour—the sum of its travels—will convey bewildered surprise: why am I here, where was I supposed to go? Either way, for those moments, you are one with the salmon's destiny.*

"It wasn't easy," Joachim shouts as he plummets down the ladder.

"What wasn't?"

"What Rib did!"

"No," she says. "It wasn't." Joachim goes into the kitchen, and Pearl hears him open and close the fridge, and then run water into the kettle.

"I'll make your coffee," he says, and he turns on the radio and whistles along to the music.

PART VI

PEARL: The Swimmer's Tale

Thousands of ordinary people understand the relationship between the human and natural world instinctively, *Cliff wrote*, because it is an unfinished relationship, among other things.

The river runs so fast and deep that Pearl cannot cross it. She has no boat, and if she had, she's not strong enough to paddle the river's invisible holes and currents by herself. Pearl looks around for Nora, but it is months since her grandmother has troubled to help her. Maybe Pearl is not meant to get to the other side?

A black and white pup snuffles from the bushes. It belongs to Nora's old friend, Walter. Although Pearl is on the verge of awakening, she follows it to a pocket in the riverbank in which the water is trapped and shallow. Salmon fry, marked with dark bars to camouflage them from predators, dart through vines that hang in loops from the overhang. They rise to snap at dragonflies. Cliff is beside her—Cliff!—whom she has not seen for a year. In the dream, they stir the water and wait to see which way the fry will swim. Towards her or towards him? In the restlessness of thoughts as Pearl stirs from sleep, she looks for Joachim instead, but from what she can hear as she opens her eyes in her room at Refuge House, Joachim is up and rattling dishes in the kitchen downstairs.

It is warm for June and Pearl has left the window open. Mosquitoes tap against the screen. Light and shadow fall trembling through the woods and a Smith's Longspur flashes across the view.

Pearl has Walter to thank for her education in local wildlife. After a winter spent in the community pool with Joachim and the rest of the Refuge House team, training for the fundraising swim down the Stemeltlanga River to the sea, they have been practising in Walter's pond. Their wetsuits have not completely shielded them from the cold. To distract them from their shivering,

Walter had made them name each living creature that happened by.

Pearl untwists the sheets, closes her eyes again, and settles in for one more minute.

On weekends, Pearl and Walter have scouted the Stemeltlanga section by section. East of town, the river is all but impassable, full of drops and chutes and grade-five cascades. The swim to the river mouth will need to launch to the west of food-fishery nets strung at the upper reach of migrating salmon. The river from that point downstream is navigable, but it will not be easy to deal with its fluctuating currents and shifting channels. Underwater rocks and snags litter the riverbed, posing dangers for the swimmers if the water levels drop; in certain spots existing whirlpools and standing waves become treacherous if the levels rise. Walter has spoken to everyone he can think of about climate, weather, and animal behaviour in the watershed. Pearl has trawled government websites for reports of mining and logging activity that could trigger slides in the area. All of it is indicated on their maps, but change is in the nature of a river, and they must be ready to adapt.

"Padma's giving you a ride today," Pearl reminds Joachim. He has made toast and the coffee is ready. She puts a pot of water on to boil for eggs. "Have you got your gym bag?"

He shakes his head. Toast in hand, he climbs the ladder to his room, retrieves the bag and hurtles down, scarcely touching the rungs. His laces are undone.

"Do up your shoes," Pearl says automatically, accepting that he won't. Joachim slumps into a chair and carries on eating. After he had understood that he would need to earn his place on the Refuge House team, and that the fundraising swim would go ahead without him if he didn't, he had begun to take practices seriously. He has put on weight and grown taller since the fall, but the added kilos are all lean muscle. Pearl, who has been training every day as well, has built muscle, too. Unlike the others, who will take on shorter relay stages, she has committed to swimming the entire distance to the sea.

While Pearl makes Joachim's lunch and gathers snacks to take him through the final after-school practice, he eats three boiled eggs and four pieces of toast, then drinks orange juice and milk straight from the jugs.

"Why can't you drive me?" he says. Padma's four by four enters the yard. He is quickly on his feet, putting his dishes in the sink. He grabs two cookies from the jar and pours a coffee for Padma.

"I've got too much to do, and you won't miss me. You've got swimming this afternoon, just time for a snack at Padma's, and then it's the community debate and pizza in the gym; and isn't the chess club setting up chairs in the band hall for the blessing?"

"She takes rice milk," Joachim says and holds out Padma's cup to Pearl who adds some from a carton. Unexpectedly, he hugs her. Her head barely reaches his chin. "You're shrinking Pearl. Sure you're up to this?"

Seeing the dolls Nora left, and hearing their stories from Pearl, has eased something in Joachim. The parts Pearl had feared would disturb him seem instead to have given him comfort. Perhaps it's because they make him feel less alone. Others, long before, suffered too, and are remembered, their lives given currency in the present. The baby wipes are gone from outside Joachim's door, but he keeps a container of them on the night table in his room. His teacher, Miss Wanda, said he is like an ex-smoker who preserves a pack of cigarettes to remind him of his struggle.

"Who would do that?" Pearl had said.

"Me," Wanda said, and she had opened her desk drawer to show her.

Pearl accompanies Joachim to the door and waves to Padma.

Padma starts her vehicle, stalls it, and tries again. It backfires as she puts it in gear and chugs out the driveway. The noise sets off Walter's dogs, and the barking ripples through the town, all the way to the mountains.

At lunchtime, having packed and re-packed her kit bag before tackling the first-aid checklist, Pearl spies Joachim's gym bag lying beneath the kitchen table. She pours herself a cup of leftover coffee and sits in Joachim's chair. He has forgotten the bag before, and she has taken it to him. She's not doing this again. He will have to borrow what he needs until she can bring it to the gym later on. With so many preparations to make, she cannot squeeze in an extra trip to school.

"Nose to the grindstone," Pearl's father, Harry, had told her recently. "It's what Joachim needs. You've got a job to do there, Pearl."

Pearl drags the bag out with her foot.

Joachim had watched her put chocolate in it, along with the sandwiches and apples. Not long ago, he would have eaten the chocolate before he got to school. Never, ever, would it have slipped his mind.

Her foot hooks the bag closer. Those simple days are behind them. He has a girlfriend, Jada, another member of the swim team. Soon he will finish middle school, and then what? To Vancouver for high school? Boarding out in the closest northern town? Or some other option neither of them has thought of yet. If they raise the money they need for Refuge House, Pearl will have repairs to oversee, applications to review, travel and resettlement programs to design, jobs to find for new arrivals; all before she's been able to think about her own future. She likes teaching, but to count on more than the occasional *ad hoc* contract, she would have to get another degree. Sure, she has magazine work, but it isn't reliable. Her piece on lichen as an emergency food and indicator of air quality was rejected by *Findable Feast*. She had written another piece about water, which *FF* is "considering." Until she did the research, she hadn't realized that bottled water could include as many as twenty-four thousand trace chemicals which interfered with the body's own chemical signalling system. Contaminants included arsenic, radioactive isotopes, fertilizer, and solvents. Where could you find pure water now? *If you ever have the privilege of being close to a glacier,* she had written, *know that pure water can be found at its centre. Drill deep into the ice, withdraw the core, melt it and satisfy your thirst toxin-free.*

The bag has slid within reach.

Nora never went through Pearl's belongings. Pearl's hiding places were left undisturbed. To Nora, privacy was a fundamental and inviolable human right. Pearl's fingers hover, but she recalls how Joachim moves through chess options in the tournaments she has seen him play: how he trusts his instincts and never overthinks.

Pearl lifts the bag onto her lap and unzips it. Towel, swimsuit, extra T-shirt and sweatpants, wallet, cellphone, a chess book from the library, the lunch and snacks she had put in. She searches further. At the bottom, underneath it all, is a hand-knit sweater. It is not a garment Pearl has seen before, but it is Nora's work. Joachim has folded it into sections. Pearl opens it out. She touches a finger to the blade of the long, decorated steel knife it enclosed. The blade draws blood. Pearl trembles as she lays the knife aside.

Tucked into one of the sweater's sleeves is a small muslin-wrapped package, the right size and shape for a doll. It smells old and musty. An aroma of oranges drifts from it, too. It is not easy, given all that Pearl would like to know and the hurt she feels at Joachim's keeping these things a secret, but she leaves the package unopened. Pearl re-packs the bag with care and closes it.

That evening, Pearl steals into the gym and stands at the rear. A debate about the future of the Stemeltlanga River is almost over. The atmosphere is tense: officials in suits are seated stage right, locals in jeans, stage left. Among the onlookers, Pearl sees Miss Wanda and the other teachers from the school. The mayor and council, the band chief and council, the doctor and dentist from the clinic, outdoor workers and tour operators, as well as the entire chess club and the Refuge House swim team and their friends—all have convened. Bob from the store, and Pinky, who runs the real estate office, turn around to see who has just come in, and acknowledge

Pearl's nods. Both have donated money and equipment to the swim.

Pinky is the only man in the village who has appeared to notice that Pearl is female. On Fridays he brings her lattes. If Joachim is away with the chess club, or visiting his mother in Vancouver, Pinky takes Pearl to dinner at the Lodge. Dead insects raisin the unused fax machine and computer in his office, but Pinky is well-known locally for tying steel-head flies with heron feathers and rabbit fur. He shifts in his seat and crosses his feet, in sandals and socks, at the ankles.

Pearl nods at Walter, but he is too busy glaring at the speakers and checking to see which of the congregants agree or disagree with him to nod back.

"I could have died on the river; and that's okay," one of the debaters, a kayaker, says. "The risk was my choice. You cannot beat the river on its own terms, but you can destroy it, no trouble at all. To me, it is sacred, inscribed on my soul. That means no to dams, diversions, or pollution from mine tailings."

"Decisions about the river should be based on economics, not emotions," the MP says. "*That* means a God-given right to stay here and earn a living, not giving in to a dictatorship of tofu eaters."

"There's no tofu on my table!" Walter shouts from the audience. "So, Mr. Big Shot—note the initials—whose salary I pay over there in Ottawa, unless you can look after yourself without your nose in the trough, you'd better stop killing off the herds with your dams and poisons! They're my meat *and* my soul!" He gives a thumbs-up to the kayaker.

"I'm not killing them," the MP protests. "I'm your representative!"

Walter leaps from his seat. "You represent mining and arsenic dumps, not us!"

"And Big Oil!" a voice cries from the assemblage.

"And Big Gas!" someone else chips in, and armpit-farts.

Padma bangs the gavel. "Manners, please! We are almost out of time. Ten seconds more to each side. Do not forget why we are here tonight. We're looking for common ground."

The MP glances at his debate mates, but they are examining their fingernails. "Look, all I'm saying is that our future is the river, and we will look after it, but the good Lord put us on Earth to make use of it, and that's our right."

Walter, still on his feet, says, "And I'm just saying, stay the sprigging out so you don't sprig it up."

Padma's brow furrows and she bangs the gavel again but fails to halt the uproar. Attendees leave their places to gather and talk, or line up for pizza.

"We should pray for the young people," a woman seated next to the kayaker says. She points to the swim team. "Here we are, sending them off to risk their lives to help others, and we can't keep peace between ourselves!"

"Thank you everyone," Padma says. "Discussions can continue informally. Anyone needing a ride to the band hall for the ceremony, please wait out front. The school bus leaves in thirty minutes. Our panels have given us much to think about as we all try to make a difference. At the moment, you can make a difference to the gym by putting your chair away after you have finished eating."

Nearly all who speak to Pearl while she eats her pizza, have advice or a word of encouragement to give her: *Don't forget the long underwear, bear grease, magic mushrooms;* and *Good for you, Pearl, you're an inspiration, we're with you.*

The gym is practically empty, tables and chairs put away, garbage tidied when Walter limps over.

"What have you done to your foot? Somebody here still angry with you?" Pearl asks.

"Nah, people get over it. Pup don't know its own strength, that's all. Stepped on my foot. It's nothing. I'm not *walking* on the river, am I?" The *pup* is his canine companion, Doggo.

"All's clear for tonight," he tells her. "You're doing the right thing, Pearl, not that I think anything will happen, but … " He trails off, embarrassed.

"Better to be safe?" Pearl helps him.

"That's it, that's the thing."

Everyone has gone except for Joachim who stands near the open exit door. Jada waits for him just beyond. He looks at Pearl and scuffs a heel on the rubber entry matting.

"You coming to the hall?" he says.

"Yes, but I'll be late, you go ahead." She thinks a moment. "If we don't meet there for any reason, can you get a ride home?"

Jada is not quite pacing, but they are both aware of her restiveness. In the parking lot, headlights snap on, veiled in mist; exhaust ascends in pale streams.

"Walter will drive me, but I don't have to go," Joachim says. He blushes. "I mean, if you don't want to be alone."

"No, go be with your friends." She holds up the gym bag he'd left behind. "Do you want it?"

"Oh, yeah, sure, guess I forgot." He takes it, glances at Jada outside shifting from foot to foot, and then at Pearl. "Thanks for telling me what you're going to do," he says.

"You've got a right to know."

"Yeah, well." He lifts the bag to his shoulder. "You're not worried about tomorrow, are you?"

"If you're there with me, no," she says.

He relaxes. "See you at home," he calls, from outside. His free arm curves around Jada's waist, and the two of them dwindle into the haze.

Pearl blinks condensing moisture from her eyelashes. In the faded light and fog, the world is brushed with indigo. The mountains are a weight, towering above the canyon. She has to force herself to move against their pressure along the dirt road that zigzags up the fell, past the church and through the reserve. Then, she tackles the final section of the steep scramble of a shortcut to the cemetery and stands back from the ledge.

Muffled drumbeats sound from the patchily-lit band hall below. Miniature cars emerge out of low cloud and park at the side of the road; doors open and shut; toy people—little more than moving shadows—come and go. But Pearl is not here for what she can see through the gloom. Walter's directions are precise. Pearl steers through the graveyard, counting her footsteps, and ducks inside the low log structure that will one day house his bones.

He had tilted his head to listen when she began to explain. "I have a problem, Walter. In a way, it's about Nora."

He had cleared his throat, interrupting, "I've been meaning to talk to you about all that, Pearl. Nora and I … well you know how I felt. I thought we might, you know, join forces, help each other out."

"Live together? Get married? She never said anything!" It had not occurred to Pearl that her grandmother might have had a private life and that it could have been important. She'd had no idea before coming to Refuge House that Walter even existed.

"We hadn't got that far," he said. "I was going to bring it up. Next time. See how she felt." Walter looked down and into an abyss of regrets. "I'll never know now, will I?"

He raised his eyes. "You said she'd never mentioned me?"

Pearl touched his arm. "Nora's work with Refuge House meant everything to her, Walter. She trusted you to keep an eye on it when she wasn't there; and she knew I'd come here after her death. She left a trail for me to follow. She trusted you with me. Isn't that enough?"

"It will have to be." He sighed. "What's this trail you're talking about?"

"Do you know about the dolls passed down in her family? They came with stories."

"Why wouldn't I? Nora and I talked, didn't we?"

"It's just a question."

He softened. "She said you would write the stories down. You doing that?"

Pearl nods. "The dolls were the trail. She left one of them, each with a message for me, in places she visited on her last trip. Refuge House is the end of the trail. I need a place to keep the dolls while I'm gone. If anything happens to me on the swim, I want Joachim to have them. I can't leave them at Refuge House, too many people have the key."

"And you can't trust the banks for important things. Me neither. There's no saying who gets let in those vaults after hours." He winked, but his demeanour was serious. "Okay, let me think. Not at my place, since I'll be on the river with you." He was silent for a minute. "What about where I'll be when the time comes? There's a little burial hut we keep in the family. Put them in there. They'll be safe as houses. It won't get many callers." He chuckles at his wit.

"If you're not around, I can tell the boy, that's what you want, huh? If I don't come back, my sister will know what to do. If half the world ends, the hut will still be here, and sooner or later somebody who gets what's what, is going to find it."

Fog sifts through the doorway and dampens Pearl's clothing. This is not a place to tread unthinkingly. Pearl places tobacco on the threshold as Walter had asked her to. The interior of the hut smells of leaves and the nests of small animals. She has no desire to disturb anything or transgress. Hurriedly, she searches for a hollow in the post Walter had spoken of.

Pearl takes the dolls from her bag and enfolds them, one by one, in the T-shirt she'd borrowed from Cliff the day they parted. Since then, a lifetime ago, she has worn it to bed to remind herself of what it felt like to lie in the choir loft with him, sustained by a next-door room of plaster saints and the carved mythic figures in the body of the church below—stratagems for living.

The last doll she wraps is Arishat. The mice have vacated the body, but wisps of straw and threadbare cloth retain their scent. Pearl tucks the bundle into the niche, listens to the distant drumming from the band hall, and to the chanted blessing for the swim, for Refuge House, for the river, and for Nora. And then she scatters the residue of Nora's ashes—north, south, east, and west—in the hut's four corners.

~

The Swimmer's Tale

The Stemeltlanga River, Northern BC

Goats clamber along the tops, and the cliffs fade into ribbons at the foot of mountains. Ghost towns and abandoned fish camps pattern both shores with derelict shacks. The river flows past spruce forests cushioned with sphagnum moss and ruffled fungi. Brush, conifers, and cottonwoods tangle with the flow until wetland hollows the flatland with bog; for long stretches, devil's club snarls in a ten-foot-high wall, its loops and rolls like barbed wire right down to the water.

It is the morning of the fourteenth day. They have shared hours of swimming, evenings trying to cook over smoky, wet-wood fires, and nights of never being able to get completely warm or dry in rain-battered tents. In a way, each of the swimmers will be glad to reach town with the adventure behind them, but they also find each time they enter the river that a layer of fear strips away. One day they might be reborn, their pain confined to a story.

The wind slithers up the sleeves and down the necks of the people in the boat. Riding along though is not as cold as swimming in the glacier-fed water; nothing like it. Droplets seep under wrist and ankle cuffs and ooze into headpieces. Even with a mask on, foreheads, cheeks, and eyes ache. Each influx from a creek brings a fresh rush of ice water, carrying with it a new batch of fingerlings to join in the flickering aura of silver-scaled fish around Pearl's body.

Pearl strokes and kicks, then rests, hanging onto the boat while the crew hauls out the most recent stage-swimmer who has accompanied her.

"You're not eating enough," Walter says. Pearl opens her mouth. He places a tasteless morsel into it.

She mimes chewing but holds the rubbery lump in her cheek.

"You're getting cold, Pearl! Do what you're told—eat!—or we'll bring you in!"

Pearl tries to swallow but whatever it is (spongy and elastic and sweet) tastes of blood, and she spits it out. She would like to ask where she is, but it would upset Walter. She is supposed to remember and stay focused.

Not long ago, a bear lumbered out of the water and onto the riverbank in a terrain of broken tree trunks and stripped branches, before turning towards her with an angry growl. She had lifted her head from the water to keep it in view until the current swept her away.

Late in the day, the river courses through heaps of moraine, hills of gravel left by the ice age. Prehistoric cairns, placed as sentinels on the pinnacles of mountains by the ancients, cast a spell into the water. The current sucks Pearl down, and she comes upon stone figures that seem as if they are about to speak. Then the flux lets her rise, and birds sketch lines in the sky.

Joachim yells at her from the boat, "Breathe, Pearl, breathe." Pearl obeys; but she prefers the underworld where the force of the river strings her through like a wire.

"Pearl?" Joachim calls again from the boat travelling beside her. "I'm coming in. You have to watch me."

"Yeah, good," she says. "You'll be fine," but the Pearl deep within the life of the river, understands that only fish swim with her—fish that do not know better—not boys like Joachim, boys with long lives ahead of them.

She stocks her mind with a glimpse of the wintergreen that springs from the moraine and reminds herself she is close to land. That helps a little, but before Joachim can get to her, she misjudges the river's depth and slashes the neoprene at her belly on a sharp-edged rock. Rapidly, the fetal blanket of the wetsuit becomes a freezing shroud.

By the time they erect tents, collect wood, and hunt through the wet-bags for supplies, it's almost dark. At night, they stay together by the fires they build to discourage the wolves that have joined their journey. Walter says that wolves are a good sign; it's useful to have them on watch; they keep off larger predators. But Walter's canine companion, Doggo, lies low whenever the wolves arrive. The fur rises along his spine, and he tucks his tail under.

They have finished eating when Walter says to Pearl, "That was too damned close. We could have lost you; I should have pulled you out earlier. You weren't really with us, were you?" The other members of the team fall quiet.

"It wasn't a problem. We planned for it. We're good at this; we were well within the margins. Everyone knew what to do. Anyway, I've got another wetsuit," Pearl says. She turns away, unwilling to discuss it further.

Joachim snatches the gym bag he is never without, and stalks to his tent. Jada follows. Chiman, who had spent months aboard a rusty leaking ship with fragments of shrapnel in his skull before Nora found him, pokes a stick at the fire. Steam purls from a kettle on the grate. Isniino, sitting beside him, scuffs at loose leaves. She had slept in a petrol dump after the murder of her mother. Nora had found her, too. Now they have new homes and new lives, but the past is not a series of chalk marks easily erased. Pearl's accident has destabilized everyone. Joachim believes it is his fault for not seeing quickly enough that Pearl was in trouble, but Pearl blames herself for a failure to self-monitor. She closes her eyes. Walter is furious. Thus far though, all has gone well. They have become close, trusted each other, watched over each other. This may be their last night together.

Twigs snap just beyond the perimeter of trees.

Doggo squiggles on his stomach until he is close enough to lick Pearl's wrist. She opens her eyes. A wolf howls, and Doggo crawls halfway onto her lap.

"What about a story, Walter?" Pearl says. The final stretches of river are wide and slow. They should finish tomorrow, or at worst, early the next day. For a change, the sky is clear. Stars sizzle and prickle; the fire crackles and pops as it devours the dry wood they unearthed in the woods from a collapsed split-shake shelter. They will replace what they have used in the morning.

"Come on, Walter."

"No, no more stories. I'm done." Walter glances at the gleam of the river ten feet away. "This used to be a good fishing place." He shakes his head.

"What happened?" Isniino asks him.

"Well, people take too much, one way or another."

"So how do we put it right, Walter?" Chiman says. "Where will we get an answer?"

"Get Pearl to ask the fish," Isniino says. "Joachim says she can talk to them."

"You got to show respect for Mother Nature," Walter says, with a glare that takes in everyone.

On this, the evening of the fourteenth day, Pearl imagines the end of the swim, the wharves and floats of the abandoned cannery at the river mouth jammed with celebrants, cameras waiting for her to appear out of the water to a heroine's welcome. Though in reality, hardly anyone is likely to be there. It is more probable that, black-headed in her wetsuit, she would be shot by a fisherman who thought she was a seal.

It is hard not to be discouraged. Padma has told them over the satellite phone that pledges have slowed to a trickle.

Doggo pricks up his ears and growls. "What is it, boy?" Walter says. Doggo stands and woofs. "I'd better go have a look." Walter deliberates, but lets the gun lie where it is, and exits the circle of firelight followed by the two young swimmers.

Pearl does not budge. She is exhausted, and Walter is right. People take too much in every way you can think of. The world is in the control of those who do not care. Bob at the general store said that aliens in reptile form have come to inhabit human bodies, which is as good an explanation as any for what has gone wrong with humanity. The *reptiles* though, are only ordinary people with cold hearts and cold minds who bludgeon and maim and kill without remorse. How else to explain what was done to Joachim and the others who had to leave their homes to survive? There are multitudes like them whom no one will ever come to aid. How had Nora stood it? All this effort they are putting in, what can it accomplish? If they succeed with the fundraising and carry on with Refuge House for a few more years, what really changes? The need for it will not diminish. War, rape, kidnapping, and torture will always generate victims. There would be no end. And the wilderness was nearing its finale as a haven.

Despair, an overcoat of stone, falls over Pearl's shoulders so heavily that she groans. The stone coat tightens at her wrists and neck.

That ocean she is trying to reach at the completion of the swim is a cesspool of chemicals. Masses of garbage converge where currents meet: vortexes of lead, cadmium, mercury, the polymer chains of BPA, and phthalates; spiralling galaxies of toxins that cause birth defects and cancers and affect the hormonal systems and immune systems of all organisms; and the growing acidity of the ocean makes the fish that swim there anxious, forgetful, incapable of being what they *are*. How can anything that she manages to accomplish make a dent?

"Yessiree," Walter says, trailed by Chiman and Isniino with Doggo slinking behind. Walter presents his flanks to the campfire and rocks on his heels. "There's nothing like the woods and a campfire to set folks thinking."

Pearl gets up and walks away. She halts at the riverbank. Insects tread her eyelids and probe her nostrils and the corners of her mouth. The atmosphere is vibrant with the electricity of stars. It pings with a bouquet of sulfur from inland mountain hot springs. The world is old and new, coming into being so it can smash itself into oblivion over and over. Human beings and all other creatures that are given life by accidents of time and place are nothing but fireflies. They are certainly not soul sparks, no. About that idea, the old stories are wrong. How can it be that those Pearl has lost will reappear? And where is the home of everything lovely? And where is the future she is supposed to shape with the purpose for which she came into the world? And yes, she knows, she should not let her spirits darken.

Pearl wipes a sleeve across her eyes, the despair-coat heavier than ever. A sudden wind swirls the insects away, and thunder rolls and rumbles, squashing her spirits further.

"In case you were wondering," Walter says, appearing beside her, "it was nothing." He scrutinizes her expression. "Nothing out there, Pearl. Nothing for you to worry about." He touches her arm. "You feeling sorry for yourself?"

"Could be, I guess. I'm tired."

"That's right. You are tired, and you don't know the half you think you do, not by a long shot. You think you want to give up, but you don't. What would …"

"Don't say it."

"Did I mention Nora?" He chuckles. "Boy oh boy, I wish she was here."

More thunder booms down the valleys.

"Better get to the tents before the rain hits," he says. "Gonna be a corker."

By the morning, the thunderstorm has cleared the air of tension. Low rays of sunlight filter through green-leafed scrub and over the camp site. It is warmer, more seasonal than the wintery temperatures they have experienced to date. Joachim chews through six oatmeal and chocolate cookies and proffers the rest to Pearl and the two girls. "Got to build up your strength," he says. He laughs and Pearl punches him in the shoulder.

"Pearl," Walter calls from where he and Chiman are loading the boat, "come here a second."

A blue grouse hoots and drums—awake early, and courting.

Walter stands where they had met by the river last night. "Look at this." He points to palm-sized prints and a mound of scat. "Mountain lion. Best not to go off by yourself anymore. You've got that boy to think of."

"Yes, I know."

"Watch out for snags today. They've cleared above high-water along one of the streams we'll come to, and they've opened a mine near the source. Could mean a bunch of debris washed down."

"Yup, got it." Pearl tugs the wetsuit hood on and enters the water to put on her flippers. The others push out the boat. Except for Pearl and Joachim who is also going to swim, they all get into it.

The stream Walter means is the Niamue: she and Walter had discussed it early on. A renewed gold and copper mine is leaching chemicals into the water, and a dredger has been ripping through the gravel beds where fish nest. The plan on file with the mining and energy ministry, shows large-scale open pit ore body extraction, as well as diversion of the Niamue and several of its tributaries to run a hydro installation. Cliff's research station is around there somewhere—she had found this out online—but it is deep in the mountains, beyond the scope of the vining tentacles of current industrial planning. Before they left on the swim, he'd sent a message through the fundraising website: *Thousands of ordinary people understand the relationship between the human and natural world instinctively, because it is a moral relationship, among other things. Best of luck to you, Pearl.* He had looked for her online as well.

For a day or two she had thought it meant something: maybe that Cliff wanted to see her; but although she had checked the messages every day for days, there was nothing more.

Dung heap, as Rib would say.

Once in the river, Pearl settles. She floats in the middle channel, her eyes on trumpeter swans flying to lakes and ponds to feed on the aquatic plants they also use for nesting. Unlike the ibises she had watched in the marshes, all swans mated for life. Unless something happened and the swan ended up alone.

Joachim eases into the water: he will swim for an hour or so and then rest. He does not have Pearl's stamina, but he never gets in the way. He has his own way of tackling currents, reading them the way he does a chessboard, able to think quickly ahead. Pearl closes her eyes and floats into an eddy. It spins her around and forces her underwater, but she is experienced at this, and drifts until the eddy releases her.

Late in the day, long after the boat has brought in Joachim and the other swimmers who accompanied Pearl in relay, clouds scoot in from the west and sink until the Coast Mountains batten down in mist. The mist condenses to drizzle, and fog rises from the plane of the river. The world is walled in white. Snow swaddles the mountaintops, and cold air leans over the layer of fog and holds it in place so that the limit of Pearl's world becomes the river's dark, wet ribbon.

The river widens and shallows, half-blocked by debris. Walter slows the boat to negotiate deposits of bedload. Trees, some containing eagle nests, have slid root first from the soaked and undermined banks.

"Pearl!" Walter calls into the fog. "Swim over."

"Pearl, Pearl," Joachim echoes.

It is more difficult than one might suppose to ascertain where the voices come from: sound is baffled by the fog and falls short. Pearl treads water and waits for the run of the engine to putter close enough for orientation, and for a spotlight to penetrate the gloom; but the sounds diminish and there is no guiding light. For a second the fog clears, and she glimpses the far bank and the waterlogged sponge of a bog dotted with willows. The current has been moving her more quickly downstream than she'd realized. It sweeps her onward, and the fog closes in again. A sudden inrush of water from a tributary smacks Pearl under and sideways. She tumbles down to where a sea lion twice her size brushes past and twists and snaps with long yellow teeth at a full-grown salmon sheltered by her body. Pink blood threads the water. Pearl kicks to the surface and repositions herself. Sea lions almost never come this far upriver, but this one has. Adrenaline doubles her strength; but the hard pull of the current keeps her in its grip. A logjam is stacked in the way, but that's okay, she will just go around it. Instead, as she powers by, she is jerked to a halt by a tangle of branches. She tugs but cannot get free. A strong push from the flow jolts her into a sitting position. She tries to drop her legs, but her flippers are caught, too. Within seconds, neck muscles straining, Pearl is having difficulty keeping her head up.

"Help!" she calls into the drifting world, "Help! Help!" The staccato duck-like call of a frog out hunting joins in. She can identify this frog: its skin is smooth, moist, and brown, and its salmon-red underbelly misinforms the small aquatic animals on which it preys that it is harmless.

A break in the fog reveals a grey desert of gravel beds beyond a channel scoured by the forces unleashed by clear cuts and dredging, and then something hard bangs into her. Pearl turns her head, and whatever it is rakes her face with its claws. The moment she lets go of the branches, her head submerges. She tries for her knife, but it is strapped on the wrong side of her body. Pearl is struggling to get to it when someone raises her head from behind so she can breathe, and Joachim says, "Grab onto the branches, Pearl. It's me and Doggo. There's a net or something; I can see where it's hooked. I've got a knife. Hold on a minute." Doggo scrambles out of the water onto the log pile, barks into the thick wool air, and Joachim disappears.

The world is made of cause and effect, although the line of its operation is a winding one. The knife is made to cut, always to cut, and this *navaja*, passed down generations from parent to child, has had a long journey. Joachim dives, and slices the plastic netting from Pearl's flippers, from her legs and then from her arm. The knife slips from his grip and sifts to the river bottom. Its job is done.

"What kind of fool sets a net here?" Pearl says after they have dragged themselves onto the logjam. Joachim sits, hands clasped round his knees, beside her.

He turns to her. "Pearl?"

"What?"

"Did you see? All the big fish have tags."

"Pink ones. Yeah, I saw them too. Those are hatchery fish, but at least they're on the move. Cliff would be pleased."

"Who?"

She sighs and looks around. "Where'd Doggo get to?"

"He jumped in the water. He's probably gone to get help."

"Right."

"He'll find someone."

"Sure."

"He's a good dog. He's smart. He left the boat and came with me. He didn't mean to scare you."

"What happened to Walter and the others?"

"I don't know." Their ears strain to hear above the rush of water. "Maybe the engine failed or something. They were having trouble with it. I didn't exactly ask if I could go." He looks pleased. "Anyway, they'll be looking for us."

"They will, but it's getting dark, and they'll have to quit. We'll need to spend the night here, so let's pile some of this stuff and dig into it. It'll be warmer."

"Like a snow cave."

"Exactly.

The jam is made of trunks and branches and river wrack, and strings of vegetation and clods of grass with small stones adhered to them. Fingernail-sized snails attach to the stones. Each is less than a gram of protein—good natural food—fit for gulls, geese, and patient raccoons, or any creature with a decent digestive system.

They cover themselves with debris to try and keep warm. The river pushes wherever it can through gaps in the wood and mud network into which they have burrowed. From there, it sounds like the world is being steam-cleaned and power-washed.

"It will be all right," Joachim says. "Someone always comes."

"Like Nora came for you and your mom." Pearl tries not to think of his scars, and how long he and his mother were on their own.

"Like Guiliam came for Yamha."

"Like you came for me."

Beaver ponds in the side streams, flycatchers in the sloughs; juncos and kinglets patrolling the borders. Frogs, smooth, moist and brown, or spotted or green; and lichen and mosses and bog laurel, and Labrador tea and salmon berry nubs on the branches. Brush, slash, and beaver-cut willow sloughing from the land into water all through the slow hours of the night. In the water, in the invisible realm, hatchery fish, streamlined and silvery, stir pink-tagged fins, and idle.

Someone is always on the way, someone always comes. But there is no guarantee about when.

Since his recent visit to Nootka where he went to clear out his lab at *SoliSunny* fish farm and say goodbye to friends before leaving for a fellowship in Japan, Cliff has had Pearl on his mind, along with lost possibilities and the swiftness of the passing seasons. He is on his way to his research station in the mountains where he has been privileged to study the cycles of the fish that spawn in the upper Kitliki: spring, chum, coho, and pink salmon as well as Dolly Varden and steelhead. He has earned his degree and found a job despite initial opposition from his supervisor. "There's no career there," he was told. "You cannot recreate the wild, Cliff, you can't teach instinct." But what else could he do? Life forms were disappearing more quickly than people could learn of their importance!

His fingers graze a paper in his pocket as he stares out the helicopter window. Fresh clear-cuts scar the passes, making way for hydro dams and power lines for which there has been no approval. The public is having its say in front of panels in far-off towns or cities while the work goes ahead.

Further north, pipeline leaks, herbicide sprays, and chemical spillage have polluted kilometres of tundra, tainting the lichens, sedges, and grasses on which wild caribou feed. From the caribou, the pollutants pass to wolves, to bears, to the hunters and their families who depend on wild herds for food—and work their way into streams and rivers. Fracking in the oil and gas industry damages the quality of the water table and aquifers. The north, a bastion of purity, has become a closed circle of human activity that transforms air, water, and food into concentrates of poison. The angels and God, perching at the zenith of an ascending evolutionary scale if they or He or She ever existed, detached themselves long ago. Perhaps they were drawing up plans for a new Creation, the evolutionary web of this one, torn.

Cliff had thought he was done with closeness to humans in general, adjusted to the necessity to be alone. His girlfriend, Tamira, had said, in a Yaletown restaurant in Vancouver, paging through the menu after they'd decided to go their separate ways for good, "You're great at what you do, Cliff, really great." She paused, tapped a finger against her lips and said, "What do you think? Maybe the duck confit? What are you having?"

None of it. Cliff will not have any of it.

And yet, the river they've been following to the limits of their fuel is his lifeline. They have heard on the radio that Pearl is down there somewhere, alone, or as good as, with one of the young swimmers missing with her. At the very least, *at the very least*, he needs to find out what happened.

The helicopter drops him in a clearing, landing, and taking off quickly through a break in the clouds. He skids down a shale slope and drops his pack at the cabin door. Fresh snow masks the peaks above the tree line, but here on the banks of a spring-fed lake, trumpeter swans swim their reflections through the dimming sunlight. The clear water Kitliki in which live the fish he has been monitoring, runs from the slough that drains the lake to the upper Niamue and then through another small lake. After that, the river splits, the main branch passing the mine works before joining the Stemeltlanga, the other fork falling westward from the north-south mountain ridge on its rapids-filled way to the ocean. Cliff passes on to the shed where he stores a canoe, checks that all is in order, and stands in the creek shallows. Pellucid water rings a bouquet of light, and ripples over his waterproof boots. Feeding fingerlings approach and scatter. The steelhead, both tagged and wild, swim in deeper waters near the monitoring station. He would have to carry the canoe there before he could paddle. Not that he thinks he would be able to find Pearl and the boy. Long before he could arrive, they would be safe, or they would drown. There is little point in trying.

Cliff's hands open and cup the fading rays of sun.

Or, if he decides to go anyway, he should wait for daylight. It's not safe to travel in the dark; if anything happens to him it will only compound the problem; whatever he does, it can't do any good.

Cliff studies the mist in the valley below. It is tinged with blue, filling in the niches of the lower slopes and smothering the dark gold and green of the forest. He will never believe this land is a prison, but after seeing nothing along the Stemeltlanga River valley but a winding lode of fog, it could seem like it. Swiftly, and without further thought, he runs to the cabin, puts blankets and rations into his pack, collects a fishing rod and rifle, and as much warm clothing as he can carry, and heads to the creek to load the canoe.

The northern lights shake green curtains above the mountains. He finds direction as he travels by listening to the way his whistles are buffered by varying thicknesses of vegetation and fly across the water ahead of him. He paddles expertly out of the first lake and into the second. Near a forestry cabin, wolves emerge from the trees to drink from the lake and scout the footprints of moose and calves in the mud. Only a day's walk from there, hot springs melt caves in glaciers. In some tales, these caves house creatures from before the Ice Age; in others, warriors wait to be called upon in time of need.

"Hello?" Cliff calls. "Anyone listening?"

The banks of the Niamue have been stripped of trees and vegetation near the mine, and the watercourse widened. New equipment—hovercraft and dredgers and diggers—sleeps in steel cages, awaiting the arrival of workers for whom a small town is under construction. Not a town on a map, with oversight and governance. Not a town for families, with schools and hospitals, but service pods for contract workers camped in bunkhouses. Three months on, then one month off to their home countries, with half their wages stripped by middlemen, and much of the rest owed for *expenses*. Since Cliff's previous trip, the company has cleared an air strip long enough for the transport planes which are coming. Soon the runway will be tarmacked. He refuses to think about the damage to spawning beds and the fish (instincts intact or not) that won't make it down the churned up Niamue river to the Stemeltlanga, let alone to the sea once the operation is running: or what this devastation means for the Stem itself—the changes in river currents, the accumulation of debris—alterations for which Pearl cannot have been prepared. If a river alters its shape and course and nobody tells, has anything happened?

Pearl and Joachim detect first light through the zipper path of a hydro cut. Carefully, they help each other out of their overnight nest of flotsam. Fog condenses the river, but there is some dispersal towards the sea.

They cut and scrape snails from clumps of detritus and suck the snail shells empty. Mucous-covered peapods of energy to force down their throats: they cannot afford to be squeamish. Heartsick, but sure of herself, Pearl lies on top of the raft, delves into a weir of debris, and hauls out a pink-tagged fish. It flips its tail and lands in her lap. With a quick slash of her dive knife, she cuts off its head. Pearl fillets the fish as Walter has taught her. "Here you go," she says, and slices off a chunk for Joachim. "Breakfast. We're at a sushi bar in Vancouver. The kind where little plates circle by on a conveyor belt and you get to pick what you want."

Doggo stands sentinel on land as he has all night against the predators which have come, assessed, and because of him, have slunk away. He barks from across a passage of fast water and piled rocks. Joachim and Pearl's shifting weight shakes the log pile, which then is speared by a speeding tree-trunk—more of the spillage from clear-cuts and eroded banks. You can start some things going, but you cannot necessarily make them stop.

"We should get in the water," Pearl says. "It's light enough. If we swim around this, they will see us."

"They'll be looking for us *in* the water, right?" Joachim says. Although that's not what Pearl means. She means they need to get moving to fight the cold; and if the raft breaks with them on it, they'll be entangled, and they will drown. They're going to have to risk a jump. They link hands and "One, two, three" leap as far from the knotted bush-waste as they can. The water boils as they splash into it, but they do not strike rocks, and they are together as they bob to the surface. Pink-tagged fish flash around them as if they've been waiting for Pearl and Joachim to lead the way. Doggo swims nearby. Clear water beckons, trembling like tinfoil below the evaporating mist. The river carries them swiftly until it broadens to where it has dropped silt and built islands for cottonwoods—nesting sites for herons. One of the large birds flaps its wings and lifts before it lands again and shrieks a protest at their passage.

Walter and the others are still upriver searching and calling, but have yet to negotiate the disintegrating jam. Boats have sailed from the port—a flotilla of craft carrying divers and medics, and the media, who overnight have latched onto the story of the missing Refuge House swimmers. Satellite phones and cameras at the ready.

Cliff arrives at the mine site at noon. He does not go near the machinery or the new buildings. He secures the canoe and strikes for the airstrip. With him is the entrenching tool he uses for digging camp site latrines, and a sack it has cost an hour of sharp-eyed trudging through woods to fill. He chips holes in the runway hardpack, scrapes loose a few inches of soil, drops in tree seedlings, and seats them firmly. He finishes one section of the runway and immediately tackles another. After he has done enough to block a plane larger than a Cessna from landing and to postpone the prospect of tarmacking for another year, he puts his tools away. By the time the company excavates the trees, regrades the strip, readies it for blacktopping, and allows the surface to cure, it will be too late to fly men in. Summer will be winding down; the metal shutters of cold about to clang shut.

In the estuary, fresh river water meets salt water, flows over it and lets fall the rich silt of rainwater runoff from forests and grasslands. Here, where the water is warmer, young salmon find abundant food: thick beds of filamentous algae, small crustaceans, insects, even other salmonids. Some types of smolts will loiter and feed for as long as four years; other kinds swim quickly from the estuary to the open sea past the gatekeepers—the gulls and terns and kittiwakes, or the murrelets which lay a single egg in mossy canopy nests far inland, nests from which the fledglings must pilot miles to the sea where medium melts to medium.

The first vessel reaches Pearl and Joachim here.

At the Harbour restaurant the next morning, now that things have quieted down, Pearl dawdles over a cup of coffee by the window while Joachim visits the washroom. His gym bag lies next to their ketchup-and-egg-smeared breakfast dishes, on top of a newspaper that tells their story. Beyond the plate glass windows, fishing boats at the marina cradle-rock on the tide. Dockside metal-carriers layer vari-coloured kayaks and canoes like paint chips. While she waits, Pearl watches a canoe approach. The paddler looks tired, backpack on, toque pulled down over his ears as he nudges the canoe against the wharf and stows the paddles.

"We should go soon," she says to Joachim, sitting across from her again. After they check out of their hotel, they will do a few more interviews, then take the bus home. It will be a long, circuitous trip. Walter and the others who have friends in the area, are taking a few days off, but with all the media attention, donations for Refuge House are coming in steadily and Pearl is anxious to sort out the accounting. She turns to look for the paddler again, but he and the canoe have disappeared, likely gone to the public canoe lock-up near the boathouse.

A helicopter whirlybirds over a container ship. Behind it, low hills, bluish in mist, emboss the edge of the northern estuary. The copter lowers over the roofs of warehouses whose outer walls are stacked with crab-traps, plastic crates, and boxes. The young men working there in gum boots and rubber aprons, ply hoses, and spray themselves and the traps clean. A customer opens the door to the restaurant and the sound of "Stairway to Heaven" wafts from the workers' boom box as the copter gentles onto the helipad next door.

"I've got something to show you," Joachim says. He opens the gym bag, fumbles through it, and brings out the small muslin package Pearl had discovered before the swim. He unwraps it for her to see, releasing the spoor of oranges. "I'm not sure what to do with it." He shunts it across the table to her. "Maybe you could keep it for me."

The doll, its costume, and its black curly hair intact, is a model of Miguel de Roca, the Aragonese, from Rosa's story. Pearl can read a line of the troubadour's song on the book it holds. *I will die if she won't have me.*

"You're not mad, are you?" Joachim says. "I would have shown you before, but Nora told me to wait until I was ready. It belonged to my father."

Pearl has so many questions, but it is not right to ask them now. The story will disclose itself in time, its jigsaw pieces assemble and reassemble, until it joins with the other stories in the pool.

"No, I'm not mad, and of course I'll take care of it. Just say when you want it back."

Pearl glances out the window, her gaze caught by the sight of a tiny green bird fluttering close to the water, but it's gone before she can clarify a thought that tries to surface. The outer door of the restaurant opens. Joachim's friend Jada comes in, followed by the man Pearl had seen in the canoe. He ducks his head as he enters, takes off his toque and polishes his glasses. Carefully, Pearl re-wraps the doll. The glasses are something new.

"Over there," Jada says to him, pointing to Pearl, and then she calls, "Joachim, come see the helicopter take off. Come on!"

Pearl brushes back her swimmer-short hair.

People are meant to find each other: they're not intended to vanish when the one they have sought is waiting. But sometimes they shift attention, or neglect to follow through on a promise, or they simply forget. People do. And there are modes of forgetting: trying to forget, pretending it didn't happen, forgetting because of embarrassment or shame; and there is also a kind of forgetfulness that can one day ease the way for another try.

The door closes on Joachim and Jada and the whine of the copter blades.

"I got your letter," Cliff says, standing at Pearl's table. His blistered hands hang at his sides, one set of fingers clinging to what looks like a square of origami. "Sandra had it. She'd made it into a *fortune teller* and forgotten about it. When I went to Nootka a few days ago, she remembered and gave it to me." He holds it for Pearl to see. "After I read it, she re-did it so it wouldn't tear it in my pocket."

Pearl's throat is dry. She motions for Cliff to sit down. He pulls a chair to the table, lays the paper aside, takes a napkin from its holder and blots the seeping skin on his palms. His eyes travel the grazes and bruises on her face and arms.

Pearl positions her thumbs and forefingers in the pockets made by the folds of the *fortune teller* and shifts the resulting *beak* in and out like a pincer. Pearl had played the game with Nora, who must have played it with Sandra. Traditionally, eight possible fortunes were written down and concealed under numbered flaps on the paper ahead of time, but there are no numbers written here. Cliff places his hands on Pearl's, gently retrieves the folded square, and smooths it out on the table. His spread fingers display the delicate webbing between them. He reads Pearl's letter aloud, "*Judy will tell you where I am if you want to get in touch. I would like it if you did.*" He carries on to Guiliam's little poem at the end and falls silent, his skin grey with fatigue.

Pearl would like to touch the line on his forehead left by his toque. Instead, she takes a drink of water and hopes it will slow her heartbeat.

Cliff closes his eyes. He opens them and says, "I wish I had known, Pearl. Why didn't you call me? Was it because of Tamira?" Colour blossoms his ears. "Sheila said she'd told you about her flying in. I wasn't expecting it. That's why I left the spare satellite phone. There's no other way to get a message to me at the station. I thought if we talked, we could work it out, but you didn't call, and I thought …"

"What phone?" Pearl asks, freeing her voice at last.

"I put a satellite phone inside one of your boots in your locker at *SoliSunny*."

"I didn't go to *SoliSunny*, I didn't open the locker; I didn't find the phone."

"But Sheila said you'd be coming in to clean the tanks. You had a job to do!"

"But I didn't. I didn't go back."

"Oh, Christ," he says, "I should have made sure."

Pearl's body aches from collisions with rock and debris, her muscles tight and sore from long days of swimming, and the cold water has drained her energy. She knows how she must look with Doggo's claw marks across her cheeks and neck, but with the shock of Cliff's words, she has lost the ability to care. What if she had done as Sheila had asked her? Why had she been adamant that she had to leave straight away? Pearl has an overwhelming desire to sleep.

"Pearl," Cliff says, "please listen to me. When you were lost on the river, I thought I might never see you again. What if we could start over?"

Start over? Pearl thinks of Nora stitching patches onto her jeans and mending her sweaters, Nora sewing a new cloak of cormorant feathers for the Rosa doll, one of the last things she did, because the original cloak was damaged beyond repair. "How do you find cormorant feathers these days?" she'd asked her granddaughter.

"It wasn't your fault," Pearl says.

"It wasn't yours," he says.

"I'm going to Refuge House with Joachim, the boy you passed on your way in. We're getting the bus."

"I'm closing the research station on the Kitliki. I'm on my way to Japan."

"You're abandoning the fish?"

Cliff grins. "They can look after themselves for a few months, Pearl. I'll be back to check on them."

Pearl's cheeks are pink. Cliff winces as she takes his hands, but Pearl needs to touch him if she is to speak. "When Joachim and I were on the drift pile in the river and I didn't know if we'd survive the night or what would happen, I wanted to tell you about the pink-tagged fish all around us. They knew where they had to go and what they were supposed to do, just like you'd hoped."

The small green bird Pearl had glimpsed earlier flits past the window. It's like the bird from the story of the boy and girl (Guiliam and Yamha) who lost each other. But this is a different time.

"I have a few days before my flight," Cliff says. "You could come to the station with me if you wanted. I'd like to show you."

"Or you could come to Refuge House with me. Is there time for both, do you think?"

"Look in the mirror," Pearl's mother, Sara, says one day when what went wrong is mended. But it is Cliff who holds the mirror in the birthing pool so that Pearl can view the widened opening to her body looking nothing like the genitals in the videos she has watched to prepare for this, but is, instead, the cup-shaped underside of a jellyfish, fringes and all. Cliff guides Pearl's touch to the wet of an infant's bony skull—another cup about to spill into the world.

"A few more pushes," the midwife says.

We come onto this Earth and we leave this Earth on a surf of tears.

Now a shoulder, another shoulder.

"Look! Its eyes are open!"

Pearl braces against the side of the pool, engages her strength and urges the baby the rest of the way from her body. The infant rises through the warm water, arms stretched towards the light, the webbing between its fingers transparent except for a tracery of tiny branching capillaries. Fronds of the tree of life.

Hands reach, so many that Pearl cannot say who first lifts the newborn into the air that prompts the baby's lungs to inflate, and the gill slits Pearl has glimpsed behind its ears, to close.

"She's perfect," Cliff says, touching the tiny fingers that are making a watery webbed flutter in his direction.

"Yes," Pearl says. "She is."

END

Acknowledgements

A novel usually involves the help of friends, family, colleagues and others of good will, and this one, perhaps, more than most. My thanks to Ingrid and the late Iain Winspur then in Santa Barbara, and to Mercedes Carbonell, Pepe Yniguez, and Juan Lacomba in Spain; to Margarita James, John Amos, and Kip Hedley who facilitated and informed my explorations of Friendly Cove; to Chief Randy Chipps for his knowledge of the impact of Spanish colonialism on Vancouver Island; to Sofia Silva Sanchez in San Blas; and to my brother David, whose long experience of the North was also an important resource.

John Black of the Alessandro Malaspina Research Foundation patiently answered questions about the Spanish presence on Vancouver Island and at San Blas, as did Nick Doe and the late John Crosse. Through Camilla Turner, I learned of Freeman Tovell's work on west coast Spanish history. My readers—Ed Carson, Paddy Grant, Ellen Godfrey, Isabel Huggan, Carol Mathews, and the late Rachel Wyatt—gave thoughtful advice. I am grateful for their generosity and friendship. My husband Michael Elcock was always encouraging and showed forbearance and insight during what turned out to be a lengthy process. I am thankful for his understanding and love, for his deep reading and editing, and his belief in what the story could be.

My thanks, as well, for the financial assistance and writing time provided by the BC Arts Council, the Canada Council, the VIU Faculty Association and the Fundación Valparaiso.

Epigraphs

Plato. "Cratylus 401E, 402A." In *The Presocratics*, edited by Phillip Wheelwright, 79–80. New York: Odyssey Press, 1966.

Parry, Idris. "Preface." In Essays on Dolls (Syrens), vii. London: Penguin Books, 1994.

Niedecker, Lorine. "My Life by Water." In *My Life by Water: Collected Poems, 1936–1968*. London: Fulcrum Press, 1970.

Attributions

A stretch of inlets … to its possibilities, near the beginning of Part IV, is from the introduction by Charles Lillard to *The Nootka*, by G.M. Sproat, published by Sono Nis Press (Victoria BC, 1987) p. ix.

Pearl's swim was inspired, in part, by Ali Howard's courageous 2009 swim from the headwaters to the mouth of the Skeena River. See the film *Awakening the Skeena* (2010) directed by Andrew Eddy.

The Tradition of Dolls

The tradition of using dolls to carry stories and identity is ancient, but I first encountered its contemporary richness in the late Adele Wiseman's memoir of her mother's creative work, *Old Woman at Play* (1978). Chaika Wiseman's dolls, which she assembled from scraps of cloth, buttons and other odds and ends, gave life to the individuals, tales, and traumatic history of her Ukrainian Jewish village in Russia.

A healing role like that in my tales, is also played by the dolls of the *Ana Collection*, founded by Syrian Lebanese sisters Marianne and Melina Mousalli to tell the stories of displaced refugees. Artist and writer Barbara-Helen Hill began making small cloth dolls "to tell more stories from our traditional ways and to make the spirit dolls." She says. "They made me laugh; they made me love them. Some are a teaching, too. I have every intention of getting back to them because there are two sitting in my head waving at me saying 'me next.'"

Glossary of the Dolls

The Aragonese (Miguel de Roca), from Aragon, Spain, is a contemporary of Beatris and Rosa. A surveyor and mapmaker, he visits and reports on San Blas to the Spanish government. He has no written tale of his own yet, but his ancestry stems from the troubadour Guiliam and extends to the refugee boy Joachim. The doll is made of wood. Its hair is glossy and black. It is fashionably dressed and holds a book on which is written a line of the troubadour's song.

Arishat, a dancer and scribe from the Goddess' Temple at ancient Cadiz (Gadir), travelled from Spain to Solomon's Jerusalem c. 950 BCE. The tale tells of the quest of her foster brother, thirteen-year-old Rib, for forgiveness after his apparent responsibility for the death of their sister, Arinna. The doll is made of cotton stuffed with straw and given painted fair hair and green eyes. Arishat is equipped with a reed pen, a scroll, and a pig bladder life-preserver.

Beatris assumes the identity of a boy on the 1789 Malaspina round-the-world expedition, to be with her twin brother,

Baruk. Together with the naturalist Tadeo, she kills the Spanish boy, Ignacio, who stalks her on Nootka Island. Her child, Rosa, is born later, in California. The doll has curly dark hair and comes with a miniature ship and a fighting knife called a *navaja.*

Guiliam & *Yamha* are two children at the Crusaders siege of Almeria, Spain (1147). The tale tells of twelve-year-old troubadour Guiliam's role in the destruction of the city, and of his rescue of the eight-year-old Muslim girl, Yamha. Their double-doll is made of bone, the girl with dark hair and dark eyes, and carrying a green bird. The boy—fair with blue eyes—is furnished with red shoes and a tiny lute.

Rosa, a fatherless adolescent and outsider in the culture of early nineteenth-century San Blas, Mexico (the Spanish naval headquarters), mistakes the kindness of a man (Miguel de Roca, *The Aragonese*) who actually loves her mother Beatris, as love for herself. After her mother's death, Rosa is marooned on an island off the Santa Barbara coast. The doll is made of whalebone and dressed in sealskin and cormorant feathers.

Theano, mathematician, teacher, philosopher, and wife of Pythagoras, lives in a fifth-century BCE Greek colony at Croton. The tale tells of an earthquake and tsunami, and the use of memory techniques to record the stories of the lost. Theano and a poet who has come to declare his love for her, argue over whose version of the value of story is correct. The doll is made of olive wood with its features painted on.